Praise for Graham Masterton

"This is supernatural horror on a grand scale, but without losing sight of the believable characters that are necessary if we are to believe the incredible events that they are experiencing." —*Science Fiction Chronicle* on *Burial*

"What places Masterton above the rest is his vivid realization of the story, and his ability to pull together all of its energy." —*Richmond Times Dispatch*

"Masterton [has a] genuinely inventive horror imagination." —*Kirkus Reviews*

"[A] chilling horror tale, deftly written and convincing. Readers who savor the taste of fear should have a field day with this one." —*Publishers Weekly* on *Master of Lies*

"Graham Masterton is the grand master of horror. . . . his genius lies in the way in which he pays homage to ancient myths, while presenting a thriller of the utmost modernity." —*Le Figaro*

"A fascinating and frightening journey to hell and back, with the fate of Hollywood, and perhaps the world, hanging in the balance." —*Horrorstruck*

"Masterton's third outing with the Manitou provides another spine-tingling excursion into the supernatural universe, the 'black infinite lake that lies beneath our feet.'" —*Booklist* on *Burial*

TOR BOOKS BY GRAHAM MASTERTON

Burial
The Manitou
Revenge of the Manitou
The Burning
Charnel House
Condor
Death Dream
Death Trance
The Devils of D-Day
The Djinn
Ikon
Master of Lies
Mirror
Night Plague
Night Warriors
Pariah
Picture of Evil
Prey
Sacrifice
Solitaire
Sphinx
Tengu
Walkers
The Wells of Hell

Scare Care (editor)

BURIAL

GRAHAM MASTERTON

TOR®

A TOM DOHERTY ASSOCIATES BOOK
NEW YORK

This is a work of fiction. All the characters and events portrayed in this book are either products of the author's imagination or are used fictitiously.

BURIAL

Cover art by Donato

A Tor Book
Published by Tom Doherty Associates, Inc.
175 Fifth Avenue
New York, N.Y. 10010

Tor Books on the World-Wide Web:
http://www.tor.com

Tor® is a registered trademark of Tom Doherty Associates, Inc.

ISBN: 0-812-53629-0
Library of Congress Card Catalog Number: 94-115

First edition: May 1994
First mass market edition: February 1996

Printed in the United States of America

0 9 8 7 6 5 4 3 2 1

New York

Naomi was right in the middle of peppering her cod chowder when she heard a sharp scraping sound from the dining room. Slowly she lowered her ladle, listening hard. A sharp scrape like somebody dragging their chair out without lifting it. But of course there was nobody there. Michael and Erwin were still at the synagogue; she wasn't expecting them back for nearly an hour.

She waited and waited; the chowder simmered, the lid covering the potatoes softly rattled. But the sound wasn't repeated. All she could hear was muffled rock music from the Bensons' apartment above her, and the echoing of car-horns from the street below. The front door was protected by three deadlocks, a chain and two bolts, so it was hardly likely that anybody could have broken in without her hearing him.

She leaned forward a little so that she could peer through the dining room door. It was only half open, so all she could see was the darkly-varnished sideboard with its crowds of framed photographs and its cream lace runners, and the corner of the dining table, and the back of one chair. The light from the candles swivelled and dipped, distorting the shadows; and for a split second she thought she saw a dark and hostile shape. But common sense told her that there was nobody there, and that it was nothing but light and dark, and the draught from an open window.

She took the strawberry shortcake out of the freezer and set it on the counter to defrost. Then she opened the oven to make sure that the chicken pieces were browning nicely. For a moment her glasses were blinded by the steam.

She closed the oven door, and it was then that she thought she heard it again. The very slightest of scrapes.

She opened and closed the oven door once more, just to make sure that it wasn't the hinges that had scraped. Then, wiping her hands on her apron, she cautiously approached the dining room door. From here she could see herself reflected in the mirror over the sideboard, a plump, pale woman with a flat Eastern European face and deep-set eyes, her rinsed hair tied with a bright red headscarf. A woman who had been startlingly pretty once, twenty-nine years ago, when she and Michael had first furnished this apartment, and who still retained a girlishness that all of their men friends found appealing. But her knuckles were reddened from housework, and from years of office-cleaning, and although she was still pillowy-breasted, too many potatoes and too much cream had made her *zaftig,* and she didn't like to go without her corset. She could diet, she supposed; but food was her only real pleasure, apart from television and singing (she loved choirs and opera), and maybe life was too short to give up such an important pleasure.

She reached out and pushed the door a few inches wider. She paused, listened.

"Who's there?" she demanded. At the same time, thinking how stupid she was. A burglar was going to say, "Don't worry, it's only me, the burglar."

She waited a few moments more. The shadows flickered, the clock ticked softly on the bookcase. She suddenly felt that she had been standing here for years, at this half-open door—that her fate was waiting for her, just out of sight. What kind of fate, she couldn't tell. She wasn't sure that she wanted to find out.

"I know there's nobody there!" she announced, and flinging the door wide open she stepped into the dining room.

She was right. There was nobody there. Only the table set for dinner for three, with its red tablecloth and its white lace overcloth. The best crystal glasses shining; the napkin rings polished; flowers arranged in the centerpiece, which was a porcelain figure of an old Hungarian flower-seller leading a donkey and cart.

The *challah* loaves were ready, covered with a cloth, the *kiddush* cup was filled with wine. She had already lit the *Shabbes* candles and said a prayer for her family, for their health, and their peace and their honor.

She walked around the table, touching everything with her fingertips—glasses, cutlery, side-plates, as if to make sure that they were all sanctified and pure. The *Shabbes* evening was one of the few times when a woman became a priestess in her own home, endowed with the ability to bless those she loved.

She looked into the living room, too. Nobody there. The big brown upholstered chairs were empty, the television cabinet closed; the whole room smelled of furniture polish and room spray. A little shabby, maybe, a little tired, but a houseproud woman's home.

Maybe it was rats again. They had been infested with rats three or four times in the years they had lived on Tenth Street. Each time the building managers had cleared the rats out and sworn that there was no way for them to get back in, but she had been raised in the Bronx and she knew about rats. They could gnaw their way through solid concrete, given enough time.

She returned to the kitchen. She dusted the chowder with a little nutmeg and decided it was ready although for some reason she wasn't very hungry any more. The chicken was doing fine: all she had to do now was to cream the potatoes.

Then—there it was again. That scraping noise. Then louder—chair legs dragging, table legs dragging. The tinkling of glasses and cutlery. She opened the drawer and took out her largest breadknife, and stood rigid and terrified—listening.

I should dial 911, she thought. There *must* be somebody here. No rat could make a noise like that. Rats may be able to chew through concrete but they can't move furniture.

She crossed the kitchen, holding the knife rigidly upright in front of her, trying to control the trembling in her hand.

She reached the telephone and lifted it off the wall. Keeping her eyes fixed on the dining-room door she punched 911 with her left thumb, then lifted the receiver to her ear.

Nothing. The phone was dead.

She replaced the receiver and tried again. Still nothing. No dial tone, no ringing tone. She tried one more time, and then hung up.

"If there's anybody there," she called out, "My husband and five other men will be home in about a minute. So if I were you, I'd get the hell out."

She listened. No reply. She hoped that if there was somebody there, that whoever it was had believed her. If six men were coming home soon, how come the table was only laid for three?

"I'm warning you," she called. She felt as if she had a thistle caught in her larynx. "You have five seconds to get the hell out, then I'm calling the police and the neighbors and God help you."

Instantly, the apartment was filled with a thunderous banging and colliding of furniture. Doors slammed, glass splintered, chairs toppled over. The huge mahogany sideboard which had once belonged to her grandmother was abruptly and noisily dragged out of view, shedding framed photographs and ornaments and most of her collection of glass paperweights.

She was too terrified even to scream. She stood breathless, gasping, listening to the last tinkling of broken glass; the muted thrumming of rock'n'roll. What kind of intruder came into your house and pushed all your furniture around? And how had he moved that sideboard? That sideboard weighed a *ton*. Michael and Erwin had once had to ask Freddie Benson to help them shift it just three feet.

Perhaps it wasn't an intruder, after all. Perhaps it was subsidence. These old houses in the Village had been pretty hastily thrown up, on the whole, when Manhattan had been forcing its way uptown almost daily—street after street, square after square, fashionable one week and derelict the next. Their surveyor had warned them that the "entire fabric is suspect: structural wood is partly-rotted and the roof tiles have become porous with age."

All the same, the house was built on solid rock, and there were no serious cracks in the walls. And she couldn't *feel* any subsidence. The floor would have had to slope at almost forty-five degrees for that sideboard to slide.

She took two or three careful steps towards the dining room. She whispered a prayer that Michael and Erwin would come home early.

"I have a knife," she said, "and I know how to use it."

She wondered if she had made a serious mistake, telling the intruder that she was armed. It was highly likely that he had a knife of his own; or even a gun. A friend of hers, Esther Fishman, had been shot in the left side of the face by an intruder, and even six years later she was still psychologically traumatised and badly scarred, and spoke like a ghastly parody of Donald Duck. She thought of Esther and almost decided to drop her knife and run for the front door.

Better to lose everything than to end up like Esther.

But this was *Shabbes* evening; and this was *her* house; the house which she had prepared for her husband and her brother. She was *Eshes Chayil,* the woman of valor, "clothed in strength and honor."

She opened the dining room door. She couldn't believe what she saw. All of her furniture was crowded against the opposite wall. Chairs, table, sideboard, bookcase, even the rug had rumpled up underneath them. Everything on the dinner table was heaped up against the wallpaper: the napkins, the glasses, the *challah* bread, the salt-shaker.

Even more disturbingly, the pictures on the walls were hanging sideways, as if gravity had changed direction and was trying to pull them towards the opposite wall. The oil-painting of Russia that her Auntie Katia had bequeathed her; the hand-tinted photograph of her great-great-uncles, on their arrival in Brooklyn, 1887; the drawing of Coney Island that Henry had given her when he was eleven. The only picture that was hanging properly was a small framed arrangement of dried flowers.

She approached the furniture with a terrible feeling of bewilderment and dread. No intruder could have done this. She had heard that the devil sometimes tried people's patience on the Sabbath, trying to shake their faith in God on the very night before their holiest day, and also to tempt them into working when work was forbidden. He would tear all the clothes in a woman's wardrobe so that she would be tempted to sew; or turn her bread into chalk so that she would be tempted to bake; or make a man's children sick so that he would have to carry them to the doctor.

There was a strange sour *smell* in the room, like nothing she had ever smelled before. She thought at first that it was the candles, that the tablecloth might have been burned, but both candles must have been instantly snuffed out when the table shifted. One of them lay tilted against the bread-basket and the other lay across one of the side-plates.

She had lit the candles for her children, for her children's souls; and for Michael's soul, too; and Erwin's.

"Oh, God protect me," she said. She didn't know what to do. She approached the oil-painting and tried to pull it down into a normal hanging position, but when she did so it immediately swung back to the horizontal. She tried again, but again it swung back.

"Who's here?" she screamed, her voice as shrill as wet fingers dragged down windowpanes.

She pushed her way back to the living room. Empty, shadowy, but still permeated with that sour offensive smell.

"Who's here?" she screamed again.

She ran around the apartment. The bedroom, with its pink quilted bed. The bathroom. Her frightened face suddenly met her in the mirror, and refused to smile. The spare room, where they kept the rowing machine. The unused, unloved rowing machine. Michael's den, crowded with books and pennants and golf clubs.

"Who's here?" she whispered. Her hands trailed along the walls, touching, pressing, as if to reassure herself that she was walking through real and solid surroundings.

She returned to the dining room. The furniture remained where it was, crowded against the wall. She stared at it for a very long time, breathless. Then she took hold of one of the dining chairs, and carried it back to the center of the room, and set it down. She watched it, half expecting it to tumble back to the wall, but it stayed where it was. She found another dining chair, and carried that back to the center of the room, too, and set that down next to the first chair.

"Nobody's here," she told herself. "Only me. It's my furniture, it goes where I want it to go."

It's my foinitcher. She hated her accent. She had taken elocution lessons, but she couldn't shake it completely. Maybe her friends didn't hear it, but she always did. Dere was a little goil who had a little coil. Besides, she didn't want to talk, not now. Somebody might be listening. Somebody might be hiding. And so long as she talked, she wouldn't be able to hear him. She wouldn't be able to hear him breathing. She wouldn't be able to hear him creeping up behind her back.

She turned, quickly. There was nobody there. There was nothing to do but to drag all the furniture back (apart from the sideboard; she'd have to leave that to Michael and Erwin, and probably to Freddie Benson, too).

She managed to push the table back, and straighten out the rug. Two of her best crystal glasses were broken, snapped-off stems. The flower-seller's donkey was missing an ear; and her best lace tablecloth was soaked in wine and water. The glass-fronted bookcase had opened, and there were heaps of books on the floor. *Exodus* by Leon Uris; *The Promised Land* by Moses Rischin; *The Golden Tradition* by Lucy S. Dawidowicz. Michael's bibles, almost. She knelt down and picked them up.

The Golden Tradition had fallen face down, spread open. As she closed it, she saw that the two open pages were blank. She turned to the next page, then to the next, and to the next. Then she riffled through the book from beginning to end. All of the pages were blank.

Maybe a notebook, she thought. A book of days. But then she picked up *Exodus* and she had read that copy of *Exodus* herself, that very same copy, and all the pages of *Exodus* were blank, too.

Desperately, she picked up book after book. Not a word inside any of them. They had all been wiped clean, as if they had never been printed. She stood up, stiffly wiping her hands together. *I'm sick. Something's wrong with me. Either I'm sick or I'm asleep. Maybe I fell asleep while I was cooking. There was so much to do, after all. If I go back to bed and lie down, and then maybe open my eyes . . . maybe this will all be a dream.*

She *knew* this had to be a dream. She would never have broken her best crystal glasses, except in a dream. She would never have broken her donkey's ear. She would never have let the *Shabbes* candles go out.

She set up the candleholders on the table, took a book of matches out of her apron pocket, and relit the candles, closing her eyes briefly with each fresh flame, praying for Henry and Anne and Leo; and for Michael, and Erwin, and for herself.

After she had lit the candles, she opened her eyes. The shadows from the candle-flames were dancing on the wall. But over on the right-hand side, one shadow remained completely still—not dancing, not even trembling, like the shadows of the chair backs. A dark hunched shape that could have been the outline of a horse's head or a kind of badly-distorted goat.

She stared at it for almost a minute, praying for it to move, *daring* it to move, but while the other shadows flickered and whirled, it remained totally motionless. Brooding; dark; engrossed in its own dreadful stillness. She lifted one of the candles so that all the shadows would swivel and sink. She moved it from side to side, so that all the shadows would shift from left to right. Still it stayed where it was, hunched, motionless, a shadow that refused to obey all the normal rules of light and shade.

She put down the candle and crossed the room to the wall. She placed her hand flat on the shadow, cautiously at first, then with more confidence. It was definitely a shadow, not just a dark mark on the wallpaper. So how come it always stayed exactly where it was?

It was then that she noticed another, smaller shadow, on the far end of the wall, almost in the corner. This shadow remained motionless, too, although it was much more recognizable as a man. He appeared to be sitting with his back towards her, his head resting on his arm, as if he were thinking about something, or tired.

After a while, the hunched shadow suddenly moved. She stepped quickly and nervously away from it, one hand raised in front of her to protect herself, *although how could a shadow jump off a wall?* Her heart was pumping so hard that she felt sure that everybody in the entire building could hear it, knocking against her ribcage. The shadow moved, dissolved, shifted and then moved again. It was still impossible for her to say what it was. It appeared to have an enormous bulky head, with strings of loose flesh hanging down from it. It reminded her of that terrible movie *The Elephant Man,* which Michael had once insisted they watch together. ("It's *culture . . .* you want to watch *The Price Is Right* for the rest of your life?")

Without warning, the hunched shadow lunged across the wall and dropped on top of the figure on the far end of the wall. She watched, mesmerized, as the two shadows appeared to struggle and fight. She kept turning her head, kept looking behind her, to see if there was anything in the dining room which could be throwing such shadows, but she was alone; she and her furniture, and her flickering candles.

It was like watching a struggle being played out in a 1950s detective movie, shadows against a windowshade. Except that this wasn't a windowshade, it was a solid wall, and shadows couldn't be seen through a solid wall.

She was so frightened that she felt like running out of the room, running out of the apartment, bursting into the synagogue and begging Michael to come home. But the hunched-up shadow was tearing the smaller shadow to pieces, lumps and strings and rags, and she had to stay to see what was going to happen.

She didn't hear a scream. The dining room remained silent, except for the pounding of her heart and the noise of the city traffic.

But when the hunched-up shadow tore off what looked like the smaller shadow's head, she *felt* something. She was sure she *felt* something. A scream as white and as silent as a frozen window; but a scream all the same.

The hunched shadow changed shape. She couldn't understand what it was doing at first, because it was dark and two-dimensional. But then she realized that it had turned around—and not just turned around, but *turned towards her*.

She backed away, two or three steps, then another. This was it. It was time to run. The shadow seemed to swell, as if it were coming closer. There was no sound, only the sensation of something approaching.

She was just about to snatch for the door when one of the dining-room chairs dragged itself noisily across the floor, caught her just behind the knees, and sent her colliding against the bookcase. Another chair slid across the floor, then another. Then the table circled around, its feet making an ear-splitting screeching noise on the wood-block flooring, and struck her on the right side of her head, so hard that it almost knocked her out. The candles were instantly snuffed out, as if a huge draft had suddenly blown through the room, and they toppled to the floor along with the bread-basket and the cutlery and Naomi's best gilt-edged porcelain plates. Naomi tried to struggle up, but the furniture pushed against her, harder and harder, all legs and arms and corners, pinning her against the wall as painfully and effectively as if it had been stacked on top of her.

She gasped for breath. The edge of the table was pressing so relentlessly against her chest that she thought her breastbone was going to crack. A chair-back wedged itself against her shoulder. She cried out *"Help! Somebody help me!!"* but Freddie Benson was playing his own guitar in accompaniment to his CD player now, and all she could hear was the deep bass thrumming of Bruce Springsteen.

She couldn't breathe. She felt one rib being pushed in further and further; and then something inside her chest made a sickening noise, halfway between a crackle and a wet sigh. She felt an intensely sharp pain, a pain that made her scream, and when she screamed she screamed out a fine spray of blood.

She felt the furniture bearing down on her harder and harder. She felt as if gravity were pressing her against the wall.

She shouted *"Help!"* again and again; but she thought about all of those times when she had heard other women shouting in the Village—muffled cries of pain and despair— and how she had always ignored them. Other women's agony hadn't been *her* business.

She smelled that deep, sour smell, like a fetid well being opened up. She twisted her head around and saw to her horror that the hunched-up shadow was heaving itself silently towards her, huge-headed, beastly, a living nightmare fashioned out of nothing but darkness.

ONE

I could never understand why I always attracted old ladies so much. Old ladies have gushed all over me ever since I was knee high to a high knee. They kissed me, they cooed at me, they patted me so often I was lucky my head didn't end up totally flat on top. They gave me dimes for candy, which I saved up and bet with at the track.

By the time I was nine I suppose it had become second nature to think that old ladies = money, just like $E = mc^2$. I ran errands for them, mowed their lawns, painted their fences, all of that Tom Sawyer stuff. In return (apart from paying me) they taught me how to play the stock-market, how to cheat at bridge, and how to blackmail major food companies into sending you heaps of free groceries, all of that old lady stuff. Don't you ever think that old ladies are innocent old dears: they have all day to sit and think of ways to rip off the system, and they do.

It was an old lady called Adelaide Bright who taught me the most profitable skill of all, however: and that was how to tell fortunes. Tea-leaves, crystal balls, star signs, Tarot cards . . . she knew them all and she showed me how they were done.

The first thing she taught me was that tea-leaves and crystal balls and astrological signs are only a ritual, a little bit of hocus-pocus to impress your client. She was one of the best, but she demonstrated without a doubt that you can no more predict somebody's future from the star sign they were born under than you can predict when a tire is going to blow out from the time of day it was molded.

Telling the future isn't magic, it's common sense. All you have to do is take a long shrewd look at your customer, come to some logical conclusions, and lie a lot. Oh—and *charge* a lot, too. The more expensive the fortune-telling, the readier your customers will be to believe you. After all, they're going to waste one hundred bucks on nonsense?

Adelaide taught me how to sum people up by the way they sat, the way they talked, their nervous habits, the way they laughed. Most of all, she taught me how to read people's personalities by the way they dressed. Two women can be wearing the same outfit, but one of them can be wearing it because it's the very best that she can afford, while another woman can be wearing it because—to her—it's cheap and casual.

"Look at their shoes," Adelaide used to remind me. "You can read volumes from people's shoes. Are they new but dirty? Are they old but well-repaired? Are they Nike trainers or are they wingtip Oxfords?"

The only thing about which Adelaide was seriously superstitious was the Tarot. She thought that the Tarot was dangerously misunderstood; not to be played with; and much more powerful than anybody knew. She said the Tarot was a window to a land which all of us could remember, but which none of us had ever visited—or would ever *want* to visit. I didn't know what the hell she meant by that, so I smiled and nodded and listened to what she had to say about detective work.

Adelaide was almost like Sherlock Holmes, the way she could analyze people; and when it came to predicting what was going to happen to them, she was almost always on the money. She even predicted that old Mr. Swietochowska's deli on Ditmas Avenue was going to go out of business, almost to the month, although I later found out that she had a nephew who worked for the planning department at Safeway, and he had told her a clear two years ahead of time that the company was thinking of building a new superstore on the waste lot right next door. But that's what telling fortunes is all about. Observation, logic, memory, and common sense. You can tell your *own* fortune if you're honest about yourself, but not many people are.

Even Adelaide wasn't. She smoked a pack and a half of Salem Menthol every day, sometimes more when she was lonely. She said they couldn't hurt her, being menthol. They kept her sinuses clear. On March 15, 1967, she complained of chest pains and shortness of breath. On April 11, she died of lung cancer at the Kings County Hospital Center and the only person who went to her funeral was me. It didn't rain.

In fact, it was hazy and uncomfortably hot, and I wished that I hadn't worn my raincoat.

I can see her face today: clear as a photograph. White hair, wound in a knot; bright green eyes; skin like soft crumpled tissue paper. She always put me in mind of Katherine Hepburn, romantic and girlish and strong, even at the age of seventy-one. And she always gave me a salt-water taffy, and kissed me before I left.

Wherever you are, Adelaide, heaven or hell or Tarotland, God bless you. It was a grilling August day and every window was open wide to let the heat in. My recently-departed lover had been friends with a very hip black gang leader called Purple Rayne who had sold me a "second-hand" air-conditioner that still had "Avis Rent-A-Car" stencilled on it. I didn't object so much to the fact that it was stolen as I did to the fact that it hardly ever worked. When I did manage to get it going, it used to sound like a Mexican rumba orchestra practicing "*La Cucaracha*" on the last train to Brighton Beach.

This morning I needed comparative quiet because I was telling the fortune of Mrs John F. Lavender, one of my most generous clients; and Mrs John F. Lavender was very demanding when it came to finding out what was going to happen to her next. This was because she was having affairs with three different men at once and she didn't want any one of them to find out about the other, and in particular she didn't want Mr John F. Lavender to find out about any of them.

My walk-up consulting rooms and living accommodation were on the top floor of a peeling three-story brick building on East 53rd, above the Molly Maguire Club, where some of the less assimilated of New York's Irishmen gathered of an evening to drink Bushmills whiskey and sing about the old country and dance a few jigs and knock each other's teeth out. The whole south side of East 53rd between Lexington and Third was in a state of dilapidation: a sorry collection of trellis-gated stores that had long gone out of business, interspersed with Cohen's Cut-Price Drugs, the Pink Pussy Sex Center, and Ned's Bargain Liquor. It directly fronted the gleaming new plaza underneath the Citicorp Center, like a hideous reminder that everything grows old one day, and that even the grandest dreams can collapse into dust. I managed to rent my premises for less than a hundred and fifty dollars a week because Citicorp was doing everything it possibly could to evict me and Ned and Cohen and the Pink Pussies and the Molly Maguires and tear the whole scabby block down. I think they were afraid we'd give their plaza some kind of architectural leprosy.

Mind you, cheap as my consulting rooms were, I'd managed to give them a certain occult tone. I'd been across to Seventh Avenue to see my friend Manny Goodman, and Manny had sold me three bolts of midnight-blue velour at cost, which I had nailed to the walls and decorated with stars cut from turkey-sized cooking foil. I still had my crystal ball from my old consulting room, plus heaps of dusty leather-bound books, which looked like ancient grimoires unless you looked too closely at the titles, *Cod Fishing Off Newfoundland* and *The Girls' Book of Lacrosse*.

My latest acquisition was a phrenological bust, on top of which I had stuck a candle. I must say it looked pretty damned clairvoyant.

Mrs John F. Lavender was lying back on the velour-draped daybed and furiously smoking at the ceiling. "I had such a terrible premonition this morning," she said. "It was like icy fingers trailing down my back."

I made notes. *Icy—fingers—trailing—down—back.* When I first started in the fortune-telling business, I used to wear a kind of occult hat and kind of shiny occult robes, but these days I found that the ladies liked it better if I wore a suit and shiny shoes and a carnation in my buttonhole and behaved more *professionally*—less like Merlin and more like a shrink. I also found that they paid me considerably more.

In a last attempt to be nice to me before her sense of humor ran out, my recently-departed lover had lettered me a very impressive certificate from the Institute of Chartered Clairvoyants, of Chewalla, Tennessee, which attested that Harold P. Erskine was a fully-qualified seer, licensed to soothsay in every state of the Union except Delaware. I don't know why Delaware was excluded; that was just an authenticating touch that she'd invented. Either that, or Delaware simply doesn't have a future.

Mrs John F. Lavender said anxiously, "I'm convinced that Mason suspects something."

"What makes you think that?"

"Well . . . I was leaving Christopher's building last Wednesday afternoon, and I was sure that I saw Mason in a passing cab. I'm ninety-nine percent certain that it was him. He looked my way, and *I think that he might have recognized me.*"

If it had been Mason (who was lover number two, incidentally) I was convinced beyond any reasonable doubt that he *would* have recognized her, instantly. Today was one of her discreet days, and she was wearing a patterned silk shirt that looked like a schizophrenic's painting of Miami's Parrot Jungle, signal-red pedal pushers, and strappy red stiletto-heeled sandals. Her hair was dyed bright henna-red and tied up into a kind of firework effect on top of her head. She was fifty-two years old, with a dead white face, turquoise eyelids, double false eyelashes and a mouth like a strawberry flan run over by a fire truck.

"We'd better go over the cards," I said. "I'm sure you don't have anything to worry about. Early Sagittarians are going through a very stable period right now . . . no disruptive vibrations. There's a possibility that something you eat may disagree with you . . . it *feels* like tortellini. But apart from that, everything's very calm. Almost cruiselike, you might say."

I brushed bagel crumbs off my baize tabletop, and laid out the cards. I didn't use the Tarot any more . . . not after all that trouble with Karen Tandy. I should have listened to Adelaide in the first place, I guess. But the Tarot is a little like crack: you can't really comprehend how dangerous it is until you try it.

These days I used Mlle Lenormand's fortune-telling cards. This is a very pretty pack of thirty-six cards which was devised by Mlle Lenormand early in 19th-century France. She used it to help her predict the rise and fall of Emperor Napoleon, the secrets of Empress Josephine, and the fate of many of their court followers. Or so the old shyster said—but then she was in the same business as me. What she *really* used was observation, logic, and common sense. The cards were nothing more than a ritual. Unlike the Tarot, Mlle Lenormand's cards have a little rhyme on them which more or less explains what they mean. Like most aids to fortune-telling, the rhymes are sufficiently ambiguous to allow the quick-witted card-diviner (i.e., me) to be able to interpret them according to his subject's immediate circumstances.

Mrs John F. Lavender noisily smoked while I laid out the cards, face up in four rows of eight cards and one row of four cards. "I don't know what I shall do if Mason has found out. He has *such* a temper! I daren't even *face* him! But then I can't live without him, either. He has such a cute ass. I mean, cute asses are *very* few and far between, especially in men of his age. Most of them look like as if they've filled their shorts with three gallons of Jell-O."

Mrs John F. Lavender's key card was number twenty-nine, an elegant woman in a long green dress carrying a bouquet of roses. Personally I thought that number fourteen, the vixen, would have been more appropriate, but then I wasn't being paid to be sarcastic.

"Here we are," I told her, laying down the last of the cards. "This is you . . . with your roses. And right ahead of you is . . . ah."

She blew smoke, and half sat up. "Right ahead of me is what? That's a scythe, isn't it? What does that mean?"

"Well . . . strictly speaking the scythe isn't altogether good news. It says here, *'The scythe looms bare, danger stalks too. Of strangers beware, they can harm you.'* "

"Danger? Of strangers beware?" snapped Mrs John F. Lavender, her mouth contorted. "I thought you said my vibrations were *calm.* That doesn't sound like calm!"

"Wait a minute," I interrupted her. "It also says, *'If some nearby cards hold a favorable view, Good are the odds you'll overcome too.'* "

"I still don't like the sound of that *'of strangers beware'* stuff," Mrs John F. Lavender protested. "God, I have a difficult enough time bewaring of people I *know!*"

"Hold on, hold on, let's not be too hasty here," I told her.

"Look, right next to you, on the right-hand side, is the clover-flower card. That means that even if something bad happens to you, you'll soon get over it."

"But I don't *want* to get over it! I don't want it to happen to me in the first place!"

"Well, for sure . . . but let's take a look here, on the left. A letter, look—lying on a lace tablecloth. *'This scented letter from a place remote . . . brings news that is better from a friend who wrote.'* There . . . it looks like everything's working out okay. The scythe card is just a warning, that's all. It's telling you to watch out for traps."

I hadn't read her the last part of the rhyme on the letter card, and I had no intention of reading it, either. It said, *"But as dark clouds loom in threatening sky, Sadness will soon much intensify."*

Mrs John F. Lavender lay back on the daybed and fumbled in her pocketbook for her cigarettes. I leaned forward and lit it for her, and she breathed tusks of smoke out of her nostrils. "What kind of trap, do you think?"

"Mason will follow you, or have you followed. That's what I think."

"The rat! But I love him."

"Just be careful, that's what the cards are telling you. Here, look at this one, underneath you. An open road. But there's a warning, too. It says *'Beware of the ground sinking from within.'* What it means is, take a different route when you visit Christopher, and when you visit Vince."

"Vance," she corrected me, "not Vince, Vance."

"Oh, I'm sorry . . . I lose track sometimes."

"I don't have *that* many men in my life, thank you!"

"I wasn't trying to suggest that you did. But four's enough to be getting along with, don't you think?"

She sucked smoke down to her red-lacquered toenails. "Do you know what my dream is?" she said. "To have them all in bed with me at one time. Can you imagine what it must be like to be taken by *four* men, all at one time?"

I frowned at the cards. "I'm afraid I don't see that particular entertainment coming along in the foreseeable future. But—well, you never know."

My intercom buzzed. I excused myself and answered it,

while Mrs John F. Lavender took out her checkbook and wrote out my fee. "Erm . . . it is fifteen dollars extra, for the Lenormand cards. I'm sorry, but that's how it is. They do take a considerable amount of psychic interpretation."

"Of course," she said, correcting the check. She signed it with her huge graffiti-like scrawl and waved it in the air to dry it.

"Hallo?" said a tiny, distorted voice on the other end of the intercom.

"Hallo, who is this?"

"Is that Harry Erskine?"

"That's me. Erskine the Incredible—palmistry, card-divining, tea-leaf interpretation, astrology, phrenology, numerology, bumps read, sooths said. As recommended by *New York* magazine and *Psychology Today.*"

Mrs John F. Lavender gave me a furry wink of her double false eyelashes, and a wide suggestive grin, from which smoke leaked.

"I read that piece about you in New York *magazine,"* said the voice on the end of the intercom. *"It said you were 'the only so-called clairvoyant who made no secret of his fakery . . . either because he thought his clients were so gullible, or because he simply didn't have the skill to make his crystal-ball gazing look convincing.' "*

"What do you want?" I demanded. "I have a client here . . . a very gracious lady who takes my divinations extremely seriously." (Here I nodded at Mrs John F. Lavender, and blew her a little kiss.) "What are you trying to do to me, ruin my reputation?"

"I need to see you," said the voice.

"Well, I'm sorry . . . I'm all booked up for the rest of the week."

"It'll only take a minute, I promise."

"I'm sorry. Why don't you put your request in writing? Enclose a clip of your hair, a tracing of the lines on the palm of your right hand, a check for thirty dollars and a stamped self-addressed envelope. I give a five-year guarantee. If what I predict doesn't happen to you within five years from the date of your reading, you get another fresh reading absolutely free, no questions asked."

"Please," the voice implored. *"I really have to talk to you."*

"You're so *popular,* Harry, that's the trouble," smiled Mrs John F. Lavender.

"Yes, Deirdre, I suppose you're right." I lifted the intercom again, and said, "Okay then, I'll be coming downstairs with my client in a couple of shakes. Just wait where you are. But I can only spare you a minute."

"I'll wait."

I frowned as I cradled the receiver. I had an odd feeling that I *knew* that voice. I couldn't think why, or how. But there was something familiar about the intonation that even the crackling of a loose connection hadn't been able to obliterate. Mrs John F. Lavender said, "Harry? Are you *okay?*"

"Sure . . . Yes, I'm okay. I'll see you down to the street."

"I'm sure that you're right about Mason having me followed," she said, hip-waggling in front of me into the hallway. I had stuck a poster of Aleister Crowley on the wall, and she peered at it in disapproval.

"Is that man any relation of yours?"

I shook my head. She peered back at me, and said, "I didn't think so. He has such piggy little eyes. He should eat less dairy products."

"He's dead," I told her.

"Well, there you are, then. Proves my point."

I opened the door for her and she clattered down the stairs on her stilettos. "I'm a little worried about Vance, to tell you the truth. He's definitely put on weight around the jowls. I don't like jowly men. They remind me of those slobbery dogs, you know the ones who leave saliva all over your velvet skirts."

The stairs down to the street were gloomy and tilted and smelled of stale cooking fat and Lysol. I'd been trying to persuade Mr Giotto the landlord to give the walls a lick of white paint. At the moment they were done in pustule yellow, which wasn't very uplifting for my clients.

"Did you give me my mystic motto?" Mrs John F. Lavender asked me, pausing on the second landing.

"Oh . . . no, sorry. I forgot."

"I do like to have my mystic motto. It always makes me

feel that I have some control over my life, do you know what I mean?"

"Yes, quite. Well . . . your mystic motto for this week is, unh, 'Many a fish should be filleted before the sun rises.' " Mrs John F. Lavender stared at me wide-eyed. I'd been giving my clients mystic mottoes for years—almost all of them insisted on it—but there was always a tense moment when I thought that they might burst out laughing.

" 'Many a fish should be filleted before the sun rises,' " Mrs John F. Lavender whispered, reverently. "That's beautiful. I can almost imagine it."

We carried on downstairs, her heels clacking loudly with every step. I had almost forgotten that somebody was waiting for me. Mrs John F. Lavender said, "I don't know why life is always so goddamned *complex.* Hiding, lying, worrying if you've left your earrings somewhere you shouldn't. And the trouble is that I absolutely adore *all* of them."

The sun was shining brightly through the grimy wired-glass panels in the building's front doors, and reflecting from the pale-green linoleum floor. The figure was silhouetted black against the reflected light, so that as I came down the last flight of stairs it was impossible for me to make out who it was.

I could see it was a woman, with a shoulder-length bob. I could see that she was very slim, and that she was wearing a simple strapless cotton dress with a red poppy print on it.

But it was only when I came right up to her, and she turned slightly towards the light, that at last I recognized her; and even then I could hardly believe it.

"Hallo, Harry," she said, with the faintest of smiles. "Very long time no see."

"Many a fish should be filleted . . ." Mrs John F. Lavender muttered. I opened the front doors for her, and she stepped out into the street. A firetruck roared past, honking and whooping, and a huge guy walked by with the largest ghetto-blaster on his shoulder that I had ever seen. The hot morning air literally throbbed. Mrs John F. Lavender blew me two ostentatious kisses and said, "You're a wonderful, wonderful man! I'll see you next week, same time!" Then—

to my visitor—"He's a *wonderful* man, dear! I can recommend him!"

I closed the doors and the hallway was abruptly quiet. Karen was still smiling in that faint, fey way she had. She was nearly twenty years older than the last time I had seen her, and there were subtle streaks of silver in her hair. I was grey, too, with a bald patch the size of a buckwheat pancake. I had a little more chin, too, although not so much as Aleister Crowley.

I took hold of her hands, and gently squeezed them. She was real, not an illusion.

"You're still doing it, then?" she asked me. "The fortune-telling."

"Oh, yes, for sure. I tried motel management for a while, up at White Plains, but that didn't really pan out. I can't be unctuous twenty-four hours a day, that's my problem. Then I tried a mobile disco. Erskine's Electric Experience. I lost over nine thousand dollars on that. I guess this is the only work that I've ever been cut out for."

"Harry," she said, "something bad's happened. Not to me, but to some friends of mine. They've tried everything. Police, doctors, rabbis. But nobody really believes them. I'm not so sure I believe them myself."

"I see. So you came looking for the one man in the world who's wacky enough to believe anything?"

"Don't say that," she chided me.

"All right," I said. "What about a drink?"

"I thought you were too busy."

"I always say that. As a matter of fact my next client isn't due until . . ." I checked my Russian wristwatch ". . . Thursday."

"Oh, Harry! You haven't changed, have you?"

I checked my wallet to make sure that I had enough money for a drink, then opened the front door and said, "I've changed, Karen, believe me. Number one, I never take anything for granted any more. Number two, I never wear tasselled loafers with a business suit."

"Before we go," she said, "lift up my hair."

"What?"

"Lift up my hair . . . here, at the back."

Slowly I approached her and lifted up her fine, soft hair. On the back of her neck, running down between her shoulder blades, was a thin silvery scar about seven inches long. I ran my fingertip down it, and then let her hair fall back.

"It *did* happen," she said, turning around.

I nodded. "I know. I keep trying to convince myself that it was nothing but a weird dream. Or maybe it was something that I imagined when I was drunk. Maybe it was a movie I saw, or a book I read. That's why I never came to see you. I knew that if I saw you, I wouldn't be able to pretend that it hadn't happened."

"This isn't as bad, this thing that's happened to my friends."

I smiled. "*Nothing* could ever be as bad as Misquamacus. Nothing."

Karen slowly lifted her hand and pressed it against the scar. Her eyes were wide with remembered fear. "Don't mention that name to me again, ever."

TWO

We sat in a booth at Maude's, on the first floor of the Summit Hotel. It was crowded and noisy with the lunchtime crowd, and we were lucky to find somewhere to wedge ourselves in. Karen had a frozen daiquiri and I had the usual: an Erskine Explosion. Maude's bar was the only bar that would make it for me. Or at least they were the only bar who knew how to make it properly. It was basically a Suffering Bastard with bourbon added. You only had to drink one and the world suddenly seemed to be a happier place. Better still, it suddenly seemed to be the *only* place. When you've glimpsed other worlds, like Tarot worlds, or worlds where invisible things go rushing down the walls, a little self-delusion can help to steady the mental boat.

I noticed a gold band on Karen's left hand.

"You're married?" I asked her.

She shook her head. "I was. A college professor from

Hartford. He was very kind to me. His name's Jim."

"So you're not Karen Tandy any more—you're Mrs Jim?"

"Mrs van Hooven."

"Oh, so you changed your nationality, too. What happened?"

"With Jim? Nothing, really. I still think the world of him. But I woke up one morning and realized that I needed more in my life than kindness."

"What else is there? Sex, drugs, and rock'n'roll?"

"I don't know. I'm trying to find out."

" *'I have known the strange nurses of Kindness,'* " I quoted. " *'I have seen them kiss the sick, attend the old, give candy to the mad!'* "

"You're a strange man, Harry."

"No, I'm not. Strange men have strange aspirations. I dream of nothing but being normal."

Karen said, "These friends of mine . . ."

"The ones you're worried about?"

"Yes. They live on East 17th Street. Their names are Michael and Naomi Greenberg. I've known Michael ever since school. They're lovely people, really lovely."

I swallowed some of my Explosion, and gave an involuntary shudder, the same kind you give when somebody walks over your grave.

"So, what's their problem?" I asked her. "This problem that nobody can bring themselves to believe, even you?"

Karen looked serious. As she spoke, she traced a pattern on the tabletop with her fingertip, around and around and around.

"It happened nearly four weeks ago this Friday. Michael went to the synagogue with Naomi's brother Erwin. Naomi cooked the supper and laid the table and had everything ready for Michael and Erwin to come home. But about half an hour before they were due to come back, all the furniture in the dining room slid across the floor by itself and crowded up against the wall. Naomi tried to stop it. In fact, she kept moving it back to the middle of the room but it still insisted on sliding towards the wall. In the end Naomi was quite badly hurt. She broke one rib and fractured two more, and her left lung was lacerated.

"Not only that, the whole experience left her totally traumatised."

"You went through worse than that," I reminded her.

She shrugged, trying to make light of it. "I wasn't alone, like Naomi. Besides, I didn't even realize what was happening to me, most of the time. How can I put it? I wasn't myself."

I leaned back in my chair. A young business type sitting close to me was laughing so loudly that I thought he was going to burst my eardrum.

"So, what's the problem? The Greenbergs' furniture moved by itself. There must be plenty of people who wish their furniture would move by itself."

"Well, there's more to it than that."

"Let's think about the moving furniture first. We have to consider the possibility that Naomi broke her rib in a different way—in a way that she didn't want Michael to know about—and so she moved the furniture herself and concocted this story that it moved by itself."

"She would never do a thing like that! And, anyway, how on earth do you break a rib in a way that you don't want your husband to know about?"

"Who knows? Maybe your friend has a violent lover. Maybe she had an automobile accident someplace where she didn't want her husband to know that she'd been."

Karen said, "No, Harry. Naomi's not like that. I can tell you that sure-and-for-certain."

"You can never be sure-and-for-certain about anybody. You know that."

"Am I hearing you right? After everything that happened at the Sisters of Jerusalem—after all of that terrible struggle—you don't believe that this could be supernatural, too?"

I finished my drink. "Karen, think about it. It's a question of scale. What happened at the Sisters of Jerusalem was virtually war—one people against another. One set of spiritual beliefs against another. At the very worst, what happened at your friends' apartment sounds like nothing much more than a minor outbreak of weird science. Maybe Naomi *is* faithful. Maybe there are such things as poltergeists. Personally, I think you have to ask the non-supernatural questions first."

Karen was upset, and the last thing I had wanted to do was upset her. But twenty years ago, in the Sisters of Jerusalem Hospital, Karen had given birth to that grotesque and stunted creature that most of us had believed to be the reincarnation of the seventeenth-century Wampanoag medicine-man, Misquamacus. It had been a devastating experience. People had died. The appearance of Misquamacus had stretched my faith and my credibility to their utmost limits, and beyond. I had been there, yes, at the Sisters of Jerusalem. I had witnessed what had happened for myself. But these days I preferred to think that Karen's unique condition had somehow been the epicenter of an extraordinary outbreak of mass suggestion. How, or why, I couldn't imagine. But I just preferred to think of it that way. Better to be nuts than have to admit that something like Misquamacus could actually exist.

Karen said, "A professor came all the way from Seattle Pacific University to check out the Greenbergs' apartment for himself. He was some kind of expert in poltergeists and people who can move things with their mind, things like that. He said that it wasn't poltergeists. At least, it wasn't like any poltergeist behaviour that *he'd* ever seen. Poltergeists are much more erratic, much more mischievous. All that happened at the Greenbergs was that the furniture all slid over to one side of the room and stayed there."

"But if it wasn't poltergeists, what did this professor think it was?"

Karen shrugged. "He didn't know. He couldn't account for it. Just like everybody else. The police saw it and they couldn't account for it. The rabbi saw it and he couldn't account for it. Naomi's shrink came to see it and he couldn't account for it. So now they've all decided that it probably never happened—or, like you, that Naomi's making it up."

I laid my hands on top of Karen's. "Karen, I wish there was something I could do. But this is way out of my field of expertise. Not that I really have any expertise, or ever will. I'm sorry."

Karen said, "You fought Misquamacus." I knew how difficult it was for her to say that name. "You fought him, and you won!"

"I don't know. Maybe it all happened a lot different from the way we remember it."

Karen's eyes glittered with tears. "Harry—Michael and Naomi are two of my very best friends. They're both going crazy. This whole thing has practically destroyed their lives. It might seem trivial to you, but to them it's the end of their marriage, the end of their sanity almost. I promised them—"

I glanced up. I had one hand raised for the waiter, to bring us two more drinks. I paused.

"You promised them what?"

"I promised them the best psychic expert in New York. In fact, the best psychic expert in America."

I didn't know what to say. The waiter came and stood beside me and all I could do was sit with my arms raised like a schoolboy and my mouth arrested in mid-pronunciation.

"Can I get you anything, sir?"

"Check," I blurted, at last. "Get me the check."

"Harry—" Karen began, but I interrupted her.

"You promised them the best psychic expert in America? You mean *me*?"

"I didn't know what else to do. I didn't know where else to turn."

"Karen, for Christ's sake! I tell fortunes! I read tea-leaves! I make it all up as I go along! I'm about as much of a psychic expert as Peewee Herman! In fact, why didn't you ask Peewee Herman? He's even loopier than I am!"

The young business type had stopped laughing all of a sudden, and was staring at me in astonishment. "You want to know *your* future, you goddamned laughing hyena?" I shouted at him. "You'll get married, deafen your wife, deafen your dog and deafen your children. Finally you'll deafen yourself. The rest is silence!"

"What's eating you, buddy?" he replied, backing away.

"Harry, please don't lose your temper," Karen begged me.

"Yeah, Harry," said the business type. "*Please* don't lose your temper."

"How would you like a smack in the face?" I asked him, but Karen snatched hold of my sleeve.

"Harry—" she implored me, "just come have a look. That's all I want you to do. Just come have a look.'

"Yeah, Harry," echoed the business type. "Do us all a favor, and go take a look."

I signed the check, drew back the table so that Karen could get out, and then ushered her towards the door. As I opened it I turned round and said to the business type, "Believe me, friend, you could go far with a laugh like that. You could go to Paterson, New Jersey, and we'd still be able to hear you."

It took us nearly twenty minutes to reach the Greenbergs' house because of a traffic snarl-up around Union Square. The fat black driver kept singing *Message in a Bottle* over and over. At least his air-conditioning worked. Outside it was eighty-seven degrees with eighty-one per cent humidity and the air was the color of breathed-over bronze.

Karen told me everything that had happened to her since I had wished her goodnight and closed the door on her bedroom twenty years ago. It was hard to believe so much time had passed. I had remembered her face so clearly—pale, elfin, with flawless skin—and now here she was grown-up, a woman with the lines of a woman.

Jim's kindness hadn't been the only problem in their marriage. Jim had wanted children, but after what had happened at the Sisters of Jerusalem, Karen hadn't been able to face it. Jim had been one of those men who desperately wants a son. He was the last of the Hartford van Hoovens: he had wanted Karen to bear him at least one heir, so that the line could continue into the next century. He was now married to a lady professor with wild, hay-colored hair, a strident line in home-knitted sweaters, and good child-bearing hips. It tickled Karen to think that both she and this academic Valkyrie shared the name of "Mrs van Hooven."

Eventually we reached East 17th and climbed out stiffly onto the roasting sidewalk. I didn't know this area very well, although I used to have a girlfriend on East 15th who wrote for the *Voice* and I often used to meet her for drinks at The Bells of Hell. I looked up and down the street. It stank of garbage and fumes and something else: something sickening and sour. A blind man with white stubble on his chin was leaning on a white stick playing *Funeral Blues* on a key-of-F harmonica.

The Greenbergs' house was a flat-fronted brownstone, with two dusty bay trees on the step outside the front door, both of them heavily chained to the stone balustrade. On the west side of the house there was an envelope factory, which looked as if it had been built around 1914, livid brown-and-white bricks and dusty blacked-out windows. On the east side stood another brownstone, much larger, with squatter proportions to its windows, and soot-scale on its brick. A red neon sign over the porch said Belford Hotel. It was the kind of hotel you would walk the streets all night rather than stay at—the kind of hotel with used needles in the lobby and all night long the sinister surreptitious rattle of people trying your doorhandle.

Karen pressed the bell marked M & N GREENBERG and after a while a strained voice said, "Karen? That you?" over the intercom.

"I've found Harry," she said, and immediately the buzzer unlocked the front door.

We climbed up the gloomy staircase. At least it was carpeted, and the smell of cooking was reasonably fresh. Somebody was having fish tonight, unless I was mistaken. Fish simmered in lavender furniture-polish.

We reached the Greenbergs' apartment and Karen knocked. The polished mahogany door was opened immediately. We were ushered in by a short balding man with a beard and black-rimmed eyeglasses. He wore a beige turtleneck and jeans that were too short for him, revealing inside-out white socks.

"Michael, this is Harry Erskine."

Michael pumped my hand. His palms were sweaty, but I guess mine were, too. "I'm so pleased you could make it,

Harry. You don't mind me calling you Harry? Karen's told us so much about you."

"She hasn't exaggerated, I hope."

"Well . . . she was very complimentary. If there's anybody in the United States who can deal with your problem, it's Harry Erskine, that's what she said."

Karen went ahead, into the living room. Michael held my sleeve for a moment, detaining me.

"Listen," he said, "my wife is a mess. She's practically gone off her head. The doctor's got her on medication; the shrink makes house calls every second day. I think she saw a whole lot more than she's been willing to tell us, but she won't say what it was. If you can be gentle with her, that's all."

"Okay," I nodded, feeling more of a fraud than ever. "I'll be gentle with her."

Michael Greenberg said, "I don't know what you did for Karen. She won't talk about it to anybody. I know it's something to do with that scar on her neck, but that's all I know. All I can tell you is that—whatever it was—Karen thinks the world of you. She really does."

"Thank you," I said. "I think a lot of Karen, too."

Michael Greenberg said, "Please . . . come this way." He led me through to a stuffy middle-class living room, with a few ornaments and knick-knacks that immediately gave away the fact that the occupants were Jewish, such as a silver Star of David on the mantelpiece and an amateurish oil painting of children working on a kibbutz. The furniture was oversized and the upholstery needed a clean. I knew a man on 53rd Street who would have brought this kind of wool fabric up really well, but I didn't think that this was an appropriate time to recommend him.

Under the window an air-conditioner was whirring away at full blast. I went over and stood in front of it for a while, enjoying the chill. Then I took a few steps into the center of the room, paused, and sniffed, and looked around. I was doing it mainly for theatrical effect: the master psychic enters the possessed property and immediately senses that some malevolence is there. But there *was* something there, some presence, I could feel it immediately. It was so strong that I felt what Mrs John F. Lavender had felt . . . *icy—fingers—down—back.*

I pressed my fingertips to my forehead. "Hmmm . . ." I said, like a wine connoisseur savoring a vintage. Poltergeist of German origin, 1979; sourish and lacking body, probably not immediately dangerous, but with a certain threatening undertone which could give you a nasty finish.

"What's the matter?" asked Karen. "Can you feel something?"

"Definitely," I said, looking around some more. "It's like a smell that you can't really smell. I mean, like the air's all thick. Can you feel it?"

"Well, kind of a *tension.* I'm not sure. Maybe it's just the humidity."

I walked around the living room, picking up various objects, books, vases, ashtrays. I picked up a framed postcard of the Mount of Olives. The glass was cracked in a curious zigzag pattern.

"I've been wondering about that, too," Michael Greenberg remarked. "It happened the same day that—" he nodded towards the dining room.

I put the postcard back on the table. "All right, then, I'd better see the epicenter." I liked the word "epicenter," it always sounded spiritually professional. I liked "paranormal" too, and "metempsychosis."

Michael Greenberg said, "Harry—before you go in there—"

I raised my hand reassuringly. "Mr Greenberg—Michael—I'm pretty experienced when it comes down to psychic phenomena. I've seen things you wouldn't even want to have nightmares about."

"Well," said Michael Greenberg. He looked dubious. "It's not just a smell in there, believe me."

"You had the police here. What did they say?"

"They didn't want to know. They said that there was no crime involved, and no public disturbance, so the whole thing was way outside of their field of expertise."

"And what do the shrinks think?"

Michael Greenberg shrugged. "I don't know. They use all this technical-type language, psycho-this, maladjusted-that.

Frankly, I don't think they know what the hell *they're* talking about, either."

I perched myself on the back of his sofa, as if I owned the place. You have to make your clients think that you're completely self-confident. I mean, we're talking about the occult here—dead relatives who whisper in your ear, mischievous gremlins who tear fistfuls of fur out of family cats. You have to give the impression that *nothing* surprises you.

"You don't think the psychiatrists fully understand Naomi's trauma?"

"No way! They're blaming her! She's the patient, she's the victim, yet they're blaming *her*! They don't seem to understand jack shit."

"Well, maybe they do and maybe they don't. But you have to understand, Michael, that if somebody's badly upset—especially a woman, for some reason—their brainwaves can actually cause physical disturbances. Minor accidents, cuts, bumps, even fires. A woman in Baltimore got angry with her husband one night two years ago and broke every God-damned window within a radius of two miles. Now that's a proven fact: you can read it in the records. She broke every God-damned window within a radius of two miles, and she didn't even leave her apartment. You saw *Carrie*. That wasn't total bullshit, by any means. In the trade we call it psychokinesis—the movement or displacement or destruction of physical objects by nothing more than mental energy."

Michael Greenberg breathed deeply, and nodded, and said, "That was one of the words the shrinks used, psychokinesis," as if I had just blasphemed.

I grasped his shoulder and gave him my best Professional Psychic's smile. "I'm going to promise you something, Michael, even before I see what's wrong. *This disturbance can be cured.* There isn't a single psychic disturbance that isn't susceptible to good psychic management. That means discipline, calm, and rational procedure. It's just like running a business. If something freaky happens in a business, if you experience a sudden and unexpected downturn in sales—well, there's always a reason for it. And there's always a way to handle it. We can do the same here—I guarantee it—I *guarantee* it—no matter what the hell is wrong. You're haunted? I can have you de-haunted. You keep hearing voices? I can shut the bastards up."

Michael glanced at Karen, as if he were questioning my competence, but Karen turned away.

"Karen told me that you were the best," he remarked.

"In this business, it isn't easy to judge. We're not talking automobile maintenance here."

Karen said, "Harry—you're good. You know you are."

"Maybe it's time you saw the problem for yourself," Michael suggested.

"For sure," I said, and followed him closely to the door.

He turned, his hand on the handle, and stared at me.

"You still have a choice. I mean, I begged Karen to get you here, but you don't have to get yourself involved with this unless you really want to."

"Michael—I meant what I said," I replied. "There isn't a psychic manifestation alive or dead that can't be dealt with. All you have to do is make sure that you apply the appropriate ritual of exorcism to the appropriate manifestation."

"All right," said Michael, and opened the door.

I stepped in, and found myself in a large family dining room. It was chilly, unexpectedly chilly, and the smell that I had noticed in the living room was very much stronger. It was a really strange smell, like burned herbs and sweat and dust. It reminded me of something ... I couldn't think what ... but something that you would never normally associate with East 17th Street on a sweaty August afternoon. It was a smell from very long ago and very far away.

The dining room was dimly lit by a five-branched chandelier, fitted with low-wattage bulbs, and that was all. The dimness did nothing to enhance the decorations, which—like the decorations in the living room—were staid beyond the Greenbergs' age—brown patterned wallpaper and thick brown carpet. But it was the furniture which caught my attention first. It was all crowded against the left-hand wall, as if it had been heaped up at a second-hand store, or a sale room. The dining table, the chairs, the sideboard—even the flower vases and the cutlery. Everything had been crammed higgledy-piggledy up against the wall.

Even the paintings on the wall were hanging sideways.

Only one chair remained in the center of the room, and on that chair sat a woman in a grubby white towelling bathrobe. Her face was grey and papery. It looked as fragile as a wasps' nest, as if you could have pierced her cheek with your finger. Her eyes were wide open but milky-white, because she had rolled her pupils up into her head. She was breathing steadily, but her breathing was fast and threatening, rather than peaceful. Her hair was wildly tangled and bone-white.

I turned to Michael in shock. The room itself had the feeling of a tightly-compressed shock.

"Who's that?" I asked him, in a hoarse whisper.

Michael took off his glasses, and wiped his eyes with the back of his hand. "That's Naomi, that's my wife."

THREE

I stepped into the dining room and cautiously looked around. This time, I wasn't acting the part of cautious psychic. I was living out the part of shit-scared psychic. The air was unnaturally chilled and the light was oppressively dim, and right in front of me sat a white-haired woman clutching her chair as if she were determined that nobody was going to prize her free from it, no matter what.

With her white, blank, terrifying eyes.

With her lips stretched back across her teeth as if she were going to snatch a bite out of anybody who tried to come close.

She was so tense, I felt that I could have hit her with a poker and she would have cracked in half. Fallen apart, like a broken bell-casting.

"How long has she been like this?" I asked Michael, leaning forward to take a closer look at her. Thinking, *Shit, give me Mrs John F. Lavender any day of the week—this is serious shit.*

"Three weeks, ever since it happened. She won't move."

"What do you mean, she won't move?"

"She won't get off the chair. She sits on it twenty-four hours."

"Has she eaten?"

"I've fed her, she allows me to feed her, and to give her water."

"What about . . . ?"

"You mean hygiene? I just have to clean her the best way I can."

"Jesus."

Karen said, "Harry . . . you must be able to help somehow."

I stepped back. "I don't know . . . can't the shrinks do anything at all? Jesus. She looks like she's catatonic."

Michael said, distractedly, "They bandaged her ribs . . . they checked her over. Then they tried to take her in for observation, but as soon as they tried to move her she threw such a fit that they decided that it would be safer to leave her where she is. I mean she went totally crazy. Arms waving, feet kicking, choking on her tongue. They keep coming up with these theories, but they still don't understand what's wrong with her. Dr. Stein visits every two or three days. He used to be senior consultant at Bellevue. He's given her every test he can think of. Every session he comes up with a different theory. Hysteria, deprived childhood. Change of life. He even tried to suggest that she was a secret alcoholic, and that she was suffering from DTs. God almighty, Naomi never drank more in her life than a half a glass of red wine at her brother's bar-mitzvah. Dr. Bradley's the same, he's been twice. He keeps saying she's manic depressive."

"Does she speak?" I asked him.

Michael nodded. "Sometimes. It doesn't always make sense."

"If I say something to her now, do you think she might answer?"

"You can try."

I approached Naomi Greenberg with considerable caution and leaned forward. Her eyes were still rolled up into her head, but her eyelids had begun to flutter.

"Naomi," I said. "Naomi, my name's Harry. I'm a friend of Karen's."

Naomi didn't show any signs that she might have heard me, but her eyelids fluttered even faster, and she began to breathe more quickly.

"Naomi, I've come here today to see what I can do to help you."

Still no reply, although her right foot suddenly shifted on the woodblock floor, making a sharp chipping sound that made me jump.

"Can you hear me, Naomi? I need to ask you some questions. I need to know what has happened to you."

"She won't say," Michael put in.

I lifted my hand behind me to shush him. "Naomi . . . I need to know what happened. I need to know what you saw."

Naomi suddenly stiffened, and her pupils rolled down into sight. They were brown, filmed-over, unfocused. She stared at me in bewilderment—not so much as if she couldn't work out who I was, but as if she couldn't work out *what* I was. Maybe she thought that I was furniture, too. I didn't have any idea how deep her disturbance went. A friend of my mother's lived for years under the delusion that her husband was a hatstand.

"Naomi," I repeated. "My name's Harry. I'm a friend of Karen's. Karen asked me to come see you. She thinks that maybe I can help you."

"You . . . can . . . help . . . me?" Naomi slurred. Her voice had no intonation at all.

"I'm going to try. But I need to know what happened to you. I want you to tell me all about this furniture."

Slowly, Naomi turned her head and stared at the heaped-up chairs and tables. "Couldn't . . . stop . . . it," she said. "Couldn't . . . stop . . . it."

"Naomi," I asked her, coming closer. "Did *you* move the furniture?"

She thought about that for a while, and then gave a quick flurrying shake of her head.

"What did I tell you?" said Michael. "Last week, Dr. Bradley kept on shouting at her, trying to get her to admit that she was acting hysterical. Like she was doing it on purpose. But how the hell could she? Why the hell *would* she?"

"Please, Michael," I told him. "I need to concentrate here."

"I'm sorry," said Michael. "But all I've been hearing is, 'Why did you move the furniture, Naomi?' 'What are you trying to *do* to yourself, Naomi?' 'Have you been sniffing any substances, Naomi?' "

His mouth tightened as he tried to control his distress. "All I know is, I went with Erwin to the synagogue that night and I left a happy, smiling, stable wife. I came back three hours later and I found this strange woman—traumatized, terrified, out of her goddamned mind. That's all I know."

"Has she told you what happened?"

"I don't know, fragments. She said there were noises. She said there were shadows. She wouldn't stop talking about shadows. But nothing that makes any sense."

"Nobody broke in?"

"Unh-hunh. The police were one hundred per cent sure about that. The windows were barred and locked, all the security locks and chains were fastened. In fact *we* had to break in, Erwin and me. We called the fire department and they jacked the front door right out of its frame."

"Naomi wouldn't have admitted anybody into the apartment of her own free will? There was no sign of that?"

"What is this?" Michael snapped. "I thought you came here to help me, not give me the third degree."

"Michael, I have to eliminate all of the natural possibilities before I even start thinking about the supernatural possibilities. It's far more likely that what happened here was caused by some kind of scientific glitch—you know, a high-voltage electrical disturbance maybe, or a localized earth tremblor, or a lightning strike."

"You're trying to tell me that Naomi was struck by lightning?"

"I have to consider it," I insisted. "She shows some of the symptoms of electrocution, right? Shock, disorientation? And all of the furniture was moved, right? They had a case like that in Cedar Rapids, Iowa, about 1977. A boy was struck by lightning and all of the living room furniture was blown into the yard. They found the couch in the next street, with the boy's Green Lantern comic still on it, open at the exact same page he'd been reading when he was struck."

"Harry, this wasn't lightning," Michael assured me, with exaggerated patience.

"Well, no, I don't really think it was."

"It wasn't an earthquake, either."

"No," I conceded. "Probably not."

"So if it wasn't lightning, or an earthquake, and nobody broke in, it must have been supernatural, whether any of us want to believe in the supernatural or not."

"There could be some element of the paranormal involved, yes."

"What do you mean, 'some element'? Look at my wife! Look at this furniture! I'll tell you what—try to move one of those chairs back to the middle of the room!"

"Michael, your wife is suffering severe psychological trauma. I can't deal with that. She needs heavyweight professional help."

Michael turned sharply to Karen, and then back to me, "I'm sorry," he said. "Karen gave me the impression that *you* were the heavyweight professional help."

"Oh, come on, Michael," I told him. "I'm a clairvoyant. I tell people's fortunes. I deal with things that look as they might be but probably aren't. I deal with Uncle Fred who wants to get in touch with Auntie Eugenie from beyond the Cypress Hills cemetery, and tell her where he left the spare lightbulbs for the icebox. This thing—this thing that's wrong with your wife . . . I can't deal with this. This is a medical problem."

"And what about the furniture?" Michael demanded. "You think the furniture is a medical problem, too? Try moving it, then you'll see how 'medical' it is!"

Reluctantly, I went across to the tangle of furniture and took hold of one of the chairs. It felt as if it were caught on one of the other chairs, and I had to tug it hard to get it free. It was only then that I realized it hadn't been caught at all. It was being drawn toward the wall as strongly as if it were magnetized.

I looked around at Michael in bewilderment.

"Take it into the center of the room," he told me. "Go on. Then put it down."

With considerable difficulty, I carried the chair to the center of the room, underneath the chandelier, and set it on the floor.

"Now let it go," said Michael.

I lifted my hands. Immediately, the chair tumbled noisily back to the opposite side of the room. No strings, no hidden mechanisms. It literally *fell* sideways, and clattered back into place with all the other furniture.

I stood and stared at it and didn't know what to do. I went back to get it, but Michael said, "It'll do that every time."

"Well," I agreed, hunkering down, and inspecting the chair closely, "that's some problem."

"And it sure isn't a medical problem, is it?"

"No, I have to agree with you. It isn't a medical problem. There's definitely some element of the paranormal involved here. Right now, I'm not too sure what it is, or what the extent of it is."

"But you can deal with it?" Michael insisted. "Five minutes ago you *guaranteed* you could deal with it. 'All it takes is good psychic management,' that's what you said."

"Exactly, exactly! But you can't exercise good psychic management until you know what kind of psychic phenomenon you're supposed to be managing."

"And you don't?"

"Not yet," I admitted. "As I said . . . we could be talking psychokinesis here. Or it might be a poltergeist. On the other hand, it might be neither of those things. It might be transmutation. Or levitation, even. Kind of *sideways* levitation."

Michael shook his head. "I see," he said, in obvious disappointment. Even Karen looked uncomfortable. I suddenly felt shabby and unconvincing, and about as professional as a door-to-door soap salesman. All the same, I turned back to Naomi and said, "Naomi . . . listen. I need you to tell me what happened."

She stared at me, her head nodding and nodding as if she

had Parkinson's Disease, saying nothing.

"Was there anybody here? Did you see anybody moving the furniture?"

She shook her head. "Nobody . . . here. Only . . . shadows."

"What shadows?"

Fearfully, she edged her eyes towards the wall. "Shadows . . . on . . . the . . . wall . . . it . . . *bit* him . . ."

"It bit him? *What* bit him?"

There was a very long silence. Naomi sat staring at the wall, breathing deeply and harshly. Then, without warning, she did something that—for some reason—utterly chilled me. She covered her face with her hands so that only her eyes looked out; and looked slowly and threateningly from right to left, and back again.

"It . . . *bit* . . . him . . ." she repeated, and made her fingers writhe and wriggle like a nest of white snakes. "It . . . *bit* . . . him . . ."

Then she raised both writhing hands so that they rested on top of her shock-white hair, like horns or antlers, or a Gorgon's snakes.

As unexpectedly as she had started this performance, she lowered her hands and resumed her grip on the seat of her chair, staring at me as if she expected me to understand exactly what she had been doing.

"Has she ever done that before?" I asked Michael.

"No, never. Not to anybody."

"Has she said 'it bit him' to anybody else?"

"Not unless she said it to Dr. Stein when I was out of the room."

I stood frowning, thinking. *Shadows on the wall.* Naomi had seen shadows on the wall. At the moment, there were very few shadows on the wall, because all of the light came from the dim chandelier suspended from the ceiling. The main shadows were mine and Naomi's, in small misshapen pools around our feet. So how had Naomi seen shadows on the wall?

"Michael . . . could you bring me a desk lamp, something like that?"

"Sure," he said, and went back through to the living room.

Karen stood in the doorway, her arms cradled, her face pale. "I'm sorry, Harry. I didn't realize how difficult this was going to be."

I grunted. "Difficult? This isn't difficult. This is so far out it's meeting itself coming the other way." I wasn't angry with her. I just felt inadequate, and seriously embarrassed.

Michael returned with a small red enamel desk lamp and I set it down on the floor and plugged it in. As I stood up again, however, it slid sharply across the room, unplugging itself as it did so, and clattered up against the opposite wall, next to the dining table.

"'A slight element of the paranormal,'" Michael quoted me.

"All right, no problem," I retaliated. "I deal with this kind of stuff every day of the week." In actual fact, I didn't *really* deal with this kind of stuff every day of the week. I had never dealt with anything like this before, ever. But I wasn't going to let Michael's skepticism get the better of me. I could understand the man's bitterness; I could understand his sense of frustration, but the fact is that there isn't *anybody* trained to cope with the supernatural, there aren't any Ducs de Richelieu or Harvard professors of Occult Goings-On, no matter what they tell you in Dennis Wheatley novels and Stephen Spielberg movies. So I was just as qualified as the next guy. Or just as *un*qualified. It depends how charitable you want to be.

I crossed the room and picked up the lamp. I had to pull at it with almost my entire strength in order to carry it back across to the far side of the room.

"Michael, I'm going to plug this in again. Do you want to hold it, please, to stop it from sliding away?"

Michael came into the room and knelt down beside the desk lamp, holding it by the neck like a live rooster—and, believe me, if he had let it go, it would have rattled away from him just as fast. He switched it on, so that it illuminated the opposite wall. I stood in front of it and did a few of my shadow-tricks. A rabbit. A dove, with flapping wings. A turtle.

"What in God's name are you doing?" Michael wanted to know.

"Shush. I want to attract Naomi's attention, but I don't want to upset her. Well, not yet, anyway."

Naomi was watching my shadow-pictures out of the corner of her eye. She flinched slightly when I made them move, but she didn't look away.

"Now, Naomi," I asked her. "Is this the kind of shadow you saw on the wall?"

She shook her head. But still she didn't look away.

I did a dog, and a giraffe, and Oliver Hardy. That was about the sum total of my repertoire. No wonder the kids always used to boo me when I tried to entertain at children's parties. But then I tried to imitate Naomi. I covered my face with my hands, so that only my eyes peered out. Then I slowly wriggled my fingers.

Naomi was staring at the wall with widened eyes. I kept on wriggling my fingers, and I gradually lifted my hands higher and higher, the same way that Naomi had done, until they crowned my head like antlers.

Naomi's scream was so high-pitched that I couldn't hear it at first. It was far beyond the normal register of human perception, like a dog whistle. But I was aware of it, I was aware of her panic, and I turned toward the wall to see what it was that had terrified her so much.

I saw my own shadow. A hunched, heavy-headed creature like a goat standing on its hind legs, with a crown of writhing snakes. If such a creature had been standing right in front of me in the flesh, you wouldn't have seen me for Reebok smoke. But I dropped my hands, just as Naomi's scream dropped from inaudible to earsplitting, and Michael let go of the desk lamp, and so the creature instantaneously turned itself back into me, and then (as the desk lamp tugged itself loose and clattered across the floor) it vanished.

Michael wrapped his arms around Naomi as she screamed and screamed and wouldn't stop. She rocked her chair violently from side to side, and drummed her feet on the floor. Her eyes rolled up again, and she began to froth and spit as if she were having an epileptic fit.

"What the fuck have you done!" Michael yelled at me.

Naomi screamed and thrashed and there was nothing that any of us could do to calm her down.

"I'm sorry!" I told Michael. "I'm really sorry! I didn't realize!"

"Forget it!" he shouted back at me. "Just get out of here! You God-damned sham!"

"Hey, who are you calling a sham?" I retorted, but Karen caught hold of my arm and said, "I'm sorry, Harry. It's better if we go. I'm really sorry."

"Just get the hell out!" Michael screamed. I didn't know who was making the most noise: him or Naomi.

But as I retreated, an odd thing happened. *Another* shadow flickered across the wall, even though there was no desk lamp to cast it. It was so brief, so insubstantial, that I wasn't at all sure that I had really seen it. But it bore a noticeable resemblance to the creature that I had created with my hunched back and my wriggling fingers.

As it passed across the wall, Naomi abruptly stopped screaming, and turned her head this way and that, as if she could sense that it was there.

"Naomi?" said Michael. His eyes were filled with tears and he was holding her very tight. "Naomi, are you okay?"

Naomi's pupils rolled back into view. She stared at Michael, face-to-face, expressionless, as if she had never seen him in her life before. Then she turned and stared at me.

"Thank God," she whispered.

"What?" said Michael. "What? Naomi—*what*?"

She ignored him. "You *know,* don't you?" she asked me, so softly that I could scarcely hear her. "You know what it is." She lifted her hands to her face in the way that she had before, so that only her eyes looked out.

Michael said, "Naomi, Harry has to leave. I really don't think—"

"No!" she interrupted him. "Harry mustn't leave. He's the only one who knows."

"Naomi—"

"*No!* He's the only one who knows!"

Her speech was still slurry and mechanical, like the speech of somebody who has suffered a mild stroke, but it was much more emphatic than it had been before, much more demanding.

There was a silence that was almost embarrassingly long, while Naomi continued to stare at me as if I was the Lone Ranger and a Chippendale's dancer and John the Baptist all rolled into one.

"What?" Michael wanted to know. "What is it? If Harry knows what it is, then don't you think I'm entitled to know, too?"

"He knows what it is," Naomi repeated. But then she turned to Michael and pressed her forehead gently against his cheek, a clear demonstration of love and affection. "It would be much better for you, Michael . . . if you never knew. I don't want to lose you, Michael . . . not now. Not ever."

Karen whispered, "Harry, do you *really* know?"

I was going to admit that I didn't have the faintest idea, but Michael had heard her, and gave me one of his narrow looks. "For sure," I said. "I had my suspicions, right from the start."

Michael took us back to the living room. He was tetchy, unsettled. But Naomi had told him that I wasn't to leave, so what could he do?

"So, are you going to tell me what this is?" he asked me, taking off his glasses. His eyes were bulgy and threatening.

I gave him the insincerest of smiles. "I'm sorry. You heard what your wife said. She'd prefer it if you were kept in the dark. I mean, it'd be safer, on the whole. Safer for you. Safer for all of us. There's more to the paranormal than meets the eye."

"You're trying to tell me this is *dangerous*? *How* dangerous?"

"Well, not so much *dangerous*," I extemporized. "More like—*unstable*."

"Let me show you something, wise guy," said Michael. He went across to the bureau and picked up a framed photograph. He brought it back and stuck it under my nose. It showed a pretty brunette standing in a New York street, holding a splashy bunch of daffodils. She wore a blue spring coat and a long white scarf and she looked happy.

"Who do you think that is?" he asked me, and his voice was harsh.

"Naomi, I guess, otherwise you wouldn't be showing it to me."

"That's right, Naomi. So when do you think this was taken?"

I glanced through the dining room at the white-haired woman clinging to her chair.

"Nineteen-eighty-five?" I hazarded. "Nineteen-eighty-six?"

"You're wrong," said Michael. "You're absolutely wrong. I took this photograph myself, on Delancey Street, April this year."

I studied the photograph hard. I gave a long, dry swallow. My larynx felt like the bowl of General MacArthur's second-best corncob pipe. Whatever this shadowy creature was that I was supposed to know about, it had done appalling things to Naomi Greenberg, and I didn't particularly relish the prospect of it doing the same things to me. I didn't think that white hair would suit me, to tell you the truth. I passed the photograph to Karen, but she had seen it before, and all she did was pass it back to Michael. I didn't particularly appreciate the small, sweet smile of confidence she was giving me. *Karen,* I thought, *I fought something supernatural for you, or what we all believed was supernatural, but once was enough; in fact, twice was enough, because I had to fight that same grisly manifestation twice. But never again. Never. Not something like this. This isn't crystal balls or tea-leaves or for-tune-telling cards. This is death, and things that make your hair turn white; and, Karen, I don't want to have anything to do with death, and things that make your hair turn white.*

Not now, not ever.

Phoenix

E.C. Dude lay back on the orange-upholstered couch in the air-conditioned Airstream trailer listening to Roxy Music's original 1971 album *Roxy Music.* He wore Randolph Engineering sunglasses, a faded black T-shirt with an Indian Head Diesel motif, second hand oil-rig boots, heavily oil-stained, and his girlfriend's white lacy panties.

His sun-faded jeans were hung over the back of his office chair, which was one of those rusted revolving office chairs with brown vinyl upholstery and half of the sponge-rubber seat dug out of it by all the bored people who had sat on it over the years. E.C. Dude was quintessentially thin, and very white-skinned considering that he had lived in Arizona all his life. His hair was curly and glossy, mahogany-coloured and very long.

His face was thin and he had the looks of a corrupt saint, like a (pre-booze) Jim Morrison painted by Giotto. His chin was prickled with soft black stubble. His Adam's apple bobbed up and down as he sang along to "Do The Strand." His legs were as white as his face, with bony knees—legs that had never ventured into the Arizona sun without the protection of Levi sun-block.

Outside the trailer, a collection of thirty-seven used cars baked in the ninety-one-degree heat. They were mostly Buicks and Oldsmobiles, around nine or ten years old, and there was a high proportion of pickups. A large hand-painted sign said PAPAGO JOE BARGAIN USED AUTOS, Nothing Over $3300. On each side of the sign a buffalo skull had been mounted, and vinyl fringes had been tacked all around it to give the impression of buckskin.

Papago Joe himself was making a court appearance today in Phoenix, trying to win custody of his sixteen-year-old daughter Susan White Feather. That was why E.C. Dude had been left in charge of the lot, with instructions not to sell anything until Papago Joe got back.

E.C. Dude was not seriously worried about that. Out here on Highway 60 between Apache and Florence Junctions, in sight of the wrinkled prehistoric skin of the Superstition Mountain, the passing trade in bargain Oldsmobiles was intermittent, to say the least. They had once gone three weeks without moving a single automobile. Papago Joe made most of his money by doing favors for men who wanted favors done: Indians, mostly, with grim leathery faces and shiny Cadillacs and mirror sunglasses. E.C. Dude never asked what. Tobacco and alcohol and a deteriorating ozone layer were quite enough of a health hazard, as far as he was concerned, without the added risk of annoying Indians with grim leathery faces and shiny Cadillacs.

E.C. Dude was trying to decide whether he had the energy to go to the Sun Devil Bar & Grill and sink a couple of cold Coors. They used to have an icebox in the trailer but Papago Joe had donated it to a family on the Salt River Reservation. It had been one of those spontaneous charitable gestures to which Papago Joe was prone; although Papago Joe could have used some charity himself sometimes. Times were difficult for everyone, especially Indians, and sometimes Papago Joe would share a cigarette with E.C. Dude and tell him about the times when "times" weren't easy or difficult, but simply "times."

"The sun came up, the clouds passed by, this way, mostly. Then the sun went down again."

"Sounds like cool times," E.C. Dude would remark, although he was never quite sure what the hell Papago Joe was talking about.

"That's right," Papago Joe would nod, his voice serious. "They were seriously cool times."

E.C. Dude had almost persuaded himself that he didn't need a beer when he felt the trailer shudder underneath him. *Shudder,* as if somebody had gently nudged a 4x4 into the side of it. He sat up, listening, waiting for the trailer to shudder again. Then he heard a knocking, scraping noise from outside, almost as if the cars in the lot were banging together.

He swung off the couch, pushed his sunglasses onto his nose, and opened the trailer door. Outside, the glare and the heat were tremendous. It was only a few minutes after midday, and the sun stabbed at him from every windshield and every door-mirror and every polished bumper. The concrete lot was dusty white, the highway was dusty white, the sky was dusty white.

E.C. Dude hesitated, and sniffed. Over the familiar smell

of hot automobiles and rubber, he was sure that he could smell something else. Like a fire burning . . . mesquite and charcoal and some kind of long-forgotten herb. A sourish smell, but a smell that strongly reminded him of when he was young.

He came down the hot aluminum steps of the trailer and stood with his hands resting on his hips, looking all around. The highway was silent, the sales lot was silent. High above his head, a turkey vulture idly and arrogantly circled on the thermal current, not even bothering to flap its wings. The red and white pennants all around the lot hung limp, as if they were soon going to melt and start dripping.

He listened. He heard a soft, high-pitched scraping noise. It came from somewhere close to the back of the lot, where the cars were parked against the long whitewashed wall of the "workshop and servicing facility."

It definitely sounded as if one automobile were being very slowly forced against another, fender to fender. Paint scratching, wheel-arches buckling, trim bending back, drip-rails being wrenched away, stud by stud. He shielded his eyes with his hand, trying to see if any of the pick-ups parked against the workshop wall were occupied. But they all appeared to be empty, and none of their motors was running.

He jumped up and down a few times, so that he could see way across the lot. But as far as he could make out, not a single car had anybody in it. It was just him, the cars, and the desert.

"Shit," he said. Then, "Shit."

He stopped jumping, because he was out of condition, and in any case he felt like he was shaking his brains up and down. He listened, his eyes tightly closed, trying to pick up the faintest sound of a footstep or a quietly-opened automobile door or a furtive whisper. Papago Joe had always taught him that you could hear much more clearly with your eyes closed.

Again, he heard that buckling, scraping noise; and then the distinctive hollow crunching of collapsing panels.

He opened his eyes. A small boy of about eight was standing by the gate, watching him solemnly. He looked like a half-caste, half-Apache and half-white. He wore a baseball cap with a picture of Michelangelo the Ninja Turtle on it, and a grubby white T-shirt that asked Who Knows What Evil Lurks In The Hearts of Men?

The small boy said, in a really snide nasal voice, "You're wearing girl's panties."

E.C. Dude looked down. He had worn out his last pair of boxer shorts months ago, and he had been wearing Cybille's panties ever since. He just hadn't bothered to go to Kmart and buy himself some more.

"So I'm wearing girl's panties?" He demanded. "What's it to you? At least I'm not wearing a stupid Ninja Turtle hat."

"Only fairies wear girl's panties."

"What do you know about fairies?"

"I know they wear girl's panties."

E.C. Dude had seen this boy before, kicking a ball around the back of the Sun Devil Bar & Grill. He probably belonged to that new waitress of theirs, the one with the short blonde hair and the rusty green Caprice. E.C. Dude didn't socialize or gossip too much, so people came and went and most of the time he never even found out their names. He always reckoned that rootless people were entitled to their privacy, just like he was.

He climbed back into the trailer and took his jeans off the back of the chair. The boy came to the foot of the steps and stared at him while he buckled up his belt. The boy crunched up one eye against the dazzling reflections from the Airstream's polished aluminum body.

"What's your name?" the boy asked him.

"E.C. Dude," said E.C. Dude.

"That's a dumb name. What kind of a name is that?"

"It's my name. What's yours?"

"Stanley."

"Your parents called you *Stanley*?"

"My mom called me Stanley, after my dad. My dad died."

"Oh, I'm sorry."

"I don't remember him. Mom said he had it coming."

"Oh, yeah?"

E.C. Dude took off his sunglasses and peered out over the lot. It seemed to be quiet now, but he thought he ought to go and look at those cars parked close to the workshop wall. They seemed to be undisturbed, in spite of all that crunching and scraping. Maybe he'd just been hearing freak echoes from Johnny Manzanera's scrapyard across the highway.

He might as well have a beer, too. Now that he had been thoroughly disturbed from his preferred position on the orange couch, E.C. Dude decided to go over to the bar and have a beer. He went to the far end of the trailer, to the kitchen, where there was a clutter of empty soup cans and instant noodle pots and half-eaten Hungry Man dinners. On the counter next to the toaster stood a smeary glass terrarium. Inside it, dry and motionless, rested a Gila monster.

E.C. Dude lifted the terrarium's lid, reached inside, and took two $20s out from under the rocks. The Gila monster licked its lips, and its eye rolled up like a camera shutter, but otherwise it ignored him.

Stanley said, "Gila monsters are bad luck."

"Oh, yes? What do you know about bad luck?"

"My mom says we always have bad luck."

"Really? Well, that's bad luck, always having bad luck."

"Gila monsters have dead people's souls inside them, and they won't let them go."

E.C. Dude stepped out of the trailer, closed the door, and locked it. He looked this way and that, just to make sure that there was nobody lurking around the lot, and then he came down the steps.

"I'm going for a beer," he told Stanley. "How about you?"

"So long as you're buying."

Hm, thought E.C. Dude. Those are the words of a kid who's spent too long hanging around bars.

They had walked only a few yards across the sun-cracked concrete when E.C. Dude heard that noise again. This time, it was much louder, much more dramatic. It sounded as if a whole car were being compressed in a crusher, panels collapsing, transmission shearing, windshield cracking.

It was immediately followed by a high, rubbery-sounding chorus of protest from all around the lot. He turned this way and that, and as he turned, a bronze metallic Delta 88 that was parked right next to him began to buck on its suspension, and then suddenly start to slide sideways. *Sideways,* without anything visibly dragging it. Its tire treads rumbled and squealed in an unholy, discordant quartet, and after six or seven feet its front bumper noisily collided with another sedan.

E.C. Dude turned to Stanley in total amazement. "Can you see that? Look at it! Holy shit, it's moving by itself!"

But all Stanley could do was stand where he was, his eyes wide, terrified.

Every car on the lot began bucking and dipping, and the shrieking of tires grew louder and louder. Their rooftops surged up and down like the backs of stampeding cattle. E.C. Dude ran to the bronze Delta 88 and tried to open the door, but the car abruptly tore away the front bumper assembly of the sedan next to it, and was pulled so forcefully away from him that he almost lost his fingers in the doorhandle.

Pulled—but pulled by *what*?

The whole collection of cars began to smash themselves into the back wall of the workshop, and into each other, in a huge unstoppable demolition derby. There was nothing that E.C. Dude could do but stand and watch them in horror and misery. Fenders ripped against fenders, doors were torn off their hinges, steering columns were forced through seats and windows. The cars were pulled toward the workshop wall with such irresistible force that they began to mount each other's rooftops. E.C. Dude watched as one of their better bargains, a two-thousand-dollar Regal, reared nose upward behind the trunk of an 88, and then rolled over on its back.

The noise was ear-splitting, a hideous cacophony of grinding and crunching and warping metal, combined with the slate-pencil squeaking of laminated glass.

Stanley clapped his hands over his ears. "What is it?" he screamed. "What's happening?"

"I don't know!" shouted E.C. Dude. "There's nobody driving them—they're just doing it themselves!"

Two sedans reared up against each other like battling

steers. With a long continuous screech of metal against metal, they pushed themselves higher and higher until they were almost vertical. Then one of them fell over sideways, and rolled over and over down the struggling, jarring chaos of other cars.

"Jesus Christ," said E.C. Dude, in disbelief. "What the hell am I going to say to Papago Joe?"

"Look!" said Stanley, pointing. "Look at the wall!"

"What are you talking about?" E.C. Dude demanded.

"Look at the wall!" Stanley shouted.

"What's the matter with the wall?"

"Look at the shadows!"

E.C. Dude stared at the workshop wall. All he could see at first were the heaving, angular shadows of the struggling cars. But then, off to the right-hand side, he saw a strange shape that wasn't part of a car at all, but more like a human figure. Except that it couldn't have been a human figure. Its head was huge and misshapen, and it ducked and dived as it hurried across the wall in a way that no human could run.

"Shit, there's somebody there!" said E.C. Dude, angrily. "There's somebody there, man, and they're smashing the cars up deliberate!"

E.C. Dude glimpsed the shadow again. It looked as if the culprit were trying to run along the workshop wall and escape unnoticed out of the back of the lot. E.C. Dude said firmly to Stanley, "Wait here, man, okay?" and dodged forward, trying to see where the shadow might have gone.

He tried to skirt around the right-hand side of the lot. Maybe he could head the shadow off. But as he approached the wall, he realized that nobody could have made their way through this battlefield of tortured, shrieking, colliding cars. Jesus, you'd be trapped and crushed in an instant.

E.C. Dude climbed cautiously up onto the back of a turned-over pick-up truck, but just as he managed to catch his balance, the truck shifted beneath the soles of his boots like something alive. He jumped back off it and stepped away. This was seriously bad news, all of this, and he didn't want to get involved. In any case, there was no longer any sign of the shadow, or the man whose shadow it might have been.

He heard a tumbling metallic noise and something struck him on the side of the foot. He jumped clear, did a hotfooted dance, and managed to dodge a shower of wrenches and screwdrivers that were rolling across the concrete to join the tangle of cars.

Every loose tool and empty bottle and thrown-away box and worn-out tire was being dragged into the heap of wrecked automobiles up against the workshop wall.

A long section of chain-link fencing began to rattle and shake, and then another, until the whole perimeter fence was jangling. The red-and-white pennants tore themselves loose, and flew towards the workshop, catching on some of the smashed-up automobiles, and fluttering wildly.

Then—to E.C. Dude's despair—Papago Joe's Airstream trailer began to creak and tilt.

"It's going to fall over!" shouted Stanley. "Look, it's going to fall over!"

Already, two or three cars had stopped on the highway, and people were hurrying from the Sun Devil Bar & Grill, including Stanley's mother, the waitress with the short blonde hair. In a high panicky voice she called, "Stanley! Stanley!" and came running across the lot barefoot.

She scooped Stanley up in her arms just as the Airstream's suspension collapsed, and the whole trailer rolled over onto its side. There was a deep crunching of broken glass and stoved-in aluminum sheeting, and E.C. Dude heard all of Papago Joe's china and glass and books and pots and pans go tumbling from one side of the trailer to the other, followed by a heavy thump and a bang which was probably his TV set.

After that, however, quite abruptly, the destruction seemed to be over. The hot noonday silence was broken by an occasional clang and rattle as another hubcap dropped off, or a capsized automobile settled on its roof, but that was all.

E.C. Dude surveyed the lot and didn't know what the hell to do. All that seemed to have been left standing was the sign saying PAPAGO JOE'S BARGAIN USED AUTOS, with its buffalo skulls. Even the "buckskin" fringes had been ripped away.

Stanley's mother came up to E.C. Dude and stood frowning at him. She was small and snub-nosed, with big china-blue eyes. He guessed that she was twenty-four or twenty-five tops, which meant that she couldn't have been very much more than a teenager when she had given birth to Stanley. She wore nothing but a white XXL T-shirt which billowed in the breeze.

"Are you okay?" she asked him.

"Sure, I'm okay."

"What happened? How did all these cars get wrecked?"

Stanley chipped in, " The shadow did it."

"The shadow?" asked Stanley's mother.

E.C. Dude grunted. "Who Knows What Evil Lurks In The Hearts Of Men? Only the Shadow knows, ho, ho, ho."

"What a mess," said Stanley's mother. "I was asleep and all the crashing woke me up."

"Yeah, well," said E.C. Dude. "It must've been some kind of magnetic storm or something, I don't know. I'm supposed to be taking care of these cars, shit."

"The *shadow* did it," Stanley insisted.

"Oh, come on, now, Stanley, ssh," his mother told him. "By the way," she said to E.C. Dude, "I'm Linda Welles. I'm working at the Sun Devil. Thanks for taking care of Stanley, he's always wandering. It's something in the blood."

"E.C. Dude," said E.C. Dude.

"E.C. Dude? That stand for something?"

E.C. Dude shrugged. "Nothing in particular," although it did. It was just that he was too embarrassed to tell her.

Jack Mackie from the Sun Devil came stalking across the concrete, the sun shining on his grey greased-back hair.

"Christ almighty, E.C., Joe's going to scalp you for this. Look at his cars. Look at his God-damned trailer. That's his *house,* man. You knocked over his God-damned *house.*"

"I just can't figure what happened," said E.C. Dude. He picked up a bent steering wheel, steered with it for a moment, then dropped it.

"The *shadow* did it," Stanley insisted.

"Oh, sure," said Jack. "Joe's in Phoenix, ain't he, trying to get custody? This won't help his case much. All his living smashed up, and no place to take his girl back to."

"It wasn't my fault, man," said E.C. Dude, mournfully. In the far distance, he heard the whooping of a siren. Deputy Fordyce, no doubt.

Jack Mackie walked around the wreckage, kicking a tire here and there, as men always do. "I never saw anything like this, E.C. Never in my natural days. I mean, what did you *do* here, man?"

"I swear on the Bible I didn't touch them," E.C. Dude protested. "I didn't touch one of them."

Stanley pointed at the wall at the rear of the workshop. "It was the shadow. I saw the shadow running along there and then it got away."

At that moment, Deputy Fordyce arrived, with his usual flourish of tires and howling siren and flashing lights. He climbed out of his car and walked towards them, a tall crimson-faced thirty-year-old with a big hat and gingery hair and a wide bottom in sharply-pressed slacks.

He took off his orange Ray•Bans, neatly folded them, and tucked them into his breast pocket.

"You again, E.C.?" he remarked. He studied the twisted wreckage, his eyes bulging and fierce. "These vehicles all look pretty well wrecked to me, even by Papago Joe's standards."

"I was just telling Jack, I didn't touch one of these cars, not one."

"The shadow did it," Stanley piped up, but his mother said, "Shush, honey, don't interrupt."

"I was thinking maybe it was a magnetic storm or something," E.C. Dude suggested.

"A magnetic storm?" asked Deputy Fordyce, with exaggerated interest. "What the hell is a magnetic storm?"

"I don't know. There was something about a magnetic storm in *Superman.*"

"Oh, really? Guess I'll have to bone up on it. You'll have to tell me which issue."

"Listen, deputy, I really didn't touch those cars."

"Got any witnesses? Anybody who saw what happened?"

"This little guy here, Stanley. He was here all along."

Deputy Fordyce tilted his hat and peered down at Stanley

like a giant suddenly noticing a morsel of mortal.

"You were here all along, were you, son? Do you want to tell me what happened?"

Stanley said, "I heard the cars banging so I came to have a look. Then E.C. Dude came out wearing girl's panties."

Deputy Fordyce gave E.C. Dude the kind of look that Arizona deputies usually reserve for the occupants of visiting UFOs. E.C. Dude said, "They were Cybille's, for Christ's sake. The rest of my shorts were in the wash."

"Go on," Deputy Fordyce told Stanley. "What happened then?"

Stanley licked his lips. "E.C. Dude put his jeans on and said let's take a look at the cars to see if there's any damage, then we'll have a beer."

"He was going to buy you a beer?"

"Listen, man, I was only kidding," E.C. Dude protested. "I was just trying to talk to him like he was grown-up."

"What happened then?" asked Deputy Fordyce, with theatrical patience.

"The cars all started crashing," said Stanley. "E.C. Dude didn't touch them. He tried to stop them, but he couldn't."

Deputy Fordyce took a long, slow look around the lot. "So, they crashed all by themselves . . . with no help whatsoever from either of you?"

Stanley shook his head.

"Well, I thought not," smiled Deputy Fordyce, carefully tugging at the knees of his immaculately-pressed slacks, and then hunkering down beside him. "So why don't you tell me exactly what happened? Did you and E.C. decide to have yourselves a demolition derby? Is that what happened?"

"No, sir, the shadow did it."

"The shadow?"

"Yes, sir, there was a shadow on the wall and I know that the shadow did it."

"How do you know that?"

Stanley shrugged. "I just do, that's all."

Deputy Fordyce stood up again. He walked around the wrecked cars towards the workshop, followed by E.C. Dude and Jack Mackie and Linda and Stanley and half a dozen locals and inquisitive strangers. He stopped when he reached the workshop wall and said, "This is some God-damned mess, I'll tell you," and everybody nodded and agreed with him. A door suddenly dropped off an over-turned sedan and everybody jumped, even Deputy Fordyce. They looked at each other in embarrassment as the door seesawed to a gradual standstill.

"Where was this shadow, then?" asked Deputy Fordyce.

Stanley pointed. "On the wall, right there. It ran across the wall." He imitated its awkward, hump-backed gait.

"But if the guy's shadow ran across the wall, you must have seen the guy whose shadow it was. He would have been in plain view. The way the sun is right now, he would have had to be *there,* right there. You couldn't have missed him."

"No, sir," said Stanley, politely. "He wasn't on this side of the wall."

"I don't understand."

Stanley walked around the back of Deputy Fordyce until he reached the rickety wooden doors of the workshop. He pressed the palm of his hand against the grey, sun-faded paint, and said, "He was on *this* side."

It took Deputy Fordyce a moment to register what Stanley was saying. Then suddenly he laughed and shook his head. "You mean he was *inside* the workshop, but his shadow went right through the brick, so that you could see it on the outside?"

Stanley looked serious. "Yes, sir."

"Oh, Stanley," said Linda, taking hold of his hand. "You make up such crazy stories sometimes! I'm sorry, Deputy. He has such a wild imagination! Sometimes he doesn't know the difference between stories and reality."

"Well, he sure ain't the only one," said Deputy Fordyce, staring beadily at E.C. Dude. "Magnetic storm, indeed. Saw it in *Superman.* Jesus!"

He was just about to turn away from the workshop doors when Stanley broke free from his mother's hand and snatched at the leg of his slacks.

"It's true!" Stanley shouted at him. "It's true! I know it's true! He was inside! He was inside!"

"Hey now, come on, pal, watch the uniform," said Deputy Fordyce. Stanley had left what looked like a chocolate mark on the immaculate twill of Deputy Fordyce's slacks. "I know you *think* it's true, but you've gotten a little mixed up, okay? It's a hot day. Sometimes the heat can get to your brain and give you wacky ideas." He spat on the end of his finger and tried to rub the chocolate off.

Stanley rushed back to the workshop doors and banged against them with his fists.

"It's true I know it's true he was inside!"

Deputy Fordyce approached the workshop doors and hefted the rusty padlock in his hand. "Is this always kept locked?" he asked E.C. Dude.

E.C. Dude nodded. "I don't think that's been opened for a year."

"Do you have a key?"

"Papago Joe has a key."

"Is there any other way in?"

"There's a window down at the far end. I guess you could climb in, but it's real high up."

Deputy Fordyce let the padlock fall back. "I think I want to take a written statement from you, E.C. And somebody better get in contact with Papago Joe. I don't know what the hell's gone down here, but I have every intention of finding out."

He began to walk back towards his car, his bottom undulating from side to side, his holster riding up and down with every step. "Everybody tells me that Papago Joe is practically a saint or something but I know the kind of guys that Papago Joe deals with. If this wasn't revenge or something, some kind of punishment, then you can eat my shorts with Dijon mustard."

E.C. Dude said, "There was nobody here, believe me. Nobody but me and the kid."

Deputy Fordyce gave him a puckered-up, disbelieving smile. "That's what I'd say, too, if the Apache Mafia told me to forget everything that happened here today. But I don't believe you, E.C., and that's just about the length of it."

At that instant, however, they heard a piercing shriek, like somebody drawing a knifeblade down a window. They turned around and saw Stanley only two or three feet away from the workshop door. His face was liverish-grey, his eyes had rolled up into his head so that only the whites showed, and he was standing in an extraordinary tensed-up posture, his knees half-bent, his fists clenched, trembling and shaking.

"He was inside!" Stanley screamed. *"He was inside, I saw him!"*

"For Christ's sake," said Deputy Fordyce.

Linda grabbed hold of Stanley and clutched him close, but he wrestled his face clear of her shoulder and kept on screaming, *"He was inside, don't you believe me, he was inside, he was inside, he was inside!"* His eyes were still white, and flecks of spit were flying from his mouth, and for the first time in his life E.C. felt like taking hold of a kid and telling him, "Don't, don't, everything's cool."

Deputy Fordyce laid his hand on Linda's shoulder. Linda looked up at him, her blonde hair tussled, her blue eyes challenging. She didn't have to speak, no need for it.

"Is he prone to hysteria?" Deputy Fordyce asked.

"What do you think?" Linda retaliated. "His father was killed when he was four. He's learned to adapt to just about anything."

Deputy Fordyce swivelled around and said, "Jack! Fetch me one of those tire-irons, would you?"

Jack Mackie kicked open the W-shaped trunk of the nearest automobile, reached inside, and yanked out the tire-iron. He handed it to Deputy Fordyce with an expression on his face which clearly meant, *You should've done this the first time, you sucker.* Deputy Fordyce took it without a word, and slid the shaft into the hasp of the padlock. He gave three hefty pulls, and the padlock burst open.

"Don't expect me to pay for that," said E.C. Dude. "There's enough God-damned damage here already."

"Be cool, will you?" said Deputy Fordyce.

E.C. Dude was outraged. "You're telling *me* to be cool? What is this?"

Deputy Fordyce swung open the workshop doors. Inside it was gloomy and smelled of burlap and oil. When Papago Joe had first taken over the business from Old Man Johnson, seventeen years ago, he had sold new Pontiacs and

Chevrolets, and used the workshop to prep and repair them. But all the new-car trade had left him for Phoenix and Scottsdale, where the displays were smarter and the discounts were higher, and where they offered your wife a set of free saucepans and your kids balloons.

The workshop was gloomy, apart from the sunlight that filtered into it from a single grimy window high up on the rear wall. There were shelves on either side, and workbenches, and a block-and-tackle for lifting out engines. The chains of the block-and-tackle swung heavy and greasy in the breeze, *chink—kerchunk . . . chink—kerchunk.*

In the center of the floor there was a deep, dark inspection pit. Deputy Fordyce approached it on flat, ten-to-two feet, and peered into it suspiciously. He peered into it for a very long time, and then he reached behind him and snapped his fingers.

"Flashlight," he said.

"Who, me?" asked E.C. Dude.

"Just get me my fucking flashlight!" Deputy Fordyce yelled at him, still without turning around.

E.C. Dude stepped back into the sunlight. Jack Mackie said, "What's going on?"

"Search me," said E.C. Dude. "He wants a flashlight."

Jack Mackie called, "Deputy, you need some help there?"

But Deputy Fordyce said harshly, "You just stay where you are! If I need your help I'll ask you for it!"

E.C. Dude opened Deputy Fordyce's patrol car and took out the long heavy-duty flashlight. The car smelled of sun-heated vinyl and the radio squawked and blurted—*we have a make on that Utah license plate now—that's correct—*. E.C. returned to the workshop and Jack Mackie let him pass without saying a word.

Deputy Fordyce took the flashlight and switched it on. The beam darted this way and that. E.C. Dude saw naked arms and legs, a bloodied torso. He saw a young woman, wide-eyed, staring up at him with such an expression of horror that he thought at first that she was alive. She was wearing what looked like a red rubber swimming cap. It was only when Deputy Fordyce held the flashlight still for a moment that he realized it wasn't a red rubber swimming cap at all. She had been scalped.

"Jesus Christ," said E.C. Dude. He felt his knees melting, and he wasn't sure that he was going to be able to stand upright.

Deputy Fordyce poked the flashlight beam all around the inspection pit. The walls were glossy with blood. There were so many arms and legs and ripped-off pieces of flesh that it was impossible to tell how many people were down there. E.C. Dude glimpsed a middle-aged man, his forehead pressed against the corner of the inspection pit, his lower jaw missing, so that his tongue lolled on the concrete. It looked like a fat purple snake that was trying to heave itself out of his throat.

He saw a black woman, with one of her eyes lying on her cheek. "Do you recognize any of these folks?" asked Deputy Fordyce.

E.C. Dude shook his head. His mouth seethed with bile.

"How about her?" The flashlight momentarily lit up the face of a freckly young woman with both of her arms torn off. "Have you ever seen her before?"

"No, sir. Never."

"Did you know these people were here?"

"No, sir. We used to have itinerants sleeping in here from time to time, but not lately. Not since Joe started to lock the doors."

Deputy Fordyce switched off the flashlight, but E.C. Dude couldn't take his eyes away from the half-darkness of the inspection pit. He could just make out the glistening of blood and bone and the terrible soft paleness of bled-white flesh.

"Come on, son," said Deputy Fordyce, and led him outside. E.C. Dude had to sit down on an oil drum and take three or four deep breaths.

Jack Mackie said, "What's happening, Deputy? You two look like you saw a ghost."

Deputy Fordyce swung the workshop doors together, and slid the tire-iron through the hasps to keep them closed.

"We have a multiple death situation," he announced.

"There are people dead in there? How many?"

"Hard to say. Five at least, could be more."

"Well, what happened to them?" asked Jack Mackie. "Have they been murdered, or what?"

Deputy Fordyce began to walk across to his car. "I can tell you for sure that it wasn't an accident. But I can't tell you for sure that it was murder. If it was some kind of animal or animals, like two or three pit bull terriers, then the animal or animals must have been crazed right out of their skulls."

"And if it was a human?"

Deputy Fordyce reached into his car window and picked up his r/t microphone. "If it was a human, then it was only a human in the technical sense. If it was a human, then you'd better start praying that you and yours never chance across him—never."

FOUR

I was waiting outside the classroom when the break bell rang and all the kids tumbled out. I stayed where I was, my arms folded, leaning against the wall, watching Amelia collect up her papers and tidy her desk. She was much thinner than I remembered her, and her hair was all pinned up in a schoolmarmish bun. She wore moon-lensed spectacles, too.

The last time I had seen her she had been wearing a crimson silk kaftan and beads and a crimson bandanna around her hair. Now she was dressed in a brown cardigan and a cream-colored blouse and a sensible pleated skirt. On the door there was a handprinted card which said *Mrs Wakeman*. On the blackboard behind her, she had written, *Words which sound alike: there—their—ours—hours.*

At last she finished tidying and closed her drawer. The classroom was filled with sunlight and a jam-jar of daisies stood on her desk. She came towards the door, folding her spectacles and tucking them into a red velvet case. She sensed me rather than saw me, and stopped.

"Harry?"

I stood to attention. "Good morning, Mrs Wakeman."

"Harry, what on earth are you doing here? I thought you were dead."

I took hold of her hand and tried to kiss her but she turned her face away. "Nay, not dead, my queen, but moved to midtown."

"You look older."

"Of course I look older. I *am* older. Mind you—let me look at you—you haven't changed a bit. Marriage must suit you."

"Divorce suits me."

"Oh . . . I'm sorry."

"Don't be. He was a commodities broker. He dressed me in Armani but he almost bored me to death."

We walked along the corridor together. The walls were decorated with bright, crude paintings, Christopher Columbus landing in the West Indies, the Pilgrim Fathers at Plymouth Rock, a splendidly gory rendition of Custer's Last Stand. Custer had fifteen fingers on each hand and about a thousand arrows in his body. The building echoed with children's laughter and the squeak-scuff-squeaking of sneakers.

"How did you find me?" asked Amelia.

"Oh, it wasn't difficult. I asked MacArthur."

"I haven't seen MacArthur in fifteen years. How is he?"

"Fat and bald. He's driving a taxi. You did yourself a favor, kicking him out."

"I should have kicked you out, too," she remarked.

"Oh, come on, can't we let bygones be bygones? It's all bourbon under the bridgework."

"You weren't very fair to me, Harry."

I took out my handkerchief and blew my nose. "I did say sorry."

She gave me a wan, indulgent smile. "Yes, I suppose you did. For what it was worth."

"Do you have time for coffee?" I asked her.

She checked her watch. "Ten minutes, no more. I have to get my next class ready."

We left the dusty fenced-off compound in front of the school and crossed the street. The morning was humid and breathlessly hot, and everything looked hazy and brown. We went into a small Italian place called Marco's and sat by the window. An immense woman with hairy armpits and a hairy mole on her chin took our order for two double espressos.

Amelia took out a cigarette and I lit it for her with the bookmatches from the table. "When did you start smoking?" I asked her.

"After *you*," she said. "I quit for a while but I started it again when Humphrey and I got divorced."

"Humphrey? That was your husband's name? What was his mother, a Bogart fan?"

"Unh-hunh. His father used to be friends with Hubert Humphrey."

"Jesus wept."

Our coffee arrived but I don't think either of us really wanted it. I would have preferred a Jack Daniels, straight up. Amelia smoked and smiled and played with the sachets of Sweet'n'Low. She still had that world-weary prettiness that had first attracted me, all that time ago. In those days, she had run a mystic bookstore in the Village, The Star Cat. That was when the world was still innocent and bright of eye, and rents were low. But in the late seventies Amelia had eventually gone broke, and that was when she and MacArthur had split up, and she and I had spent some time together. I don't know whether you could call it an affair, or even a relationship. I was somewhat less than sane in those days: given to drinking and nightmares and bad temper, and Amelia had suffered more than she should have.

Amelia had deserved somebody much kinder than me, and I had needed somebody much stronger than Amelia. In the end I hurt her, just to get myself free.

"MacArthur said you'd been teaching for nearly six years," I remarked.

She nodded. "The remedial class. The poor little kids who can't tell the difference between 'cat' and 'hat.' I love it, though. It's very rewarding."

"You don't do any of that occult stuff any more?"

"Never. What about you?"

"Oh, I'm still telling the fortunes. Reading the palms, laying out the cards, probing the entrails."

"I thought you were finished with all that."

"Well, it's a living. And people still need to feel that the real world isn't all there is."

Amelia sipped her coffee. "I can't stay very much longer," she said. "Was there any particular reason you wanted to talk to me? I mean, apart from old times' sake?"

"There was something," I said, cautiously. "Kind of a favor, really, for a friend of a friend."

"A girlfriend, no doubt."

"You know her, Karen Tandy. Well, Karen van Hooven these days. She's divorced, too.

"Go on," said Amelia, with a warning note in her voice.

"It's hard for me to explain. You really have to see it for yourself. Karen has some friends called the Greenbergs. They live on East 17th Street, not a particularly salubrious area but their apartment's okay. One Friday evening about three weeks ago Mr Greenberg went off to the synagogue, and when he came back he found that something strange had happened."

"Harry, if this is something weird, then I don't want to know."

"Amelia, I don't know who else to ask!"

"I don't care, I don't want to have anything to do with it! Don't you think the last time was bad enough? It took me *years* to get over the nightmares, you know that. I still can't look at a table without feeling frightened of what might come out of it—even now, even today!"

I sat back and lifted my hands in surrender. "I'm sorry. You're right. I shouldn't even have come here."

"Harry," said Amelia, "You seem to think that you can use people like characters in your own TV series. You seem to think that when you ask me a favor, I'm going to come running. In spite of how you treated me; in spite of the fact that for fifteen years you haven't written or telephoned or even sent me a Christmas card. In spite of the risks, too. Especially in spite of the risks."

I looked down at my coffee, trying to appear as chastened as possible. To tell you the truth, I would have done anything not to have had to ask Amelia to help me. But whether I liked it or not, there was nobody else. She was the only person I had ever come across who could do for real what I could only pretend to do—contact the spirit-world. She was spiritually sensitive to the point where she could hear whispers when she walked past cemeteries. The dead, if you can believe it, whispering to each other in their sleep.

Amelia said, "You can't ask me, Harry. It's simply not fair."

"You're right," I agreed. "I should have tried to find somebody else. It's just that we don't know where to turn next."

"Did you tell Karen you were going to ask me?"

I shook my head. "I didn't want to raise her hopes. Or Michael Greenberg's hopes, either."

"How is Karen these days?" I could sense that Amelia was circling around this conversation, anxious to know more, yet equally anxious not to commit herself.

"Karen's fine." I touched the back of my neck. "She still

has a scar there, but that's all. I guess we all carry some kind of scar."

"You said she was divorced."

"That's right. She couldn't face the idea of having children. I guess it's understandable."

"And these friends of hers—what's this strange problem they've been having?"

I touched her hand; her long pale fingernails. It's very unsettling, touching somebody you used to hold so intimately, after so many years of separation.

"Amelia, if you don't want to get involved, I'd rather you didn't know."

Amelia eyed me narrowly through the ribboning sunlit smoke of her cigarette. Out in the street, a young Hispanic kid pressed his face to the window and made a squint-eyed, mouth-blown-out expression. "Nice neighborhood," I remarked, nodding to the kid, who didn't run away, but pulled ever-more-grotesque faces.

Amelia smiled. "Tell me what's wrong. Maybe I can make some suggestions. Maybe I can recommend somebody."

"Well," I said, "I guess the most accurate way of describing it is to say that it's a poltergeist manifestation. When Michael Greenberg got home that night from the synagogue, his wife didn't answer the door. He had to call the fire department to rip it down. He found his wife in the dining room clinging to this single chair, and the rest of the furniture up against the opposite wall."

"The furniture seemed to have moved by itself?"

"Not seemed, did."

"How can you be so sure? It's possible that she moved the furniture herself, isn't it?"

"Amelia, I've seen it for myself. It's up against the wall and every time anybody tries to move it away from the wall it just slides back again. On its own."

Amelia frowned at me. "I don't understand. The furniture's *still* up against the wall?"

"That's right. And nobody can shift it. Naomi Greenberg's sitting on this one chair, keeping it anchored by her own weight in the center of the room, and she's not going to let it go for anything. She's been sitting on it for nearly four weeks, God-damnit. Eats on it, sleeps on it, won't let it go."

"Can't they move her?"

"Michael's arranged for regular visits from two different psychiatrists. They're both worried that she'll have some kind of catatonic fit if they try to move her."

"So what on earth can I do? I'm a sensitive, not an exorcist."

"Naomi says she saw shadows on the wall . . . some kind of creature."

"And?"

"I think I may have seen it, too."

Amelia rearranged the sachets of sugar again. "I have to tell you, Harry, this doesn't sound at all like poltergeists. Poltergeists don't pull things across the room like that, and they certainly don't keep them there. They're very erratic and temperamental. They're the spiritual expression of somebody's anger. Nobody stays angry for three weeks, do they? Not unless they're a very disturbed character indeed."

I didn't want to tell Amelia about the way in which Naomi had covered her face with her hands. It was too strongly reminiscent of the events that had taken place at the Sisters of Jerusalem Hospital, especially since Naomi had insisted over and over that I knew what she was trying to describe. It gave me too deep a feeling of dread to think that there might be any connection. I didn't really believe that there *could* be any connection. But all the same, I didn't want to frighten Amelia and I didn't particularly want to frighten myself, either.

What I had seen at the Greenbergs' apartment had already been frightening enough.

"Any suggestions?" I asked Amelia.

"I'm not sure," she said. "I've never heard about anything like it before."

"Maybe it's nothing to do with spirits," I said. "Maybe it's just some kind of electrical fault."

"Electrical fault?" she asked me, in the tone of voice that she probably used when one of her less bright remedials asked her the difference between cartoon characters and real life. I remember we had a kid at school who insisted that Mr

Magoo lived at home with him, but I guess that's another story.

"I just wanted to make sure that it *wasn't* spirits," I said. "That's why I threw caution and good manners and human decency to the winds and came round to ask you a favor."

Amelia unfolded a paper napkin and took out a pen. "Listen," she said, "there's a man I know who lives on Central Park West. His name's Martin Vaizey. He's very sensitive, and particularly good at contacting wayward spirits. I think he may be able to help you even better than I could."

I tucked the napkin in my pocket without reading it. "Well," I said, "I knew I could count on you."

"Don't make the mistake of underestimating Martin. He's very, very good. He's talked to John Lennon a few times. Of course they were practically neighbors."

"He's talked to John Lennon? You mean *after* he was shot?"

Amelia nodded.

"Did he get his autograph?" I asked her.

"Harry—don't underestimate Martin, please. He's kind of eccentric, but he's a brilliant man. He's a better sensitive than me. He can tune himself, almost. It's fantastic to watch."

"Okay, then," I agreed. "I'll give him a try."

"Don't look so disappointed."

"I'm trying my damnedest not to."

She checked her watch. "I have to get back to my class. It was good to see you again, Harry. Sorry I couldn't help you personally."

"Well, me too. How about dinner sometime? They opened this terrific Korean restaurant on 52nd Street, close to my office. Have you ever tasted *ojingu chim*?"

Amelia gave me a long, level look. "Why do I have the feeling that *ojingu chim* is going to be something awful?"

"Come on, Amelia. What's awful about squid's bodies stuffed with pickled cabbage and chopped-up tentacles?"

She stood up and went to the door, and waited for me smiling, one hand shading her eyes. I paid the check and came out after her and stretched.

"I still miss knowing you," she said, lightly kissing my cheek. "But not that much."

I called back at the Greenbergs' apartment before I attempted to get in touch with Martin Vaizey. When he answered the door, Michael looked sweaty and yellow, like a man with malaria. Karen was sitting by the window with a freshly-brewed jug of iced tea.

"Any luck?" Michael asked me.

"I don't know yet. Amelia wouldn't do it; she said she gave up mysticism years ago. But she gave me the name of a sensitive on Central Park West. Highly recommended, that's what she said."

I nodded towards the dining room. "How is it in there?"

"Awful . . . cold, scary. She keeps singing some song. The psychiatrist said that if she doesn't show any signs of recovery by the end of the week, they're going to have to pull her out of there whether she throws a seizure or not."

Karen came up. She was wearing a loose silk shirt of saffron yellow and a loose pair of silk pajama pants. Her hair was clipped back with yellow plastic barrettes. "Do you want some iced tea?" she asked me. She knew I didn't really want any; she was simply trying to show how concerned she was.

"I'll find somebody, don't worry," I told Michael, grasping his shoulder. "I guaranteed that I was going to clear your apartment, one way or another, and I will."

I was on the point of leaving when I heard Naomi singing from the next room. Her voice was shrill and keening, with loud ululations at the end of every line. It went on, and on, echoing a little, and every line seemed to be different. I approached the half-open dining-room door and listened hard, but I couldn't make out a single word she was saying.

"Is that Hebrew?" I asked Michael.

Michael shook his head. "It's no language that *I* ever heard before."

"How about you, Karen?"

Karen said, "Me neither." But the singing went on and on, high and insistent, until at last Michael came forward and closed the door.

"She was doing it all night," he explained. "I can't take too much more of it."

"Will you do me one favor?" I asked him. "Will you record it for me? You have a tape deck, don't you?"

"You think it'll help?"

"I don't know. Maybe it will, maybe it won't. It can't hurt, whatever."

I gave Karen a peck on the cheek, squeezed Michael Greenberg by his sweaty hand, and then left the building and hailed a taxi. The cabbie had just arrived in New York from Swaziland or someplace like that, and he drove backwards and forwards across midtown for almost fifteen minutes before I discovered that he was looking for "Sanitary Parts Waste."

"Central Park West, for Christ's sake," I snapped at him. I told him to stop on the corner by Radio City, climbed out, and gave him some interesting physiological ideas about what he could do with his blatant request for a tip. I walked the rest of the way. By the time I reached the Montmorency Building my shirt was clinging to my back and my boxer shorts had twisted themselves into a sumo-wrestler's loincloth. A dense hot sour-smelling smog covered everything. The park was bronze. Up above me reared the forbidding bulk of the Montmorency Building, an uglier cousin of the Dakota, all red brick and mansard roofs and cupolas and gargoyles. A plaque on the wall announced that it was the first apartment building in New York to have been wired for electric light.

Inside the mahogany swing doors, I was met by semi-darkness and a deep refrigerated chill. A large circular table stood in the center of the brown-and-white mosaic floor, and in the center of the table there was an extravagant arrangement of huge white arum lilies. I had the feeling that I had entered the foyer of a funeral parlor, rather than somebody's home. On the far side of the foyer, there was a small niche in the panelling, in which a sallow potato-faced man with ears like a troll was smoking a bright green cigar and reading the sports section.

I approached the niche and rapped on the ledge. "Can you help me? I'm looking for Mr Vaizey."

The man took the cigar out of his mouth with an exaggerated flourish. "Do you have an appointment?"

"No, I don't. But if you call him and say that I'm a friend of Amelia Wakeman, then I don't think there'll be any kind of problem."

"Mr Vaizey don't see nobody without no appointment. Strict instructions."

"Will you just call him, please?"

"Well I don't know. He's not too keen on being disturbed none."

I leaned on the ledge. "You want a shit-hot tip for the four o'clock or what?"

The concierge narrowed his eyes and blew smoke out of his nostrils. "Who *are* you?" he wanted to know.

"Harry Erskine, Erskine the Incredible—palmistry, card-divining, tea-leaf interpretation, astrology, phrenology, numerology, bumps read, sooths said."

The concierge rolled his eyes up toward the ceiling, presumably in the general direction of Martin Vaizey's apartment. "You're another one of these clairvoyant characters, huh? What's this, the annual fortune-tellers' get-together?"

"You want the tip or what?"

The concierge didn't answer, but punched out a number on his telephone. After a while, he said, "Sorry to disturb you, Mr Vaizey, but I got somebody called Bearskin down here, wants to talk to you."

"Erskine!" I hissed, in a stage whisper. "A friend of Amelia Wakeman!"

The concierge conveyed this revised message upstairs, waited, and then nodded.

"He'll see you," he said. "Apartment 717."

I walked towards the elevators, and pressed 7. The concierge stuck his head out of his niche and called, "Hey!" in an echoing voice. "What about that tip?"

"Oh . . . don't bet on Perfect Favor."

"I wouldn't've bet on Perfect Favor anyway. Everybody knows that nag is only one race away from the glue factory. I want to know what's going to win, not what's going to lose."

"Don't we all, friend." I smiled, and rattled open the elevator gates. "Don't we all."

To my surprise, Martin Vaizey was waiting for me in the corridor when I appeared. I had imagined one of those roly-poly asthmatic types with plastered-down hair and a purple silk bathrobe, rather like Zero Mostel in *The Producers.* Instead, I was greeted by a very tall, heavily-built man with wavy grey hair and a big open face, wearing a green plaid short-sleeved shirt, and jungle-green slacks and open-toed sandals.

"Mr Erskine, come on in."

He led me into a large, airy apartment, decorated like a feature for *Architectural Digest.* You know the kind of thing—glass-topped tables with arrangements of marble pyramids and expensive books about artists you've never heard of, pale velvet drapes with fancy swags and tie-backs, exquisite flower arrangements and a couple of inexplicable abstract paintings that look like somebody's digestion rebelling against a double portion of crab claws in black bean sauce.

"Attractive place," I told him.

"I was lucky. It used to belong to my parents. Would you care for a drink? You look hot."

"Is that a jug of margarita I see before me?" I asked him, nodding towards a collection of elegant Swedish crystal on an elegant silver Swedish tray.

"Sorry, no, it's passion-fruit crush. I don't drink alcohol. It disturbs my sensitivity."

"Yes, well, I guess it disturbs everybody's sensitivity. That's what it's for."

Martin Vaizey sat down on the white hide couch opposite me, and crossed his legs.

"As a matter of fact, Mr Erskine, Amelia called me from the school. She told me to expect you. She also gave me some idea of what it was you wanted."

"Did she tell you how serious it was?"

"It's obviously too serious for you to be able to handle it on your own."

"Mr Vaizey," I told him. "I'm a fortune-teller, a freelance consultant in future options. The skills I have are showmanship, observation, a tireless ear, and the ability to tell anxious menopausal women exactly what they want to hear."

Martin Vaizey slowly nodded. "Those are not inconsiderable skills."

"I didn't say they were. But they don't include psychic sensitivity. I know that there are spirits all around us, just longing to get in touch, but whatever it takes to talk to them, I simply don't have it. I'm like Alexander Graham Bell's mother. How can I call him up and ask him if he's invented the telephone yet? I don't have the wherewithal."

Martin Vaizey steepled his fingers in front of his face and looked at me intently. *He covered his face so that onlie ye Eyes look'd out.* "You're honest, at least," he told me, "and even on *my* side of the business you don't find much of that."

I didn't know whether I should have been insulted by that remark or not. Probably yes. But right at this moment, I needed Martin Vaizey's assistance a whole lot more than I needed my professional pride, so I decided to say nothing. I gave him my famous mail-slot grin instead, and nodded stiffly.

"Do you know why Amelia wouldn't help you herself?" asked Martin Vaizey.

"She said she'd given it up. You know, contacting the spirits, stuff like that. Besides, she and I had a thing going once. It was a long time ago, but it didn't end too happily. I guess she didn't want to risk an action replay."

Martin Vaizey nodded, as if Amelia had already told him that the reason for her refusal was partly personal. "She also said that what you were asking her to do sounded dangerous."

I raised an eyebrow. "*Dangerous?* Is that what she said?"

"Mr Erskine . . . all spirit contact is dangerous, to a greater or lesser extent. Even *you* should know that."

"Well with this particular case, with Naomi Greenberg, I guess there could be some kind of minor risk involved. But as you say, there's always a risk, pretty much, when you contact the spirits. I mean, they're not all cheerful, well-meaning souls, are they?"

Martin Vaizey took a long, patient breath. "I am not an

amateur, Mr Erskine. I have seen and talked to spirits that would astonish you, and I have been seeing them and talking to them for nearly forty years."

He poured himself a glass of passion-fruit crush. He didn't offer any to me—not that I wanted any. I guess that he proved he *was* psychically sensitive, after all.

"Let me tell you a little about myself, Mr Erskine. I first discovered that I was a sensitive when I was only five years old. My ten-year-old brother Samuel died of pneumonia the day before my fifth birthday. But—even after his funeral—I continued to see him in his room, and talk to him.

"Our relationship continued for years, and each time he appeared his image became clearer, until it was hard to tell that I wasn't speaking to a real boy. Only the faint images of the bedside light that shone right through his body showed that he was a spirit.

"Samuel introduced me to scores of other spirits, some of them clear, some very faint—some so old that they were nothing more than creaking voices in the darkness. He showed me a world that exists beyond death; what you might call the landscape of immortality. It's very desolate sometimes, but at other times it's very beautiful—almost picture-postcard beautiful. The sort of heaven that over-enthusiastic young Catholic girls like to imagine. It's *always* strange.

"I wasn't often afraid; although some of the very old voices were quite sinister. I wasn't afraid of my brother, of course, because he never grew older than ten, and he visited me nearly every day. One evening my father caught me talking to him in my room. Samuel vanished, but my father had caught the briefest glimpse of him. It nearly drove my father insane, but when I explained, he began to calm down. I suspect that my father may have been slightly sensitive, too—and that I inherited my sensitivity from him.

"He didn't say anything else, and he never asked me to get in touch with my brother on his behalf. But he bought me some books on psychic skills and psychic phenomena; and without saying a word he encouraged me to develop my sensitivity, and to learn how to use it with skill, and above all with accuracy. My father believed that whatever natural gifts one had, however arcane, one should stretch them to the utmost."

I sat back. I didn't know whether I believed any of this or not. The landscape of immortality? Creaking voices in the darkness?

"You're skeptical," said Martin Vaizey.

"Are you surprised? You're talking more like me than me."

"Perhaps I am. But if you really want to know what's troubling Mrs Greenberg, then I'm sure I can help you. It's my forté, identifying the spirits that are troubling people, and bringing them into the open. Most of the time, people aren't aware that spirits are trying to get in touch with them. They feel a sense of irritation, perhaps; or discontent, without even realizing that a spirit in the spirit-world is doing everything it possibly can to attract their attention. For instance, there is a spirit that is troubling you.

"Me?" I asked him, in disbelief. Now I knew that he was a quack. The only spirit that was troubling me was the chronic lack of a cold dry vodkatini, or maybe a tequila slammer with lots of lime.

"I noticed it when you came along the corridor," smiled Martin Vaizey. "You have a spirit who walks close behind your right shoulder. He is always there, always close. He is trying to protect you and also to attract your attention, both at once. He is trying to warn you, too, if I'm not mistaken."

I whipped my head around. All I could see was the headless legless torso of a bronze nude with a pretty sizable pair of gazongas, and a fussy arrangement of blue irises.

I grunted in amusement, licked my finger, and chalked up a mark in the air. "All right. One to you. You made me look."

"Of course I made you look. Don't you believe that there's anybody there?"

I was about to say, *oh, for sure, like hell I do,* when something stopped me. It wasn't just natural bet-hedging, either. I looked into Martin Vaizey's eyes and I saw such clarity and focus and sheer self-confidence that I almost began to think that he might have seen somebody walking behind me; that he might be able to see somebody, even now.

"Don't you want to know who it is?" he asked me.

"Can't you tell me?"

"Of course not." He smiled. "How should I know who it is?"

"Can't you *ask* him? It? Whatever it is?"

"I can do better than that."

He finished his drink, then shifted himself forward on the white hide sofa until he could reach the stack of art books on the glass-topped coffee-table. The top book was *The Art of Velazquez,* with a reproduction on the front cover of Philip IV in his field marshal's uniform. Martin Vaizey said, "Here lay your right hand flat on top of this book. That's right. Now, I'll lay my hand on top of yours."

I pressed my hand against the glossy book-jacket. I was still quite warm and sweaty and I could feel my fingers sticking to it. Martin Vaizey laid his hand flat on top of mine and his fingers were very very cool and dry.

"What are we doing this for?" I asked him.

He kept glancing over my right shoulder, which I found quite irritating. "Whatever spirit is following you . . . I'm inducing it to make its face known to you. We have to work together, all three of us. I don't know what the face looks like, you don't have the capability of recreating it in the real world, and the spirit can't make an appearance without our help. It's like molding a Hallowe'en mask out of plastic. Your hand is the mould, my hand is the injector pump, and the spirit is the plastic."

"What makes me think you've used that analogy before?" I asked him.

His eyes flickered. "I have used it before, yes. In fact, I've used it many times. But it's an accurate analogy."

We sat there, face to face, hand over hand, for what felt like a quarter of an hour, but was probably no longer than three or four minutes. I was beginning to feel stiff-backed and uncomfortable, and I was sure that my sweaty hand was cockling the jacket of his expensive art book. I looked at Martin Vaizey, but he wasn't really looking back at me. I looked at the crab's claws painting on the wall behind him. I listened to the whispering whirr of the air-conditioning, and the constant grumbling of the traffic outside. An elevator whined—stopped—then whined again.

Martin Vaizey suddenly exclaimed, "Spirit!"

"What?" I jumped.

"I'm addressing the spirit, not you," he snapped at me.

"Oh I'm sorry. I'm sorry. I didn't realize."

"Spirit," he went on, "take hold of my hand, let me lead you out of your formlessness. Be not afraid, o spirit, for we will protect and guide you. Show yourself, spirit, that we may know you."

There was another lengthy silence. But, skeptical as I was, I began to feel that there really *was* somebody standing behind me. Maybe it was the way that Martin Vaizey kept glancing over my shoulder. If somebody keeps on glancing over your shoulder, in the end you *have* to start believing that there could be somebody there. It's the same as staring at people's shoes as they pass you in the street. They almost always lift their feet up to see if they've stepped in something.

"Spirit, we know that you are trying to speak to us. Show yourself, spirit, take my hand. We will guard you and keep you, have no fear."

Maybe the sun had been covered by a cloud, as well as smog. But by scarcely-perceptible degrees the whole apartment darkened, and the air began to smell different, fresh but highly-charged, like ozone. I felt a deep sonic resonance, no louder than the dying vibrations of the lowest tuning-fork; but a resonance all the same. There was a feeling that time had shifted, that the room had changed, that there was somebody else here.

"Spirit, show yourself," whispered Martin Vaizey. "We are friends and protectors, we mean you no ill."

We waited. The apartment grew darker still. A small prissy clock in the hallway chimed four. *Ning, ning, ning, ning.* I raised my eyes and looked at Martin Vaizey with growing impatience.

It was then that I felt a totallly cold hand on my right shoulder. A hand that pressed against me for the briefest of seconds, as if a dead man were standing right behind me and were trying to attract my attention.

Instantly I turned round, almost ricking my neck in the process. There was nobody there. Only the well-developed torso. Only the irises. *Icy—fingers—trailing—down—back.*

I turned back to Martin Vaizey and said, "What—?" but he lifted an admonishing finger and said, "Wait, quiet! It's now! It's happening now!"

A numbingly-cold sensation passed down the entire length of my right arm, from shoulder to wrist, as if all my veins were being gradually filled with liquid oxygen. I was already suffering from tennis elbow—not from playing tennis, but from paint-rollering the ceiling of my office—and I grunted "Unh!" out loud as the coldness flooded down to my forearm.

"Please—don't be afraid," Martin Vaizey told me. "All spirits are cold. They have no need of body-warmth, after all."

I winced and nodded, trying to feel reassured, even though a spirit with no body-warmth whatsoever had just flowed down my arm and turned my work-strained tendons into strings of icy-cold agony.

I felt my fingers fill up with cold. And then immediately I felt an extraordinary sensation that made me catch my breath, and prickled up the hairs on the back of my neck. The book jacket seemed to be rising up in my palm, filling my hand with contours and bumps. The book jacket was taking on a shape. An oval shape. A nose shape. A chin shape. A mouth shape.

My hand wasn't pressed against a flat book cover any more. *It was pressed against a man's face.*

FIVE

I tried to snatch my hand away, but Martin Vaizey wouldn't let me go. He pressed his hand down harder and harder and there was nothing I could do but wait for the lumps on the book to rise higher and higher, and with every rising second to feel more like a cold, soft human face.

I tried to struggle free for a second time, but Martin Vaizey said, "No! Please! Not yet! You could hurt him!"

I was helpless. I certainly didn't want to hurt the face that had formed inside my hand, but much more critical than that was the fact that Martin Vaizey was so much heavier and stronger than me, and I simply couldn't tug myself free.

At last, the rising process appeared to have stopped. But I could still feel this chilled living face filling the palm of my hand. Worse than that, I could feel his eyelashes flickering against my skin. Even worse than that, I was sure that I could feel him *breathing* thin, steady breaths against my heart-line.

"All right," breathed Martin Vaizey. "You can take your hand away now. He's ready. Come on, take your hand away."

Carefully, cautiously, I lifted my hand from the book.

"There," said Martin Vaizey, his voice soft with triumph.

"Jesus," I whispered.

The cover had formed itself into the shape of a human face, a man's face, with a short straight nose and a sharp-cut mouth and a severe-looking forehead. It was impossible to tell whether the man was black or white, because his features stood out in relief from Velaquez' painting of Philip IV. His cheeks were tattooed with the orange silk and lace of Philip's field marshal's uniform, his chin bearded with Philip's black triangular hat, his right eye covered by Philip's pale featureless Hapsburg face.

What made the apparition so incredible, though, was the fact that it was breathing; that its eyes were open; that it was moving its lips.

"Spirit, can you hear me?" asked Martin Vaizey, leaning over it.

I heard a fluffing noise like wind blowing across a microphone; like beech-trees rustling; like dune-grass seething with fine grey sand. And then a voice, blurred and small, the voice of a man speaking over unimaginable distances.

"*. . . couldn't drive you back . . . they couldn't . . .*"

"What's he saying?" I asked Martin Vaizey, in sheer fright. "Who the hell is he?"

"I thought *you* could tell *me* that," said Martin Vaizey. "I never saw him before in the whole of my life."

"He's just a book!" I almost screamed at him. "He can't talk, for Christ's sake! He's just a book!"

"Mr Erskine, please—I thought I'd explained. What you're seeing is a simply a death-mask. Unlike your usual kind of death-mask, however, it's taken from a man's immortal spirit, rather than his dead flesh, which is why it can move and breathe and speak. I used the book because it was convenient, that's all. We could just as easily have molded his face on the wall, or on the table, or on the floor."

"So this isn't his real face, just a replica?"

"Well, it is and it isn't. Usually, a spirit is everywhere and nowhere. It just happens that, right now, we've arranged for *this* spirit's facial likeness to appear on this book."

ssshhhhh . . . "*. . . little too late . . . didn't understand that you can't use spirits to fight against spiritless men . . . so now they're going to . . . every place where . . . not a trace of . . . nothing left . . . until they have it all back . . . all of it . . . the way it was before . . .*" . . . ssshhhhh—

Although I was still upset—and although I wasn't at all sure just how dangerous this death-mask might be—I gingerly leaned a little closer. It was unnerving to watch Philip IV's orange silk uniform rippling like real material as the death-mask breathed and spoke, and to watch Philip's miniature face bobbing up and down with every twitch of the death-mask's eyelid.

"You're sure you don't recognize him?" asked Martin Vaizey. "It must be somebody you've met, somebody whose face you remember, otherwise we couldn't have created this manifestation."

"I don't know . . . it's kind of difficult to tell, with that blotchy painting all over his face."

sssshhhhh . . . "*. . . warned you . . . warned you . . . now they're going to purge the whole . . . now they're going to drag you all down . . . everything . . .*" . . . sssshhhhh—

"He's very distressed, don't you think?" Martin Vaizey remarked. "It sounds like he's trying to tell you that somebody's out to get their revenge. And a pretty radical revenge, at that. 'Nothing left—they're going to drag you all down—not a trace.' That sounds like radical revenge to me."

"Okay if I touch the book?" I asked him.

"Sure, you can do what you want with it. You can even read it, if you like."

"Okay if I turn it around?"

"Go ahead, do what you like."

I reached out and touched the spine of the book with my fingertips. I don't know what I was expecting. Maybe I thought that the face would suddenly turn around and bite my fingers. But instead, all I felt was a soft electric chill.

Carefully, I swivelled the book around, so that I could examine the face from all angles. All the time, it kept on whispering, but its voice was so faint that it was impossible to make any sense out of it.

"Do you have any enemies?" asked Martin Vaizey seriously. "Anybody who might want to hurt you?"

I shook my head. "Maybe a couple of husbands who got the idea that my consultations were more than just palm reading. I should be so lucky. My prettiest client looks like Bette Midler's twin brother."

"This is a great deal more serious than anything like that," said Martin Vaizey. "This spirit is very deeply troubled. In fact, I can't remember seeing a spirit so anxious, not in twenty years."

The whispering went on and on. *". . . whatever you do . . . remember what he promised . . . remember what he promised . . . even outside . . ."*

"Did anybody promise you anything?" Martin Vaizey asked me.

"I don't know. My landlord promised to kick me out if I didn't settle the rent. But that's about all."

Suddenly, the whispering voice said *". . . not in this world . . . not in this world . . . rock, don't you remember . . . have you hidden it so well? . . . stored it in mudballs . . . ing rock . . . don't you . . ."*

I stared at the face in rising horror and disbelief. I thought: no, not again. Not any more. I couldn't take another experience like that. Once in a lifetime was more than enough; twice almost drove me crazy. Not again, God.

Don't tangle me up in all this stuff again.

Martin Vaizey was watching me acutely. "You know who it is, don't you?" he said. "You've suddenly remembered who it is!"

I stood up, wiping the palms of my hands against my pants. "Listen, Mr Vaizey, I'm beginning to think that maybe this little experiment was kind of a mistake. If you could just . . . get rid of that face?"

"You came here asking for help," said Martin Vaizey.

"Well, yes, you're right. But that's all to do with Mrs Greenberg and Mrs Greenberg's furniture. Nothing to do with *this*."

"You don't think so?"

"I know so. This—this face here is something to do with my past. Something that I got myself involved in, years ago. This is *my* ghost, not Naomi Greenberg's. I don't know why it should still be following me around."

"Mr Erskine, it's following you around because you're involved in some kind of psychic struggle. It's not trying to warn you about jealous husbands or landlords dunning you for rent. It's trying to warn you about something *beyond.* 'Not of this world,' that's what it said. 'Not of this world.' And it talked about 'outside.' 'Outside' is common psychic parlance for the realms of the spirits."

I raised my hand emphatically. "Mr Vaizey, believe me, this has nothing to do with Mrs Greenberg."

"What other psychic manifestations are you handling right now, apart from Mrs Greenberg's?"

"One or two."

"Like what?" Martin Vaizey challenged me.

"Well, just one, as a matter of fact. A lady on East 86th Street."

"And what precisely is the nature of the psychic manifestation on East 86th Street?"

I glanced at the face on the Velazquez book. It was still whispering, still opening and closing its eyes. "Her piano plays by itself. At least, she *thinks* it plays by itself."

Martin Vaizey was silent for a while, watching me. I glanced at him two or three times, trying to smile. I don't think I had much success.

"You want to tell me who he is, our spirit friend?" he suggested, at last.

"Can you take off the book jacket? Just to make sure."

Martin Vaizey carefully picked up the book, and held it up facing me at eye level. Then he slipped off the illustrated jacket and let it drop to the floor. I was confronted with the same living death-mask, only this time it faced me at the same height as the real man might have faced me, and its skin was a pale marble-effect cream color, the color of the book's inside binding. The gold-blocked name *Velazquez* encircled its forehead like a headband. Its eyes blindly blinked at me, its mouth kept on whispering.

There was no doubt about it. No doubt at all. I was filled with the most unmanageable mixture of grief and cowardice.

The first time I had seen this face was on a slushy spring day nearly twenty years ago, when I had gone to La Guardia Airport to meet a flight from Sioux Falls, South Dakota.

The first time I had seen this face I hadn't known what butchery lay ahead of me; what cans of writhing spiritual worms were going to be opened up.

The first time I had seen this face, I hadn't understood magic, or death beyond death, or what total shit-freezing terror was.

It was Singing Rock, real-estate developer, part-time medicine man—dead now, and dead for a very long time.

Singing Rock went on whispering *". . . clear the land from sea to . . . back to what it was . . . any idea what . . ."*

"You want to tell me who he is?" Martin Vaizey repeated, more gently. It was only then that I realized I had tears in my eyes.

I swallowed hard. "He's a—friend of mine. Well, acquaintance of mine. I can't say that we were really ever friends. His name's Singing Rock."

"An Original Person, I assume, with a name like that?"

"That's right."

"Can you think of any reason why he might be trying to warn you?"

"I can, but I'm not sure that I want to."

"Do you want to try calling him by name? Maybe we'll get a clearer response."

I hesitated, but Martin Vaizey nodded encouragement, and so I stepped nearer to the face on the book. I looked into its blind cream marble-effect eyes and said, with a catch in my throat. "How're you doing, Singing Rock?"

The eyes opened and closed. *". . . Harry . . . you can hear me . . ."*

"Sure I can hear you. But very faint. Where are you speaking from?"

The face almost smiled. *". . . what you would call the Happy Hunting Grounds . . . what I call the Great Outside . . ."*

"I see. We've got a pretty bad connection."

". . . and me . . . always had a bad connection . . ."

"Singing Rock, something's bothering you. Singing Rock? I said, something's bothering you. Something's making you edgy. That's right. I can hear some of what you're saying, yes, but I don't understand what it is. I don't understand what's going down."

". . . every trace . . . they're clearing the sacred lands of every trace ."

"What do you mean? I don't understand you."

". . . very little time . . . believe me . . ."

His voice faded altogether, and all I could hear was a thick stream of static.

"Singing Rock?" I called him. "Singing Rock!"

Singing Rock's eyes closed, and he began to breathe more rapidly.

Martin Vaizey said, "We're losing him. Something's happening, I can feel it! There's something around him: some other presence."

"What? What do you mean? What presence?"

"Something's circling around him. Something dark. Something *black*."

"Jesus! Is he all right?"

The face on the book suddenly opened its eyes and stretched its mouth wide and screamed at me. I was so frightened I practically wet myself. Martin Vaizey shouted out, "Aaahh!" in terror and flung the book into the air.

The book tumbled onto the floor, and as it did so, its

cover was ripped off, as if by a hurricane-force wind, and tossed across the room, still screaming. The title page was raised up into Singing Rock's face, too, and that was screaming. It was torn out of the binding, and tossed after the cover. Underneath that was the acknowledgments page, and *that* was shaped like Singing Rock's face, and *that* was screaming. The unfelt wind snatched it away.

Page after page was torn out of the spine, and each page carried Singing Rock's death-mask, and each death-mask was screaming. The pages whirled across the room, fifty faces, seventy faces, a hundred faces, two hundred faces. The screaming grew louder and louder with every face that was torn off into the air, until Martin Vaizey's apartment screeched with a choir of more than three hundred agonized voices.

"Spirit-go!" bellowed Martin Vaizey. But still the blizzard of shrieking pages flew furiously around the room, and still they screamed. Somebody was banging and ringing at the door, too.

I fought my way through the flying pages with my hands over my ears. Martin Vaizey was still standing in the thick of them, shouting, "Go! Do you hear me? I command you to go!" I snatched a copy of *The New Yorker* from the magazine rack, loosely rolled it, and tucked it between my knees. The screaming went on and on, so loud and harsh that I began to think that I would never be able to hear properly again.

But I took out a book of matches, struck one, and managed to light the pages of *The New Yorker* like a torch.

"Mr Erskine, no!" Martin Vaizey shouted at me, but I stood up, brandishing my blazing magazine, and there was nothing he could have done to stop me. I knew what we might be up against, and he didn't. Not yet, anyway. Or not at all, if we didn't get rid of these shrieking faces.

I strode through the living room, waving my torch from side to side. The flames thundered softly with every wave. I caught two or three whirling death-masks, and set them alight. They blazed up instantly, screaming with even greater ferocity. I caught another, and another, face by face, until the whole apartment was filled with blazing, whirling, screaming death-masks of Singing Rock.

Whoever was pounding on the door, they were doing it even more furiously now, and bellowing, "Come on! Come on! Cut out the God-damned noise, will you? I'll call the cops!"

But I turned around and strode back again, touching every death-mask that plummeted past me. They flared and crumpled in the air; they spun around and around, smoking blackly; they fell on Martin Vaizey's white hide couch, they fell on Martin Vaizey's ice-blue rug. They fell on Martin Vaizey's glass-topped coffee-table and into his half-finished passion-fruit crush. The air was thick with smoke and black smudgy fragments of ash.

I was surrounded by a circus of fire and screaming faces. The heat lifted the burning pages so that they swooped and flew. I saw Singing Rock's face wherever I turned. Singing Rock with his nose burning off. Singing Rock with his hair alight. Singing Rock screaming out fire.

They were nothing but masks, nothing but Xeroxes of a human soul. But all the same they were the faces of a man who had protected and defended me—a man who had sacrificed his life so that his people and our people could both forget about the past.

"My God," said Martin Vaizey. "What the hell have you done to my apartment?"

I ignored him, and searched around and around, brandishing the stub of my burning *New Yorker*. I seemed to have caught almost every flying page, and those that I hadn't caught had been ignited by other pages. Martin Vaizey stood and watched me, his arms folded, as if he were posing for a painting called The Importance of Controlling Your Anger.

"I'm sorry," I said. I dragged over the Boda glass ashtray and messily crushed out the butt of my burned magazine. "I couldn't think of any other way."

He brushed ash from the back of his couch. "Well," he said, "I suppose you did the right thing, under the circumstances."

"I know some very good upholstery cleaners," I told him.

He used a long silver cocktail spoon to fish ash out of his

drink. He stared into it to make sure that it was no longer contaminated, and then decided not to drink it after all.

"I don't think our first priority is to worry about cleaning the upholstery," he said. "It seems to me that you and your Mrs Greenberg are both in serious trouble."

"How serious is your interpretation of serious?'

"You're in physical danger, that's my interpretation of serious." He looked at his watch, a 1930s Rolex. A watch like that could have paid my rent for two years. "Give me fifteen minutes to shower and change. Please—try to clean up as best you can. Don't rub ash into the fabrics."

"Excuse me?"

He had already half-turned toward the bathroom. "Yes? What is it?"

"Do I understand from this sudden burst of activity that you've agreed to help me with Mrs Greenberg?"

His face was very grim. He had a muscle in his right cheek that kept twitching, over and over, as if he were grinding his teeth, which he probably was.

"Mr Erskine, what we witnessed just now was the most flamboyant display of psychic intervention that I have ever seen in my *life*. And, as I've said, you're in serious trouble."

South-East
Colorado

Wanda heard her small brother whooping and calling so she left off shelling the peas and came out onto the verandah. The wind was up, and the screen door slammed so loudly behind her that it made her jump. Joey was sitting on his swing, swaying wildly backwards and forwards and shouting, "Lookit! Lookit! Lookit! The sky!"

Wanda went over to the verandah rail and lifted her eyes to the clouds. They were so low that they looked almost as if they were resting on the roof of the house, like a huge oppressive quilt. There was an ominous circular swirl in them, too, the kind of swirl you saw when a cyclone was stirring. *Wizard of Oz* weather. But it was the *color* of the clouds that made them so extraordinary. They were dark crimson, almost blood-red, like no clouds that Wanda had ever seen before, even at sunset.

All around them the grasslands were rustling, silvery-bright. There was a strange feeling of anticipation in the air. The chicken-coop door was bang-*pause*-banging, and small dust-devils were dancing across the yard. A flock of sharp-tailed grouse feathered their wings against the wind, and angled southwestward.

"Joey!" called Wanda. "You'd best come in!"

"It's only the sky!" Joey protested.

"You come on in. Mom said I was in charge and there's an end to it."

"But it's only the sky!"

"Could be a twister and then what? You'd be sucked up into the air. 'Member Mr Begley's sheep. They found it all the way over in Bent County, six days later, with its neck broke."

Joey reluctantly spun and swang, spun and swang. The grasslands were beginning to lash like the sea, and the flying dust stung Wanda's eyes.

"Joey McIntosh you come inside!"

But Joey kept on spinning and swinging, sometimes facing Wanda and sometimes turning away.

Wanda clattered down the verandah steps and crossed the windy yard. She was a small plain girl of nearly fifteen, thin-wristed, skinny-legged, in jeans and a black-and-white checkered shirt. Her mom had left her in charge and as far as she was concerned that meant that she was in charge, no ifs and ands.

She looked up at the clouds and they were whirling, rotating, like she'd never seen them whirling before. And they were so low! She could hardly believe they were real.

Just as she reached Joey, an upstairs window dropped on its sash and loudly broke.

"Joey . . . come on, there's a cyclone coming. We'd best get down in the cellar."

Joey clung tight to his swing-seat. Blond-headed, eight years old, impish, in a grubby blue T-shirt and grubbier shorts. "This ain't no cyclone. Can't you feel it?"

"Feel it?" asked Wanda. "Feel what?"

"This sure ain't no cyclone!" Joey repeated, in triumph, while the clouds roiled over his head.

"Joey!" snapped Wanda. "You have to come in!"

Already, her mother's painstakingly-cultivated vegetable garden had become clogged up with dust. The lettuce leaves had been filled with dust and then buried, the tomatoes would be next, then the beans.

Wanda crossed the yard with her hand raised to shield her eyes. She snatched hold of the swing-rope and said, "If you don't come in, I'm going to tell Mom that it was you who broke the milk jug."

Joey tried to carry on swinging, tilting sideways with every swing. He sang at the top of his voice, *"It ain't no cyclone, no, no way! Doo-dah! Doo-dah! It's Old Man Chopper come to stay! Oh, doo-dah-day!"*

Wanda took hold of his T-shirt and pulled him off the swing-seat. "What's the matter with you?" she demanded.

"It ain't no cyclone, that's all," Joey insisted. "It's something else."

The screen door slammed, making Wanda jump for a second time. But again, it was only the wind.

Lightning crackled on the western horizon, over towards Kim, in the heart of the Comanche National Grassland, and beyond, where the Sangre de Cristo Mountains rose dark and secretive and haughty—twelve, thirteen, fourteen thousand feet above sea-level. But this lightning wasn't like the usual lightning. This lightning was fine and thousand-branched, almost *hairy*. This lightning advanced across the prairie like blazing timbers, crackle-pop-crackle, or like the blazing organza petticoats of suicidal chorus-girls. This lightning was *fire*. This lightning was Armageddon coming today and not tomorrow.

Wanda snatched Joey's hand. "Come on, Joey! We have got to get into the cellar!"

"But what about Mom?" Joey demanded, dragging and scuffing his heels.

"Mom's okay, for God's sake. She probably took shelter in Springfield."

She took hold of Joey's wrist and dragged him arguing back towards the house. The wind was whooping and whistling now, and she heard another upstairs window break. A harness jangled, even though the horse was long gone.

"I sure hope Mom doesn't think those windows are *our* fault!" said Joey.

"Of course she won't, she'll know how windy it's been."

They struggled into the house. The screen door banged violently behind them. They went directly to the cellar door, but to Wanda's consternation it was locked, and the key was gone. She rattled the handle but that was no use. Joey kicked it and that was even less use. Where was the key? She tried the hall table but that was crammed with visiting cards and bills. She stood on tiptoe and ran her fingertips along the architrave. No key nowhere.

"What're we going to do?" asked Joey. He seemed to be much less skeptical now. The house was creaking and stirring and giving unsettling little shifts and judders; and if that didn't mean cyclone coming then they didn't know what else it could be.

Through the window Wanda saw yards of fencing torn up and flying through the air. Then the chicken-coop went through the air. Then the chicken-coop went over, and there were feathers and chickens and flapping tarpaper.

"What're we going to do?" Joey repeated, much more anxious. "S'posin' the cyclone sucks us up? Then what?"

"How should I know?" said Wanda, with the irritability of real fear. "I was never sucked up by a cyclone before."

All the same, she took hold of Joey's hand and the two

of them stood in the middle of the living room, in bloody and darkened shadows, while the wind gradually rose to screaming-pitch, and the shingles started to rip off the roof. The windows were filled with crimson light, so dark and glutinous that it looked as if somebody had been horribly slaughtered in an upstairs room, and their blood was running down the windowpanes.

"Wanda, what's happening?" asked Joey, his voice tiny and tight. "Everything's gone red."

"It's the dust, that's all," Wanda reassured him. "Storms always have colors. Brown or grey or green or black. It depends on where they come from, what dust they whup up. We learned that in Weather."

"It's *red,*" whispered Joey, in awe. Even his eyes shone red, like the eyes of a Stephen King vampire. "I never saw a *red* storm before."

They heard the long-case clock in the hallway beginning to strike twelve; but before it could finish striking the whole house lurched beneath their feet, and they heard the pendulum knocking and the chimes sound only once more, muffled and flat, before the clock fell sideways onto the floor. Pictures dropped from the walls; the curtain-rail collapsed. The big Zenith television set slewed around on its axis and knocked against the red-brick chimney-breast.

"I want Mommy," said Joey, in a tight, breathy voice. "Wanda, I want Mommy."

"It's okay, Mommy's sheltering too. She'll be back when the storm's blown over."

Wanda didn't know whether she believed that their mother was safe or not. She had seen electric storms and hurricanes and two or three rip-roaring twisters, but she had never seen anything like this before. It felt like the whole world was being pulled sideways—like standing on a rug that somebody was forcefully dragging away beneath her feet.

"Look!" said Joey, squeezing her hand. "Mr MacHenry's pick-up!"

As if in a dream she saw Mr MacHenry's old blue Chevy pick-up sliding through their yard. There was nobody driving it, and it was sliding *sideways,* its tires digging deep furrows in the dirt. It was followed by a slowly-tumbling junk-pile of wheelbarrows and shovels and farming equipment, even a rusty engine-block turning over and over. Wanda could hear the sound of it over the shrieking of the wind. A jangly, bumping, knocking, dragged-along sound, like some strange ritual funeral procession. It gave her a feeling of fear like nothing she had ever experienced before—a slow-burning chill that ran through every nerve-fiber in her body.

I was standing by my window
On a cold and cloudy day
When I saw those hearse wheels rolling
They was taking my mother away . . .

What had made her think of that song? Why did that jangling, tumbling junk sound so much like a burial? She thought of ashes to ashes and dust to dust, and black sashes and black veils, and grim white faces gliding through the bloody half-darkness.

It was then that something collided with the corner of the house. Something huge and heavy, that splintered the verandah and cracked the frame around the kitchen door. They heard furniture falling all through the house. Upstairs, their mother's huge mahogany wardrobe slammed flat on its face. Windows broke, china smashed, rows of books softly thundered onto the floor. Both Wanda and Joey were knocked off balance, and toppled onto the rug. All around them, chairs and tables and china came sliding across the room, to heap themselves up against the wall.

"Wanda!" screamed Joey, climbing to his feet, and balancing himself like a slack-wire walker. "The house is falling down! The house is falling down!"

Wanda managed to get herself up onto all fours, and then unsteadily stand upright.

"We'd better get out!" she shouted at Joey. "Try and get to the door!"

They struggled towards the living room door. Wanda couldn't believe how difficult it was just to walk. The floor was perfectly level, but it felt as if it were tilting uphill at forty-five degrees. All of the furniture in the house wanted to slide towards the western wall. The living room door was already clogged with kitchen chairs and stools and pulled-open drawers from the kitchen hutch; and up above her head Wanda could hear the beds rumbling across the the the polished board floors.

Joey tried to clear the tangle of chairs in the doorway, but as soon as he pulled one chair aside, it slid back to where it had been before.

Wanda shouted, "We'll have to climb over! Quick!"

Awkwardly, they managed to scale the chairs and climb down the other side, into the hallway. The front door was open, and outside they could see the yard and the highway beyond. They should have been able to see Mr MacHenry's house, but that seemed to have vanished altogether.

By pulling themselves along the walls, they managed to reach the doorway. The force of the storm seemed to grow every second so that by the time they had reached the door-way, and were clinging onto the frame, they felt as if they were hanging by their fingertips from the top of a building. The floor stayed as level as ever, but Wanda knew that if she lost her grip on the doorframe, she would literally fall.

Peering through the doorway, their eyes narrowed against the wind and the flying grit, they could see why Mr MacHenry's house seemed to have disappeared. The whole building had been wrenched free from its brick foundations, and had slid right across their yard and collided with theirs. The two houses were now crushed together like a monstrous traffic-accident; with stove-in boarding and broken windows and collapsed rooftops.

And all around them they could feel their own house shuddering against its supports; its whole frame tense, its mitres and dovetails strained to the limit; its nails being gradually dragged out like wisdom teeth.

"Wanda, we're not going to die, are we?" asked Joey. All the hysteria had gone out of his voice. His words sounded like clear water.

Wanda swallowed and clung on tight to the door frame, and didn't know what to say. This wasn't a storm at all. This was hell on earth.

The noise was enormous and overwhelming, but quite un-

like any noise that the children had heard before. Apart
from the funereal jangling and clanking, and the keening
and whistling of the wind, there was a deep arrhythmic
crashing. It was the sound of cars and trucks rolling over
and over—not fast, as they would have rolled over in an accident, but *slowly*—roof, fender, trunk, wheels—jouncing
on ruined suspension—as if they were being heaved over
and over by a mob of protesters. Except that there were no
protesters. There was nothing but the wind and the grit and
the bloodily-swirling sky. These cars and trucks were rolling
on their own.

The cars and trucks were accompanied by a tumbling,
dancing tide of rubbish. Wanda saw a half-crushed telephone booth; and a bashed-up Coca-Cola machine, its cans
brashly sliding around inside it; a jumble of newspaper
racks performing clattering handstands. She saw iceboxes
and display counters and shelving and magazines and bright
red packs of frozen food and shoes and sunglasses and broken bicycles and sacks of dog food.

She began to see people, too. One dark-blue Ford wagon
slid eerily past with its tires screaming an off-key Hallelujah
chorus, its windows totally blanked out with blood. A few
moments later, Mrs Hemming from the Hemming General
Store appeared. She was sliding along the highway on her
back, dead or nearly dead, her eyes open as if she were staring up at the sky. Her auburn wig was clotted with blood
and a big whitish bulge of brain-tissue, as if she had pinned
a cauliflower to her hair. Her pink floral dress was torn to
tatters, so that Wanda could see her blood-soaked corset
and her bruised and bulging thigh.

Soon after, a tall thin man in OshKosh dungarees slid
past, face down. He looked as if he had been broken, like a
marionette. Nobody could lie with their arms and legs
angled like that, not unless their arms and legs were all dislocated, torn out of their sockets, shoulders, and hips.
Wanda thought she recognized him as one of Mrs
Hardesty's farmhands from the Grasslands spread. He left a
wide glistening trail of blood on the road surface, but the
blood was soon covered over by newspapers and gum-
wrappers and Kentucky Fried Chicken boxes.

Wanda glimpsed children amongst the rubbish—children who must have been dead. She saw broken baby-buggies and dead dogs. She saw Leroy Williams, the janitor from Pritchard Elementary School, lying on his side with his face like a bright red Hallowe'en mask.

Joey started to scream. Piercing, high, in utter panic.

"Joey!" Wanda reached across the doorway and snatched at his wrist. "Joey, it's all right, just hold on!"

"But it's Mommy! Look, it's Mommy!"

"Mommy's in Springfield, I told you!"

"She's not, she's not! It's Mommy!"

Wanda stared at Joey, wide-eyed. *"Look,"* he said. But she didn't want to look. All this wind and noise and blood and deafening chaos were enough for her to cope with.

She couldn't face the idea that she might have lost her mother, too.

"It's not Mommy," she whispered. "Mommy's in Springfield."

But then that capillary-fine lightning crackled from the clouds; crackled like cellophane; crackled like blazing hair.

Its charge was so strong that Wanda could feel her blouse sticking to her skin. Her fingertips snapped with tiny sparks of static. The lightning crackled again, and rubbish whirled and shopping carts bucked and bounced and tumbled. Stray sheets of newspaper suddenly caught fire.

In the sudden darkness that followed the lightning, Wanda turned toward the highway. There—slowly borne along on a river of garbage and paper and broken vegetables—her mother lay, white-faced, dead, like Ophelia.

Her mother's hair was spread out all around her, blonde and fine. Her eyes were wide open, her fists possessively clenched around bunches of paper and plastic bags. What can you take, when you go? When you go to Heaven even the humblest of plastic bags is too much of an earthly self-indulgence.

Wanda watched her mother pass with a terrible feeling of loneliness and desperation. What was she going to do now? She would have to bring up Joey; she would have to fend for herself. How were they going to eat? How were they going to get to school? Who was going to buy their clothes? What about the rent? She couldn't bear it, couldn't believe it.

She called, "Mommy! Mommy! It's Wanda!"

But her mother was gradually being dragged away, one arm lolling, one cheek lacerated by asphalt. Her jeans were torn at the knee and her yellow-checkered shirt was splattered with brown dried blood.

She can't be dead. She can't be. She's my mother.

Wanda shouted to Joey, "Wait here! Cling on tight!"

"Where are you going?" Joey screamed at her. "You can't leave me! You can't leave me!"

"Wait here!" Wanda insisted.

She pulled herself out of the doorway and took three staggering steps across the verandah. It was only then that she realized how strongly everything in Pritchard was being dragged towards the west. She managed to catch the verandah-rail, but all the same she could hardly stay upright. Lightning spat all around her; garbage and newspapers blew in the wind. She turned back to Joey and shouted, "Stay there! Stay there! I'm going to rescue Mommy!"

"You can't!" screamed Joey. "You can't save her, you can't!"

"Just stay where you are!" Wanda yelled at him.

She stood up as tall as she dared. Her mother's body was moving slowly but unceasingly away from her. If Wanda allowed herself to be dragged away too, then perhaps she could catch up with her; and find a place for them both to cling on to; a house or a shed or even just a fence; at least until this storm had blown itself out.

"Mom!" she shouted. "Mom, it's Wanda! I'm coming to save you!"

Her mother's body rose and dipped in the tide of garbage. For a moment, Wanda lost sight of her. But then another crackle of lightning caught the yellow plaid of her bloodied shirt; and Wanda could see that she had already been carried away as far as Waldo's Food Mart, on Main and Comanche.

Joey screamed at her, "Don't! Don't leave me alone!"

Wanda turned. "Joey, I have to! Somebody has to!"

"Don't leave me alone! Don't leave me alone!"

"Joey—"

"Noooo!"

At that instant, with a sharp ripping noise, the nails were tugged out of the verandah rail, and flew towards the west. The rail collapsed, with a barking, planklike echo, and Wanda was thrown head-over-heels into the dusty yard. She rolled over, rolled over again, thought: *this isn't so bad.* But then she found herself rolling over and over again, and again, and hitting a fence post, and tumbling over grit and shingle, and tumbling again, and hitting a hitching-rail, and—winded—colliding with boxes and reels of cable and bedding-posts and cans of paint.

She caught hold of the hitching-rail and pulled herself onto her feet. She took a deep breath, and then tried to walk towards her mother.

She managed three or four tottering steps, but then she couldn't stop herself. The ground was level but she had to run. She felt as if she were bounding down a steep hill, faster and faster, until her legs were whirling so fast that she couldn't keep up with the pull of gravity. She tripped, stumbled and fell—only fifty or sixty feet away from her mother. She was showered in cans and papers and garbage and broken bottles. She scraped both knees, and they stung like fire. She was almost drowned in rubbish. A cat jumped past her, end over end, an acrobat cat, even though its eyes were yellow and staring, and its legs were rigid with *rigor mortis.* She screamed, helpless, scrabbling against the tarmac with lacerated hands, trying anything to prevent herself from falling any further.

"Mommy! Mommy!" she cried. *"Mommy!"*

She got up on her knees; fell; got up again; fell. Lightning snapped and exploded all around her, cans and papers pirouetted with static. She opened her mouth to scream but her lips crackled with living electricity.

She fell, waded, fell again. But she had nearly reached her mother. "Mommy!" she shouted, but stumbled. Trash poured over her like a surging tide. A supermarket cart struck her on the side of the head. *Mommy, it's me! Please, Mommy, it's me!*

She was dragged at last into her mother's arms. But her mother's arms were lifeless: lolling and loose.

Through a blizzard of Styrofoam cups and ripped-up *Time* magazines, Wanda could see without doubt that her mother was dead; smiling but dead; nothing but a heavy jiggling body in a yellow-checked shirt, grinning, sightless, and blissfully ignorant of Wanda's fear. She wasn't Mommy any more; she was a lifesize imitation made of dead meat; horribly flawed; horribly carefree. Wanda screamed and pummelled at her mother's arm. Her mother vanished under showers of torn-up plastic bags and rubbish; then reappeared ten or fifteen feet further away, still smiling, a woman happily swimming in the sea of oblivion, all responsibilities forgotten.

Wanda screamed, "Mommy! Mommy!" But she knew that her Mommy had already left her. The smiling woman in the yellow-checked shirt was nothing but a mockery of Mommy. Her real Mommy was in heaven; or someplace else, where Wanda could never find her; and Wanda had been left to survive on her own.

She climbed to her feet again, stumbled, and toppled. All around her houses were moving like ships that had dragged their anchors. Chimneys dipping; balconies swaying. Even the Exxon gas station had collapsed, and its roof was being pulled westward like the black triangular fin of a killer whale. She looked up, and saw that the sky to the west of Pritchard was black as night; black as sin; and that even the clouds seemed to be drawn towards it.

She saw a house grinding past her, a mustard-painted house; and recognized the Allisons' place from almost a half a mile east. She struggled upright, ran and fell; but ran again, and managed to clamber up onto the Allisons' porch. The house was moving beneath her feet, and slowly turning as it moved, but at least she wasn't being pulled along the highway.

She circled the Allison house, clinging tightly to the verandah posts to keep herself from being pulled off. It was two-story, clapboard, a typical Pritchard house. Some of the folks who moved away from Pritchard took their houses along with them, on the back of a flatbed trailer. Almost all of the downstairs windows were broken and the door was hanging off its hinges. Wanda struggled into the hallway, snagging her hand on a broken hinge. She sucked blood, and wrapped her handkerchief around it. Then bracing herself against the wall, she shouted out, "Hallo! Is anybody home? Hallo!"

There was no reply. The house whistled with wind and echoed with banging doors. The wallpaper in the hall was yellow and brown, like French and American mustard all mixed up; but most of the pictures had dropped off the wall and all of the furniture had slid right through to the drawing room, so that the hall was oddly bare for a town where people habitually over-furnished. In Pritchard, furniture meant affluence, the same as it had when the town was first established, back in 1865. Big color TVs and coffee tables and couches and display cabinets crowded with crystal and china, they all stood for solidity, and community pride, and success.

Wanda's feet crunched on broken picture-glass. "Hallo?" she called again. "Is anybody there?"

She was just about to make her way through to the kitchen when she heard a thin, distorted cry from upstairs. She froze, her hand on the bannister post, and swallowed hard. She heard the cry again. *Aaaooooooohhhhh,* with a chilling echo to it. She couldn't make up her mind if it were an animal or a human.

"Is anyone there?" she shouted; her voice tight and piping. "Hallo? Is there anyone up there?"

She heard the cry once again, and this time it sounded distinctly like *"Help me."*

She hesitated for a moment, listening to the wind and the dreadful banging of trucks and automobiles, and then she mounted the stairs. She had to grasp each bannister rail tightly to prevent herself from being dragged away. It was more like scaling a steeply-tilted ladder than climbing upstairs. She whimpered as she went, partly out of grief, partly out of fear. But she was desperate to find somebody alive, somebody who could help her, somebody who could tell her what to do.

"Aaaaaoooohhhhhh," came the cry; lower this time, and somehow more frightening than it had been before.

Wanda pushed open a bedroom door. The four-poster

bed had slid across to one side of the room, along with the nightstand and the dressing-table and tangled heaps of clothes. A dressmaking dummy lay tilted against the wall, stiff and dowdy and headless. It was wearing a half-finished summer frock with bright splashy poppies on it—a frock which now would never be finished.

"Aaaaoooohhhhhh," the voice wailed again.

Wanda called, "I'm here, I'm coming! Where are you?"

"Aaathrroom," the voice called back.

"What?" asked Wanda.

"Baaatthhhrooommm. I'm in the baaatthhrooommm."

Shaking with delayed shock Wanda made her way along the landing until she reached the very last door, which was the only door which was closed. There was a clutter of broken pictures up against it, as well as a bentwood chair and a small semicircular table and a shattered glass lamp. One of the pictures was an amateurish oil painting of Pritchard in pioneer days, when it had been nothing much more than a general store and a post office and a haphazard collection of farms.

"Oh, God, please help me," the voice begged, from beyond the door.

Wanda turned the handle, and the door opened. Immediately, all of the debris that had been piled up against it tumbled eagerly into the bathroom, and collided with the bathtub.

The bathroom window had fallen inwards, and the wind was blowing the flowery curtains into rags. Even though the glass was gone, however, the sky had grown so bloody and dark that it was difficult for Wanda to see what had happened. She could make out a big white bathtub, and a cork-topped seat lying on its side, and heaps of shattered glass. But at first sight the bathroom appeared to be empty.

"Where are you?" she called, uncertainly. "I can hear you but I can't see you."

"Bath," the voice echoed. *"Please help me."*

Wanda half-slid, half-crawled across the floor, until she clumsily fell against the side of the high old-fashioned tub. It felt icy-cold, and it made a dull booming noise when she banged it.

"Please God help me," the voice repeated.

Wanda climbed up on the side of the bath. Inside, the entire tub was awash with blood. A naked girl of about sixteen or seventeen was lying in it, her skin so white that it looked like ivory soap, one hand clinging to the handgrip, the other pressed hard against the tiles. Her hair was soaked in blood, so that it was impossible for Wanda to see what color it might have been. Her breasts and shoulders were streaked and mottled with blood, both fresh and dried. Her bloody handprints had stencilled Rorschach prints all over the tiles, nightmares in living colour.

Wanda said, "Maggie, is that you? *Maggie?*"

She could scarcely recognize this bloodied mermaid as the second-eldest Allison daughter, the girl who used to babysit her when she was small. The last time Wanda had seen her, Maggie Allison had been sitting sidesaddle on the back of Rick Merrick's motorcycle, brightly laughing, her head thrown back so that her long cornsilk-colored hair had flowed and whipped in the slipstream.

"Maggie, what happened?" said Wanda. "You're covered in blood."

Maggie looked up at her and her face was grotesquely smeared, as if she had been taking part in some terrible tribal initiation. Her eyes glistened in the gloom; the bloody water thickly lapped against the sides of the bath, and made a gurgling noise.

"Window . . . the window broke. The glass fell into the bath. I tried to get it out but I cut my legs and the back of my ankle. Sliced right through. I just can't move, and I can't stop bleeding, and there's so much blood. Oh, Wanda, I think I'm going to die. I think I'm going to bleed to death."

"Is your mom here?" asked Wanda. What was she going to do? Even if she were strong enough to lift Maggie out of the bath, how could she stop her from bleeding?

Maggie said, "I called and I called but nobody came. Mom was in the yard when the storm blew up . . . I didn't hear her after that."

"It's not just a storm," said Wanda. "It's something else."

"Oh Wanda, get me out of here," Maggie pleaded.

Wanda hesitated for a moment, then tugged at the waste-lever. There was a sharp clonking noise but that was all.

"Doesn't it empty?" asked Wanda.

Maggie coughed a bloody bubble. "It's broke . . . we always used to pull out the plug by hand—but don't! There's too much glass. You'll cut your fingers off."

"Maybe I can lift you up," Wanda suggested.

"You could try, but don't drag me. There's a huge piece of glass and it's sticking in my side."

Wanda looked around the bathroom in desperation. All the while, Maggie continued to cling to the handgrip, her breathing thin and unsteady, the blood in her hair congealing into a hideous fright wig.

The house trembled all around them, and they heard a sharp clattering landslide of shingles falling off the roof above their heads. The main support beams groaned, tiles cracked like castanets, and nails began to pop out of the flooring. As the house slowly swivelled, the blood-red light from the window slowly moved around the bathroom.

Wanda said, "I know what I'll do . . . I'll fill the bath with towels, push them underneath you. That way, I can get you out without you cutting yourself."

Maggie said nothing, but coughed, and coughed again.

Wanda fought her way across the floor, straining against the unnatural gravity that had dragged away her mother, and was threatening to drag away everything—people, cars, houses, maybe the sky itself. She clawed her way to the linen-cupboard, opened the catch, and was immediately caught on the forehead by the door swinging open, and then half-buried under an avalanche of Sears bath towels.

Winded, coughing, she shuffled crabwise back to the bath, pulling the bath towels along with her, although there was scarcely any need. All of the contents of the linen-cupboard came sliding and tumbling across the bathroom floor, and ended up heaped against the tub.

"Wanda, I'm so cold," whispered Maggie. "Wanda, please save me. I'm so cold."

Wanda picked up a towel and plunged it deep into the bloody water. It bulged with air for a moment, then sank. Wanda heard the glass squeaking and crunching on the bottom of the tub, and Maggie gasped, "Careful, careful."

When she tried to pull the towel further down the bath, Wanda felt a quick sharp sensation across the heel of her hand. She snatched her hand out of the water, and saw bright red blood running in feathery patterns all down her wrist.

She unfolded another towel and pressed it against her hand. The cut was clean and curved and quite deep. Every time she dabbed the towel against it, more blood welled up. She dabbed it again and again, but it kept on bleeding.

Maggie whimpered. Wanda took out her handkerchief and tied it around her hand, tightening the knot with her teeth. Then she plunged another towel into the bath, and another, and another.

"Maggie," she urged her. "Maggie, can you hear me?"

Maggie nodded. "I'm so cold," she breathed. She had sunk so far down into the water that her words bubbled.

"Maggie, I've covered all of the glass next to you with towels. All you have to do is to roll over onto the towels, then I'll help to lift you out."

The house gave a groan that sounded almost human, and part of the bathroom ceiling collapsed, showering them both in plaster-dust. They heard other windows breaking, and a heavy lurching noise which sounded like the verandah roof caving in. The bloody red light waxed and then waned, but the wind persisted.

"Maggie, you have to try!"

Maggie turned her head and stared at Wanda in pitiful desperation. *"I feel like . . . there's no blood left in me . . . none at all."*

"Maggie, you must . . . You don't want to die here!"

Wanda reached across the tub and prized Maggie's fingers away from the handgrip, one by one. It wasn't difficult: Maggie was so weak now that she was barely conscious. Forcing back an urge to gag, Wanda cautiously lowered her arms into the water. She hesitated, swallowing bile. Maggie's back felt like a freshly-slaughtered pig's carcass, gutted and singed and hung up to chill—hardly human at all. Wanda gripped her cold, yielding flesh and tried to turn her over, onto the towels.

"Come on Maggie, you'll have to help me," Wanda urged her. "Try to pull yourself up the side of the bath . . . I can't lift you all on my own."

Maggie stared at her. White eyes, bloody face.

"No, Wanda, you'll have to leave me here."

"I can't! I can't leave you!"

"You'll have to. I'm as good as dead already."

"No!" Wanda shouted at her.

Maggie shivered and closed her eyes. *"No!"* Wanda screamed at her. *"No!"*

She plunged her hands back into the bloody bathwater, and tried to heave Maggie up the slippery side of the bath. She strained and strained, grunting and tugging and letting out little screams of effort.

She sat on the floor beside the bathtub, pulling Maggie higher and higher. At first she thought she would never be able to do it, but then Maggie seemed to grow inexplicably lighter. Soon Wanda had managed to balance her right on the edge of the bath, one blood-streaked arm swinging. A last effort dragged her over, right on top of Wanda, wet and bloody and chilled.

"I'll dry you . . . bandage your cuts." Wanda panted. She climbed to her knees, and steadied herself on the side of the bath. "There must be a doctor somewhere around . . . somebody must have called for help."

It was only then that she realized why Maggie had grown so much lighter, as she pulled her up the side of the bath. The left side of her belly had been sliced right open. A huge triangular shard of window-glass had cut through skin and fat and membrane and muscle, from her ribcage to her mound of Venus. The way she had been lying in the bath, with her left side pressed against the side of the bath and her knees drawn up, the wound had kept itself closed. But as soon as Wanda had lifted her up the side of the bath, it had gaped wide open.

The bath was filled with knives of glass and cold bloody water and Maggie's emptied-out intestines. Soft glistening coils, in fawns and blacks and lurid scarlets, with all the pungency of blood and the sourness of stomach acids and the overwhelming truffle-mustiness of human excrement.

Wanda closed her eyes. She knew now that she would probably die today, too. She didn't have the strength to move away from the side of the bath, not against that unyielding, irresistible force. All around her, the Allisons' house shuddered and shifted and collapsed, and it was so dark now that she felt sure that today was the end of the world. The bathtub slopped and plopped, and quietly crunched with broken glass. Through the window, she could see the clouds boiling and swelling, more like a speeded-up movie than a real sky.

She pressed her hands over her face and said, "I wish for God's good spirit from above, to shed within my heart His holy love. I wish that—rescued from the power of sin—His love may make and keep me pure within. I wish it may with sweet and strong control, from glory unto glory change my soul."

She wasn't sure how long she knelt in the bathroom with her eyes tightly closed, but after a while she became aware that somebody else was standing close by. She *sensed* their presence, rather than hearing it, and she took her hands away from her face and looked around the bathroom with a slowly-growing feeling of apprehension.

"Is there somebody there?" she called out. Her voice sounded flat and muffled in the blood-colored gloom.

At first there was no reply. But then a tall dark figure separated itself from the shadows in the doorway, like a black amoeba splitting itself in half. It was a black man, almost skeletally thin, dressed up in a tailcoat and striped grey formal trousers, with a high wing collar and a watch-chain.

His appearance would have been ludicrously dandified if his shoulders hadn't been so stained with dust, and his shirt hadn't been so discolored. Around the neck it was so greasy that it was almost orange. His eyes glittered in the gloom like two shiny black-beetles feeding on his eyelids, and his mouth was stretched tightly back over yellowing teeth.

He stepped up closer. Wanda gripped the cold, sticky side of the bath, and climbed awkwardly and fearfully onto her feet.

"Are you afraid of me, child?" the black man asked her.

His words were husky-dry, like corn-chaff sifted through somebody's fingers.

"Who are you?" she asked him. "What are you doing here? This isn't your house."

"I know," the black man nodded. "This is your friend's house, and I can see that your friend is dead. I'm sorry for that. That's a sorry sight to see."

"What do you want?" Wanda asked him.

He shook his head. "Nothing in particular. I was passing, that was all, and felt your prayers. They was such strong prayers I was minded to listen for a while, because in these days people rarely pray so strong."

He paused, and then he said, "If more of your people had believed in things that can't be seen and can't be locked up in the bank then maybe this never would have come to be."

Wanda said, "What's happening? Is it the end of the world?"

The man thought about that and then nodded. "Yes, it is, in a manner of speaking. For most of your folks, anyway, with some exceptions. As for you—well, I think very highly of your faith, as a matter of fact, and hallelujah."

He reached into the pocket of his vest, and produced a small silver pendant on a thin silver chain. He offered it to Wanda, but at first Wanda was reluctant to touch it.

"Go on," the black man coaxed her. "Wear it, and you'll stay safe, even when you walk through the valley of the shadow of death. Do you know who gave me that? Toussaint L'Ouverture gave me that, the leader of the black slaves."

Wanda reluctantly held out her hand and the black man took hold of her wrist, and let the chain and pendant trickle down into her open palm. She looked down at it, and saw a tarnished silver cockerel, its neck broken, its wings spread.

"Wear it," the black man urged her. "And if anybody asks you where you came by it; you say it came from Toussaint L'Ouverture himself, and was a gift to Jonas DuPaul, and that Jonas DuPaul gave it to you, and said hallelujah."

Wanda didn't know what to say, but the black man coaxed her, "Put it on, child. Put it on. It'll keep you from harm. That's a voodoo necklace . . . and whoever wears it, they give it all of their character, all of their strength—so that when they pass it on, the next person who wears it gains all of the character too.

"When you put it on, child, you'll have all of my protection from the evil spirits that walk this land, and the evil spirits that walk the land beneath; and you'll have all of my wisdom, child, and all of my magic."

Hesitantly, cautiously, Wanda lifted the necklace over her head. The black man watched her with a yellow-toothed smile, and nodded, and said, "Hallelujah. That's the way of it, child. Hallelujah."

SIX

Karen opened the door for us. The last triangle of sunlight was creeping out of the window like a furtive visitor who has been kept waiting too long in the hallway, and has decided to call it a day. Michael Greenberg stood a little way away, wearing a baggy bottle-green turtleneck. His eyes were swollen with tiredness, and his whole attitude was cagy and skeptical. When I introduced Martin Vaizey to him, he gave a quick, who-cares kind of nod and said, "Sure, pleased to know you." I didn't blame him. He'd suffered two psychiatrists; dozens of disbelieving relatives; a clairvoyant who looked like a men's fashion buyer for J.C. Penney; Karen, who had always been over-romantic and a little screwy; and now this tall Boy Scout figure in a woven linen suit and a Panama hat, carrying a three-hundred-and-fifty-dollar Abercrombie & Fitch briefcase.

Martin stepped into the apartment and sniffed the air. "Curious," he said, after a sniff or two.

Michael unscrewed the cap from a bottle of Absolut Vodka. "Anybody want a drink?"

"No, no, no thank you," Martin told him, lifting his hand to his ear, as if he could hear something that the rest of us couldn't.

"Erm . . . alcohol disturbs his psychic sensitivity," I put in.

Michael shrugged. "You don't mind if I do?"

"No," I replied. "And I don't mind if *I* do, either."

Michael poured out two overgenerous vodkas-on-the-rocks. "What about *your* psychic sensitivity?"

"Mine is the kind of psychic sensitivity that for some reason thrives on alcohol. *Nasdravye.*"

Martin circled the room slowly, moving in and out of the shadows. He seemed to make Karen nervous, and she came up close to me and held my arm.

"Very curious," said Martin. "This is quite unlike anything that I've ever had to deal with before."

"Oh, yes?" I asked.

He nodded, eyes narrowed. "Its transcommunicational vibrancy is *totally* different."

"I see," I replied. I swallowed vodka. "In—unh—what particular way?"

Martin stopped circling and blinked at me. "I'm sorry?"

I coughed. It was strong stuff, that Absolut. "I said, in what particular way?"

"In what particular way what?"

"In what particular way is its trans—? Well, in what particular way is it different?"

Martin stared at me for a long time and made me feel even more awkward. When he spoke, he spoke very slowly and patiently, as if he were trying to explain to a six-year-old how a ballpoint pen worked. "A spirit's transcommunicational vibrancy is the distinctive, individual way in which it contacts the physical world. Its psychic voiceprint, if you want to draw a comparison.

"In this case, the transcommunicational vibrancy that I can feel is very strong and it's probably human, although not *certainly* human. There are nonhuman spirits which are very skillful at imitating humans. It *feels* human, but it's not communicating in the way in which I would normally expect a human spirit to communicate. Do you understand me?"

"Yes, of course I understand you," I replied, a tad too aggressively. I turned to Karen and Michael and gave them a look that was meant to convey, "Understand him? Is he kidding me, or what?"

Martin continued his ethereal prowling around the room. "With very few exceptions—such as murderers and suicides—most spirits *adore* getting in touch with the living. As soon as you start reaching out for them, you can feel them reaching out for you in return. It's almost like immersing yourself in a pool, and finding scores of willing hands trying to pull you out. They love us, the dead. They love the world they have left behind them. Quite beyond reason, sometimes, considering the suffering that many of them experienced before they died.

"Still—they miss it, and they appreciate every effort that we make to contact them. That's what makes my life as a medium so pleasurable. You may be skeptical about those who talk to the dead—present company excepted, of course—but almost anybody can do it, to a greater or lesser extent, because the spirits are so keen to talk to us. They want to tell their loved ones that it's true—that there *is* such a thing as life after death. They want to tell their loved ones that they're waiting, patient and sad, for the day when they can walk together, once again.

"They want to tell us that there's hope, and happiness, and relief from suffering."

Christ on a bicycle, I thought, this guy could use a violin.

"I thought you said this spirit was *different*," I interrupted him.

I hoped Michael Greenberg wouldn't misinterpret the sharpness in my voice as meaning that I didn't have very much faith in Martin's talents. The only reason I was being sharp was because I had heard all of this sales pitch about "hope, and happiness, and relief from suffering" so many times before—mainly from me.

Quite honestly, as far as I was concerned, Martin didn't need to sell himself. He had more spiritual skill than anybody I had ever met, Amelia included. I had seen him raise the face of my late Indian compadre Singing Rock out of a book about Spanish painting. I had seen it, touched it, heard it talk, and that was good enough for me.

Martin said, "By now, I would have expected to hear the spirits talking—even *calling*. But all I can sense so far is—" he half-closed his eyes, as if he were trying to hear the strains of a very distant train-whistle *"—darkness."*

"Darkness?" asked Michael.

Martin hesitated. "Darkness, yes. Extraordinary darkness. And the movements of those who live in darkness. The movements of those who *are* darkness."

Karen squeezed my arm. "This won't be too dangerous, will it?"

"Oh, no, not especially," Martin reassured her. "Not unless you happen to be afraid of the dark. Not unless your own shadow makes you jump." He gave a brittle little laugh. "I'm not talking about the Prince of Darkness."

"You'd better be introduced to Naomi," I told him. "The

sooner we can find out what's wrong with her, the sooner this gentleman can get back to leading some kind of normal life."

"Of course," agreed Martin, rubbing his hands together with supreme confidence.

Michael opened the dining room door and took two or three paces back, leaving it open.

"In here?" asked Martin, and stepped cautiously forward.

If anything, the dining room was even gloomier and colder than it had been before, and it certainly smelled sourer. The furniture was still piled up against the opposite wall, and Naomi still stubbornly clung to her single dining room chair. She was wrapped in a dark plaid blanket. Her hair was wild and she was beginning to look emaciated. Her eyes were red-rimmed with exhaustion and stress. To be truthful, she stank.

Martin crossed the room and hunkered down to Naomi's eye level. At first her eyes were rolled up white in her head, but Martin patiently waited for her, his hands clasped together, and after a while her eyelids began to flutter and her pupils reappeared. She focused on Martin in perplexity, and then she glanced over at me.

"Hallo, Naomi," said Martin, touching her blanketed knee, as if she were an old friend whom he hadn't seen for years and years. "How are you feeling?"

"I feel—*worried*," said Naomi, hoarsely.

"Worried?" asked Martin. "What have you got to be worried about?"

Michael said, "She talks to him, she talks to you, why won't she talk to me?"

"Ssh," said Karen, and I said, "Ssh."

Naomi said, in the tone of an irritable little girl, "I'm worried about what's going to happen when . . ."

Martin said nothing, but waited for her to search for the words.

"I'm worried about what's going to happen when I die."

"Why are you so concerned about that?"

Naomi glanced quickly from side to side, as if she were trying to make sure that nobody else was listening. "Supposing I die in the night and fall off this chair?"

Martin thought about that. "All right," he said at last, "supposing you do?"

"Then they'll get everything, won't they? Then they'll have shown us how strong they are."

"Who's 'they,' Naomi?"

Naomi jerked her head towards the wall.

"The people next door?" Martin asked her.

Naomi shook her head. "*He* knows," she said, jerking her head toward me. "And *she* knows," jerking her head toward Karen. She looked like a pecking barnyard chicken.

"Mr Erskine knows who it is?" Martin pressed her. "*And* Mrs van Hooven?"

Naomi covered her face with her hand, so that only her eyes looked out. Martin stared at her in fascination; but there was no doubt that she was disturbed too.

"Now I'm beginning to understand what your friend Singing Rock was trying to warn you about," he said.

"You've seen that sign before?" I asked him. "You know what it means?"

He stood up, touching Naomi on the shoulder to indicate that he appreciated her help. "It can signify several different things. It has a meaning in clinical psychiatry as well as folklore and spiritualism."

Michael put in, "Her analyst thinks that it's an indication that she's developing a split personality. A form of mild schizophrenia."

"Well, he's quite correct," Martin agreed. "Psychiatric patients who cover their faces or who make improvised masks are often trying to indicate that they're 'someone else.'"

"And you think this is Naomi's problem?" asked Michael.

Martin gave him a wry smile. "Let's be honest about this. Naomi is exhibiting several tell-tale symptoms of schizophrenia. A progressive withdrawal from the real world. Hallucinations, in the form of threatening voices and images. A tendency to remain rigidly in the same place. I can understand why her analyst thinks that she could be schizophrenic."

"But?" asked Michael.

"But look around you," smiled Martin. "How does her analyst explain this furniture? How does he explain these pictures?" He tried to straighten one of the pictures so that it hung downwards, instead of sideways, but as soon as he let it go, it swung back up to a horizontal position. "There is so much paranormal activity in this room, it makes Amityville look like *The Wonder Years*. And it's so *tenacious*. I never saw such tenacious activity before. Usually, a mischievous spirit grows tired of the game after a while and goes off to make mischief someplace else. But this spirit is *determined*. This spirit is like a pit bull that won't take its teeth out of your leg, even if you break its back."

He said to Michael, "Have Naomi's doctors offered any kind of explanation for any of this?"

Michael shook his head. "Dr Stein seems to think that she's doing it herself—I don't know—out of spite, or menopausal derangement. He won't say *how*. I never saw a change of life that could make a thousand-pound sideboard move across the room. He keeps talking mumbo-jumbo about psychokinetic influences and mind-over-matter. I don't know whether he really believes in it, but he hasn't offered any other suggestions. Dr Bradley prefers to ignore it."

Martin looked around the dim, rancid room, his breath fuming from the chill. "He prefers to *ignore* it? How can he ignore it?"

I made one more attempt to straighten up one of the paintings. It stayed vertical for a moment or two, then dragged itself back to the horizontal.

I said, as lightly as I could, "I guess he ignores it the same way that you and I ignore muggers and junkies and guys sleeping in cardboard boxes. That's what you call self-absolution, isn't it? If you ignore it, you don't have to worry about it. Doctors are good at that kind of thing."

Martin touched the walls, touched the furniture. "Well . . ." he said, "whatever your Dr Bradley believes, there's something here. We'd better start trying to find out what it is."

"How are you going to do that?" asked Michael.

"I'm going to communicate with it."

"You're going to get in touch with it?" I asked him. "You're going to hold a séance?"

Karen looked anxious. The last time that she and I had been involved in a séance, she had come face to face with the spirit who—eventually—had almost killed her.

"Harry . . ." she said. "Not for me, please."

"Don't worry," Martin told her. "I'm not holding a séance in the conventional sense—you know, everybody holding hands, knock-knock, is there anybody there? They're not very effective, in any case, séances like that. The more people you get involved, the more psychic resistance you build up. If you want a really clear message, then it has to be one-to-one."

"Can I help?" I asked him.

Martin glanced around the room, his eyes quick and analytical, searching for anything amiss, his hand pressed thoughtfully over his mouth. "Yes, you can. I'll be going into a transplanar trance. There's a possibility that I may have to go in pretty deep to locate the spirit that's responsible for this. It's being very unresponsive and it may be hiding in a very complicated way—taking on the shape of another spirit, for example, or dispersing its mind through several levels.

"In spite of your self-deprecation, Harry, you *do* have quite impressive sensitivity. I want you to be my anchorman; the guy who belays me."

"What does that mean?"

"It means that if you sense that anything is going badly wrong, you should bring me back. No questions, no arguments—no matter what I appear to be saying to you, you should bring me back."

"How am I supposed to know if anything's going badly wrong?"

"You'll *know,* believe me."

"And what do I do to bring you back?"

"You simply shake me and wake me."

I puffed out my cheeks. "I sure hope you know what you're doing."

Martin smiled. "That's what I enjoy about being a psychic sensitive, Harry. It's different every time. You *never* know what you're doing."

He took off his coat, and nonchalantly dropped it. Instead of falling on the floor, it dropped sideways and draped itself over one of the legs of the Greenbergs' dining table. I was impressed by that. That was what I called style. That was like Norman Schwarzkopf using a blazing Kuwaiti oil well to light a cigar.

He unfastened his silver cufflinks and rolled up his shirt-sleeves. "There's one thing I think I need to clear up before I start. Naomi here said that you and Ms van Hooven both *knew*. What exactly did she mean by that?"

I looked across at Karen, but Karen turned her face away.

I said, with some reluctance, "Karen and I were both involved in a serious psychic disturbance once, that's all."

"How long ago was that?"

"Twenty years. A little more."

"Was it anywhere near here?"

"Unh-hunh. It was up at the Sisters of Jerusalem Hospital, on Park Avenue."

"Do you think it could be in any way connected to what's happening here? Even remotely?"

"How could it? Who knows? The spirits move in mysterious ways, you should know that."

"Oh, come on, Harry. How often does your average man on the street get himself involved in a serious psychic disturbance? Once in a lifetime? You're more likely to meet the Pope in the Chock Full o' Nuts."

"You want my honest opinion?" I retorted. "I've been racking my brains, but I can't see how *this* psychic disturbance could possibly be connected to *my* psychic disturbance. I accept that Singing Rock was trying to warn me about something, but I don't see how or why he could be warning me about *this*."

Martin lifted both hands in apology. "I'm sorry. I didn't mean to upset you."

"You didn't," I told him, cooling down. "It's just that— well, it was pretty damn harrowing, that's all. It took me a long time to get over it. Maybe I should have had therapy.

Karen went through years of it. She doesn't like to talk about it, even now. So you can see why we don't take very kindly to the suggestion that we might have to go through it all over again."

"All right," Martin conceded. "But if there *is* a connection, I want you to understand ahead of time that we're going to find out about it very quickly indeed. In fact, it's essential that we find out about it very quickly indeed. So it's better that you're prepared for it. The more I know, the quicker I can locate this spirit. The more I know, the *stronger* I can be."

I couldn't take my eyes away from Karen. One hand half-covered her eyes and the other hand was pressed against the back of her neck. I went over to her and said, quietly, "It's going to be okay. I guarantee it."

"Just like you guaranteed you could help Naomi?" Michael put in.

I tried to control my temper. "I'm doing my best, *capisce*? Martin's the very best there is."

Martin said to Michael, "If you don't object, Mr Greenberg, I would find it easier to cope with this disturbance if you and Ms. van Hooven were to leave the room. You are obviously feeling tired and hostile—no fault of your own. Ms. van Hooven is obviously feeling afraid. Neither of those feelings is very conducive to safe transplanar trancing."

"What about Naomi?" asked Michael.

"She'll be fine. I'll take good care of Naomi, believe me. That's what I'm here for."

"All right," Michael agreed. "Is there anything you need?"

"Yes, please," said Martin. "A bowl of water. An ordinary kitchen mixing bowl would do."

Michael went to fetch the water. He handed it carefully to Martin, and Martin set it down on the floor. To my surprise, it stayed where it was.

"Spirits have no influence whatsoever over water," Martin told me. "I'm surprised you didn't know that."

"What about the bowl?"

"They can't move the bowl because the bowl is holding

the water. There's a very interesting chapter on spirits and water in *Daneman's Psychic Phenomena.*"

"You're the genuine goods, aren't you?" I asked him.

"I do my best," he said, without much of an effort to sound modest. "Now, if we could be left alone . . . ?"

With obvious reluctance, Michael and Karen left the dining room. Karen gave me an intense, anxious look, and blew me the smallest of kisses, and then closed the door behind her.

Naomi whispered, "I'm worried . . . I'm worried about dying in my sleep . . . I'm worried they'll take my chair . . ."

Martin laid a hand against her cheek. "Don't upset yourself, Naomi . . . You're not going to die in your sleep. Before you know it, this will all be over, and you'll be able to put your chair any place you want to."

"Really?" asked Naomi, in almost pathetic hope.

"Really," he smiled. Then he turned to me and said, "First of all, I'm going to try to contact that spirit guide of yours, Singing Rock? I want to find out exactly what he was trying to warn you about . . . and whether it's connected with Naomi Greenberg and what's been happening here."

"All right," I agreed. "If you have to." I didn't like the sound of this at all. It gave me a cold, dreadful feeling that I hadn't felt for twenty years, and which I had hoped that I would never feel again.

"Harry," said Martin. "If there was any alternative . . ."

"I hear you," I told him.

"Spirits don't warn you for nothing. They don't make phony alarm calls."

"All right. I said all right, all right?"

"All right, fine." Martin sniffed, and looked around. "Do you smell that?"

"I don't know. I have rhinitis."

"Do you smell herbs, and maybe smoke?"

I sniffed loudly. "Kind of, yes."

"Did you ever visit the prairie?"

"Any special prairie?"

"I don't know. Sagebrush prairie; that's what this smells like. Sagebrush and balsam-root. And outdoor fires."

"Don't tell me. We have a spirit who barbecues."

Martin ignored that remark. He must have learned by now that my first response to anything frightening was to laugh. If you go to a horror movie, you hear people laughing, and not because they think the film is funny. Laughing is one of the first things that human beings do to chase away the devil.

"Singing Rock was an Opie, right?" Martin asked me.

"He was an Indian, yes, an Oglala Sioux. He ran some kind of insurance business. But he was a medicine man, too."

Martin sniffed again, and thoughtfully closed his eyes, but he didn't say anything more.

"Will we see him again?" I asked, at last. "Like we did with the book?"

Martin opened his eyes. "That's what the water's for."

"Oh, sure, yes. I nearly forgot about the water."

Martin approached the wall where all the furniture was heaped, and cleared aside two chairs so that he could reach it. He stood staring at it for quite a long time. I stayed where I was, trying to smile at Naomi, and glancing at the bowl of water from time to time. Nothing had happened yet, except that the surface was faintly rippled. That could have been caused by nothing more than the draft under the door, or Martin's footsteps jarring the floorboards as he walked. Quite honestly, I felt embarrassed about looking at it. I had never heard about spirits and water, and I didn't have the slightest idea what to expect. Martin made me feel even more like a charlatan than Karen, and that was saying something. Karen had always come to me with such earnest pleas for help—with such *belief* in my psychic abilities—that I almost hated her for it. But you couldn't really hate a girl like Karen. Well, I couldn't, anyway. She was so trusting, so childlike, so darn *defenseless*.

Martin raised both hands and pressed them flat against the wall. This seemed to agitate Naomi, who jiggled and swayed in her chair, although it was obvious that she wasn't going to leave it, no matter what. She stared at me, wide-eyed, and begged.

"What's he doing? What's he doing? Tell him to stop!"

I laid my hand on her shoulder. "Ssh, don't worry,

Naomi. Martin really knows what he's doing. Like, he's the Craig Claiborne of spiritualism."

"Tell him to stop." Naomi repeated, in a voice like glass.

"Naomi, sweetheart, we're trying to help you. We're trying to find out what's made all your furniture move, and we're trying to get rid of it for you. Come on—don't get anxious. Don't fret. This is all going to work out good."

"But the shadows," Naomi fretted. "What about the shadows?"

"I don't know," I told her. "What about the shadows?"

"They bit him. They *bit* him!"

"They bit him? Who?"

Naomi nodded wildly toward the left-hand side of the wall. "He was there and they bit him!"

"The shadows bit him?" I asked. "How can a shadow bite anybody?"

"They—" Naomi began, but Martin turned around and said, "Quiet, *please*. Transplanary trance is difficult enough, without you talking all the time."

"Sorry," I told him. "Sorry." And when Naomi tried again to tell me how the shadows had bitten somebody, I said, "Shush, shush. Tell me later."

"But I should tell you *now*," she hissed. "Before it's too late."

"*Please*," Martin asked us, and I pressed my finger tight against my lips so that Naomi couldn't possibly misunderstand me.

"He's doing something very complicated," I whispered. "Something that needs his complete concentration. We mustn't say anything, because he's going into a special kind of trance, and if you break somebody's concentration when they're in this special kind of trance, it can be really dangerous. You can leave half of their psyche in the spirit world and half—"

Martin said, with huge self-restraint, "Harry, do you mind, please, shutting up?"

"Oh—sure," I said, and gave him my obliging *Columbo*-style salute. "Anything you say. I was just telling Naomi that—well, never mind. You go ahead. You go right ahead. Don't pay any mind to me. I'm just helping."

"Is that it?" Martin asked me. "Is that the end of the conversation?"

I nodded, and saluted again. It has always amazed me, how much concentration other people need. I can go for weeks and never have to concentrate once.

Martin turned back to the wall and pressed his hands flat against it.

"I am summoning a spirit called Singing Rock . . . a spirit from South Dakota, a wonder-worker from the Sioux. I want to feel his presence; I want to touch his hand. I am summoning him to help me, to guide me through the levels. I am asking him to show himself, so that he and I can hunt down the spirit who has possessed this room."

We waited for or four or five minutes, although it seemed more like four or five years. The room remained chilly and silent, except for the distant cacophony of traffic, and the thumping of rock'n'roll from the Bensons'.

Naomi began to hum, and then to sing that high, keening song that I had heard before, although not so loudly this time. Martin stayed where he was, his head bowed, his hands still pressed against the wallpaper. I had no idea whether he was angry, bored, or simply waiting for Naomi and me to stop making distracting noises.

"I am summoning a spirit called Singing Rock," he repeated. "I am asking Singing Rock to help me."

Again, there was no obvious reply; although Naomi continued to keen and ululate under her breath. *"Aye-aye-aye-aye-wejoo-suk,"* she changed. *"Aye-aye-aye-aye-alnoba-na'lwiwi."*

I wondered whether Michael had managed to record any of this singing, and I was just about to stick my head out of the dining room door and ask him when Martin suddenly said, "I hear you. I see you."

"Excuse me?" I asked him.

"I want to talk to Singing Rock," said Martin. His back was still turned. "A Sioux Indian called Singing Rock. He came across—Harry, when did Singing Rock die?"

"What?" I said, confused.

"When did Singing Rock die?"

"I, uh—seventy-nine, summer of seventy-nine. Lake Berryessa, California."

Martin repeated this information as if he were talking to somebody else on the telephone. I stared at him in perplexity. Was he really talking to the spirit-world? To *dead* people? It all seemed incredibly casual. Why did everybody make such a fuss about dying, if you could get in touch with the living as easily as this? Next thing we knew, the dead would be sending us faxes. Having a great time, wish you were here, Uncle Chesney.

"I can hear you," Martin repeated. "I can see you, too, but not very clearly."

I edged back slowly to Naomi's side, watching Martin all the time. Naomi was chanting, *"Aye-aye-aye-aye-wejoosuk."* Then, *"Aye-aye-aye-nayew."*

"Shush," I told her. But she kept on singing and rocking on her precious chair, and in the end I decided that she wasn't worth worrying about. I was much more interested in what Martin was doing. He seemed to be talking to somebody—quite fluently and cogently—even though his face was turned to the wall.

"I want you to bring me Singing Rock. Yes. He knows me. He's seen me with Harry Erskine. Tell him Harry Erskine wants him here."

I stared at Martin in fascination; and as I did so, I saw shadows appearing on the smoothly-plastered wall. One of them danced and skipped very quickly and lightly; another was taller and thinner and much more hesitant; a third was huge-headed and silent.

Naomi rocked wildly backward and forward, screaming, *"Aye! Paukunnawaw! Aye! Wajuk! Aye! Nish! Aye! Neip!"*

"Martin," I cautioned. "Just take care of yourself." But when I stepped closer, it suddenly became obvious that he was no longer with me. He was with me in body but not in spirit. His hands were pressed so firmly against the wall that his knuckles were spotted with white; his cheek-muscles were rigid; his teeth were gritted together. His eyes were open but he wasn't looking at the wall. He was focused on something way beyond it. He was still talking—and, better still, he was still breathing. But when I walked around and stared at his face, I didn't see the man I had brought into Michael Greenberg's front door, smiling and nodding and packed to the ears with *joie-d'ésprit.* His face looked like a death-mask, greasy and unreal, as if it had been molded from yellow-ochre wax. And there was the faintest of auras around him; a foggy veil of dim blue light; a *phosphorescence,* as if he were dead already, and rotting. You know what they say about rotten herring, shining in the dark.

"Martin," I said, with huge uncertainty.

"I want to speak with Singing Rock," he said; but he certainly wasn't talking to me.

"Martin, talk to me! Are you okay?"

Martin turned his head sideways and stared straight in my direction, but his eyes didn't see me at all. "I can see you clearly. I saw you before, in my book. I have to know what you want."

"Martin, this isn't funny. How can I help you if I don't know what the hell's going on?"

Martin nodded, as if he had understood me. But then he said, "Why?"

"Why?" I asked him. "What the hell do you mean, why?"

Martin said, "I'm not afraid, no. He's only a spirit, after all, just like you are. There isn't a spirit in God's creation who can hurt me."

"Martin," I appealed to him. "Who are you talking to? There's nobody here!"

"I want his name. I want to know where to find him."

I was about to say something else, but then I knew for sure that Martin could neither see me nor hear me. He was in a trance, talking to spirits, talking to dead people.

It may be hard to understand, but at that moment I was jealous of him. Jealous of his sophistication, jealous of his culture, jealous of his psychic sensitivity. He could do for real what I could only pretend to do—and, brother, didn't the difference show. More than anything else, I was jealous because he was talking to dead people, as plainly and clearly as if they were standing right in front of him. He was talking with people who might have fought with Grant; or talked to Lindbergh; or simply lived in America when there were log cabins and hard winters and marauding Indians.

They survive someplace; the dead survive. Their ashes enrich the earth, and their spirits enrich the air. They're always with us, all around us, but it's a rare talent to be able to talk to them. Martin Vaizey had that talent, and yes, I admit it, I was jealous as hell.

I could only stand helplessly next to him while he walked through worlds that I had never even seen, and never would.

All the same, I surprised myself. I could feel some presence in the room, even though my own perception was very blurry, like trying to see moving figures through a frosted-up windowpane. I could sense their movement. I could even *hear* them: not as distinct voices, but as soft blurtings and rustlings.

I glanced back at Naomi. She was still clinging to her chair, rocking and dipping her head, although she had stopped chanting for the time being.

"I want to talk to him," Martin repeated, even more insistently than before. "We have much to discuss."

"Martin," I asked, "are you okay?" I very much doubted if he could hear me, or even if he wanted to answer me. But I was supposed to be his anchor-man, and I thought that the least I could do was let him know that I was still here, still watching him.

"Yes, parley," he said, and this time the eeriest thing happened. He spoke without moving his lips, like a ventriloquist. I heard his voice quite clearly but I swear to God that he didn't move his lips.

"Martin?" I urged him. "Is everything okay?"

It was then that I heard a noise like somebody slowly emptying a large sack of shingle onto the floor. On the wall in front of Martin, the shadows rose and swelled; and the large-headed shadow appeared to approach him, and raise its own hands to meet Martin's hands, so that to all intents and purposes it *became* Martin's shadow.

Martin began to quiver. "It's you," he whispered.

"It's who?" I asked him.

"It's you," Martin repeated. His voice was flooded with fear and awe.

He turned slowly around to face me. Then he stepped back, so that his back was pressed flat against the shadow so that he and the shadow became one. A visible *darkness* seemed to flow over him, as if a black veil were being lowered over his head. His eyes closed, and the skin of his face began to pull back over his forehead and his cheekbones, so that the contours of his skull became startlingly obvious. His lips were drawn back over his teeth in the thinnest of grimaces, almost a snarl. If I hadn't known that he was travelling from one psychic plane to another, and that he was somewhere further away in time and reality than I could even begin to think about, I would have said that he was dying.

He grew darker and darker. It wasn't so much that his skin was changing color. It was his whole aura. There was a feeling of terrible *oldness* about him; a feeling of black and bitter nights, long before any of us here had been born. There was a feeling of tragedy and dread. I could smell not only sagebrush but blood.

Naomi started to chant once again, but very softly, so that I couldn't really hear what she was saying—not that I could have understood her, even if I had. But there was always a chance that—when we played back Michael's recordings—somebody might be able to translate them, even if she was only chanting "The Camptown Races" backward.

Martin held out both hands, and pointed toward the bowl of water on the floor.

"You seek to trick me, as you have always sought to trick me?" he asked. His voice was remarkable. It was very deep, very vibrant—so vibrant that I heard it through my jawbone, more than my ears. "You seek to insult those very spirits on whom your civilization is built?"

I didn't realize at first that he was talking to me, so I didn't answer. But then he abruptly opened his eyes and roared at me, "You bring this water into my lodge? You seek to insult me?"

"Er, no, I'm not seeking to insult you," I told him. Then, very gently, very diplomatically, I said, "Pardon me, but are you still Martin?"

Martin stared at me and his eyes were so strange that I physically shivered. They looked as if they had been cut out of an old black-and-white photograph and pasted onto his eyelids. In other words they were real and they were focused but somehow they weren't real at all. More like a memory of somebody's eyes: somebody very long dead.

So that onlie ye Eyes look'd out.

"You must take this water away," Martin directed me.

"Is that you?" I asked him. "First of all you wanted the water and now you don't want the water?"

"It has no spirit."

"Oh, so that's it. Maybe you'd like a little bourbon with it."

"It has no spirit," Martin repeated. "It is white man's water. Dead water."

I took a step nearer. All this talk of lodges and white man's water could mean only one thing: that Martin had contacted Singing Rock, my old medicine-man buddy. Well, buddy isn't really the right word. It's almost impossible for a white man to be buddies with a Native American, not real buddies, not soulmates; and it's even harder for a white man to be buddies with a medicine-man. How can you be buddies with somebody who can see the ghosts of his ancestors in every hill and every tree and every puff of wind? Especially when you and your kind have been responsible for decimating those trees and laying eight-lane highways over those hills and filling those puffs of wind with sulfur dioxide?

I'll tell you what kind of relationship I had with Singing Rock. Once I showed him my grandparents' tombstone in Newark, and he asked me very politely if he could piss on it. "After all, you white men have been pissing on my grandparents' graves ever since you got here."

At first I had been seriously angry. Did I say angry? I thought he was sick, and I told him so. "You're one sick Sioux," that's what I told him. I told him that he was bitter and vengeful and that he was taking history far too personally. Was it my grandparents' fault, what had happened to the Indians? Was it *my* fault?

But sometimes you need to be angry before you can understand. Singing Rock had calmly explained that his twenty-one-year-old great-great-great-grandmother, a

Northern Cheyenne, had been killed at Sand Creek, near Denver, in the summer of 1864. Raped, scalped, mutilated. Was it wrong for him to feel bitter and vengeful about that?

As for taking history too personally—well, she hadn't been killed by history but by Captain Silas S. Soule, Company D, First Cavalry of Colorado.

Singing Rock said that you couldn't find the history of what happened to the Indians in libraries, or John Wayne movies, or even Kevin Costner movies. You could only find it in all of those tribes of shadows, which no longer had Indians to cast them.

I still wasn't too sure that I *agreed* with Singing Rock. I wasn't even sure that I *sympathized* with him. I understood most of what he was talking about, and I respected his point of view. But that wasn't exactly the stuff of buddydom, was it?

"Singing Rock?" I asked, circling around him. Those photographic eyes followed me without blinking once. "Singing Rock, is that you?"

"I know you, foolish," Martin replied. "I know your name."

His voice seemed even harsher now. Whoever was talking out of Martin's mouth, it definitely wasn't Martin. This must be a spirit whom Martin had encountered during his psychic wanderings around, and he was using Martin's mouth and breath and lips to talk to me. I backed away. He might have called me "foolish" but I hadn't been born after breakfast. Martin was one of the most skillful mediums I had ever come across—and what's more, he was *alive,* which meant that he should be very much stronger than anybody who had passed over. So whoever *this* spirit was, he must be one powerful mother; and he didn't seem to like *me* much, either.

"Singing Rock, is that you?" I asked him again. It *could* have been Singing Rock. He had always been modest about his wonder-working, but he was as good as any other medicine-man I had ever come across.

But Martin let out a harsh, unexpected laugh. "Singing Rock will never speak to you again. Singing Rock has been punished beyond your wildest imagination. He has been given the soul-torture—and no man, living or dead, has ever returned from the soul-torture with the ability to speak."

Naomi was chanting much louder now. *"Nish-neip, nish-neip . . . Nepauz-had . . ."* She was rocking backwards and forwards so violently that the feet of her chair were drumming unevenly on the floorboards, and I was afraid that she might topple over.

"Remove the water!" Martin demanded, with ill-concealed rage. "Remove the water or I will kill you all!"

"No way, fella," I told him. "That water stays."

Martin practically growled with temper, but he made no attempt to move away from the wall. "I warn you," he breathed, "this is just the beginning . . . We will swallow you all . . . everything, you and yours! From shore to shore, and all across the Plains, the lands will again be free, and nothing of the white man will ever be heard of again!"

He suddenly turned his head and stared at Naomi, rocking and chanting.

"Here!" he commanded—and without any hesitation at all, the chair slid noisily across the room towards him, with Naomi still sitting on it. She was about to collide with his shins when he seized her hair and twisted her deftly around. She screamed and tightly clenched her fists.

"My chair! Not my chair!"

I took three strides across the room and seized hold of the chair, with Naomi still on it, and tried to pull her clear. Martin stared me fiercely in the face and said, "You would really dare, foolish?"

I heaved at the chair but it could have been screwed to the floor for all I was able to shift it. Naomi screamed and screamed and rocked herself backwards and forwards. "Naomi!" I told her. "Naomi, get off the chair!"

"She cannot," said Martin, in a terrible husky voice. His breath was sourish-sweet and actually *cold.* It was like opening an icebox door and smelling month-old melon.

"Let her go," I snapped at him.

"Alive or dead, which do you prefer?"

"I said, let her go!"

"You are as foolish and as weak as ever."

I kept my grip on the chair, and kept trying to pull it

away, but at the same time I scrutinized Martin's face for
any tell-tale signs of what was possessing him. I could feel it,
I could talk to it, but I couldn't clearly see it. It could be a
man, it could be a woman. It could be something that wasn't
human at all. The story goes that there was a trapper in the
1920s in Immokalee, Florida, who was regularly possessed
by a giant alligator. He tore his wife and his three children
apart with his teeth before he was hunted down by the state
police and a Miccosukee wonder-worker, and shot.

But that was another story; and this was frightening
enough, and this was real.

"Who are you?" I asked Martin.

Those terrible dead eyes closed, and then re-opened.
"Don't you recognize me? I'm the one who knows you the
best."

"What the hell are you talking about?"

"Come on, Harry . . . I know you better than you know
yourself. I can remember things about you that you've forgotten about."

I was beginning not to like the sound of this. The room
seemed gloomier and chillier than ever, and Martin had
taken on a darkness that was even more overwhelming than
the shadows that I had first seen flickering on the wall. His
darkness was three-dimensional—a frigid and tangible
darkness. I felt that there was every possibility that the sun
had set for good; and that the Earth had already started on
its long and final journey into endless night.

I gave Naomi's chair a quick, forceful pull, hoping to
catch Martin off guard. But he must have been able to read
my mind, because he held on to it as tightly as ever.

"What the hell do you want?" I shouted at him. "Is it you
who moved all of this furniture? What the hell are you doing
it for?"

"Now then, foolish; learn your place."

"Let her go," I insisted.

Martin slowly shook his head, and gave a taut, unpleasant grin, like somebody peeling back the skin of a strange
dried-up fruit, to reveal the structure underneath. "Now it's
our turn. I will never let her go. I will never let any of you go.
Not until you have been dragged from the face of the earth,

and every last trace of you has vanished as if you had never been, and you have been imprisoned in the place of shadows to which so many of *us* were once condemned."

"What are you talking about? Who are you?"

"I am the one who knows you the best."

"Let the woman go. That's all I'm asking. She never did anything to you. She never hurt a fly."

Martin shook his head again. "How can I let her go? How can I release just one of you, when *all* of you have to die?"

"For Christ's sake, Martin—whatever you are, whoever's inside of you, let her go!"

With a fierce expression on his face, Martin raised his right arm and tugged at his shirtsleeve, so that his cuff tore open. He rolled back his sleeve in three quick jerky movements. He turned his bare forearm this way and that. Then he seized hold of Naomi's hair with his left hand and violently pulled her head back.

Naomi let out a gargling squeal and kicked on the floor with her heels. Almost at once, the dining-room door was snatched open, and Michael came in. He stared at Martin, then he stared at me.

"What in God's name is going on? What are you doing to her?"

"Michael—it's okay," I told him. "Please, just back off."

"I heard Naomi cry out. Listen—what are you doing? Get your hands off her hair. Listen, did you hear me? Get your hands off her hair!"

"Out!" Martin commanded him.

But Michael stalked forward and tried to prize Naomi free. "Listen, pal, I gave you permission to hold a séance, not to—"

Karen was standing in the doorway. "Harry?" she said. "Is everything all right?"

Michael had stopped talking in mid-sentence. He was staring at Martin and quaking all over, as if he were being shaken.

"Not that," he said, thickly. "You can't bring that back."

"I can bring anything back," Martin told him, wrenching Naomi's hair back even further. "I know you the best, after all. I know everything about you. *Everything.*"

Michael dropped slowly to his knees. He pressed his hands over his eyes, and I could tell by the way that his shoulders were shaking that he was sobbing.

"What the hell have you done to him?" I asked.

"Nothing," said Martin, turning his attention away from Michael as if he were quite confident that he wasn't going to give him any more trouble. "I have shown him *himself*, that's all. And I can do the same to you." I went over to Michael and helped him up. His face was smothered in tears. "Nobody could have known that," he wept. *"Nobody."*

"Come on, Michael, I think it's better that you stay out of here."

"What about Naomi? What's he *doing* to her?"

"It's okay," I reassured him, although it wasn't okay at all. I had expected to confront some kind of apparition. I had even been prepared for voices; or glowing ectoplasm; or faces that appeared out of the floor. But I hadn't expected Martin to be taken over so completely. I felt helpless. If Martin couldn't control this spirit that was using his body, then how the hell could I?

Michael said—more to himself than to me—"Nobody could have known that. Nobody."

I put my arm around his shoulder. "Maybe it's better if you leave the room. This is kind of a critical moment."

"I was only seven when it happened," he sobbed. "How could anybody know?"

"Please, Michael," I insisted. "Take care of Karen for me."

Michael sniffed and nodded and smeared his eyes with his fingers. "I'm sorry. I apologize. It took me so much by surprise, is all."

I led him to the door, and Karen reached out for him. But at that moment, Martin called, "Wait! Why shouldn't he see?"

We turned. Martin looked thunderously dark. He seemed to be bigger than before, his head throwing a shadow as heavy and ungainly as a buffalo's. His face was transfigured—his eyes wide, his skin stretched back over his cheekbones, his teeth snarling.

Before any of us could move, he had thrust his right hand into Naomi's mouth, his fingers hooked around her lower teeth. Then he wrenched her mouth wide open, audibly dislocating her jaw. Naomi choked and gagged and gave a muffled scream, but Martin was gripping her hair so tightly that she couldn't move.

Without a word, I ran across the room and threw Martin back against the wall. I managed to catch him with one awkward punch, but he swung his right arm and hit me so hard on the side of the head that I toppled over sideways. My head sang and for a split second I didn't know where the hell I was, or what I was doing. I stood up, staggered toward him, and he hit me again, right on the checkbone.

I fell backwards, stumbled, and sat jarringly right on my tailbone. For a moment I saw nothing but darkness, with needle-prick stars.

"Stay away!" Martin roared at me. "You changed the course of our history; now it is our turn to change the course of *yours*!"

Without hesitation, he pushed his hand into Naomi's mouth, and took hold of her tongue. She was struggling and kicking and letting out high, rabbit-like screams. But Martin's strength—or the strength of the spirit which possessed him—was enormous. I had been in fights before, plenty of fights—you know how it is: jealous husbands; political disagreements after too many martinis; parking-lot tussles over who got to which space first. But nobody had ever knocked me down with two straight punches, not like that. And I had a strong suspicion that he hadn't even hit me as hard as he was capable of hitting me.

"Martin!" I shouted at him. But the spirit was in full control now, and the spirit didn't answer to the name of Martin.

"Singing Rock," I breathed. "If you can help me now, in the name of all that you hold sacred, then do it."

Karen, in the doorway, screamed in fear.

Michael bellowed, "No!"

Martin had grasped Naomi's tongue in his fist, so that it bulged out dark and distended, like a huge purplish slug. He started to pull it out of her mouth with hard, insistent tugs. I could hear the floor of her mouth tearing with every tug: the crackle of skin and membrane parting company.

Michael flew forward, his arms like windmills, his fears forgotten, but Martin was more than ready for him. As Michael rushed up, he let go of Naomi's hair, and hit him with a left that snapped his head back and stopped him dead. Michael dropped to the floor as if he had been hit by a .45.

"Harry—stop him!" Karen screamed. But I knew there was nothing I could do. The spirit was far too vicious, far too strong.

"Dial 911," I told her.

"What?"

"There's nothing I can do! Dial 911, for Christ's sake, before he kills her!"

Martin gripped Naomi's hair again and gave her tongue one last vicious yank. It was ripped away in a welter of blood and Martin tossed it onto the floor. It made a slapping sound that I won't ever forget.

"It's your turn now," Martin breathed. "You thought you were mighty, didn't you? You thought you were superior! You thought that your laws were more just, that your gods were more powerful, that your destiny was written in letters of fire! Well, you should have killed us all while you had the chance. You should have wiped out every last one of us. At least we would have gone with pride.

"But you imprisoned us on our own land; and degraded us; and brought us low. And that was your greatest mistake. Because the prisoner craves release, my friend; and the degraded dream of walking with a straight back; and those who have been brought low think of nothing but revenge."

He stared at me for a very long time, almost as if he were willing me to name him. I had already suspected who he might be. I had already spoken his name in my mind. But I had been hoping with the same unreasonable hope that had made me bet on the New York Yankees year after year that I was wrong; that this couldn't be.

As soon as I had seen Singing Rock's face on that book, I had realized who was threatening me, maybe even sooner— when Karen had first walked into my office.

It wasn't a coincidence. I didn't believe in magic and I didn't believe in what the tea-leaves told me and I didn't believe that I hadn't found myself here in this apartment by accident. I had faced this spirit before and this spirit now wanted to confront me again, face to face, and show me at last who was stronger.

"We won't make the same mistake as you," Martin told me. "We won't wish on you the living death that you wished on us. We won't pretend to protect and revere your culture while treating your people like filth.

"By the time we have finished, you will be gone. *You will be gone.* There will be no trace of you, no single footmark, anywhere."

I touched my swollen cheekbone. I felt as if I had been hit by a hammer. "What are you talking about?" I asked him, in a cotton-packed voice that sounded like Marlon Brando in *The Godfather*. "What the hell are you talking about?"

Martin smiled. "I am talking about *this,* foolish," he said. "I am talking about turning your whole world inside out."

With that, he thrust his whole fist down between Naomi's dislocated jaws, straight into her throat. She heaved and retched, and her eyes goggled as his arm blocked off her windpipe. But he continued to push and push, until he had forced his arm right down her throat to the elbow. Blood ran from her lips like overflowing soup: dark blood, arterial blood, which soaked her dress. Martin's invading arm swelled her throat up obscenely, so that she looked as if she were goitered.

"What can I feel?" he asked, twisting his arm around. "I can feel her lungs; I can feel her belly, warm as a cut-open buffalo."

Michael, stunned, had managed to struggle onto his knees. First of all he tried to focus on me, then on Naomi.

"What's—what's—" he began. But Martin had hit him so hard that he couldn't see properly and he couldn't understand what was going on. He sat back on his haunches with his hands over his face, while only a few feet in front of him Naomi was dying.

I managed to climb onto my feet, and stood in front of Martin. I guessed I must have been swaying, because the whole room seemed to be tilting from side to side like a showboat, and Martin kept advancing and receding, advancing and receding.

"Singing Rock," I whispered. "Help me."

Martin thrust his arm deeper into Naomi's mouth. Her cheeks were grey from oxygen starvation, her eyes were almost bursting out. But one hand still feebly flapped, as she tried to fight against this monstrous invasion of her body—the most complete and devastating rape of a human being that I had ever seen. Tiny bubbles of blood frothed around the corner of her mouth as she tried to drag air into her lungs past Martin's arm.

"I can feel a heart, beating its last frantic beats," said Martin. "I can feel a liver, slippery and dark. I can feel a womb, like the softest of fruits."

Singing Rock said, *"The water."*

I turned around, still half-poleaxed, almost losing my balance. Singing Rock was standing by the door, his arms by his sides, in his horn-rimmed spectacles and his sober business suit; yet his face was as hawklike as ever.

"The water," he repeated, in a voice that sang in my ears like the dying reverberations of a tuning fork. *"Spirits have no command over water; that is why your friend brought it here."*

I turned back in horror to Martin and Naomi. Martin had plunged his arm into Naomi's mouth right up to his bicep. Her lips were stretched so wide that she looked like a snake swallowing a sheep. He had plunged his hand deep into her intestines and was stirring them around, so that even beneath her dress her stomach rippled and churned.

"Singing Rock," I said, softly. Then, *"Singing Rock!"* But as I turned around again, he disappeared through the open doorway, as silently as a switched-off light.

I staggered after him. *"Singing Rock, help me!"* My shoulder collided with the doorframe and I bruised the back of my hand on the handle.

The living room was brightly lit, another world. Karen was just putting down the phone. "They're coming as quick as they can," she told me, her face white.

"Did you see him?" I demanded.

"Who? What are you talking about?"

"Singing Rock was here—he just came through the door."

"Harry, there was nobody."

"I saw him! He was here!"

I heard a coarse, jerky tearing sound behind me. I looked back, and saw that Martin had reached forward with his left hand and ripped open Naomi's floral dress. Karen came hurrying across the living room but I said, "No—stay there. Wait for the cops."

"But, Harry—"

"Stay there, for Christ's sake!" I shouted at her. She had already seen more than enough: I didn't want her to see this. I blundered back into the dining room and slammed the door behind me.

"Inside out," said Martin, his breathing as thick as the lowest of organ-pipes. He pulled apart Naomi's dress, then dragged her pantyhose halfway down her thighs, exposing white skin, veined with blue, and a bush of black pubic hair. With a grin of sheer triumph, he said, *"Watch."*

At first I couldn't understand what he was going to do. I stood blinking, swaying with concussion. But then, blurrily, I saw Naomi's stomach bulging, just above her mound of Venus. Then her thighs parted and I saw her vulva running with blood. Her vaginal lips peeled apart like the mouth of a freshly-clubbed fish, and Martin's fingers emerged, glistening with blood, his fingernails snagged with fragments of internal tissues.

He had thrust his arm down her throat right up to his armpit, so that blood was soaking his shirt, and now his entire hand emerged from her widely-stretched vagina, a sight so surreal that I felt I was going to suffocate from shock. I couldn't breathe, couldn't move. I felt hysteria rising up inside me as if my lungs were filling with iced water.

"Inside out," Martin thundered; although I *felt* him rather than *heard* him.

His fingers dug into the plump, hairy flesh around her vagina, and then he *pulled.* I heard a hideous suction sound, and a repetitive snapping of ribs, and then Martin dragged Naomi's stomach and lungs and liver and endless yards of intestines out of her mouth. It heaped and slithered all over the floor; I thought it was never going to end. The stench of blood and bile and half-digested food was unbearable.

At the very end, Martin slowly withdrew his fist from Naomi's bloody, gaping mouth. Between his fingers he was still clutching the hairy flesh of her sex, which he had pulled up through the whole length of her abdomen and thorax. He held it up, triumphantly, and said, "What warrior has ever taken a scalp like this?"

He opened his hand and Naomi's shapeless body fell from the chair on top of her own insides, one sightless eye staring in perplexity at her own bladder.

Michael lowered his hands. He was still punch-drunk, and I doubted if he could see anything. I prayed very much that he couldn't. He crawled on all fours towards Naomi's body and touched it. He must have been able to smell it. He must have been able to feel its slime.

"What's happened?" he asked. "Naomi?"

"No more Naomi," Martin told him, rolling his sleeve back down his bloodied arm. "No more of you, or any of your kind."

"Naomi?" said Michael, blind with shock. "Naomi?" He crawled around her grisly remains, dragging guts and lungs after him. "Naomi?"

Martin gave him a contemptuous sideways look. He buttoned up his cuff. Then he hit him on the back of the neck with the edge of his open hand—so fast and hard that I scarcely saw it. Michael's head dropped at an odd angle, and he rolled over onto what was left of Naomi's thighs. He lay there quivering for a moment and then he was still.

"You've killed him too," I said, hoarsely. "Jesus Christ, Martin, you've killed him too!"

"As I shall kill all of you, foolish. And you shall be next."

With that, he raised both his fists and threw back his shadowy head and let out the most chilling cry that I had ever heard in my life. It was joyful, bloodthirsty, and overwhelmingly frightening. It was a cry that didn't belong in this age. Not in this city, not in this house. It belonged on wind-furrowed prairies; or on snowcapped mountains; or in the smoky, mysterious twilight of river banks, among the lodges of the cruel and the proud and the warlike. I had heard it only once before. I had never thought I would ever hear it again.

I had woken up sweating in the night and prayed that I would never hear it again.

"Ak! Ak! Ak! Ak! Ak! Akkkrraaaaaaaaaaaaaaaa!"

SEVEN

As the war cry died on Martin's lips, another war cry was taken up. It came from the streets outside, and it echoed for block after block. It was the whooping and screaming of police sirens, as Karen's 911 call was answered.

Martin lifted his head. For the first time since the spirit had taken possession of him, he looked uncertain.

"You hear that, you bastard?" I challenged him. "That's the cops."

Martin gave me a dark frown. "I promised you death, foolish. I always keep my promises."

I lurched backward. I wished to God he hadn't knocked my sense of balance out of kilter. "Just this once," I said, "I'll take an IOU."

Martin stepped away from the wall, clearing aside Naomi's bloodied remains with the side of his foot. Her head turned over to face me, her mouth still gaping. I could scarcely bear to look at her.

"I promise you pain, foolish. I promise you soul-torture. I promise that you will kiss my feet and plead with me to tear you inside out, as I did with this woman. Compared to what you are going to suffer, her fate will seem like pleasure."

I took another step back, and as I did so, my heel touched the bowl of water, and almost tipped it over. Martin came nearer and nearer, his feet dragging on the floor as if he were climbing a very steep hill. "You will beg me to die even more slowly than she did, as long as I give you the certainty of dying."

I heard tires squealing in the street outside. Doors opening. Feet running upstairs, and men's voices shouting. I heard the doorbell, and somebody beating on the door with their fist.

"You hear that, Martin?" I asked him. "It's too late for you now, that's the *polizei.* You touch one hair on my head and they won't even give you time to say honest Injun."

Martin was still coming towards me, but a whole lot more slowly now. The further away from the wall he walked, the more effort he had to make. His steps were very slow and deliberate, and after only five or six steps his face was masked with sweat.

"I will destroy you, foolish," he said, in a breathless rumble that was more like distant traffic. "I will tear off your hair and carry your scalp around my waist for all eternity."

I knew then for certain who he was. I knew then for certain why it had been Singing Rock, of all dead spirits, who had warned me about him.

The water, Singing Rock had told me. *Spirits have no command over water.*

I bent down, picked up the bowl, and held it up in the palm of my hand. Martin glanced at it uneasily.

"I'm warning you," I told him, in a shaky voice. "One more step and I'll—"

"One more step and you'll *what*?" Martin asked me. "Soak me? Drown me? You were always foolish, foolish. You don't even know what to do."

Of course he was absolutely right. I *didn't* know what to do. I took two or three more steps back, and Martin took two or three more steps forward.

There was a loud knocking on the door behind me, which made me jump.

"Mr Erskine? This is the police! Are you okay in there?"

I looked cautiously at Martin and Martin looked contemptuously back at me. "Tell them," he smiled. "Tell them how you are. Tell them I'm going to hurt you badly. Tell them I'm going to turn you inside out."

"Mr Erskine?" the cop repeated.

"I'm fine," I called back. "Just take it easy, okay?"

"What's the situation? Can you talk?"

"Not right now."

Martin kept on smiling, but now his face was running

with sweat, and his eyelids kept flickering. "Tell them—" he began. Then, "No."

He clenched his teeth and shook his head from side to side like a dog worrying a rat. The darkness seemed to be draining out of him in the same way that the color drains out of a dying man. His face looked greasy and pale, and spit began to fly from his lips.

"Tell them, tell them—*No! Don't tell them anything!*"

The police shouted, "We're going to give you a count of three, Mr Erskine, then we're coming in!"

"Tell them, tell them, tell them—*No, damn it! The water! We have command of the water!*"

"Hold it!" I called to the police. I had suddenly realized what was happening. Away from the wall, away from the shadows, the spirit that had taken control of Martin's body had very much less influence; and now Martin himself was fighting back.

"*The water!*" he gasped, his whole body shaking, as if he were being violently thrown from side to side by a man twice his size. "*Think of anything—think of anything—something that frightens him*—No!"

"What the hell's going to frighten him?" I screamed at Martin. But the spirit had taken control of him again, and was struggling to crush his mind and his will.

"Mr Erskine, that's it, we're coming in!" the police barked at me, from the other side of the door.

"Not yet!" I shouted. "For Christ's sake, not yet!"

It was then that I had about the first and only brilliant inspiration of my whole life. I remembered a color illustration in one of my childhood cowboy books, of a Cheyenne medicine-man recoiling from a rattlesnake. Eyes wide, shadows looming up behind him. His own buffalo-headed shadow; and the vicious S-shaped shadow of the rattler.

I held out the bowl of water with trembling hands, splashing it all over my cuffs, and thought: *rattlesnake.*

Martin screeched and grunted as he fought the spirit inside him. Veins wriggled like speeded-up tree-roots on the side of his head; and his neck swelled with strain. He started to jerk his head backwards and forwards, as if he were trying to break his own neck; and I was so horrified by what he was doing that I didn't see the water in the bowl beginning to rise. It was only when I felt the bowl stirring in my hands that I looked at it, stared, and then dropped it in shock.

The bowl fell to the floor, and tipped over. Immediately a long glistening snake poured out of it—a full-grown rattlesnake, with stretched-open jaws and viciously curved fangs and a sleek, thick body. The incredible thing about it was that it was totally transparent, and it shone as bright as glass. It was formed out of water, and nothing else. White man's water—*dead* water, as the spirit had called it—had suddenly come to life.

The rattlesnake gave a sharp, watery rattle. Without hesitation, it lunged at Martin's leg. Martin shouted, *"No!"* in tones of thunder. But then he suddenly stopped shaking, and lowered his head, and stood like a man who has won the greatest of battles, but lost everything he held dear while doing it.

I looked down. There was no rattlesnake, only a narrow splash of water where the bowl had tipped over.

"Coming in!" yelled the police, and kicked open the door, splintering the doorframe. Two officers, one black and one white, hustled into the dining room with guns held high. "Police officers! Put your hands up!"

Being an innocent bystander, I didn't think I had to put my hands up, and Martin obviously hadn't heard them, so neither of us did.

"Put your hands up!" the black officer screamed at me, and so, slowly, I lifted them.

The other officer frisked Martin quickly, then looked around at the bloody carnage that had been Michael and Naomi Greenberg. "Jesus, what happened here?"

Martin said, "It wasn't me."

The black officer stared at Martin's gory right arm. "You're all covered in blood and it wasn't you?"

"It was my body that did it. It was my arm that did it. But it wasn't me."

The officer unhooked his handcuffs and said, "Put your hands behind your back. I'm arresting you on suspicion of homicide. You have the right to remain silent, but anything you say can and will—"

"Officer," I interrupted. "I know it sounds wacky, but he's telling the truth. It wasn't him. I promise you."

The officer stared at me without blinking. "You can promise me whatever you like, sir. I'm charging you with homicide, too."

They finally let me leave the precinct house at a quarter after six the following morning, after they had questioned Karen and after the medical examiner had assured them that it was Martin alone who had killed both Naomi and Michael.

Martin was charged with two counts of first-degree homicide and refused bail. When Karen came to collect me, the precinct was crowded with newspaper and TV reporters and ENG cameras. The killings were already being called The Black Magic Murders. "Evil spirit made me do it, protests alleged slayer."

Karen drove me in her red VW Jetta to her aunt's apartment on East 82nd Street. Her aunt was nearly ninety now, and spent all of her summers in New England, with Karen's parents, because she couldn't stand the heat and the pollution. Karen unlocked the door and I stepped inside. The apartment hadn't changed much in all of the years since Amelia and MacArthur and I had first held a séance here. It was a big, grand place, decorated in a wealthy but anonymous style—big upholstered armchairs and couches, thick red velvet drapes, antique tables and paintings.

It had once been warm and bright but now there was a feeling of neglect and emptiness about it. Some of the brocade fabric on the arms of the chairs was wearing out, and there were threadbare patches in the carpet.

I went to the window and looked down at the trees and sidewalks of East 82nd. Karen came up behind me and said, "Do you want some breakfast?"

"Hmm? No, coffee'll do."

She was wearing a white linen blouse with patch pockets and a short twill skirt. Her hair needed washing so she had tied it back. There were plum-colored circles under her eyes but I thought she looked as delicate and pretty as ever. She was about two houses, a BMW 5-series, an account at Saks Fifth Avenue, and $1.23M out of my league, but she had a natural sweetness about her which made the social and financial differences between us irrelevant.

I followed her into the pale-green kitchen. In the 1950s, it must have been the last word in fitted units, but now it looked like something out of an early episode of *I Love Lucy*. It even had a dome-topped Westinghouse icebox.

"Espresso?" asked Karen.

I leaned up against the counter next to her. The extraction fan above the range slowly rotated. It reminded me of that movie *Angel Heart*. I very rarely went to see movies like that because I happened to know how much of that kind of stuff is real. One of the things I tried to do after Singing Rock died was to write a book about Indian magic, a true book, explaining all about manitous and wind-spirits and devil-dolls, but when I showed it to a literary agent she said that my viewpoint was all wrong. I couldn't possibly assume without any demonstrable proof that Indian magic was— ahem—*real*.

She should have been with us in the Greenbergs' apartment, that literary agent. Then she could have asked me about demonstrable God-damned proof.

"Are you all right now?" Karen asked me.

"Tired, I guess. Shocked. How about you?"

"I'm not sure. I can't yet believe that it actually happened."

"Oh, it happened all right. Something took over Martin's body and soul completely—something very strong. And when I say very strong, I mean we're talking major league here. The Hulk Hogan of evil spirits."

I took the coffee mugs and carried them through to the living room. The sun was well up now, and it lay across the well-worn carpet in gilded rhomboids.

We sat side by side on one of the huge overstuffed couches and propped our feet on the coffee table. There was a 1920s statuette of a leaping Isadora Duncan–type dancer next to my foot. She was pointing accusingly at the large hole in my sock.

"You said you saw Singing Rock," Karen remarked, without looking at me.

I nodded. "I saw him in Martin's apartment, too. Apparently he was following me around. Martin sensed him the moment I walked in. He kind of—well, conjured him up, I suppose you could say. He made his face appear; he even made him *talk*."

"What did he say?" Still she wouldn't look at me.

"He gave me some sort of a warning. I can't say that I really understood it too good. It was something about the Great Outside, and clearing the sacred lands. Martin said something similar last night. Well, I don't mean Martin, but the spirit who was in him. He kept saying that he wanted to get rid of every trace of us . . . whoever he meant by *us*."

I paused, sipped coffee, and managed to scald the roof of my mouth. "I thought at first that it might be a Nazi spirit—the Greenbergs being Jewish and everything. The Nazis dabbled a lot in spirit-travel and reincarnation. I think I was almost *hoping* that it would be a Nazi spirit."

Karen turned and looked at me at last. "It isn't, is it?"

I shook my head. "It's an Indian spirit, no doubt about it."

"It's *him*, isn't it?" she said, unconsciously lifting her hand and touching the back of her neck.

"I think so. I won't be able to tell for sure until they let me talk to Martin."

"When will that be?"

"Not for quite a while. Not till he's talked to his lawyer, anyway."

Karen said, "I feel terrible about dragging you into this. If I'd had any idea . . ."

I took hold of her hand. "If you ask me, you and me were going to get dragged into it whatever. We've been involved in all this before, we *believe* in it. That makes us much easier for him to manipulate. Besides that, I think he's after some good old-fashioned getting-his-own-back."

Karen, unexpectedly, leaned across the couch and kissed me on the lips. I stared at her. "What was that for?" I asked her.

"Bravery."

"Bravery? The only award I deserve is the Father Karras Award for Total Stupidity in the Face of the Supernatural."

"Don't be so modest. Not many people would have faced

up to any of that. Not many people would have faced up to what happened to me. Besides," she said, "I happen to have realized that I like you. I always did."

I didn't know whether Karen felt genuine affection for me, or whether she was clinging to the only other person on the planet who knew for certain what had happened to Michael and Naomi Greenberg. Maybe it was a little of one and a little of another, with a dash of tiredness and shock thrown in for good measure. I don't usually think about love, not in the context of *my* day-to-day relationships. Love was something that got bored with sitting on the end of my bed, and which one day just got up and walked out, without even bothering to close the door behind it.

After I had finished my coffee I went into the spare bedroom for a couple of hours' sleep. I didn't want to go back to my consulting rooms on East 53rd because I knew that there would be more reporters lying in wait for me; and I wanted to forget about the Greenbergs for a while. I could still see Martin's fist clutching Naomi's bloody, hairy flesh; and I thought that I would probably go on seeing it for ever.

The spare bedroom was small but pretty, wallpapered with faded gilt flowers. I looked at myself in the dressing-table mirror. The left side of my face was hugely swollen, like a cartoon character, and my eye was almost closed. I hadn't realized I looked so bad. I slowly undressed and climbed into bed, and eased my cheek onto the cool, slightly musty-smelling pillow. Next to me, on the wall, there was a gold-framed engraving. It depicted a fierce nineteenth-century lady traveller in a large ostrich-plumed hat staring through opera glasses at a Red Indian in a magnificent war-bonnet. The caption read *Our Feathered Friends*.

I couldn't help smiling at its naïveté. The Indians had never been our friends and never would be, and we would never be theirs.

I closed my eyes and fell asleep almost at once.

After about a half hour, I began to dream. I dreamed that I was running upstairs in the Greenbergs' apartment building. Their front door was ajar, and a cold bluish light was shining out of it, like a television flickering in a strange motel room. I could hear people talking in muffled voices, and somebody saying, *"Neeim . . . neeim . . . Nepauz-had . . ."* again and again.

Then I realized that somebody was standing close behind me—so close that I could feel their chill, even breathing on the back of my neck. I tried to turn around but I couldn't. A hand had gripped my hair and was tearing it out by the roots. I felt panic more than pain, but I knew that my assailant was hurting me badly. He might even be disfiguring me for life.

The next thing I knew, my head had been pulled back, and somebody was trying to cram their fingers into my mouth. I gagged, struggled, and tried to wrench my head away. I shouted, "Get off me! Get off me! I can't breathe! You're choking me!"

At least I *thought* I was shouting "Get off me!" I was probably screaming "Gruggle-uggle-grogghh!" instead. Suddenly I opened my eyes and said, *"Ah!"* because I found Karen lying right next to me, smoothing my forehead. She whispered, warmly, "Ssh! You've been having a nightmare. You've been screaming and groaning at the top of your voice."

I let my head drop back onto the pillow. I looked up at her. It didn't take much waking-up for me to realize that she was naked. All she was wearing, as far as I could make out, was a thin gold chain around her neck, with a gold S-shaped pendant dangling from it. Singing Rock had sent her that pendant, after he had helped to save her life. It was the prehistoric Algonquin hieroglyph for "secret sign"; and according to Singing Rock it was supposed to have the same deterrent effect on evil Indian spirits as crucifixes had on vampires.

Karen kissed my forehead and ran her hand through my hair.

"I'm not sure that I'm ready for this," I told her.

"Why not?" she smiled. "I've always liked you, right from the moment I first met you."

"Karen, you don't owe me anything. You know that. Besides . . . you and me, they didn't exactly find us under the same bramblebush, now did they? I'm a Bronx boy, always will be. Sniffy suburban Bronx, with the fancy lace curtains, but Bronx all the same. And what are you? New England and Upper East Side. Private education, designer duds."

She reached across to the nightstand and produced a square foil envelope. "I took the liberty," she said. "Do you want me to put it on for you?"

"Karen . . ." I protested, as she drew back the sheet, "think of the age difference. If I'd married your mother when I was fifteen, I could have been your father."

"My mother doesn't like younger men," she said, biting open the condom packet.

"I'm not talking about your mother, I'm talking about you. I don't even know if I feel this way about you."

Karen grasped my cock in her hand and gave it three arousing rubs. "It *looks* as if you do."

"Karen—"

"Ssh, this is the difficult bit."

She stretched the rubber over my swollen glans, and then carefully unrolled it down the shaft. I was disconcerted to see when she'd finished that my cock had turned bright emerald.

"They come in colors," she said. "Green was all I had left."

She climbed over me and kissed me again. Her small breasts brushed against my bare chest, and her nipples crinkled. They were pointed and pale pink, with just a hint of brown, like dying rose petals.

We kissed deep and long. I brushed back her hair, and looked into her eyes. She was so close that I could see every crinkle of her irises; every stray fleck of color.

"I never thought of you this way," I told her.

She smiled. "I never thought of you any other way. Besides—what choice do we have?"

"I don't understand you."

"After what happened, how could any of us possibly form any kind of relationship with anybody else? We're the only ones who know, the only ones who really saw. When I was standing at the altar with Jim I was promising to love him in the name of God, but all the time I was wearing this pendant around my neck to protect me from the spirits that I *really* believed in."

"Karen—"

She kissed my eyelids, kissed the tip of my nose. "Harry, I'm not Karen Tandy any more. I'm not that innocent young girl who first came to you for help. I've grown up, I've married, I've learned what's what. I'm Karen van Hooven who fancies your body, if only for once."

With that, she lifted herself over me, took hold of my cock in her right hand, and positioned it up between her legs. She excited me. I can't say that she didn't. She was very slim and very small, and whatever she said she was still a child-woman. I reached up and touched her breast, and gently rolled her nipple between finger and thumb, and kissed her chin and her neck and anywhere else I could reach.

When she sat down on me, she felt very tight and very slippery and very warm. She threw back her head and closed her eyes and rode up and down as if she were crossing the prairies on a slow and faithful horse. I kept thinking to myself, *you shouldn't be doing this . . . this girl believes in you, this girl has faith in you, you're supposed to take care of her, not screw her. What would her aunt think?*

But I looked down and saw her lean hips rising and falling over mine; and the neatly-clipped triangular bush of her pubic hair; and my shiny emerald-green cock sliding in and out of her swollen pink lips. And I was turned on, I admit it. Green cock, pink flesh, it turned me on.

I reared up and turned her over onto her back. I kissed her and snuzzled her neck. I squeezed her breasts and tugged her nipples between my fingers. Then I pushed myself deep inside her, and deeper, until she lifted both her legs in the air and gasped and cried out, and made other noises like suddenly-disturbed doves.

She cupped my balls in her hand and I could feel how scrunched-up they were: all ready to shoot. I wished to God that condoms hadn't been invented, or better still, that communicable diseases hadn't made them necessary. But that was the last complicated thought that I had before I filled the condom in three bulging bursts, and Karen dug her nails into my back and held me tight.

At last I dropped back onto my side of the bed. I kissed

her. I was sweating so much that my hair stuck to my forehead like Julius Caesar. All I needed was a laurel wreath. "I'm sorry," I said.

She kissed me back, licked my sweat. "What are you sorry for?"

"Well, I could have lasted longer. It's been a while, that's all. Gives a man an itchy trigger."

"What are you talking about? I came."

"You did?"

"Just because I didn't scream and throw myself around."

"You actually had a climax?"

"Of course I did. I wouldn't lie about it."

I stared at her. I couldn't believe it. All of the ladies with whom I usually consorted made such a song-and-dance about climaxing that you would have thought that their sexual responses were choreographed by Leo Karibian—you know, the guy who did *West Side Story*. Maybe they were trying to give me value for money. Maybe they were faking it.

But Karen simply smiled and kissed me again and said, "I came, okay? I really did. As soon as you got on top of me."

"Oh," I said, feeling pleased.

"It was gorgeous," she said, and snuggled under my armpit.

We lay like that for almost an hour. We both dozed. I had more intermittent dreams about the Greenbergs' apartment, and I was sure that I could see a snake gliding transparently beneath the bed, with just the faintest hint of a rattle. I opened my eyes and the sun was still shining through the drapes, and the telephone was warbling.

"You want me to answer it?" asked Karen, in a blurry voice.

But I said, "No, I'll answer it. You stay where you are."

It was Sergeant Friendly, from the 13th Precinct. He sounded tired. "You asked me to call when your friend had seen his lawyer."

"Oh, sure, thanks. I owe you."

Karen was sitting up in bed, bare-breasted. I didn't know whether I had known her long enough to be permitted an eyeful or not. Sometimes even long-term ladies get upset if you stare too open-mouthed at their gazongas. Not that Karen's were gazongas, more like modest-sized meringues with cherries on top.

"What is it?" she said.

I tugged on my pants. "The police. I can talk to Martin."

"What time is it?"

"Ten after eleven."

"Do you want me to come with you?"

I thought about it, but then I shook my head. "I don't think so. I don't want you to get mixed up in this for a second time."

She looked at me with eyes like dark smudges. "You're still so sure that it's him?"

I nodded. "It all fits. I didn't want it to fit. I tried to think of a hundred possible ways in which it wouldn't. But it does, and I don't even know what I'm supposed to do next. That's why I want to talk to Martin."

"Okay," she said, with determination, and her little breasts jiggled.

Martin was waiting for me in a stuffy interview room with windows that were covered in dented steel mesh. Outside I could see rooftops and warehouses and water towers, and a thin stratum of idle clouds. There was a hot, glazed look to the Lower East Side that for some reason reminded me of that poem, "By the old Moulmein Pagoda, looking lazy at the sea." You'd never believe it, but I first came across that poem in an old *Pogo* strip, and it wasn't until fifteen years later that I realized that it wasn't Walt Kelly who had written it, but Rudyard Kipling. Goes to show, doesn't it. I've got all the style, but none of the education.

A bored Hispanic police officer with Elvis Presley sideburns (Las Vegas era) leaned against the flaking green wall and tried to beat the world chewing-gum-noise record. Martin sat at the cheap sun-faded table looking diminished and grey. They had given him a clean denim shirt and jeans, and allowed him to shave, but he still looked haunted and strange, as if his face was a half-assembled jigsaw.

The chair made a scraping noise as I pulled it out. Martin looked up. "Harry," he said.

"Are you okay?" I asked him.

He shrugged. "As well as can be expected. My lawyer's already started to make lateral noises about pleading insanity. He was my father's attorney, yet there he was screaming at me. 'You pulled her muff out of her mouth, and you want to plead *what*?' "

I drummed the table with my fingertips. By the old Moulmein Pagoda. "How are you going to plead?"

"You know how. You know what happened. I was *possessed*. I was taken over completely."

There was no point in being ridiculous about it. I said, "Yes, I know you were. If I had any way of proving it, they'd let you out of here in three minutes flat."

"It's never happened to me before. Usually, I can control any spirit from any age . . . the older the better. They're usually so gentle, so sympathetic. But this one—my God, you have no idea. This one hit me like a locomotive. It was big, it was dark, it was powerful—and it was so *vengeful*. I've never felt anything like it. It wanted to tear my heart out, and everybody else's heart out, too."

"How did you reach it?" I asked him. "Through Singing Rock?"

"Unh-hunh." He shook his head. "I felt Singing Rock . . . Singing Rock passed me by, like a wind. Singing Rock didn't want me to go any further. But of course I knew better. Don't the living always know better than the dead?"

"So what did you do?"

Martin wiped the sweat from his forehead with the back of his hand. His eyes shifted quickly and furtively from side to side, as if he were afraid of being overheard. "I didn't have to do anything at all—which is very unusual. I was approached. A man in a blue cavalry uniform came up to me. His head was all bone and blood, like he'd been scalped. I've never been approached by a spirit like that before. He was angry: calm but angry. He had a moustache and his moustache was all stringy with blood. He couldn't look at me directly. It was very unusual. He said that I should have stayed away; but since I hadn't, he'd show me the cause of all the trouble."

I narrowed my eyes. "What kind of condition were you in then? I mean, were you dreaming, were you in a trance?"

Martin hesitated. "It's very hard to explain to somebody who's never experienced it. I call it my ghost phase. It's when I'm here in body but someplace else in mind. I was conscious of the room, conscious of you . . . but at the same time there's this total darkness, this total singing emptiness, and the spirits come walking out of the emptiness like people coming off a plane."

"Were you scared?"

"Is the Pope Polish?"

I sat back in my hard folding chair. By the old Moulmein Pagoda, looking lazy. I was supposed to be reading Mrs Herbert Bugliosi's tea-leaves in less than twenty minutes— what had involved me in all of this? Where had my peaceful existence suddenly disappeared to? The smiles, the flirtatious thigh-crossings, the fluttering eyelashes, the money, the idle afternoons? Today Mrs Herbert Bugliosi's tea-leaves, tomorrow Aqueduct. Leastways, that had been the game plan.

"What was it like?" I asked Martin, in a low voice.

He pulled a face. "I don't remember particularly well. It was dark. It was very dark. It was like a shadow and a magnet and a dead body. Cold, you know? Dark and cold. But alive, too, the same way that electricity's alive. Plenty of lethal voltage; plenty of sparks; but no soul."

"Did you see it?" I asked him.

He stared at me. "*See* it? I *was* it! It took me over completely."

"When it took you over like that were you conscious? Were you aware of what it was doing to you?"

Martin emphatically nodded. "You bet I was aware of what it was doing to me. That was part of its ploy, if you ask me. To kill, yes—as a grisly lesson that we shouldn't interfere. But to show us, too, that it cared so little for any of our lives that it would turn us inside out, without a moment's hesitation. Rip, glug, splutch, Geronimo."

"Was it a Red Indian spirit?"

"I don't know . . . I wasn't aware of it being Red Indian. Then again, I don't know very much about Red Indians. I never met one, not in the flesh. I think the only Red Indians I ever saw were in Jeff Chandler movies."

"Just now, you said 'Geronimo.' "

He brushed his sleeve, crossed and recrossed his legs. "People who jump off twenty-three-story buildings say 'Geronimo.' It's a figure of speech, that's all."

"What did he look like?"

"I told you . . . he was dark and cold. A shadow, that's all I saw. And *felt,* too, right inside my body, if you want to know the real preposterous truth."

"But you had no feeling that he might be an Indian?"

Martin shook his head. "No. But that doesn't necessarily mean that he *wasn't.* You and I don't normally go around thinking, 'Oh, we're Caucasians,' do we?"

"I guess," I acknowledged. I sat back and looked at him. I had the oddest feeling that he wasn't being straight with me. I couldn't think *why.* He had already been charged with murder in the first degree, and it must have been worth his while to think of *anything* that could prove his innocence, no matter how unlikely it might be.

"My lawyer isn't exactly optimistic," he said. He gave a cynical, lopsided smile. "Proving demonic possession to twelve good people and true is going to be uphill all the way, believe me."

"You're really going to use that as a defense?"

"What else can I do? I turned that poor woman inside out. I slaughtered her husband in cold blood. If I plead insanity, they'll send me to the maximum-security insane asylum and throw away the key."

I didn't know what to say. I felt as if Martin's plight was entirely my fault. Of course I was quite prepared to stand up in his defense and tell the court that he had been totally possessed by a vengeful, rampaging spirit, and that he hadn't been responsible for anything that he had done. But what would that achieve? They would probably send *me* to the funny farm, too.

I stood up. "I guess I'd better go," I told him. "If you think of anything—anything at all—then, please, don't keep it to yourself. I know that it wasn't you who killed the Greenbergs, and Karen knows that it wasn't you. But we have to find a way of proving it."

"Listen," said Martin, without looking up. "If you're

thinking of trying another séance, don't. That spirit is really very dangerous indeed—and what we saw last night . . . that's just the tip of a very black iceberg."

"Go on," I told him.

He took a deep breath. "Something's happening, Harry. Something major. I've never felt such spirit disturbance ever. I can feel it even now. It's like the whole damned spirit world is in turmoil. You know when there's an earthquake, the way people rush around in a panic? Well, that's what it's like in the spirit world."

"And what happened to you yesterday? That was part of it?"

He didn't answer. I stood looking at him but he wouldn't raise his eyes and he wouldn't speak. After a while I nodded to the cop with the Elvis Presley sideburns and he unlocked the door for me.

"Harry," said Martin, as I was about to leave. "Thanks for coming. I don't blame you for what happened. I was always aware of the risks."

"We'll get you out of this," I assured him. "I guarantee it."

He smiled. "Nobody can make guarantees in our business, Harry."

I left the precinct. I felt worried and sweaty and disoriented. I particularly didn't like what Martin had said about turmoil in the spirit world. I had seen turmoil in the spirit world before, and how it could spill over into the world of the living. The living and the dead exist side by side, cheek by jowl, and when something goes wrong in one world, it can have a catastrophic effect on the other world, too.

People can die before their time has come. People whose time has already come can walk the streets. There's only the thinnest of lines between dead and alive. Sometimes I wondered if it wasn't good old-fashioned cynicism that made me the worst of fortune-tellers, but my fear of crossing that thinnest of lines and mingling with things that didn't concern me. Like death. Like shadows. Like women turned inside out.

I hailed a taxi on Broadway and asked the driver to take me uptown. The day was varnished with heat, and the driver

had a short-sleeved drip-dry shirt and some of the strongest
body odor that I had smelled in years. He told me his son
played bass in a heavy metal band. I fretted on the sticky
back seat and kept dabbing my forehead with a balled-up
Kleenex. "Sure," I kept saying. "Oh, really?"

Out of the cab windows, as we drove up Broadway, I kept
catching people staring at me. Bagel-sellers, cops, shoppers
with too many bags. It felt as if I was under surveillance. I
knew that it was nothing more than my imagination, but all
the same I found it disturbing. The cab driver's eyes floated
disembodied in his rear-view mirror, and he was watching
me, too. By the old Moulmein Pagoda.

The only feeling of pride and security I had was that Martin hadn't said "*my* business" but "*our* business." At least
he considered that we were both mediums together, in the
same wacky profession. At least it showed he had some confidence in me.

I wished to God that I had half his confidence.

Amelia listened to me gravely. The classroom was flooded
with dusty golden light. A small boy with spiky hair and
Coke-bottle eyeglasses stood a little way off, clutching a
crayon drawing of bombers destroying a city. It looked a
damn sight better than Picasso's *Guernica.*

Amelia said, "I can't, Harry. I gave it all up."

"I know. I know you did. But who else can I turn to? If
he's lucky, Martin's going to end up in Attica for ever. It'll
kill him."

"I heard about it on the news this morning." Amelia said.
Her eyes were pale as agates. The sun turned her hair into
filaments of gold: the kind of gold that Rumpelstiltskin used
to spin, before they found out his name. And when they
found out his name, he stamped his foot, and he plunged
right through the floor to the world of shadows underneath,
for ever. What did I tell you? Thin-skinned place, this
planet.

"Amelia," I said, "I could help him if I had half of your
talent."

She looked at me acutely. "If the truth were known,
Harry, you probably have more."

"Amelia . . . please."

The small boy with the spiky hair came anxiously forward and presented his drawing. Amelia took it and examined it carefully.

"It's very well drawn, Douglas. Don't you think it's kind of violent?"

Douglas shook his head. "That's not a town, with people or anything."

"Oh, no? But there are buildings here. Who lives in these buildings?"

"The IRS."

"The IRS?"

Douglas nodded. "Daddy said that somebody ought to drop a bomb on the IRS. So that's what I did a drawing of."

"I see," said Amelia. "So you want to take this home, to show your daddy?"

She watched him go, and close the classroom door behind him. "Cute kid," I remarked. "He could grow up to be something big in corporate finance."

Amelia smiled. "He's severely disturbed. His mother abandoned him when he was five, while his father was away in Alaska, working for Exxon. He was left to look after his two-year-old sister for nearly two weeks, all on his own. He cooked for his baby sister, he bathed her, he told her stories. He even went shopping. It was only when he burst into tears in the middle of class that anybody realized that anything was wrong."

"Shit," I said.

"Yes," smiled Amelia. "Shit. But we can't help everybody, all of the time, no matter how much we may want to, and no matter how hard we may try."

"Meaning that you won't come and help me now?"

"I don't know, Harry. It sounds like trouble. It sounds like such bad trouble."

I dry-washed my face with my hands. "All right, Amelia. I understand. It's your life. When it comes down to it, I don't even think that I had any right to ask you."

"Harry—"

"Forget it. I don't want you doing anything for old times' sake. There isn't any worse reason for doing anything than that. I'll find somebody else. There are dozens of spiritualists in the yellow pages."

Amelia said, very softly, her words falling through the afternoon sunlight like tissues, "You think it's Misquamacus, don't you?"

"Yes," I said. "Who else?"

"You told me that Misquamacus had sworn to kill you."

"He did. In no uncertain terms."

"So why don't you let things lie? Forget about Martin; forget about the Greenbergs; forget about the whole damned thing? Whatever you do, it's only going to make matters worse."

"But Martin said there's something major going down. Something serious. He said the spirits were rushing around like blue-assed flies."

"And you really think that it's anything to do with you? For God's sake, Harry, stop trying to be responsible for the whole damned world! Go home, read your fortunes, flirt with all your old ladies. Forget it."

"But Martin—"

"Martin knew the risks. That's what he told you. Every medium knows the risks. There's nothing more that you can do."

I paused, then threw up my hands in acceptance. "Okay . . . if that's the way you feel about it."

"Harry, I'm sorry. But that *is* the way I feel about it. I'm not going to jeopardize this—any of this—my life, these kids—just to rub a little feel-better ointment on your conscience."

"All right," I told her. "I completely understand. Karen and I will just have to manage the best we can."

"You won't put Karen into any danger, will you?" Amelia said, in a sharp voice.

"Amelia, please. I wouldn't risk hurting one hair on Karen's head. Karen and I are—well, Karen and I have become close."

Long pause. Kids singing in the corridor outside. *"Round, round, rosie, cuppie, cuppie shell, the dog's gone to Charleston, to buy a new bell."*

"Close," Amelia repeated, as if she didn't understand what the word meant.

I didn't say anything. But I could see the thought of Karen and me getting together gradually working its way down through Amelia's brain like one of those puzzles where a marble drops out of a hopper and rolls down a ramp and then spins down a helter-skelter and then counterbalances a seesaw and then drops down a chute.

I shrugged. "You know, friendly. Why not? For old times' sake."

"You shouldn't do anything for old times' sake," Amelia retorted. "There isn't any worse reason."

"Well, *touché,*" I told her.

She picked up the workbooks on her desk, and shuffled them straight. "I'll come take a look," she said. "I'm not making any promises. I can't give you any guarantees. But I'll come take a look."

I leaned over and kissed her. "That's what I was hoping you'd say."

Colorado

The turbulence was now so severe that Deke tapped Willard on the shoulder and said, "Time we headed back! We'll just have to look for the rest of the strays tomorrow!"

Reluctantly, Willard said, "Guess you're right. Those clouds up ahead don't look none too healthy, do they?"

"Never saw nothing like them," Deke confessed. "And that lightning . . . what kind of lightning would you call that? It ain't fork and it ain't sheet. It's kind of like falling rain, almost."

Willard eased the Jetranger's cyclic stick to the right, and the helicopter began a wide, bumpy turn. They were flying at less than five hundred feet over the sagebrush, and for the past twenty minutes they had been buffeted by some of the most aggressive and unpredictable gusts that Willard had ever encountered. He had flown through thunder-squalls that had killed cattle by the score, and in Vietnam he had lifted Hueys in and out of Saigon in every kind of tropical storm that the Lord God had ever whipped up.

He and Deke were looking for almost thirty head of cattle that had strayed through a broken fence on the Peterson ranch, and had now been scattered wide across the Yampa River valley. Usually strays kept close together, but the winds and the lightning must have frightened these cattle into running every which way. So far they had only found twenty-three of them. The remainder seemed to have vanished across the plateau without trace.

Deke had been punching cattle for the Petersons for over twenty-five years. He was a thin, leathery-skinned man with very little hair, which he grew as long as he could and combed meticulously sideways over his sun-freckled scalp. He wore faded denims that were soft with wear, and the same pair of orange-tinted sunglasses that he had been issued by the Army in 1967. He was a man of long practical experience, monastic ways, and almost no sense of humor whatever, except for that grim, dry bunkhouse wit for which cattlemen had been celebrated for more than a hundred years.

Willard was a natural helicopter pilot. Deke had once remarked that he must have been born with a collective lever instead of a penis. That was about as close as Deke ever got to admitting that he admired Willard's flying skill. Willard was only two years younger than Deke but he looked about half his age, podgy and boyish, with a jet-black quiff that was higher and greasier than anyone else's in Moffat County. He wore a drip-dry khaki shirt and drip-dry khaki pants, and his pockets were always arrayed with different-color ballpoint pens.

He had almost completed his 180-degree turn to the east when Deke touched his shoulder again. "Look there, Willard, you see something moving?"

Willard kept his left pedal depressed so that the helicopter continued its turn and circled right around.

"Just there," Deke pointed.

Struggling to keep the Jetranger steady, Willard followed the sloping plateau towards the river. Something *was* moving down there, and it wasn't just the wind blowing through the sage. Something heavy and wide was plowing its way slowly through the brush, leaving a track of broken vegetation behind it. Deke took off his sunglasses and saw that, whatever it was, it had already covered more than a mile and a half, possibly more, because the beginnings of the track were obscured behind a low range of hills.

The northwest squall abruptly dropped—as abruptly as if a huge door had been slammed shut—but then another door was flung open and they were hit by a squall from due west. The helicopter bucked and dived and spun around on its center of gravity.

"Jesus Christ," Deke swore, snatching for the grabhandle.

Willard juggled with levers and pedals, trying to bring the Jetranger level again. The engine ground and growled and sang out of key.

"Have you got this fucking thing under control or what?" Deke demanded.

Willard sniffed, and coughed. "Okay so far," he said tautly, glancing at his instruments.

The helicopter swayed pendulum-like from side to side as Willard followed the track towards the river. He had to make constant adjustments to the tail-rotor to compensate for the unexpected chopping and changing of the wind.

There were sudden down-drafts, too, immediately followed by fierce, unmanageable gusts from behind and below. Willard had never experienced anything like it.

Up above them, the clouds were the color of skinned beef, black and bloody, and growing darker all the time. They reminded Deke of the time when they had put out a grassfire by shooting and skinning a bull, and then dragging its bleeding carcass backward and forward through the flames. Rain began to patter against the Jetranger's windshield, and Willard switched on the wipers.

"There's the highway," Deke remarked, pointing to the dim grey line of Highway 40 beyond the river. "We'll be hitting Maybelline as soon as makes no difference. We can put down there if you druther—wait till this blows itself out."

The helicopter bounced and moaned and whinnied like a kicked horse. Deke was thrown from one side of his seat to the other, and knocked his earphone against the doorframe.

"What the hell are you trying to do?" Deke yelled. "I thought you said you had this thing under control!"

"It's all right, it's all right, I can handle it," Willard reassured him.

"Well, I put on a clean pair of shorts this morning and I want them to stay that way," Deke told him.

"Don't worry about it," said Willard. "I've been flying these bastards since sixty-six, when they first brought them out, and only one of my passengers ever shit himself, and he was only three months old."

They had almost reached the Yampa River. It was all but dried up this time of year, and right here, close to Maybelline, it meandered in wide, idle loops of tan-colored mud, thinly overgrown with needle-grass. Deke could see the shallow water gleaming as bloody-black as the sky, and crisscrossed with ripples from the changing wind.

Off to his right, through the scattering rain, he could still make out the slowly-moving object that was dragging a track through the sagebrush. The track must have been thirty or forty feet wide, maybe wider, so whatever was causing it must be *huge,* wider than a combine-harvester. Deke could glimpse something brown and white, but even when Willard angled the helicopter over it, he still couldn't understand what it was.

His brain simply couldn't make any sense of it. It was a tangle of shapes and objects, a jigsaw of colors and textures. He saw things that slid and things that jiggled. He saw things that glistened and things that shone. He saw fur and bone and flesh and lots of blood.

"What the fuck?" he asked himself.

It was animal, it had hair and hide and legs and eyes, but what kind of animal was it? There was no animal as wide as this; no animal that dragged itself along the ground, leaving a forty-foot track in the sagebrush. He could make out a head, but the head was only as big as a cow's head. He could see scores of legs, but they were all sticking out at different angles, and some of them were obviously broken.

"Jesus H. Christ," whispered Willard. Willard had flown Hueys in Vietnam. Willard had seen grey-faced boys slip-sliding into body-bags and Marines caught by booby-trapped mines. Willard had seen women and children caught by Vulcan fire. It's extraordinary what six thousand rounds a minute can do to the human body.

Willard knew what happened when several living bodies were violently dismembered—what kind of impossible anatomical puzzles you ended up with. Heads here, legs there, guts over yonder, and bucketfuls of what the corpsmen used to call goop. Goop looked like pale pink semolina, almost appetizing, but in fact it was soft human tissues emulsified by blast.

What he saw below them on this rainy, squally day wasn't human, but it was just as terrible. It was a raft of dead cattle, all of the twenty-seven strays they had been searching for. They had been hideously torn to pieces, and mixed up together, and yet somehow they were still dragging their way through the sagebrush.

Deke whispered, "This is a nightmare. This is a fucking nightmare."

Willard circled round, trying to keep the Jetranger stable. The gusts were even more ferocious over the cattle, and one down-draft was so strong that Willard felt as if the helicopter were being deliberately pressed towards the ground by a giant hand.

"Deke—we're going to have to call it a day!" he shouted. "These squalls are going to bring us down if we don't!"

Deke stared at him, his eyes almost mad with alarm. "But they're *moving*! They're dead, they're all chopped up, but they're *moving*! For Christ's sake, Willard, how can they *move*?"

"Freak weather conditions, who knows?" said Willard. "Maybe the riverbed's caving in."

Deke pressed his helmet against the window, looking down at the grisly piebald shambles that was sliding its way westward.

"This is a nightmare," he repeated.

Willard circled the animals once more. Their mutilated bodies had emerged from the sagebrush, and were now heaving themselves across a flat grey mudbank beside the river. They left behind them a sickening trail of blood and legs and udders and pieces of ripped-apart hide.

Turning his head, Deke said, "Let's head for Maybelline. That way we can catch up with them on foot."

"You're the boss," Willard replied.

He lifted the helicopter off to starboard, fighting a sudden burst of contradictory crosswinds. The clouds were blacker than ever, and lightning crackled all around the helicopter in fine fiery curtains.

"Are you okay?" Deke asked Willard. "Listen—if you want to ditch this thing, you can ditch it any time that you want to. I'll bear witness for you. There ain't no helicopter on God's earth that's worth losing your life for."

"It's okay, it's okay," Willard told him, as they flew low and crabwise across the Yampa River. "I think I'm beginning to get the hang of these damn squalls. They jump from one side of the compass to the other, then up, then down."

All the same, the Jetranger dipped and danced so wildly as they crossed to the opposite side of the river that Deke was sure they were going to fly straight into the ground. He kept having mental flashes of TV news pictures of helicopter crashes. All he could think of was bodies, still strapped in their seats, and a framework of twisted, insubstantial wreckage.

"Only about a mile!" Willard told him. "Maybelline's just beyond the ridge!"

The helicopter skimmed the sagebrush, less than fifty feet above the ground. Lightning showered all around them, and sparks were flung from their rotors like Catherinewheels. They saw grassfires burning all across the dark horizon, and the helicopter's ventilation system took in the aromatic smell of charring balsam-root.

"Never saw a damn storm like this before, never," said Deke.

It was then that Willard leaned forward in his seat and peered ahead of them into the gloom.

"Do you see what I see?" he asked.

Deke peered, too, and then shook his head. "In this rain, I can't see squat."

"No Maybelline," said Willard.

"What? What do you mean?"

"Look for yourself! No Maybelline! There's supposed to be a town there, ain't that right? Right there, right on the bend. Maybelline, Moffat County, population four hundred and nineteen. So where is it?"

"We missed it, must have overshot."

"What the hell do you mean, overshot? There's the highway and there's the river and Maybelline's supposed to be *there.*" Willard jabbed his finger directly in front of them.

"Jesus," said Deke, in awe, looking around at the clouds, as if he expected to see houses and barns whirling above their heads. "You don't think that—? Not a whole *town!*"

"It's gone," said Willard. "Frank's gas station and Charlie Butcher's stables and the church and everything! There was houses there! Four houses, maybe five!" As they flew in closer to the town center, however, they began to come across traces of what had happened. The highway was littered with windblown debris, pieces of broken automobiles, chairs, couches, display stands, tires, baby buggies.

They saw a dead horse and two dead dogs: then they saw their first human victims. A woman lying face down with her flowery dress immodestly dragged up. A man with no head, just a neck like a bloodied drainpipe.

Even in the storm they could see that all of this debris was gradually moving; at the same gradual but relentless speed as the dead cattle had been moving.

Lightning crackled, and the helicopter skittered disobediently sideways, with sparks jumping and spitting down the windshield, and falling from the landing-skids. One of the instruments abruptly fused, and the smell of burning balsam-root was sharply mixed with the smell of burning plastic.

"I'm going to try to bring her down!" Willard yelled. The engine screamed and they heard an ear-splitting screeching noise like gears shearing.

Deke was about to say something, but couldn't. He was clinging onto the grabhandle so tight that he bent it.

The Jetranger stuttered and bounced into the center of Maybelline less than thirty feet above the highway. The town square was a slowly-creeping forest of furniture and abandoned automobiles and bashed-in iceboxes, with flying newspapers everywhere. Willard turned desperately from left to right, continually nudging back the collective lever to give himself a few feet of height.

"Look for someplace clear to land!" he shouted.

Deke strained his eyes in the darkness. A sheet of wet newspaper flapped against the window beside him, and for a moment he couldn't see anything at all; but then the wind plucked the newspaper away again.

"There!" he said. "There!"

About a hundred feet ahead of them a small open space appeared. It was strewn with papers and broken glass, but it was free from tumbling automobiles and furniture. Willard steered the helicopter unevenly toward it, fighting for power now as well as control. The engine was coughing, suddenly racing and then coughing again, and it was all he could do to keep them in the air.

They had almost reached the landing-space when Deke grabbed at his arm again. *"Look,"* he said. "For Christ's sake—*look*!"

Only twenty or thirty feet further ahead, on the edge of what had once been Maybelline's small public park, the very *air* was stained as black as ink. It looked as if the ground had opened up, because everything that had been sliding along the roadway—fencing, sheds, trucks, road-signs, *everything*—was disappearing into this blackness like vegetable peelings down an endlessly-grinding sink-disposal unit.

As their Jetranger lurched and dipped above the landing-space, Deke and Willard saw the half-collapsed wreckage of an entire family house slide across the road and vanish into the ground, its walls splintering, its windows shattering, its chimney collapsing into its roof. Lightning spat all around it as it was finally lost from sight, followed by a cascade of torn-up railings and a battered Winnebago Chieftain and a hurrying collection of cans and bottles and crates.

Deke glimpsed some bodies go, too. Three children, a dog, and an elderly man. He saw one arm uplifted for a moment which suggested (to his helpless horror) that one of the children wasn't yet dead. What would happen to it beneath the ground, he couldn't even guess.

He shouted, "For Christ's sake, Willard! We can't land there! We'll be sucked in with all the rest of that shit!"

But the Jetranger's engine had developed a blurting, terminal cough, and the cockpit was filling with eye-watering smoke. Willard could scarcely keep the helicopter from spinning round and round on its own axis and tipping over.

"I can't hold it no more!" he yelled. "We'll just have to hit the doors and run like fun!"

They were hovering over the landing-space now, tilting and teetering, only ten feet or so from the garbage-strewn ground. Just as Willard was about to push forward the collective lever, however, Deke screamed, "No! No! There's a kid down there!"

"What?" yelped Willard, his voice white.

"A kid! There's a kid down there!"

Willard dragged back the lever, and the helicopter gave a last blurt of power and jounced up into the air. Through the rain-blurred windshield, Willard glimpsed a young pale-faced girl standing right in the middle of the landing-space, her arms by her sides, watching them.

He was too shocked to wonder what she was doing there; or why *she* wasn't being dragged off into the blackness. All he could hear was the Jetranger's engine knock and bang, and then the wind and the rain buffeting against the fuselage. Then he heard Deke screaming, really screaming like a man who knows that he is just about to die. The helicopter windmilled inelegantly forward, overshooting the landing-space, and plunging straight into the inky blackness at the edge of the park.

Willard had been in crashes before. He had broken both legs in Saigon, and only the second time he had flown for Mr Peterson he had clipped a power line and fractured his skull. But this wasn't like a crash at all. This was violent and noisy beyond all imagination. The helicopter was crushed into the blackness like a man crushing a lightbulb into a bowl of molasses. Willard heard the windshield collapse; then the bulkheads; then suddenly the helicopter was torn away from all around him, doorframes, instrument panel, pedals, levers, floor—even his seat—and he had the extraordinary feeling that he was being swung upside down, so that he was hanging by his boots from the ceiling.

"Deke!" he shouted out. *"Deke, are you okay?"*

He reached out into the blackness, trying to find something to touch, something that would help him to orient himself. It was like inching his way along the pitch-dark landing of a strange house, trying to find the light switch. His eyes were open but the black filled everything. He felt that black was pouring into his head and into his lungs and drowning him.

"Deke, where are you?"

He heard tearing noises, collapsing noises, crunches and smashes. He tried to take two or three steps forward, but he still felt as if he were hanging head-downward, and that he could easily fall. He stayed where he was, his arms outstretched, blinded, trying to balance himself.

It was then that he saw something pale approaching him through the blackness. Something pale and very tall.

He must be dead. There was no doubt about it. He must be dead.

The pale creature came closer and closer, and as it did so Willard realized that it was somebody riding a horse. Somebody or some*thing* riding a horse—because it looked hunched and strange and it seemed to have a monstrously huge head.

If it was a man on a horse, he must be half a mile away at least, half a mile away in total blackness and *upside down*.

The vision was so eerie that Willard started shivering with fear. He tried to close his eyes but he couldn't, they refused. They were too filled with blackness. All he could do was stand and wait for the man on the horse to flicker nearer and nearer, a spectre with all the blurry pale uncertainty of an early movie.

Above the crashing and the tearing, he heard, very faintly, the light, hard rhythm of hoofbeats.

It seemed to Willard that the man on the horse took an age to reach him. Willard no longer tried calling out for Deke. If Deke had survived the crash, he would have shouted out himself by now.

Mind you, thought Willard, *there was always the possibility that Deke had survived the crash and that he hadn't—that he was dead, and that this was Purgatory, or wherever you went when you tried to land your Jetranger with a sheared engine and found that a girl was standing in your way.*

The hoofbeats sounded louder now, more distinctive. But it was like listening to the sound of somebody running down the staircase of a thirty-story hotel. You couldn't believe that they would ever get there.

Eventually, however, the vision flickered quite close. A white negative image in the blackness. It appeared to be a man, but if it was, he was either wearing a monstrous box-like helmet, or else his skull was hugely deformed. He sat on his white negative-image horse with both hands holding the reins, watching Willard with eyes that were little more than shadowy blurs.

His horse twitched and circled and appeared to change shape. "What are you?" Willard demanded. "Am I dead, or what?"

The whitish vision circled all the way around him. Willard turned his head to follow him, not trusting himself to move his feet, in case he fell from the ground and into the blackest of skies.

"I feel like I'm dead," said Willard. "I don't know, either dead or unconscious or something."

The vision came so close that Willard could feel its cold, charged aura. Willard said, "Can you speak? Do you know what I'm saying to you?" He looked up at that whitish, misshapen head and he wasn't even sure that he was talking to anything human, let alone anybody who could answer him in English.

There were more crashes and creaks and collapsing noises, somewhere in the blackness. Willard said, "Thing of it is, I don't know what's happening. I can't understand where I am."

The vision seemed to lean forward. Willard narrowed his eyes against its brightness. He smelled the oddest of smells, like fires and burned grease, a smell that was disturbingly reminiscent of—what? He couldn't decide. He stepped cautiously back. But—as he did so—he felt something snatch hold of his right arm, and twist it around as violently as an airplane propeller. He felt an explosion in his shoulder. He heard his shirt tear. Not only his shirt, but his skin and his flesh and his arteries. He was too startled even to scream. He staggered sideways in the blackness, blind, agonized, not knowing which way to turn—not even understanding what had happened to him.

"Shit! What have you done? Shit! What have you done to my shoulder?"

He tried to flex his right arm but he couldn't. He kept staggering and losing his balance. He felt warmth and wetness flooding his shirt. He reached across with his left hand to find out whether the vision had dislocated his shoulder, and it was only then that he felt strings of skin and slippery worms of tendon and pumping blood.

The white negative rider had torn his arm off.

Willard choked. His mouth filled with sick. He dropped to his knees in the overwhelming blackness and shivered and shook and that was all he could do. *This isn't happening. This isn't real.* But he kept seeing those maimed and bloodied young Marines in Vietnam, those boys with no legs and those boys with no arms and those boys with no faces.

What did they do, when a soldier lost his arm? Tourniquet?

How? How did they stop the blood from pumping out of his body and into the blackness—pumped out forever into oblivion?

But he didn't have to think about it for very long. Because the white shimmering vision dismounted from his white shimmering horse and approached him with terrible swiftness.

"Help me," Willard pleaded. But without hesitation the vision swung around and hit him across the side of the head with something heavy and clublike and soft.

Willard tipped to the ground. He was clubbed again, and then again. He tried to lift his left arm to protect himself, but the vision was beating him in a frenzy. He felt blood spraying everywhere, his own blood. He felt his ribs snap, three of them, and then his jaw was dislocated, so that he couldn't do anything to express his agony but gargle.

The vision was beating him to death with his own arm. It was done vengefully, the way you might club a dog to death if it had bitten your child.

There came a time when Willard decided that he could no longer distinguish between light and dark, up and down, pain and pleasure. He thought he heard the vision chanting; but perhaps it was nothing more than his own heartbeat, dutifully pumping his blood out of his severed brachial artery into the darkness.

Oh God our help in ages past, he thought to himself. Then, for some reason a ribald little nursery rhyme he hadn't thought of in thirty-five years: "Papa loved Mama,/Mama loved babies,/Mama caught two,/With Papa at Creybie's."

But his ordeal was not over yet. Just when he believed that the beating might have stopped, he felt his head wrenched upward by the hair. He was crowned with white blurry light, so that he felt almost holy, almost sanctified. But then something that felt like fire cut across his hairline.

Inch by inch, with a noise like tearing calico, his scalp was wrenched from the top of his head—hair-roots crackling, skin pulling free.

It was like having his hair burned off, but very slowly. It was so painful he couldn't understand how God could have made him capable of feeling so much pain. He might have been screaming then but he simply didn't know.

EIGHT

It was still light when Amelia arrived at the Greenbergs' house. Karen and I had been sitting on the stoop outside waiting for her. The air was thick and hot and tasted like a mouthful of pennies.

She climbed out of a sagging red Cadillac, waved to the driver, and mounted the steps. She was wearing the same orange Indian-cotton dress that she had been wearing that afternoon. She carried a straw purse and a straw hat, and her eyes were concealed behind oil-slick–colored sunglasses.

"Amelia!" said Karen, and hugged her. "It's so good to see you!"

Amelia came up to the top of the steps and stood over me. Someone in the distance was shouting, "Manny! Manny! You come back here right this instant!"

Amelia said, "I promised I'd come."

I tried to smile. "I knew that you wouldn't let us down." Almost as soon as I'd uttered it, though, I wished to God that I hadn't said "us." It didn't seem like all that long ago that Amelia and I had been "us."

But Karen was so pleased to see her that somehow all the sting was taken out of it. "You haven't changed a bit! Well, you *have* changed, but only for the better! Harry tells me you're teaching."

"That's right. Slow and disturbed children."

"That must be so rewarding."

Amelia was looking at me, rather than Karen. "It can be," she said. "At other times, it can be very frustrating."

"Harry told you about the Greenbergs?"

"Yes. I'm so sorry. It's a terrible tragedy."

"Do you think you can help?"

Amelia took off her sunglasses and stared up at the building's brown-painted brick facade. "I don't know. It depends what we've got here. If it really *is* Misquamacus then we could be at very considerable risk."

Karen was beginning to look tired. "I thought Misquamacus was dead."

Amelia replaced her sunglasses. "Oh, no. Misquamacus was never dead. Even when we first met him he wasn't dead. But then he wasn't properly alive, either. He moves around that kind of limbo-land which we call Purgatory and which the Indians call the Lodge of the Moon."

Karen glanced up at the apartment, too. "Do you want to take a look?"

I took hold of Amelia's wrist. "There's no compulsion about this, Amelia. You can just turn your back and walk away. I won't think any the less of you."

Amelia gave me one of her real old-fashioned looks. "And I won't think any the more of you."

Karen opened the front door and that kind of settled everything. Together we climbed the stairs to the Greenbergs' apartment. Up until lunchtime, a cop had been standing guard on the door; but now the apartment was guarded by nothing more effective than tape saying POLICE LINE DO NOT CROSS.

I took out my Swiss Army penknife and cut the tape.

"I hope you realize that what we're doing is illegal," said Amelia.

"Trust me," I told her. "Besides, there's no other way."

I opened the door and we stepped inside. The apartment was warm but gloomy, and I could faintly detect the smell of death. Amelia must have picked it up, too, because she shivered and reached out with her right hand to steady herself against the architrave.

"My God," she said. "I never went anyplace where anybody died so recently. It's like a battlefield."

The living room wasn't untidy. When Amelia said "battlefield," she meant a spiritual battlefield: a war in that other, closely-adjacent dimension, where men could run like dogs and women could be slaughtered and still desirable. Karen reached out for my hand and don't tell me that Amelia didn't notice it. But all the same she kept her composure. She was many things, Amelia Crusoe, but she wasn't petty or spiteful and she didn't care for living in the past.

She reached out her left hand towards the dining-room door.

"In there," she said, and it wasn't a question.

"That's right," I said. "Do you want to take a look?"

She humphed in amusement. "I *have* to take a look, I'm sorry to say."

She eased open the dining-room door, and there was all the furniture heaped against the opposite wall, including the bloodied chair to which Naomi had clung for so long. The living room had been warm, but this room was nearly fifteen degrees colder, and illuminated by the kind of bluish-green radiance that I had seen in my dream. The glow of death, the glow of decay. This room was something else altogether. This was a room where spirits had emerged into the real world, and where people had been mutilated and hideously killed.

Amelia took two or three very cautious steps into the room, then stood quite still and silent, looking around. I stood very close behind her. I could smell school and perfume on her clothes, one of her old favourite perfumes, Joy. I wondered for a moment how she could afford it on a teacher's wages, but then I remembered that MacArthur always used to send her a giant-sized bottle for her birthday, July 6, and probably still did. Just because somebody doesn't love you any more, that's no excuse for not sending them perfume.

"I used to love that woman so much," MacArthur had once confided in me, "I could have cut my eyes out, rather than see her going around with another man."

But times change. And I knew from my own experience that Amelia wasn't particularly easy to get along with. People who are good with children tend to find it difficult to manage their relationships with other adults. MacArthur had been sweet and almost childlike, and maybe that was why their affair had lasted so long. Our affair, on the other hand, had been fractured and almost unreal, like watching an Ingmar Bergman movie in the wrong order. Or even the *right* order.

"Tell me what happened," said Amelia; and I told her. I didn't give her all the gory details, but I didn't really have to. She understood.

"There was a shadow on the wall?"

"That's right. I mean it *looked* like a shadow, but there

was nobody standing in front of the wall to throw it."

"And what happened? Martin went up to the wall—and the shadow kind of joined him?"

"That's the only way to describe it. It was like Martin and the shadow turned into one person. Martin went very dark, and his skin looked strange, and there was something weird about his eyes. They looked more like a photograph of someone's eyes than real eyes."

Amelia glanced at me. "You wouldn't like to say whose?"

"Whose what?"

"Whose eyes they were. Were they Martin's, or did they look like someone else's?"

I tried to think. "I don't know, I—"

She covered her face with her hands *so that onlie ye Eyes look'd out.* "Think Martin. Think about Singing Rock. Were they *his* eyes?"

"No . . . I don't think so."

"What about Misquamacus?"

"The last time I saw Misquamacus was a very long time ago."

"Don't tell me you've forgotten how he looks."

"I've done my best."

"All right," said Amelia. "We'd better get down to it. I think it's safer if we form a conventional circle, all holding hands, than try to follow Martin's technique. Martin likes to enter the spirit-world like a potholer. I'm not sure that I have the courage to do that. I prefer to call the spirits and wait till they come to *me.*"

"I'll drink to that," I told her. "What about the table?"

"We'll have to do without. The spirit will only drag it across the room, and heap it up with everything else."

The three of us stood facing each other and held hands. Almost immediately I could feel an electric tingle go through me, as Amelia closed the circuit. She was always conscious of the spirits around her, all the time. Some days they used to light up her brain cells like a telephone exchange. Personally, I would have hated to be *that* sensitive. It was irritating enough listening to other people's Walkmans, let alone other people's souls. I would have told them all to lie down and get some rest, but Amelia had once told me that many recently-dead people can't even grasp the fact that they're dead. They wander around Purgatory or whatever you call it, wondering what time's lunch, and when are they going to get out of these pajamas.

Amelia closed her eyes. I gave Karen a last reassuring wink and then closed mine too. I don't know why I was trying to reassure her. I had stood in this same room less than twenty-four hours ago, and seen a woman reduced to a grisly parody of a rubber glove. My mouth was dry and my heart was cantering like a yearling. Bom-bom, bom-bom, bom-bom, bom-bom. They say that the second "bom" you hear is the echo of the first "bom," bouncing off the inside of your skull. They also say that one person's guts, properly dried and prepared, could be used to string every tennis racket used in the Wimbledon Tennis Tournament; and let me tell you, they use literally hundreds of rackets every year.

I was trying to think of some more "Believe-It-Or-Not"-type facts—just to keep my mind off malevolent spirits—when Amelia suddenly said, "George Hope and Andrew Danetree, room 212—"

"What?" I said. "Who?"

I opened my eyes. Karen had opened her eyes, too; but Amelia's were still closed. She looked extremely pale, as if all the blood had drained out of her cheeks.

"Asked to meet me," said Amelia, quite clearly.

"Who asked to meet you?" I urged her.

"George Hope. Andrew Danetree. Room 212, Friday. Six o'clock."

"Amelia, who are George Hope and Andrew Danetree when they're at home?"

But although she was talking, Amelia didn't seem to be able to hear me. "I never knew your father. I thought you knew mine."

I was about to say something else, when Amelia half-opened her eyes and looked at me. "Harry," she whispered. "They're coming."

"But—"

"Quiet, Harry, they're coming. They're very distressed."

She closed her eyes again. I glanced across at Karen, but now Karen had closed her eyes again, too. Personally, I preferred to keep my eyes open. I'm not cowardly by nature. Cautious, maybe. Self-protective. But I could see shadows stirring on the wall. I could sense a cold, encroaching darkness. If Amelia was going to be possessed in the same way that Martin had been possessed, then I didn't want to be standing there with my eyes tight shut while it happened. I had many desires, many hopes, many ambitions. Being turned inside out by an ill-tempered spirit wasn't one of them.

The temperature in the dining room dropped even further. I could see Amelia's breath fuming out of her nostrils. Her hands grew colder, too, and she clutched me so tightly that I didn't think that I would be able to prize myself free.

"I am calling on the spirits who are wandering in this place," said Amelia. *"I am asking them to show themselves."*

I heard a very faint sound like a cat yowling. The atmosphere began to feel as if it were charged with static electricity. Bright steely sparks crackled from Amelia's hair; and Karen's hair began to lift, too, the way it does when you comb it too much. I felt an electrical buzzing sensation in my teeth, and pins and needles in my wrists.

Then—for some reason that I can't really describe—I began to feel seriously frightened. I'm not talking apprehensive or vaguely worried. I'm talking about the bowels melting, and the feeling that death was standing in the room with us. It was just like the feeling you get when you've been wading in the shallows of a chilly lake, and suddenly the bottom shelves away beneath your feet, and leaves you shocked and gasping, out of your depth.

The air in front of me seemed to bend and distort. Again, I heard that cat-yowling sound. *Yarrrooowwwww.*

"Amelia?" I said; but Amelia couldn't hear me. Her eyes were tightly closed and there were sparks dripping from her hair like crystal-bright raindrops.

"Amelia?" I repeated. This time my voice sounded slow and blurred. *"Ahhhmmmeeeellliaaaahhhhh . . ."* But she kept her eyes closed; and she gripped my hand as tightly as before, if not tighter, and I knew that there was no disturbing her. She was closely in touch with the spirits, and even if it wasn't dangerous to wake her, it was damned difficult.

The spirits demand so much attention. In their sad, frightening way, they're worse than children. They want everything, and they want it now. They seem to forget that they have all of eternity.

As I've said before, I'm not particularly sensitive myself. Psychically sensitive, that is—although you can show me a movie with kids in it, and I'll get all choked up before you can say *Boys' Town.* But Amelia was arousing something and I could feel it coming. *I could feel it coming.* It was tortured and cold and very strange and it was in pain. *It was in pain.*

It was writhing the way that a worm writhes when you crush it on a concrete path. *Wagging,* rather than writhing, so that I felt horror and disgust as well as sympathy.

It was a man. No, it wasn't. It was *men*—two men, butchered and grisly and eyeless. I could scarcely see them. It was like watching a broken-up image on a dying TV. There was blood and bone and I could see a stump-like arm waving. And those eyeless eyes, begging for sight, or begging for extinction. But then the image wavered and disintegrated, and all I could see was a vague outline of that waggling motion, that hideous waggling, and hear those anguished voices. *"Yaaaooowwwwwww, yarrrooowww"*—so agonized that they didn't even sound human.

In the summer of 1957, on the Sawmill River Parkway, I saw a station wagon burning, with a family inside. Father and mother and three kids. They were screaming for help, but the fire was so fierce that nobody could get close. All that anybody could do was stand around and watch the windows blacken, and the smoke roll up, and hope that the screaming would stop. My father had stopped the car and rolled down the window and stared for almost a minute without saying a word. Then he had driven on to Katonah, where my aunt lived, with tears in his eyes.

This was the same. This was real people, suffering more than people were ever meant to suffer. You can read about pain in the papers but when you see it and hear it it's something else.

Amelia quivered. Karen grasped my hand even more

tightly. Amelia said, in the strangest of voices, *"Who are you? What did they do to you?"*

But then there was the highest of high-pitched shrieks, and for a split second we saw a *face* hovering bright and foggy right in front of us, a man's face, just about to turn, just about to speak. He looked like a man in young middle age, with a broad forehead and deepset eyes, and maybe a moustache—although this could have been a shadow.

"Killing us," he blurted. *"Killing us."* Then, *"Never knew ... Hope and Danetree ... never ever knew ..."*

The head began to shrink, smaller and smaller, until it was only the size of a puppet's head. Yet it continued to cry out, continued to plead for mercy. It shrank so small that it was not much bigger than a point of light.

There was a moment of charged silence. I could feel through her clutching fingers just how tense Amelia was. Every fiber in her body was tightened to the point of squeaking, like sisal cords tightened in a tourniquet. Then suddenly she shrieked out, *"Aaaaaaahhhhhhh!"* and the point of light exploded in front of us and we were sprayed with pints of warm, half-congealed blood.

Drenched, disgusted, we broke the circle. Amelia, wiping her face, said, "Quick—I want you out of here—please."

"This is *blood,*" said Karen, in disbelief, looking down at her black-sprayed blouse. "Amelia, this is *blood.*"

Amelia closed the dining-room door behind us and made a sign in the air that I didn't understand.

"What was that?" I asked her.

"Clidomancy," she said, tight-lipped.

"*Clidomancy?* What the hell does that mean?"

"God, this is revolting," she said, smearing the blood on her cheek. She went through to the kitchen and came back with towels so that we could wipe ourselves clean. I wiped blobs of jellyish blood onto a view of Niagara Falls. Next to me Karen was sickly silent.

When Amelia had finished cleaning herself up, she dropped her towel and then went back to the dining room and vigorously shook the handle. It was obviously locked.

She said, "Clidomancy is key-magic. My mother taught me how to do it. Lock, unlock. It's very easy. You see all these movies where people can't get out of the house because the doors have suddenly and mysteriously locked themselves . . . that's what is is, clidomancy, although of course not many moviemakers have the slightest clue that it is.

"Keys are iron and iron is the metal of the gods. Iron protects you from demonic possession. Iron protects you from disease, too. And if you place a key on the Fiftieth Psalm, and close the Bible tight, and bind it with a virgin's hair, and then hang it by a hook, the Bible will turn and twist whenever you mention the name of somebody who has hurt you or stolen something from you."

"Don't tell me you really believe that," I said.

She stared back at me without flinching. "Do you want to try opening that door?" she challenged me.

I hesitated. Then I said, "No, I guess not."

Karen was drying her hands. "What *happened* in there?" she asked. "I was so scared!"

"I'm not totally sure," said Amelia. "But the moment I tried to make contact, I could feel a spirit reaching out for me. I felt as if it had actually been *waiting* for me to make contact."

"Do you know who it was?"

"Unh-hunh. It didn't identify itself. It was strangely weak . . . but at the same time it wanted very much to help me. How can I put it? It felt like a guide. It felt like somebody who *belonged* here—somebody who knew this land and its history very well."

"An Indian spirit?"

"More than likely."

"Could it have been Singing Rock?"

"I'm not sure. You saw him here before so it's highly probable. I had the feeling that it knew who I was, and why I was here. On the other hand he was very weak, very vague and indistinct."

She paused. "How did Singing Rock die? You never told me."

I made a throat-cutting gesture with my finger. "Misquamacus—ah—took his head off." I hadn't meant my voice to sound choked up. I hadn't realized that it would.

But sometimes your emotions can ambush you when you're least expecting it.

"Oh, Harry, I'm sorry," said Amelia. "I didn't mean to upset you."

"It's okay, forget it. What's a little decapitation between friends?"

Amelia said, "The point is, if he died that way, that might account for how weak his spirit seems to be. When a person suffers a traumatic death that often makes them very restless and erratic spirits."

"He was always so damned pragmatic," I said. "Can you imagine that? A pragmatic medicine-man?" I tried to make a joke of it, but I was already worried that all of those nightmares that had plagued me after Singing Rock's death wouldn't come creeping out from under my pillow again. I hadn't thought about the way in which Singing Rock had died for a very long time, and I didn't want to start thinking about it again. I had a sharp mental picture of it that never faded and never grew any less horrifying. To watch somebody's *face* flying away from you with an expression of total fear on it . . . to see them still looking at you when their head is ten feet away from their body—well, that's more than some of us can happily live with.

Amelia said, "I don't usually like to make uninformed guesses, but I'm almost sure that we're dealing with some kind of Indian magic here. Either Indian or early Spanish. It has a completely different *feel* from white and European magic. It's very *pictorial,* if you know what I mean; and it's very much concerned with elemental things like fire and water, darkness and light, wind and rain.

"Indian magic is the magic of life and death—whereas white man's magic is usually all about things like money and revenge on your employer and making people love you. 'O Great Satan, I want to be irresistible to men.' Indians are much more concerned with basic survival."

"The noble savage strikes again," I remarked.

"Not so noble in this case," said Amelia. "Those two men we saw in there were the victims of a recent murder. It wasn't any ordinary murder, either. They were killed in such a way that neither their bodies nor their souls will ever be able to rest. They will suffer that torture forever. Even if we manage to find out what's going on, and what commands they were given, we will never be able to release them. To be released, you need either a whole body or a whole spirit. They don't have *either*."

"What do you mean?" asked Karen, in bewilderment.

"I mean that whoever killed them didn't just take their bodies to pieces. It took their souls to pieces, too."

"Is that *possible*?"

"I wouldn't have thought so not until now. But I don't know yet what kind of force this is. You mentioned a shadow."

"Yes," I told her. "But this time I didn't sense the shadow so strongly. It was there, hovering in the background, but that was all."

"In that case it was probably away someplace else, working out its temper on somebody else. Just as well, too."

Karen said, "What about the furniture? Do you have any idea why all the furniture slid across the room like that?"

"I don't know," said Amelia. "I've been thinking about that. The last time I saw anything like that was in a house in Poughkeepsie, years and years ago when I first started contacting the spirits.

"The owner of the house was a man called Grant. He was a real psycho. He killed one of his daughters by pressing her face onto an electric hotplate."

"Oh, *no*, I don't believe it," said Karen.

"Oh, people do worse," said Amelia. "Mr Grant said he was only trying to teach his daughter a lesson because she was so vain about her looks. She thought she was God's gift to men. He wanted to see how sassy she could be without a face.

"Anyway, I was asked to go to the house to help clear it, because after Mr Grant had been sent up the river the new owners kept hearing terrible screams in the middle of the night, and smelling a strong smell like burning liver. Yes, I know, it's disgusting, isn't it? But it was true."

"What has this to do with our two friends in the dining room?" I asked, glancing without too much confidence at Amelia's magically-locked door.

"I'm not altogether sure. But when I visited the Grant house I found that dozens of small objects like books and hair ribbons and bobby-pins were all crowded against the skirting-board in the girl's bedroom. No matter how I tried to move them, I couldn't. As fast as I took one book away another tumbled back in its place. It then occurred to me that all of the objects were in direct line with the place by the cooker where the girl had been killed. It was like they were being *drawn* towards it; as if they were being pulled by a magnet.

"I couldn't work out what to do about it, but a couple of months later I struck lucky. I met a professor from SUNY Utica Rome, Madron Vaudrey. One of his specialties was to see how many vital influences survived in the human mind and body after clinical death—such as the discharge of electrical impulses, the sending-out of viral codings, things like that. Purely by accident, he had found that in *scores* of recorded cases, objects belonging to dead people—particularly objects that they had regularly worn during their lifetime—would measurably move towards the place where they had died.

"He said that in his experience the more violent or painful the death, the further the objects would move. In one case, an eighty-two-year-old man was murdered by his two sons. After his death, his spectacles moved across the floor towards him, nearly twelve feet, I think it was. It was all recorded on police video. I don't know—it's almost as if, when a soul goes, it leaves a vacuum, and sympathetic objects try to fill it. Or maybe they're trying to follow their owners into the other world."

"But how about Naomi Greenberg's furniture?" I asked her. "It didn't belong to either of those two murdered men—George Hope and Andrew what's-his-face—not unless they were sent here from the finance company to repossess it, and that's not what you call 'sympathetic.' So why should it move when *they* were killed?"

Amelia shrugged. "I really don't know. But what I *do* know is that they probably died on the other side of Mrs Greenberg's dining-room wall; and very violently. Maybe they were killed so brutally that enough negative force was set up to cause the furniture to move. After all, we're not talking about any ordinary kind of killing here. Those men were taken to pieces, and their souls put into *sokwet*. That means 'eclipse' in MicMac. Total darkness in any language."

"What's on the other side of that wall?" I asked Karen.

"The Belford Hotel," Karen told me. "This whole row used to be residential, when it was first built; but it was one of those neighborhoods that was fashionable one week and not-so-fashionable the next."

"So that's a hotel room, on the other side of there?"

"I guess it must be."

"All right," I said, briskly chafing my hands together. "The best thing we can do is go take a look."

Amelia said, "Harry, you ought to understand how dangerous this is going to be. We're not dealing with poltergeists or bad-mannered demons who make you puke custard. We're dealing with some very strong and some very determined people who just happen to be dead."

"What about the shadow thing?"

"I don't know. Maybe we could get some expert advice on that."

"That shadow thing turned Martin into a psychopath."

"I know." Amelia looked tired. I was tempted to put my arm around her but then I thought about Karen and I decided that it probably wasn't the best thing to do, not right now. It was difficult enough fighting the wrath of a murderous shadow thing, without fighting the wrath of two women.

"Come on, let's go," I said, and we left the Greenbergs' silent and abandoned apartment to deal with its ghosts on its own.

NINE

The Belford Hotel wasn't quite as scabby as I had expected it to be. It wasn't one of those cabbage-smelling roach-infested flophouses you see in Robert de Niro movies. In fact it turned out to be reasonably clean and smart—the kind of old-fashioned family hotel that used to be favored by travelling salesmen and out-of-towners who couldn't afford the Sheraton or the Summit. But it had an atmosphere, you know what I mean? An atmosphere of polish and disinfectant and sneaky peeking into communal bathrooms. Prim, but creepy.

A man sat behind the high mahogany reception counter, reading a book. He was sixtyish, with thick white hair and a bulbous nose and tortoiseshell eyeglasses that magnified his eyes like freshly-opened clams. He wore a well-pressed short-sleeved shirt with surfers and hula girls on it. When I stepped up to the desk he carefully took out a red leather bookmark, and folded it into the book. He was reading *The Clocks of Columbus,* the biography of James Thurber. I guess the guy was entitled to read anything he liked but somehow this struck me as incongruous.

"Can I help you folks?" he inquired. I could see by the expression on his face that he was seriously hoping that I wouldn't ask him for a room for three: Mr and Mrs and Mrs Smith.

"Well, we're getting a little tired of all the noise."

"I'm sorry? What noise?"

"We live right next door, and the noises we've been hearing. You'd think somebody was being murdered."

The man took off his eyeglasses and laid them on the desk. "I'm sorry, sir. I don't know what noise you could be referring to. We run a real quiet establishment here. Some people think we're a little old-fashioned, to tell you the truth, because we're so darn quiet."

"Well, I'm sorry," I snapped back at him. "I've been

hearing noises like you wouldn't believe. Screams, yells, banging. It's been terrible."

"Where do you live, sir?"

"Right next door. Second floor. I don't know which of your rooms it could be, but it's right next to my dining room."

"And does your dining room overlook the street or does it overlook the back?"

"The back."

"That's Room 212, sir. I'll have a word with them, when I see them. Tell them to keep the noise down."

"I think I'd like to have a word with them myself."

"I'm sorry, sir, you can't go up there less'n a guest invites you."

"Well, let me talk to them on the house phone, at least."

"They're not in, sir. I'm sorry. They're very rarely in. In fact I don't think I've seen them for over a week, maybe longer."

"Can you tell us their names?" asked Amelia, in her softest, most dove-cooing voice.

"I'm sorry, miss. I'm not at liberty to give out private guest information like that. You do understand."

"All right," said Amelia. "But is one of them called George Hope, and is the other one called Andrew Danetree?"

"I'm real sorry, miss," the man told her, shaking his head. "I'm really not at liberty to—"

"Sir," said Amelia, "if those are the names of the people occupying Room 212, then there's every likelihood that those men have been murdered."

The man's cheek twitched. "Murdered? You don't mean *here*, in this hotel?"

Amelia nodded.

"What are you, the police or something?" the man demanded. "I think I need to see some ID."

I smiled at him. "We're not police, sir. We're just concerned neighbors. Now, would you mind if we went up to see if Mr Hope and Mr Danetree are actually there?"

"You can escort us, of course," said Amelia.

The man looked hesitant. I guess he was worried that we

were going to take him upstairs and mug him. We did look slightly less than respectable, after all. We had sponged blood from our clothes, so that they were spotted with rusty-colored damp patches, and none of us had been sleeping too good.

Amelia said, "It's just that we've heard such awful noises. We couldn't bear to think that they might be lying on the floor in pain, or anything like that."

After a lengthy think, the man took down his bunch of keys, buttoned up one more shirt-button, and called to some invisible woman in the room behind him, "Alma! I'm taking some people up to 212. Don't let those kids come in again!"

He came out from behind the counter. He had an artificial leg, so that he walked with a ducking, swinging motion, and creaked loudly with every step. "Damn kids," he complained. "They come in here and they steal anything that isn't superglued to the floor. See that square mark on the wall? Last week they stole a steel engraving of the Croton Reservoir. What's a nine-year-old kid going to do with a steel engraving of the Croton Reservoir?"

We crowded into a tiny elevator that felt as if it had been designed by Mr Otis to fit into his daughter's doll-house. The man kept creaking his leg and suppressing burps of gas. The elevator took about nine years to reach the second floor. Karen reached behind me and squeezed my hand, partly out of intimacy, I guess, but mostly out of claustrophobia. Amelia kept her eyes on the ceiling, as if willing us to rise faster.

The elevator doors juddered open. Then we were led along a gloomy, green-carpeted corridor lit by low-wattage bulbs. At last we reached Room 212, and the man gave a curiously old-fashioned Oliver Hardy–type knock.

"Mr Hope? Mr Danetree? Is there anybody in?"

He did this three times before he was satisfied that nobody was going to answer. I suppose he was trying to impress us that this was a real respectable hotel where a guest's privacy was paramount.

He held up his key and announced, "Pass key."

We all nodded. He unlocked the door and opened it wide.

"Mr Hope? Mr Danetree? It's Mr Rheiner, the manager."

Still no answer. The room was completely dark, and very cold. We sniffed the air and again we smelled that strange flat herbal aroma—the sort of smell that belonged to the open air and to vast distances. Karen shivered.

Mr Rheiner switched on the light. We found ourselves in a room that was almost exactly the same size as Naomi Greenberg's dining room, except that it had been partitioned off to create a small bathroom and a closet. There were two single beds, both of them covered in faded green candlewick throw-overs. The walls were decorated with combed plaster, painted pale yellow. The lemon-colored Venetian blind was closed tight.

"See, what did I tell you?" said Mr Rheiner, holding out his hands. "Nobody here. Whatever those two gentlemen are doing in New York, they certainly aren't doing it here."

I went to the closet and slid open the door. Inside hung three or four jackets, several pairs of slacks, and half-a-dozen clean shirts. Four of the shirts were fifteen-and-a-half-inch collar, the other two were seventeen. Mr Hope was obviously bigger than Mr Danetree, or else it was the other way about. There were five pairs of leather shoes on the closet floor, and one pair of canvas loafers.

"Hey—what are you doing?" demanded Mr Rheiner, swinging around. "You can't go nosing in there!"

"I'm sorry," I told him, sliding the door shut. "Forgot where I was for a moment." I wandered over to Amelia, and said, "Anything?"

Her eyes were glittering. She seemed extremely tense, highly charged up. "You bet there's something. Something very strong indeed—even stronger than the Greenbergs'."

I looked around, and sniffed. I could still smell that herby smell, but I couldn't sense anything else. "I don't feel anything," I said. "Nothing at all."

"That coldness?" she asked, her eyes narrowing in concentration.

"Sure, I can feel that."

"That *pain*?"

I shook my head. "I'd like to say yes, but I really don't think so."

Mr Rheiner shifted uncomfortably on his artificial leg. "Are you people quite finished now? Murder, for crying out loud. I ought to call the cops."

"I'm sorry," I said. I took out my wallet and gave him two crumpled-up portraits of Honest Abe. We left the room and then endured the endless elevator journey down to the lobby.

"I want to thank you for your help," I said, as we left the hotel.

"Do you want to leave a number or something?" Mr Rheiner asked me.

"A number?"

"You know, for when Mr Hope or Mr Danetree gets back."

"Oh, no. Thanks all the same. That won't be necessary."

"I'll tell them to keep the noise down."

"Thanks," I said. "You do that."

He watched us with deep suspicion as we pushed open the swing doors and stepped down into the street.

"Let's get ourselves a drink," I suggested. "I'm dying from a surfeit of spirits and a dire lack of booze."

We crossed the street and went into a bar called La Bohème. It was painted all in black, with plastic ivy hanging from the ceiling and black-painted chairs and tables, and Frenchified squeeze-box music coming out from behind a four-foot model of a cancan girl. It was one of the few remaining beatnik hangouts from the 1950s, when beatniks wore berets and beards and stripey sweaters and said "like" in front of every sentence. We sat down in the corner and ordered a bottle of red wine.

It was then that Karen reached into her purse and produced a small red plastic-covered diary.

"Look what I found," she said.

"Where did you get this?" I asked her.

"It was right there on one of the nightstands. He didn't even see me pick it up."

"You should take up house-breaking for a living. You're a natural-born burglar."

I ruffled through the diary with my thumb. It belonged to Andrew W. Danetree of Pocomoke City, Maryland. He had rounded, grade-school handwriting, and his diary entries were sparse and less-than-literate—but they turned out to be some of the most mysterious and fascinating reading I had ever come across.

While I was reading, Amelia said, "There's some force in that room, for definite. I could feel it. It's very cold, very *negative*. I don't quite know how to explain it, but in spiritual terms it feels like somebody's left the door wide open."

"The door to where?" asked Karen. "Or maybe I should ask *from* where?"

"If I knew that, I think I'd know exactly what this disturbance is all about."

I swallowed a mouthful of Paul Masson's worst. "Listen to this," I said. " '*Tuesday morning 4:25 pm stopped car outside of Salisbury & knew I had to go to NY. No reasonable explanation but I knew I had to.*' And here, listen '*Told Billie it was business, guess if I try to tell anybody about it they'll think I've flipped.*' "

I turned over a few more pages. " '*Arrived NY Thurs pm from Baltimore, taxi downtown. Had to locate the Belford Hotel on foot but here I am. Around 9 pm George H. a total stranger to me arrived from Brooklyn Center MN and said that he had experienced the same feeling too, right in the middle of work. He just had to come to NY whether he had liked it or not. He found the Belford by walking, too—experienced the same feeling of being drawn.*' "

"How about *that*?" said Amelia. She opened her purse and took out her cigarettes. "Here are two men who didn't know each other. One came from the back end of Maryland and the other from less-than-beautiful downtown Brooklyn Center, Minnesota. But suddenly they both got the inexplicable feeling that they *had* to go to New York."

"Not only inexplicable but irresistible," I said. "Our friend Andrew W. Danetree even lied to his wife so that he could come here. And these guys don't just get a *vague* feeling 'go to New York.' Oh, no. These guys have a compulsion to go to the exact same hotel. They're *drawn*."

Amelia lit her cigarette and said, "Read some more."

"Here we are. '*Spent most of Thurs nite trying to decide what made us both come here. We have nothing in common as far as we can work out. I was born in Baltimore and George was born in Cleveland, OH. My father was a painter and decorator, George's father was a captain in the Army. My background is German originally, George's family was probably Irish. I've been to NY before but George hasn't. So why are we both here? Why did we both feel exactly the same feeling?' "*

I turned over the next and last entry. " *'Woke up early Fri am feeling anxious & threatened. George reports the same. In fact he said he thinks we're going to die. He can't explain it. He says he had a nightmare about men and women being killed and mutilated, little children, too. Then he felt that there was a dark shadow standing close behind him, and he was too scared of it to turn around. I had a dream like that, too. My dream was so real I didn't know if I was asleep or awake. There was a shadow in the corner but it was much, much more than a shadow. It was watching me and it wanted to kill me.' "*

I closed the diary.

"Is that it?" asked Amelia, and I nodded.

"I have to see that room again," she said.

"Oh, yes? And how do you propose to do that? Especially with Rheiner the Whiner on the desk."

Amelia looked at me with those challenging eyes—the same challenging eyes that had eventually led me to look for somebody a little less demanding. "Do you have a head for heights?" she asked me.

"You're not expecting me to climb up a drainpipe?"

"No, but the fire escape from the Greenbergs' apartment and the fire escape from the Belford Hotel are only about five feet apart. All we have to do is jump from one to the other, and we can reach the back window of Room 212."

"Amelia—"I warned her.

But Amelia said, "Harry, we can't turn our backs on this now. We can't turn our backs on Martin Vaizey, either. We got him into this mess and now it's up to us to get him out of it. The only way we can do that is to *prove* beyond a shadow of a doubt that he was possessed."

" 'Shadow of a doubt,' hunh?" I said, sardonically. "And what if *we* get arrested for breaking in?"

"Under the circumstances, Mr Erskine, I think that's a chance we'll have to take."

I'm very uncomfortable with heights. I don't mind flying. I don't mind tall buildings. But I hate looking over cliffs at the sea foaming about two hundred feet below me; or standing on twenty-fifth floor balconies and looking down at the tops of people's heads and tiny cars and buses. For some weird reason, I'm always seized by this terrible urge to throw myself off—to find out what it's like to fall. They say that you're conscious right till the instant of impact. The trouble is, very few spirits have any clear recollection of how they died, especially the ones who died violently, and so you can't really ask them what it was like. Or so Amelia told me. Maybe they *do* remember but it's just too harrowing for them to talk about it.

The Greenbergs' window had been screwed into place, and it took us almost half an hour to free it. Eventually, however, I managed to prize out all of the screws and chip six or seven layers of dried paint away from the frame, and lift the lower sash two or three inches. When I couldn't force it up any further I pushed one end of Naomi Greenberg's ironing board into it and knelt on the other end with all of my weight. With a shuddering groan the window lifted and I overbalanced onto the floor, knocking my head against the leg of the couch. I used some spectacular language.

We climbed out onto the fire escape. Below us, the yard was shadowy and dark except for litter and broken glass. The fire escape groaned as Karen stepped onto it, and we all stood stock-still and listened.

"Are you sure it's safe?" asked Karen.

"No," I told her.

The Belford Hotel fire escape had looked pretty damned close when viewed from the inside of the Greenbergs' apartment. But now I was out here, seventy feet above a junk-strewn concrete yard, it mysteriously seemed to have shifted itself two or three feet further away.

I climbed with some difficulty over the railing of the Greenbergs' fire escape. By holding onto one of the rusty iron uprights I could then lean way out until I could grasp the railings of the Belford Hotel fire escape. That was the theory, anyway. In practice it looked way too far away; and way too high up; and way too God-damned dangerous.

I leaned further and further out. Below me I could make out the cinderblock wall that separated the Greenbergs' yard from the yard of the Belford Hotel. It was thickly encrusted with glittering slices of broken glass. I swallowed and looked up again. I didn't need to look down to know what would happen to me if I fell.

"Harry, are you okay?" called Amelia, in a loud stage-whisper.

"I don't know," I admitted. My grip on the rust-scaled upright seemed to be even more tenuous than ever, and I felt the strength in my knees gradually washing away like mud being hosed off a sidewalk. I thought: Jesus, I'm not going to make it. I'm going to fall. I'm going to hit that glass-topped wall and it's going to cut me in half. My legs are going to end up in the Greenbergs' yard and my torso's going to end up next door.

"You can reach it easy," Amelia urged me. "You only have to stretch out two or three inches further."

I closed my eyes for a moment and listened to the grumbling ambient roar of Manhattan's traffic, the sirens and the car-horns and the grinding of the trucks. I said a kind of prayer which involved God granting me the strength of Arnold Schwarzenegger, the balance of Blondin, and the bluff self-confidence of Teddy Roosevelt, if only on a purely temporary basis. Then I opened my eyes and focused on the fire-escape railing opposite and lunged for it.

And caught it. And swung across, barking my shin on the rusty cross-tie. And lost my footing, and swung around, barking my elbow and catching my ribs against the railing.

"Harry be careful!" called Karen, but I managed to snatch the railing and cling on tight.

"Holy shit," whispered Amelia. I don't know whether she was impressed or terrified.

I heaved myself over the railing and onto the fire-escape landing. My hands were smothered in rust, and my eyes were furiously watering.

"Are you okay?" asked Amelia. "We're coming across now!"

I leaned over the railing and helped Amelia and Karen to climb over. Then all three of us stood on the fire escape and looked at each other as if we'd achieved something really tremendous, like climbing Everest.

" 'I hope you realize that what we're going to do now is strictly illegal,' " I quoted.

Amelia was unfazed. "I think we're all fully aware of that. I think we're also fully aware that nobody else can do anything to save Martin but us. I think it's worth the risk, don't you?"

Karen glanced at me in that Bambi-admiring way of hers, and there was nothing else I could do but say, "For sure, of course I do. That's why I'm here."

I took out the screwdriver and wedged it into the Belford Hotel window. The frame was pretty rotten, and when I levered the screwdriver upwards, splinters of wood dropped onto the fire escape. But, miracle of miracles, the window was actually unlocked—and even though it took some strenuous pushing to slide it upwards in its sash, it wasn't long before I had heaved it up enough for us to climb inside.

The bedroom was dark and cold and filled with the same herbal aroma. We stood by the window for a moment, so that our eyes could get accustomed to the gloom. Then I said, "Karen—can you lock the door and put on the security chain? Then listen out for Gimpy Rheiner."

Amelia was standing between the two beds. She looked very pale and still. "Anything?" I asked her.

She nodded. "There's something here. Something close. I have a very strong feeling about a door being open."

"You mean, like a spiritual door?"

Again she nodded. "But it's not like anything I ever felt before. It feels *dangerous,* if you know what I mean. Like a roller-coaster ride in pitch darkness."

"I went on one of those in Disneyland."

"This is a hell of a lot more dangerous than Disneyland."

She closed her eyes. "I feel it. It's very, very close. It's there, to the right."

"I can't see anything," I told her.

Her eyes were still closed. "It's there, right there!"

"I still don't see anything!" I said, beginning to panic.

But then she opened her eyes wide and pointed at the bed. *"It's there!"*

With a huge surge of fright, I dragged back the blankets; there was nothing there but a rumpled sheet. "Where?" I demanded. "Where?"

"Under the bed!" Amelia shrilled at me. *"It's under the bed!"*

I stared at her. I was trying hard not to hyperventilate.

"Under the bed?" Her eyes stayed tight shut. Her cheek-muscles were taut. Her jaw was rigid. "Umh-humh," she said.

I turned back to the bed. All of my life I've been afraid of things lurking under beds. Even when I was a kid I didn't let my toes peek out from under the covers, because I knew for an absolute fact that trolls with razor-sharp teeth were hiding and waiting, and as soon as I peeked my toes out they would bite them off.

When I grew older I could never quite shake that feeling off. Under the bed was a dark space where anything could lurk, where anything could wait for you while you were asleep, ready to snatch at your unprotected ankles.

Karen, from the door, said, "Ssh! I think I can hear the elevator!"

"The bed, Harry," Amelia repeated. "It's under the bed."

I thought: what the hell did I come here for? Why the hell did I allow Karen to get me mixed up in all of this? I thought of Martin, under arrest for a surrealistic murder that he hadn't really committed—that's if you believed in psychic possession. But what if you *didn't* believe in psychic possession? Supposing the whole jury was made up of James Randis? What then? I was risking my life for nothing, and for somebody I hardly even knew.

Erskine, I thought, you've already donated quite enough sweat and adrenalin to other people's good causes—not to mention all that pleasurable and profitable business that you've sacrificed. How about taking care of yourself for a change? I hadn't known either of the Greenbergs; I hadn't been acquainted with Martin Vaizey, not until Amelia sent me round to Central Park West. I was an innocent by-stander, that's all, and it was only my emotional involvement with Karen and Amelia that was keeping me here.

But—*"The bed!"* screamed Amelia—and I seized the end of the bed and hefted it over to the right.

What I saw under that bed made me stumble two paces back; and then another pace; and stand with my back hard against the wall. I was trembling and sweating and I had to keep coughing to clear my throat. I was like a man who has nearly stepped over a precipice, except that this was much more frightening than any precipice. This was *forever*.

Beneath the bed, there was a narrow trench in the floor, as narrow as a freshly-dug grave; but this grave was totally black and totally cold and apparently bottomless. I couldn't understand where it went. Down through the floor, down through the room below, and the room below that, and then thousands and thousands of feet, down through the solid bedrock? How could that be?

A thin icy wind keened almost silently through the hole, more like a memory of a wind than a real wind.

I didn't understand how such a hole could exist, and I didn't particularly want to understand it either. I turned to Amelia and said, "What? What the hell is it?"

She opened her eyes. "It's the door," she said, with great simplicity.

"The door? The door to where?"

"The door that somebody opened and then forgot to close. Or didn't *want* to close."

"But what's *down* there? Where does it go?"

Amelia leaned over it for a long time, making sure that she didn't stand too near to the edge. Her hair flew out behind her, proving that the grave was wide open; and that some kind of wind was blowing through, whether it was real or imaginary.

"It's remarkable," she said, standing up straight. "It's truly remarkable. It's one of the largest openings I've ever come across."

Karen said, "Sssh! I'm sure I heard the elevator!"

I glanced down at the empty black hole under the bed. "You've seen something like this before?" I asked Amelia.

"Oh, yes. They're quite common. But they're usually very, very small. Like a reflecting puddle, maybe; or a chip of broken glass; or a mirror; or a miniature picture. They're like windows. They happen everywhere. In the street in the countryside, everywhere you look. They let us see right through to the world of spirits; and in return, the spirits can see us."

"So—these windows—these doors—they work two ways?" I asked her.

"That's right. They're better than television, better than a book. If you can keep a window open for long enough, you can watch somebody's life, year after year."

I looked down at the cold black hole. "There's nobody down there—not as far as I can make out."

Amelia said, "I don't know *what's* down there. The last hole I saw was about the size of a pinprick. I never saw anything like this before."

"So what do we do?" I asked her.

"I don't know," she said. "This is way beyond the limit of my expertise. I mean, this is spirit activity on a massive scale. It's powerful, it's sustained. It obviously has some purpose, but I don't know what."

At that moment, there was a knock at the door, and Karen hissed, "Harry!" and backed away from it quickly.

A voice called out, "Mr Hope? Mr Danetree?"

"Oh, God, it's Hopalong Rheiner," I said. "Time we made a graceless exit."

Mr Rheiner knocked again. "Just want to check your bathroom, gentlemen. Some of the drains have been backing up."

There was a lengthy pause, and then we heard a passkey turning in the lock. The door jarred open on the security chain, and Mr Rheiner said, "Mr Hope? Mr Danetree? Who's in there?"

The door rattled violently, and Mr Rheiner shouted, "Who's in there? Who is that? If you don't open the door, I'll call the cops!"

"What are we going to do?" asked Karen, on the verge of panic.

"We'll play it straight," I told her. "We'll let Mr Rheiner in, we'll show him the hole and tell him what we're doing. Look at it, there's no denying its existence! A hole, right, six feet by three feet, and it goes down for ever!"

"But he'll call the police, or make us leave," said Amelia. "And we *have* to find out what this hole is."

I lifted my hand reassuringly. Have no fear, Erskine's here. I went to the door and stood in front of it for a while, watching it furiously shake and rattle, and then I said, "Mr Rheiner?"

"Who the hell are you? How d'you know my name?"

"Mr Rheiner, it's Harry Erskine, from next door. My friends and I visited this room a little earlier today."

"Oh, it's you! I said to my wife, there's something I don't like about those people. I didn't like you the moment I clapped eyes on you."

"Mr Rheiner, we're not trying to cause trouble. But we've discovered something important—something that may explain what happened to George Hope and Andrew Danetree."

"Listen, friend." Mr Rheiner raged, "either you get out of that room *now,* this minute, or else I'm going to call the cops and have you arrested for trespass."

"Mr Rheiner, you don't understand."

"You're damned right I don't understand! I run a respectable hotel here! Nobody got themselves murdered here and nobody did anything illegal or immoral! So get the hell out while I'm still feeling generous about it!"

I drew back the security chain and opened the door. Mr Rheiner was standing in the corridor with a furiously scarlet face. He was brandishing a policeman's nightstick.

"Right," he said, swinging his way into the room. "I want you out, and I want you out now, no arguments!"

I pointed to the hole in the floor. Black, empty, keening and cold. Mr Rheiner stared at it and then he stared at me. His eyeballs glistened with disbelief.

"You see?" I challenged him. "I was telling the truth."

"You pulled up the floorboards," he said, accusingly.

"No, sir. No way."

"You pulled up the goddamned floorboards! Do you have any idea how much that's going to *cost* me?!"

"Mr Rheiner, look at it. Nobody pulled up the floorboards!"

Mr Rheiner peered at the hole. Then, slowly, he eased himself down on his knees next to it and stared right into it. He poked his nightstick into it, as far as it would go. The hole was dark and deep and totally empty.

"Give me that book," he said, jerking his head towards the windowsill. A dog-eared copy of Ogden Nash poems was lying on the nightstand. I reluctantly picked it up and passed it over. Mr Rheiner took it and flipped it without hesitation into the hole.

He peered down after it. "It's falling," he said, in awe. "It's falling."

Amelia glanced at me impatiently.

"It's not your ordinary kind of hole in the floor, Mr Rheiner," she told him.

"The book's still falling," said Mr Rheiner, in awe. "It must be a hundred feet down, and it's still falling."

I was tempted for a split second to give him a kick up the backside, and send him tumbling down the hole to fall as far as his book was falling—which as far as I could see, was forever. I checked my watch. I looked at Amelia, but Amelia must have guessed what I was thinking, because she shook her head. I could guess what she would say to me: that if I kicked a living man down a spiritual hole, I'd disrupt the equilibrium of the spirit world so violently that all human existence could stop dead, right here and now, as if it had never happened.

I remembered Adelaide Bright telling me that for every psychic success we have a psychic bill to pay, and sometimes that bill is almost more than anybody could bear.

Mr Rheiner stood up. "There's a hole here," he said, in an oddly matter-of-fact voice. "A damned great hole, all the way down to the basement. All the way down to the god-damned *sewers*."

He stood up and faced us, brushing his pants. "I think you people owe me some kind of explanation, don't you? In one afternoon, you've dug a damned great hole, all the way down to God knows where? And you dug it so's I didn't even hear? What about the Kinseys, in the apartment below. You think *they're* going to tolerate such a hole? I just had their ceiling replastered."

"Mr Rheiner—"I began, but he loudly shushed me.

"You listen to me, feller, I don't want to hear anything you have to say. All I know is, you've wrecked at least three of my best rooms. Either you agree to have them all repaired—and I mean repaired quick—or else I call the cops. In any case, I don't want to see you or your lady friends in my hotel ever again, and I mean *ever,* period. What these two ladies see in you, I can't even begin to imagine."

"Mr Rheiner—" I began again, but I knew that there wasn't much point. It's always sad and embarrassing when people start being personal.

Amelia, said, "Harry, I need to try some tests," but Mr Rheiner stood defensively in front of the hole and folded his arms.

"You're not coming anywhere near. I want your names and I want your addresses and I want to hear you say that you're going to make all of this damage good."

"Mr Rheiner, I don't think you understand what this is all about," said Amelia. "There's a hole in this room, for sure; but if you go downstairs to the apartment below, I don't think you'll find that there's any hole at all."

Mr Rheiner pugnaciously folded his arms. "Lady, this hole is hundreds of feet deep. What the hell do you take me for? Some kind of retard?"

"You're a retard if you think we dug our way through three floors and hundreds of feet of bedrock in a couple of hours, without machinery and without spoil and without making any sound at all."

Mr Rheiner pointed at her accusingly, and then at me. "I'll find out how you did it. You mark my words. I'll find out how."

Even as he spoke, however, I saw wisps of what looked like black smoke drifting out of the hole, and sliding in a curious sideways motion under the bed. The smoke grew thicker, until it was blowing around his ankles. Amelia began to back away and took hold of Karen's arm so that she retreated, too.

Mr Rheiner said, "There's no use in your trying to duck out of this. You're going to pay for this damage no matter what."

"What *is* that?" I whispered to Amelia, as the smoke around Mr Rheiner's ankles billowed denser and blacker. It didn't smell like smoke. It didn't dissipate like smoke. It seemed to swell, and to grow denser, until it loomed over Mr Rheiner like a hugely-exaggerated shadow.

It *was* a shadow. It wasn't smoke at all. It was the raw stuff of darkness; the raw stuff of fright and fear. It grew heavy-headed and forbidding, until it loomed behind Mr Rheiner in a hideous parody of his own lumpen disabled shape. It *was* him; and yet it was something more, something *other*. It was like all that was blackest in his own soul, climbing above him in a threatening theater of mockery and destructive hatred.

"Now, what do you propose to do about this damage?" he demanded. "Because sure as eggs you're going to make it good. That's nearly two thousand bucks' worth of damage, believe you me. Maybe more, new rug and all."

Amelia said, "Mr Rheiner—step this way. Very gently. Don't worry about why. Just step this way."

Mr Rheiner frowned at her. "What the devil are you talking about, young lady?"

"Just step this way, Mr Rheiner, there's something dangerous behind you! Something—!"

For a moment, Mr Rheiner just stared at her—unable to understand what she was saying. But then the coin dropped and he slowly turned his head and looked behind him.

His head turned *and continued to turn*. It went round the full 360 degrees like Linda Blair in *The Exorcist* but it didn't turn smoothly and it didn't stop there. It turned with a hideous crackling and tearing noise; the skin of Mr Rheiner's neck was twisted around like yellowish-pink rope. His face came around for a second time and he was still staring at us in disbelief. Technically, he was already dead, but his eyes were still showing pain and terror and surprise.

The shadow curled and fumed around his legs as if it were the slithering tentacles of a giant squid. Quickly, with obscene haste, two tentacles probed the front of his shirt, tearing aside buttons and sliding inside. His whole body shuddered and shook as the tentacles dragged apart skin and muscle and layers of whitish belly-fat, ripping him open as easily as a sodden paper shopping-sack—and then continued relentlessly to pour inside him.

"*Harry!*" screamed Karen. "*Harry, it's killing him!*"

But of course it was already too late for me to help him—even if I'd had the courage to try. His head nodded wildly from side to side, an epileptic puppet. Then thick black shadow gushed out of his mouth, and wound itself around his face, like a suffocating scarf. Karen screamed again and again as Mr Rheiner danced in front of us, much nimbler in death than he had ever been in life. His artificial leg collapsed inside the leg of his pants, clattered to the floor. But still he danced.

"*Out of here!*" I shouted at Karen and Amelia.

For a split second Karen stood paralyzed, but then, with her arms stretched out defensively in front of her, she made a sudden and frenzied run for the open door. She was too late. A shadow whiplashed across the door and slammed it furiously shut.

Karen tugged at the handle and screamed out, "Harry! Help me!" I came up and yanked at it too, so hard that I almost pulled off the handle. But whatever was holding it shut was much more powerful than both of us.

"*I command you open!*" cried Amelia. "*By salt, by fire, by mirror, by key!*"

I wrenched at the door again, but it stayed adamantly shut.

"*Open once! Open twice!*" Amelia screamed at it, "*Open demon! Open ghost! Nail this devil to the post!*"

Behind me, I heard an appalling rumbling noise, as if the entire building were collapsing. I looked around to see the monstrous shadow *ripping Mr Rheiner's scalp off,* blood and hair and ragged skin. Then, almost as an afterthought, with all the casualness of true cruelty, it twisted off his arms and legs.

There was a moment's lull, and then we were scourged by a fierce, cold wind, full of blood and grit and pungent, eye-stinging smoke. Karen and Amelia were both screaming. Blood streaked Karen's cheek and poured from her chin. Blood dripped from Amelia's hair.

"*Open once! Open twice!*" Amelia was shrieking.

Amelia may have been able to lock doors, but she sure as hell couldn't open them: not when she was up against a spiritual force as violent as this. I kicked at the door and kicked again, and at last one of the lower panels began to split.

"Harry, for God's sake!" Amelia urged me.

I quickly looked over my shoulder. As I did so, I caught sight of my face in the mirror on the bedroom wall. I had seen Karen and Amelia smothered in Mr Rheiner's blood, but I hadn't realized that *my* face, too, had been turned into a scarlet and grisly mask. I shouted out loud in horror and surprise, and Amelia demanded, "What? What?"

"Jesus," I started to say. "I thought I was—" But behind us the shadow was filling the room, darker and colder, looming over us like cruelty and menace made visible. I didn't have time to think. I had to kick.

I slammed my foot into the door again and again. The left-hand lower panel splintered and burst. Then I managed to kick out the center rail. I could hear Karen screaming almost continuously, but there was nothing I could do but give the door two more kicks until it cracked into pieces.

"Out!" I shouted, catching hold of Amelia's arm. Bloody-faced, dazed, Amelia stepped over the broken framework and scrambled into the corridor.

I turned round to help Karen. But Karen had suddenly stopped screaming. She was standing with her arms by her sides, blood-smeared and bedraggled and rigid, staring at me with a peculiar expression—not so much an expression of alarm, but something much more frightening—an expression of *hopelessness,* as if she had already given up.

"Karen?" I said.

The shadow was all around her. It seemed to pass across her face like a cloud passing over the sun. I looked up at it, swallowing in fear, and I swear I could see the shape of a huge distorted *head,* nodding slightly, as if it were too heavy and overcalcified for its owner to carry. I heard a low groaning sound, too, a vibration so low that it made my teeth buzz.

"Karen, are you okay?"

Karen didn't answer. I wasn't sure if she could hear me or not.

"Karen, all you have to do is walk towards me. One step at a time."

Beside the bed, Mr Rheiner's bloodied torso rolled without warning, and disappeared into the empty hole. There was a slight flicker of light that reminded me of summer lightning out on the plains. Mr Rheiner's scalp slithered into the hole, too, like an obedient rat, leaving a glistening maroon trail. Then part of his stomach twitched after it, some terrible scarlet part that I couldn't even identify. Then his artificial leg. Another slight flicker of light.

Karen stood beneath the shadow and her eyes were wide.

"Karen," I said, reaching out my hand. "Just take it real easy, everything's going to be fine."

Still she said nothing. I didn't even know whether she could see me or not. Her eyes didn't appear to be properly focused.

"Karen, I want you to take hold of my hand. Everything's fine. It's only a shadow, right? It's nothing. If it has any power to hurt you, that power comes from *you,* from inside your own head." I tapped my forehead, in case she didn't understand. "All you have to do is say, 'It can't hurt me, it's only a shadow,' and then take hold of my hand."

Karen's eyes turned glazed and dreamy. One second she had been screaming-hysterical. Now she looked as if she were high on magic mushrooms. Slow, strange, otherworldly.

"You took her away from me before . . ." she whispered. *"This time you will not be so lucky."*

"What?" I said. 'What are you talking about? Karen—come on!" I reached out and tried to snatch her hand from her side.

But the hand I touched wasn't Karen's hand. It surely didn't *feel* like Karen's hand. It felt cold and dry and wrinkled, like a man's hand, a man with rings and beads around his fingers. I felt something else, too. The spidery tickling of something hairy that must have been invisibly dangling round this man's wrist.

I jerked my hand away and stared at Karen, bewildered.

"You can do nothing, white devil—nothing at all. You have no power over me now. I have learned my warcraft well."

"Harry!" called Amelia, from the corridor outside. "Are you all right in there? Where's Karen?"

"Just wait up!" I called back. "Please, Amelia—stay where you are! I'll be out in a minute!"

I tried to sound confident. I tried to sound as if I was in control. But in actual fact my heart was thumping slowly and painfully, and my mouth was filled with the sharp penny-dreadful taste of fear.

Karen said, *"Once I travelled like the shadow of the eagle over many thousands of moons to reclaim what truly belonged to my people."* Her voice was extraordinary, as if five or six people were all speaking at once, in chorus. Her face was still veiled in shadow. *"I was reborn, and I sought my just revenge. But I did not understand how much you had changed our world. I did not understand that you had destroyed not only our lodges and our hunting-grounds, but our sacred places, too. The lakes and rivers in which our water-spirits once thrived are now as dead as your souls. The air in which our wind-spirits once flew is poisoned as your hearts are poisoned. Even the grasses and the trees have been suffocated, like unwanted children."*

Karen paused, and then she said, *"In such a world, I had no power. So I called on more of my kind; and more of my spirits; but still we had no power. You had done more than murder my people; you had murdered a cosmos. You had murdered spirits which will never walk this earth again—fragile spirits, subtle spirits—spirits which can tell a hunter where a deer is concealed, or how a stream will flow. You had murdered spirits of lightning and rain.*

"The sadness is that you destroyed all of these things before you ever had a chance to encounter them. You laid waste an entire world—and you were not even aware that it was there."

I looked Karen directly in the eyes. Her pupils were darkly dilated, and I knew that he was there. He was using her to speak in the way that he had used her to speak before. Those without substance have to speak through those who have.

"Misquamacus," I said, my voice shaking with emotion and rage. "Misquamacus the greatest of all Algonquin wonder-workers. Misquamacus to whom time and space mean absolutely zilch. Misquamacus who kills innocent people without any guilt whatsoever; and who hides himself like a jackrabbit in the souls of children and defenseless women."

Karen's eyes flared. *"Do you want me to take this woman's scalp, right in front of your eyes?"*

"Are you brave enough?" I challenged him. Thinking— please God, don't let him be brave enough. Please God, make him proud and arrogant, rather than cruel.

And please God, shoehorn him out of her, would You, please, and then connect him up to all of the lightning bolts in heaven above, and cremate him for good and all.

"Harry!" called Amelia, in high anxiety. "What's happening?"

I held out my hand yet again. "Misquamacus, this woman has no quarrel with you. None of us do. Please, let her go."

Karen raised both hands, and covered her face so that only her eyes looked out. *"I have need of her. She was once my host and my protector. She will be so again. She will speak for me; and she will be my hostage, too, until my work among the shadows is all done, and the sacred lands are sacred again, and my people can ride in the wind."*

"Misquamacus!" I shouted at him. "You can't take Karen, not again! It'll kill her!"

"When you speak of one woman's death, think of Sand Creek. Think of Wounded Knee."

"Don't take her, please," I begged him. Thinking: come on, God, come on, God. For Christ's sake, come on, God. Lightning bolts, earthquakes, anything! "Listen—don't take her, take me." Shades of Father Karras!

But Misquamacus had lived and died and travelled through long shadowy centuries to avenge and protect his people. He had suffered agonies of body and agonies of spirit. Even if there was anything left in him that was still human, there was nothing left in him that was at all forgiving. Not towards the white devils, who sat in automobiles all across his hunting-grounds, polluting the air so that the wind-spirits fell out of the sky like suffocated doves. Not towards the white devils, who had poisoned the very last ghost

in his sacred lakes, and turned water into his enemy rather
than his friend.

I almost wished I could sympathize with him. But I was
me and he was him, and tepees and buffalo-hunting were a
little behind the times as far as world economics went. We
couldn't fight the Japanese electronics industry with wind-
spirits and ethnic sentiment and a few hundred Navajo
blankets.

Karen kept her hands over her face. Her eyes glittered like
other eyes. *"I have learned much, white devil. Now it is your
turn to learn. You have your Day of Judgment—we have ours.
Soon you will discover what it is like to live, as we have, in the
Great Outside, without light or hope."*

"Misquamacus, let her go."

I tried to grab her. I caught the sleeve of her blouse. But
then the shadow collapsed on top of me like five sackfuls of
coal, and I was buried in blackness. I heard Karen cry out.
Not so much a scream, but a heart-rending cry for help. *Not
again, not again, not that hideous nightmare again!*

I managed to raise my head just in time to see the shadow
funneling back into the empty hole in the floor, and Karen
sliding in with it.

"Karen!" I snatched her hand, and for a long, strained
moment I managed to keep a tenuous, three-fingered hold
on her. *"Karen, fight back!"*

I tried to adjust my grip, get a better hold. Karen was
being dragged away from me with almost irresistible force,
as if she were being sucked into a giant vacuum-cleaner. She
wasn't crying; she wasn't screaming. She was concentrating
every last ounce of strength on holding onto my hand.

I felt myself being dragged along the floor, too. I
managed to hook my left foot around the leg of the left-
hand bed, and that slowed us down a little. Karen had actually *disappeared* into the hole, right up to her waist, and she
was twisting her body from side to side. I didn't know
whether this hole bore any resemblance to quicksand—
whether you sank more quickly if you struggled—but I
shouted, *"Keep still! Keep still! Just pull!"*

Right behind me, Amelia came back into the room, and

without a word she took hold of my belt in one hand and seized hold of the bed with the other.

For a few seconds, I believed that we were winning. Karen managed to lift one knee onto the brink of the hole, and I reached out with my other hand and caught hold of the shoulder of her blouse.

"Pull!" I told Amelia. "One big effort and we should get her out!"

I grunted and strained and we gained an inch; and then another inch.

"Give me your other hand!" I told Karen. "Here—give me your other hand!"

I offered her my right hand. She reached out for it.

"That's it, you've almost done it!"

But then she looked at me with wild piggy-eyed triumph, and harshly laughed in my face. Her hand was cold and hard as a claw, a man's hand, and she twisted my fingers around until I heard the cartilage crunch.

I roared at her, *"Stop, Karen, don't let him do it!"* But she twisted my left hand, too, almost crushing my fingers. The pain was incredible. I had to let her go.

"Karen!" I yelled. But with a sharp *ffwwooossshhh!* she slid across the rug and into the empty hole. Immediately, the rug closed up around her, and the last I saw of her was an upraised hand, clutching, clutching, like the hand of a swimmer going down for the third time.

I hammered on the floor with my fist but it was solid, and I knew that I had lost her.

Amelia touched my shoulder. "Harry," she said. "I'm sorry, Harry. I wish I could have helped more. I wish I *hadn't* helped at all."

I knew what she meant. I slowly stood up and looked around the smoky, blood-spattered room.

"Misquamacus," I repeated. "I really hoped and prayed that I'd seen the last of him. The great Indian crusader. The great Red hope."

"Harry, there's nothing more you can do."

"Jesus!" I shouted. I punched the wall in anger and grief and blinding frustration. "Doesn't he understand that it's all over? The buffalo hunts and the war-parties and the

God-damned pow-wows? It's all over—gone!—whether we're sorry about it or not!"

Amelia put her arms around me and held me very close. "Come on, Harry, let's just get ourselves out of here before somebody calls the police. We've got enough trouble on our plates, without the law."

I turned back and stared at the place where the hole had been.

"That Misquamacus is damned to hell," I said, in a voice like mashed-up glass. "That Misquamacus is damned to hell. Even if I have to take him there myself."

Chicago

Behind the brightly-lit theater of the Revlon cosmetics counter at Marshall Field, Nann Bryce waited with tightly stage-managed patience while the woman tried Caribbean Glow for the third time, pressing her lips tightly together, and then pouting at herself in the magnifying mirror. "I don't know," the woman told her. "I still think it's *way* too dark for me."

"Maybe you'd like to try the Tropical Kiss again," Nann suggested. It was seven after one, seven minutes into Nann's lunchbreak, and she was anxious to meet Trixie to see if the results of Trixie's test had come through. She was supposed to be meeting her at Orlowski's Coffee Shop at a quarter past, and she didn't want to be late. Trixie was volatile at the best of times. All this trouble with Nat had made her ten times more jumpy and irritable than usual.

The woman turned her face from side to side. "I don't know. Do *you* think it's too dark?"

Nann said, "It depends on how you want to present yourself. Do you want to have that sultry, exotic look; or do you want to look bright and outgoing?"

"Well, exotic," the woman declared. "I mean *mysterious,* you know? I want my husband to think, 'Here's a woman with something more about her than I ever knew.'"

Nann smiled. "In that case, Caribbean Glow's the one for you, no question." Pause. "Is that cash or charge?"

It was almost twenty-five past one by the time Nann dodged through the jammed-up traffic on Washington Street and hurried into Orlowski's. The midday sun was brassy and uncomfortably hot, and the city was unusually airless. This morning's weather forecast had predicted high humidity, smog pollution and electric storms. No wind off the lake.

At least Orlowski's was cool, mirrored and mosaic-floored, with palms nodding in the air-conditioned draft.

Trixie was sitting in the far corner next to the wall-mirror, drinking coffee. She was nineteen years old, skinny and startlingly pretty—her hair back-combed and spritzed up. She wore black pedal-pushers and three layers of T-shirt and black cotton jacket. Nann thought that Janet Jackson had nothing on Trixie; but while Janet Jackson danced and sang and made millions, Trixie courted nothing but trouble. The latest trouble, of course, being Nat.

"Oh, honey . . . I'm so sorry I'm late," Nann told her, parking her bag and sitting down next to her. "It was Caribbean Glow or Tropical Kiss and she couldn't make up her mind for hard cash. 'I want my husband to think, "Here's a woman with something more about her than I ever knew." ' "

Trixie gave her a slanted, humorless smile. She looked like her father when she did that. Her father had died four years ago in a stupid car accident on Dundee Avenue, by Santa's Village. A huge delivery truck had charged out of a side-turning like a dinosaur. Oil, snow, and blood on the highway. Nann still missed him sorely, and still cried at Christmas. Some people died and the space they left in the world seemed to close and heal, but the space that Trixie's father had left behind him was still vacant. In Nann's heart, at least, and probably in Trixie's, and Marshall's, too. Marshall was Nann's younger child and only son.

"Coffee," Nann told the waitress. And then, to Trixie, "You eaten?"

Trixie shook her head. Nann said, "What's the special?"

"Meatloaf."

"Bring me two turkey on rye."

"Momma," protested Trixie, "I don't want anything."

The waitress hesitated. "You deaf?" Nann demanded. "Two turkey on rye."

The waitress left. Trixie had tears sparkling in her eyes. "Momma," she said, shaking her head.

"You're pregnant," said Nann, taking a clean handkerchief out of her purse and unfolding it. Trixie still wasn't old enough to unfold her own handkerchiefs: at least, not the way that Nann saw it. Trixie dabbed her eyes and looked distraught.

Nann said, "You're sitting in the corner with nothing but coffee and a face like a funeral, and I can't guess you're pregnant?"

"It's due February fourteenth, St Valentine's Day."

Nann sat back in exasperation. "How appropriate. The St Valentine's Day Fiasco."

"Momma, we were so *careful!*"

"Oh, *sure* you were careful. Careful to enjoy yourselves. Careful not to think about the consequences. Careful not to consider that poor baby you're carrying, what its future is going to be, with Nat the Hat for a poppa, and Trixie the Airhead for a momma. Are you going to give birth to this child? If so, how are you going to take care of it? And what about your education? What about you? What about everything we planned?"

Trixie banged down her coffee cup. "The next thing you're going to tell me is that I've betrayed poppa's memory, is that it?"

Nann covered her eyes with her hand. "I'm sorry. I guess I'm disappointed, that's all. I feel like it's my fault."

Trixie held her mother's hand. "Momma, Nat loves me and I love him. I know you think that he's no good at all; but then your folks didn't like poppa, did they? What happened—it's nobody's *fault.* You were younger than me when you had me, weren't you? We made a mistake, for sure. We shouldn't have had a baby so soon. But we'll work it out, one way or another."

Nann took her handkerchief back and wiped her eyes. "How many times do you think mothers have conversations like this, all over the world? Every day, I shouldn't wonder, in every town and every city you can name."

She looked up. "I don't know. I guess times change. What you hoped for yourself, what you wished for your children, that can't always be. Sometimes what happens is what's best."

The waitress brought their turkey sandwiches. They both looked down at them, then up at each other. "Go on," smiled Nann. "You have to eat for two."

Trixie picked her sandwich up and stared at it. Nann took a bite out of hers, and started to chew. But her mouth refused to produce any saliva, and she was just chewing and chewing, a big wad of turkey breast and dry bread that wouldn't be swallowed, no matter what.

Nann started to sob. Tears ran down her cheeks and down the sides of her mouth and plopped on to her plate. She couldn't help herself. She didn't know whether she was

happy or sad or shocked or just plain silly. But in the end
she had to take out her mouthful of sandwich in her napkin
and put it in the ashtray, and dab her eyes again, because
she was only thirty-eight years old, God help me, and she
was going to be a grandmother.

Trixie said, "Momma—don't cry. There's no use to cry.
Everything's going to work out, one way or another. At
least this baby's got himself a future."

Nann was still sobbing and Trixie was still holding her
hand when the world became a different place.

They couldn't understand what had happened at first.
They thought that somebody had thrown a brick at Orlowski's window, because it cracked diagonally all the way
across, and palms tipped over, their china planters shattering on the mosaic floor. Plaster sifted from the ceiling,
chairs tipped. *Earthquake?* they thought. They'd read about
earthquakes, seen them on the news. But then all the wall-
mirrors warped and exploded, and women were screaming,
and glass was sparkling everywhere. *Earthquake!* somebody
screamed (or maybe they didn't—maybe they all just
thought it, all together—like the crowd that watches an airplane crashing, and thinks *oh, no, dear God, oh, no!* but nobody can actually manage to speak).

Trixie clutched her mother's wrist. Her mother's wrist
with its silver charm bracelet. All the charms that her father
had given her—the lucky horseshoe and the wedding bell,
and the strange crooked salamander. But then they didn't
have a moment to say anything; or even to look at each
other, because out of the window they could see Marshall
Field's store collapsing—the whole building *collapsing,* as if
it had been dynamited.

The summer fashion displays in the State Street windows
vanished completely. Windows burst, mannequins flung up
their arms in grotesque gestures of despair. Then they were
gone, drowned in concrete. Above them, floor after floor
came thundering down—steel, glass, concrete—thousands
of tons of building and goods and elevators and staircases,
all dropping into the subways beneath, and then deeper, and
deeper still, with hundreds of shoppers and sales assistants
dropping down with them. It was like the *Titanic* sinking on

land—a huge building full of wealthy shoppers disappearing into the bedrock, as if it had struck an iceberg.

Nann stood by the cracked window of Orlowski's with her mouth open and watched Marshall Field's roar thunderously into oblivion. Trixie stood a little way behind her. The cloud of dust and concrete shone like fog, gilded and choking. Gradually, it sifted to the ground, and the sun began to penetrate, but Orlowski's and all the surrounding area was oddly silent, as if the world had suddenly come to an end. It was only when they heard sirens in the distance that people began to move, and talk, and hurry outside.

Nann stood on the sidewalk and stared at the rubble-strewn site where Marshall Field's had once been. Trixie came up and stood beside her. They could barely see each other through the dust.

"This is ridiculous," said Nann. It was all she could think of to say.

Trixie was in shock, the back of her hand pressed to her forehead.

"This is ridiculous!" Nann screamed at her. *"A whole building doesn't just vanish!"*

"Earthquake," said Trixie. She took her hand away from her forehead and covered her mouth, as if she were about to retch. "Didn't you hear those people say earthquake?"

Nann stared at her. "This isn't any earthquake! This building is *gone*! All of my friends, all of the people I work with! They're *gone*! Look at it, there's nothing left! Only bricks, and bits and pieces! Where's the building gone, child? Where's the people who were in it? Where's it *gone*, Trixie? Where's the whole damned block gone to? This was Marshall Field's! This was *Marshall Field's*! Where does Marshall Field's disappear to, all of a sudden?"

"I don't know," said Trixie, turning her back, shivering, chilled with fright. "I don't *want* to know."

All around them, almost overwhelming the whooping and honking of firetrucks and ambulances, they heard deeper rumbling noises. Chunks of concrete and masonry began to rain down heavily onto the streets, some of them bouncing and shattering on the sidewalk, some of them noisily crushing taxis and automobiles.

Buildings were falling everywhere; but not just falling, they were *vanishing,* disappearing into the ground as if they had never been built. The noise was huge: worse than an earthquake. Drumming like mad drummers; thundering like summer thunderstorms. Nann put her arm around Trixie's shoulders and clutched her tight; but for some unaccountable reason Nann *knew* she knew why this was happening, just like her grandmother had told her, just like her great-grandmother had told her grandmother: she *knew*.

This was the time that the slaves had predicted. This was the fulfilment of the prophecy that they had brought across from Africa. We can suffer these centuries of bondage and woe; we can suffer this captivity, o Lord. Because one day this land will fall. One day this civilization will crumble. A house that is built on suffering is built on sand, that's what her grandmother used to say, over and over, and Nann had never understood what she meant, until now.

A gigantic block of reinforced concrete dropped from the building above them, twenty or thirty tons of it, but instead of shattering when it hit the sidewalk, it *vanished*. More concrete rained down; then huge panes of glass; then window frames and ducting and zig zag flights of concrete stairs.

A man was running along the sidewalk towards them when Nann glimpsed something flash in the dusty sunlight just above his head. It wasn't until it had actually hit him on top of the head, edge-on, that she realized it was a sheet of glass. It went down him at a slight diagonal, from the left side of his skull to his right knee, slicing him completely in half. Then it instantly disappeared, with an odd ringing noise, into the concrete flagstones.

The man continued standing in the same position for a slow count of three. His eyes were wide open, his glasses had been sheared in half at the bridge of the nose. His short-sleeved shirt and his pale grey slacks were marked with a fine toothbrush-splatter of blood.

Nann whispered, "Lord," and crossed herself; and when she crossed herself the man slid in half, becoming two butchered men instead of one. His insides dropped onto the sidewalk in a glistening, profligate heap; and Nann saw his actual heart, and his ribs red-and-white like a rack of pork chops.

She grasped Trixie's hand tightly and turned around. "Run, child," she said.

At first Trixie seemed to be too stunned to understand her. But Nann fiercely yanked her hand and said "Run!" and together they started to jog along the concrete-littered street, amid smashed-up automobiles and overturned buses. Their feet crunched on acres and acres of broken glass. It was so bright and brittle that it was like running on diamonds.

"Come on, child, run!" Nann insisted.

"Where are we going?" Trixie shouted. A shower of medium-sized concrete boulders rumbled into the street just ahead of them; and then a garage wall collapsed, bringing down half of the buildings on East Washington between State and South Wabash.

"If we—can make it to the lakeshore—" Nann gasped.

They ran hand in hand; then Nann began to fall behind. Hundreds of other people were running all around them, grim-faced but peculiarly silent. Most drivers seemed to have abandoned their automobiles, but a few still swerved in and out of the traffic. Nann saw a young red-haired woman running with a baby in her arms. A green Granada came around the corner out of East Randolph Street, its tires shrilling, and hit her as she ran across the road. Nann saw her flying, saw her baby fly. She called to Trixie to stop, and she limped and panted across to where the woman and her child were lying.

The woman was already surrounded by a crowd of onlookers, but between their jostling shoulders Nann could see that she was already dead. Her face was very white and blood was sliding out of her broken skull and into the gutter. The baby lay face-down, not moving. The driver kept repeating, "She practically dived into me, she practically dived into me," over and over.

Meanwhile, all around them, Chicago was collapsing. Nann had never seen an earthquake before so she didn't know if this was some kind of earthquake or not. There was something unreal about it. Although she would have expected this overwhelming thunder as millions of tons of steel and concrete fell into the ground, she wouldn't have expected the buildings to collapse so systematically and so completely. The Prudential Building went; then the Amoco Building went; then the Rookery and the Monadnock Building; and even the Gothic-styled water tower, which had survived the Great Chicago Fire of 1871.

They all came rumbling down—huge avalanches of steel and glass—and they all vanished into the ground like subway trains vanishing into a tunnel. Thousands and thousands of people vanished with them, with no chance of escaping. Nann saw faces pressed desperately to office windows as entire thirty-story buildings roared into oblivion. The John Hancock Building dropped to the ground, leaving a high plume of black funereal dust that hung over North Michigan Avenue for ten minutes afterwards; and then gradually shuddered its way out over the Oak Street Beach.

Nann and Trixie ran and hobbled across Grant Park until they reached the lake shore. There were crowds of people there already—people who had been working or sailing around the harbor, or people who had fled from the tall buildings around the Loop and the Civic Center. They were all dusty; some of them floury-faced like zombies. Some of them were sobbing or shouting but most of them were silent. Chicago was still falling and there was nothing they could do but stand and watch it.

Nann held Trixie in her arms as the skyline vanished, building by building, like the targets in some huge shooting gallery. The Dirksen Building, the Tribune tower. Then a deafening bellow of masonry as the Merchandise Mart collapsed into the Chicago River. When it was built, the Merchandice Mart had been the largest building in the world. Now it was nothing but slowly drifting dust; and a memory.

"I never knew we could have earthquakes in Chicago," said Trixie.

Nann shook her head. "I don't think this *is* an earthquake. I think this is the time that my great-grandmother and my grandmother and my mother always told me about."

"What time? What do you mean?"

"I mean they always said that the day would come when the white people would get their punishment in hell, and that the ground would open up and all the white man's shining buildings and all the white man's wealth and glory would just be swallowed up, like it had never even been."

"Oh, come on, momma, you can't believe any of that old superstitious talk. Look at it, this is an earthquake!"

"Well, I'm not so sure about that," said Nann. "If this is an earthquake, how come the ground isn't shaking none? Look at the lake, calm as milk."

Trixie frowned and turned round. The surface of Lake Michigan was eerily placid, with only the very laziest of swells. In fact it was so calm that the film of dust which had fallen onto it was unbroken, except where occasional ducks had left little foot-paddled swirls. The sky over the lake was burnished and brown, the same livid saddle-bronze color that realtors chose for their Cadillacs.

They heard another percussive rumbling; and the Wrigley Building went, followed almost immediately afterward by Marina Towers.

Marina Towers collapsed, one floor on top of the other, like a stack of old 78 records, and then thundered into the river in a chaos of spray and overturned boats.

"God-damn it, it's the end of the world," said one old lady standing close to Nann.

"Well, ma'am, I think you're probably right," Nann replied. "Maybe we should be kneeling now, and making our final absolution. On the other hand, maybe we should be cheering and waving our arms around and shouting Hosanna!"

Nann was shocked and distressed by the deaths and injuries that she saw all around her. A staring woman was being piggy-backed towards the lakeshore by a man whose cheek was hanging open, baring his teeth. Blood was running down the woman's legs in thin rivulets, and dripping from her heels. A truck driver with a crushed pelvis was lying on the grass in an ever-widening pool of bright shining blood, and as the grass grew redder his face turned greyer. There were many children dead, children and old people. A woman in her late sixties lay on her side staring at the grass with filmy blue eyes. She was being guarded by a boy of about twelve, who told Nann to keep well clear. He had been walking with his grandparents across Federal Center Plaza when Alexander Calder's steel "Flamingo" sculpture had dropped into the paving stones. His grandmother had been shocked but unhurt. His grandfather had been instantly guillotined. Scarlet sculpture, scarlet blood.

In spite of these tragedies, however; in spite of seeing her home city collapsing all around her, Nann felt a fierce emotion that was something very close to joy. She stood with her fists clenched and her eyes wide, watching the towers of the wealthy and the privileged brought low. At last the cruel and the careless were being punished. At the very end, this was where their manifest destiny had led them.

The Sears Tower was apparently still intact. It stood almost alone now, reflecting the dull unburnished metallic color of the sky, nearly one-and-a-half-thousand feet high. Everybody was watching it, as if its collapse would signify not only the final collapse of Chicago—the city of big shoulders—but of the greatest monument that men had built anywhere to their own superiority over nature and over everything.

Nann had always thought that the Sears Tower looked dead and aloof: more like a gravestone than a building. This afternoon it presided over the destruction of Chicago and didn't fall. Not yet, anyway. Nann thought she understood why.

The whole city lay in eerie silence for a while; and then the wind began to rise off the lake, and the brown sky grew thicker and browner with building-dust. Huddled by the shore, they heard sirens whooping, and after a while the *flacker-flacker-flacker* of helicopters.

"Oh, God," said a woman standing close to Nann. She must have been quite elegantly groomed when she set out from home this morning. Now her pale-lemon suit was smudged with dust and splattered with blood, and her pink-rinsed hair was blown awry. "Oh, God, my husband."

Nann didn't know what to say to her. Instead she took hold of Trixie's hand and started to walk south through Grant Park. More helicopters flew overhead, big military

Chinooks. They heard the rumble of another building falling, off to the north-west, maybe the Civic Opera House or the Northwestern Atrium Center.

Miraculously the Buckingham Fountain was still working, although the darkness of the sky had turned the water muddy-coloured and grim. Nann washed her face with her hands while Trixie stood close beside her and watched the plumes of spray from the fountain's central island, and the sparkling jets from the sculptured seahorses.

"What are we going to do now?" Trixie asked her mother.

Nann dried her face with a Kleenex out of her purse. Then she snapped the purse shut and said, "Time to see your grandmama."

"Grandmama? What for?"

"To make sure she's not in any trouble. And to see what we have to do next."

"Momma—" Trixie protested. But Nann touched a fingertip to her lips to silence her. "It's time, honey, I know it's time. Your grandmama will tell you all about it, same as I should have done when you were smaller."

Once they had passed East 26th Street they found, quite suddenly, that the atmosphere was calmer. Although they could still hear the low thunder of falling buildings and the odd throbbing noise made by scores of sirens all howling in unison, they found automobiles driving almost complacently through the streets, and people standing on street corners talking and laughing almost as if nothing were happening.

By Dunbar Park they were able to hail a passing taxi. The driver said laconically, "South Side only." He looked disturbingly like a reincarnation of Sammy Davis, Jr.

They climbed in. The driver had his radio on. A frantic news reporter was grabbling, "—building after building collapsing—almost the whole of the Loop devastated—people wandering the streets in a state of total shock—"

"Worse than San Francisco," the taxi-driver remarked. "They can't even count how many dead."

Nann said nothing but sat in the back of the taxi with her fists clenched tight. Trixie glanced at her from time to time but said nothing.

"What I say is, Nature always has the last laugh, that's what I say," the taxi driver added. "We can build whatever we like, as high as we like, but if *Nature* don't like it, then down it has to come."

He turned around in his seat and grinned at them. "Just so long as I ain't standing underneath when it happens, if you know what I mean."

Nann said, "Don't worry. You'll be all right."

"I got your guarantee?"

"You'll be all right," Nann insisted. "That's your destiny, because of what you are."

The taxi driver eyed her in his rear-view mirror for block after block. Then he said, "You some kind of fortune-teller, something like that?"

Nann shook her head.

"You into voodoo, maybe?"

"Maybe," said Nann. "If that's what you want to call it."

The taxi driver lifted his index finger and his pinkie in the sign of the horns.

"You just keep that Baron Samedi off my back, then, that's all. I don't care for voodoo but I respect it, know what I mean?"

"You'll be all right," Nann repeated.

The taxi driver took them right to the door of the brown brick house near Avalon Park. Nann offered him ten dollars but he refused to take it. "Just call it my contribution to the Baron Samedi birthday fund."

They climbed out. Nann pressed the doorbell while Trixie stood a little way away, as if she had discovered something about her momma that she didn't understand, and which made her feel unsettled and afraid. After a while, they heard her grandmama saying, *"Yes? Who is it?"* on the intercom.

Her grandmama's sitting room was cluttered and gloomy, and even more gloomy now that the sky had turned to bronze. It was wallpapered in browns and crimsons, and furnished with heavy, elaborate furniture with tassels and fringes and embroidered cushions and antimacassars. The old-fashioned fireplace was no longer used for fire, but as a religious shrine, crowded with plaster figures of Jesus and Mary and gilded statuettes of sightless angels. There were also swathes of brightly-painted papier-maché beads and chicken feather headdresses and complicated black arrangements of nails and wire and broken glass.

On both sides of the fireplace were pinned scores of postcards and photographs of relatives and friends and grandmama's saints and heroes: St Sebastian, Haile Selassie, Jesse Jackson, Martin Luther King, St Luke, Papa Doc Duvalier, Otis Redding. There were also garish prints of demonic green and blue faces with blotchy scarlet lips. Demons from Haiti and Dominica, hair-raising zombies from the bayous and snarling loogaroos from the swamps and Spanish Quarters.

Grandmama sat in her favourite armchair, a little grey stick insect in a long grey dress, her silver hair brushed back and fastened with combs decorated with shells and beads and knots of twine. Her face was all sunken in these days. She was only seventy-two, but she had always smoked too much and Nann knew that she regularly took something which she called "the seeing drink" to induce hallucinogenic trances. Nann had never discovered exactly what "the seeing drink" was, but she had heard of Dominican mystics who drank an infusion of yage and human ashes in order to talk to their ancestors.

Nann made a tray of tea and set it down on the table beside her mother's knee. Her mother watched her with filmy eyes. In the opposite corner the television was flickering, but with the volume turned right down. Trixie was standing staring at it—at the jumpy aerial views of the Loop and Lincoln Park and West Wacker—all of them flattened and devastated. It looked as if the Sears Tower were the only major skyscraper left standing. Trixie had tried twenty or thirty times to get in touch with Nat at the hi-fi store near Normal Park where he worked, but the phones were down. She held her hands clasped over her stomach as if trying to protect her baby from the prospect of being fatherless.

Grandmama watched Nann pouring the tea. The steam from the teapot twisted in the dim afternoon sunlight. "How did *you* know the time had come?" she asked. Her voice was low and thick and rasping. "On the TV, all they said was, earthquake."

Nann gave the slightest of shrugs. "I just *knew,* that's all. You always told me that one day the buildings would disappear. Even when I was small you told me that over and over. 'One day, all of the buildings are going to up and disappear, just like they never were.' I couldn't imagine it, I couldn't imagine how it was going to happen. But they did, they disappeared. And they didn't just *fall.* They disappeared. Marshall Field's, the whole block, everything, all of my friends, too, everybody who worked there, and customers, and everybody. They went right down into the ground like they never were."

The terrible elation that she had first felt was beginning to wear off. Her voice trembled erratically and her eyes glistened with tears.

"My *friends*—I mean, what's happened to them?"

Grandmama reached over and took hold of her hand. "Nann child, this was spoke of from mother to daughter for ten generations. Carried down, mouth to mouth, family to family. 'The time's gonna come, the time's gonna come,' even Martin Luther King understood that the time had to come, and what we meant by 'the time.' It never exactly meant free, although free was a part of it. It never exactly meant equal, neither, although equal was part of it, too.

"It didn't mean sitting in the front of the bus. It didn't mean sitting alone in the bus. It meant no bus at all; because the bus is *their* way, not ours. It meant nothing of theirs, none of their houses, none of their automobiles, none of their technological gimcrackery. It meant the way things were *meant* to be. Slow, true, and back to nature."

Trixie said, "This is all crazy."

Grandmama turned around, her neck stretching like an egret's. "Who are you to say crazy?"

"It's crazy. It's old women's crazy talk."

Nann said, "Trixie, you listen to me—" but Grandmama shushed her.

"It's easy enough for you to say it's crazy, young lady. But this was always meant to be, from way, way back, when the black man and the red man first faced each other and knew what their common destiny was. There was the famous day we still call Soul Day, when a voodoo priest called

Doctor Hambone met a Red Indian magic-man called Maccus, and they shared a trance for twenty days and twenty nights and when they came back they was neither of them really human no more, because they'd been to places where only dead men can go, and they'd learned all of the dead men's secrets, and what was going to happen to the world."

"Come on, Grandmama," Trixie protested. "This is the twentieth century."

"That's right," Grandmama nodded. "This is the twentieth century, and the time has come at last, and I praise God and all of his spirits that I lived to see it."

Trixie said, "I'm going across to West Normal. I have to, Momma. I have to make sure that Nat's okay."

Nann said, "Trixie, you can't. Supposing more of those buildings fall?"

Almost as if the words she had spoken were a spell, the television screen suddenly jumped to a long shot of the Sears Tower. The sound was turned down but they didn't need sound. They could hear the rumbling even from here, on East 83rd Street.

With dreadful majesty, the tower began to slide into the ground. As it slid, it gathered momentum, faster and faster, until it was vanishing into its foundations like a high-speed elevator—one thousand four hundred feet of steel and glass and concrete thundering into the bedrock in an unstoppable rush.

It took less than two minutes to disappear. In Grandmama's apartment, they felt the aftershocks warping and rippling the floor beneath their feet. Grandmama's voodoo bells tinkled and jangled, and her beads swung, and one of her postcards dropped from the fireplace. It was the ghastly grinning powder-blue face of Chief Lorgnette, one of the most frightening of all of Grandmama's voodoo deities.

"Hosanna and hallelujah," said Grandmama. "At long last we brung them low."

TEN

We heard the news as we sat in my consulting rooms eating Korean take-away. It was a few minutes after noon, and quite suddenly Amelia lowered her chopsticks and said, "Listen!"

I was chasing the world's liveliest dead shrimp around its carton. I was never much of a hand with chopsticks: as far as I was concerned eating with chopsticks was about as sensible as apple-bobbing.

"Listen!" Amelia repeated, and I stopped shrimp-chasing.

"What is it?"

"Can't you hear it?"

I listened. There was nothing. "I don't hear anything," I told her.

"That's the whole point," she said. "It's so quiet. No traffic, no automobile horns, nothing at all."

I listened again, and frowned. I put down my shrimp and went to the window and opened the blind. Amelia was right. Most of the traffic in the street outside had come to a standstill, even the buses. All around the plaza of the Citicorp Building, people were standing like store-window dummies. It was truly weird, like a scene out of one of those 1950s sci-fi movies where the whole population is paralyzed by an alien ray.

Amelia came over and stood beside me. "Something's happened," she said. "Turn on the TV."

"Maybe somebody's shot the President," I said. I couldn't think of anything else that could turn midtown Manhattan into a game of statues in the middle of the lunchbreak.

I switched on my Sony portable, and immediately heard *"—thirty or forty major buildings have collapsed, and those killed or missing already run into tens of thousands—"*

Amelia and I watched in silence as CBS News brought jagged, jerky aerial pictures of downtown Chicago.

"—refugees streaming out of the metropolitan area in all

directions—but a strange calm prevailing mainly because peo-
ple have found this sudden disaster so hard to believe—"

An ENG picture of a tearful elderly man. *"I step from the*
building into the street . . . my wife's just behind me in the
hallway—then bricks are falling, and I hear this crashing
noise—and I turn round and the building is gone, just gone. No
rubble, just flat, like it was never there—"

A serious-faced earthquake expert, speaking by satellite
linkup from Santa Cruz, California: *"—most remarkable is*
the way that the buildings appear to have dropped directly
downwards into the bedrock—leaving no mountains of rubble,
as I would normally expect, nor semi-collapsed structures—if
there were any other possible explanation for what's going on
here, I'd say that this wasn't an earthquake at all, but a totally
different kind of natural phenomenon."

I sat down. "Do you see that?" I asked Amelia, at last.
"Do you see what's happening? The buildings are disappearing into the ground. Disappearing. It's weird."

She stood behind me, and put her arms around my neck.
We watched Marina Towers dropping into the Chicago
River. We watched the John G. Shedd Aquarium vanish in
front of our eyes.

"Maybe the lakebed is collapsing, something like that."

"God," I told her. "I can't believe this is happening. I
can't believe it."

Like everybody else in America that day, like everybody
else throughout the world, we spent the whole of the afternoon and most of the evening in front of the television.
Manhattan was a hot, smoggy cemetery. Hardly anybody
was out on the streets, except for occasional police cars and
firetrucks. It was almost impossible to make a phone call. I
was glad that I didn't have any friends or relatives in Chicago; but for those who did, the TV channels regularly
reeled off scores of emergency numbers, and numbers of all
the Chicago hospitals.

At 3:25 pm the President declared a national emergency.
All flights, national and international, had to be rerouted
away from O'Hare and Meigs Field, and the whole area
within a twenty-five-mile radius was evacuated.

I think the most stunning moment was when the Sears

Tower went. The tallest building in the world, the pinnacle of American capitalism. It was like the Eiffel Tower collapsing, or Buckingham Palace being demolished. In some ways, it felt worse than all the hurt that was inflicted by the Vietnam war, and it induced the same helpless anger and frustration.

When it happened, of course, we weren't even aware that it *was* a war. A war of shadows, and of terrible revenge.

At about 9:00, I walked down to the drugstore on the corner of 50th and Lex and bought a newspaper. The front page showed the Sears Tower collapsing, and the headline said simply QUAKE. I stopped off at the liquor store on 51st and bought two bottles of cold Chardonnay, and walked back to my consulting rooms feeling as if the world was coming to an end.

I still hadn't come to terms with what had happened to Karen. I had spent all night blaming myself for getting her involved with Misquamacus, for getting *myself* involved. Amelia had tried to rustle up some of her spirit-guides in a vain attempt to find out where she had gone and what had happened to her. But the spirit world had been in turmoil, like listening to a radio disturbed by sunspots; and she had picked up nothing but blurted messages of panic.

The only clear voice she had heard was that of a previous occupant of my consulting rooms, who appeared to have been an Armenian tailor. He had lost his seven-year-old daughter and couldn't locate her. Just another tragedy, as painful for him as losing Karen was painful for me. Not helpful, just sad.

In the small hours of this morning Amelia had sat beside me, smoking a cigarette, and said, "I don't think she's dead. From what Misquamacus said, I think he'll keep her alive. He needs her. He needs a voice."

"Maybe it wasn't Misquamacus at all." I replied. "You know what these spirits are like. Always playing tricks. Maybe he was only pretending to be Misquamacus, just to frighten me."

"Harry," said Amelia, "it *was* Misquamacus, believe me. I recognized his aura. I recognized his power. It was the same power he showed me when he came out of that table

the very first time we saw him. Overwhelming. Totally overwhelming. He's laughing at us now, playing games with us.
But it's him all right, no question about it. I can *smell* him."

I had nodded. Amelia was right, and I suppose in a way I
should have been reassured. Better the supernatural enemy
you know than the supernatural enemy you don't. But Misquamacus had always been vicious and cunning and spectacularly cruel, and out of all the clutches in the cosmos, the
very last that I would have wanted Karen to have fallen into
were his.

Maybe he was right about white men destroying his
lodges, but, you know, time marches on, and those Indian
lodges weren't exactly squeaky-clean villas. The way Singing Rock had described it to me, those Plains Indians en-
campments had reeked of woodsmoke, rotting meat,
burning fat, human waste and body odor so strong that they
didn't need to knock over the buffalo with bows and arrows,
all they had to do was lift their armpits.

Maybe Misquamacus was right about the Indians' sacred
places; maybe he was right about their trees and their
grasses and their rivers. But the buffalo-jump wasn't the
greatest way to preserve the species, by any means; and
some of those southwestern tribes could strip forests faster
than Agent Orange.

Maybe Misquamacus was right about the spirits, too: the
spirits that had haunted rocks and rivers and forests. But
there had been just as many malevolent Indian spirits that
had brought disease and madness and early death. Every
idyll has its downside, just like every one of Mlle Lenormand's cards had its warning as well as its promise.

In a mixed-up way, I had always understood Misquamacus' thirst for revenge. At times I had nearly sympathized. But my sympathy had ended with his taking Karen.
Her first experience had nearly driven her over the edge.
God alone knew what she was suffering now; or where; or
how I was ever going to get her back.

Have you ever felt like smashing the wall with your fist?
That's what I felt like then.

I opened the wine and leafed through the paper while
Amelia watched the news. It was all Chicago, Chicago, Chi-

cago. Slow-motion replays of the Sears Tower collapsing. Interviews with grieving relatives. Looting, and scenes of panic. After a while, the sheer magnitude of what had happened made me feel numb. I turned to some of the newspaper's back pages.

That was when I saw it. A four-paragraph item from Phoenix, Arizona. BODYSHOP MASSACRES. I poured myself some more wine and read it slowly.

"Pinal County police were today trying to identify the dismembered bodies of seven men and women discovered in a disused automobile body shop.

"The remains were discovered after a deputy was called to investigate complaints of a 'demolition derby' at a used-car dealership.

"Scores of cars were crushed in what the deputy called 'an orgy of auto-wrecking.' It was afterwards that the bodies were discovered in an oily inspection-pit in the body shop nearby.

"So far only two of the victims have been identified. Sheriff Wallace said that all of them were out-of-towners, as far as he could determine, and that they had 'nothing obvious in common.' One of the victims came from Anaheim, California, and the other, a woman, from St Louis, Missouri.

"Sheriff Wallace appealed for anybody who may have friends or relatives missing in southern Arizona to contact him. He would make no specific comment on the injuries sustained by the victims but said, 'They looked like they were attacked by a psychotic sushi-chef.'

"E.C. Dude, a twenty-two-year-old man who worked at the dealership, was questioned by police but later released. He denied involvement in the slayings or with the auto-wrecking. Dude claimed that the cars 'wrecked themselves.' 'They were all dragged across the lot like somebody was pulling them with a giant magnet,' he claimed. He says he glimpsed 'shadows' but did not see the auto-vandals face-to-face.

"Police described his explanation as 'spacey, but so far we have no evidence to the contrary. We're more concerned with catching a multiple killer.' "

I read the news item twice over, and then I passed it to

Amelia. She glanced at it distractedly and asked, "What?"

" 'The automobiles were all dragged across the lot like somebody was pulling them with a giant magnet,' " I quoted. "He says he glimpsed shadows. "Doesn't that remind you of something? Like the Greenbergs' apartment?"

"I don't know," she said. "Where was this?"

"Someplace near Phoenix, Arizona."

"What possible connection could there be between a mass murder in Phoenix, and what happened to the Greenbergs?"

"I'm not sure, but it's this business about things being dragged along that makes me wonder."

Two pages later, my attention was caught again, and this time I could sense that I was onto something. TWISTERS FLATTEN TWO COLORADO TOWNS. It was obvious that this had probably been the paper's intended front-page story until Chicago started to collapse. It had been patchily edited and cut down, and jammed in next to an advertisement for J.C. Penney's Summer Picnic Sale.

"Freak tornadoes hit two small towns on opposite sides of Colorado today, wrecking homes and leaving 'hundreds' killed or missing.

"State emergency services were called to Pritchard in the southeast and Maybelline in the northwest after unexpected storms raged through both communities. The extent of the damage is reported to be 'severe to very severe' and all utilities are cut off.

"Early eyewitness accounts say that the tornadoes pulled whole buildings for hundreds of feet, along with vehicles, fencing, animals, and human beings. In Maybelline, where there were only a handful of survivors, rescue crews talked of houses being dragged into the ground.

"They said that, at one point during the storm, the sky turned dark red 'like something out of the Old Testament.' "

I put down the paper. *They are clearing the sacred grounds.* First Mrs Greenberg's apartment; then a used-car dealership in Arizona; then two Colorado townships; then Chicago. And the same characteristics every time. Darkness, and dragging down. Buildings not collapsing, but vanishing into the ground. Even *people* vanishing into the ground, like Karen had vanished into the floor.

I had a terrible feeling that America was no longer safe beneath our feet—that we were all standing on a huge darkness that was threatening to swallow us up.

I stood up, and switched off the television. Amelia was looking very tired.

"What did you do that for?" she asked.

"Because we're not helping by watching."

She reached for her cigarettes, but I caught hold of her wrist and said, gently, "Don't. Maybe it was me who started you smoking. In which case I think I have a right to wean you off it."

"Harry Erskine, you have no rights as far as I'm concerned. Your rights were all used up a very long time ago."

"MacArthur once told me that you were the most beautiful woman he had ever met."

Amelia said nothing, but lowered her eyes.

"MacArthur once told me that you threw linguine at him."

"He was lying, it was fettucine."

I kissed her awkwardly, half on the left temple and half on the frame of her spectacles. Middle age, it makes adolescents out of us all over again.

"Look at these news stories," I said. "Arizona, Colorado, and now Chicago."

She did me the courtesy of looking at them and I waited patiently while she read. Then she took off her glasses and said, "You really believe they're all connected?"

"The same dragging, the same disappearing," I pointed out. "When has that ever happened before? Have *you* ever heard about that happening before?"

"It may be happening all the time, for all I know. I don't usually read the newspapers."

"Well, I think there's a connection here and I think that connection is Misquamacus."

"You seriously think that Misquamacus is bringing down the whole of Chicago?"

"I don't know. I don't know what the hell to think. But what a coincidence, all these similar-type disasters, all within a matter of days."

"Perhaps we need some expert advice," said Amelia.

"Oh, for sure. But the only expert I ever knew was Singing Rock."

"No, it wasn't. What about Dr what's-his-name, up at Albany? The one who first found Singing Rock for us."

"Oh, you mean Dr Snow. I don't know. He's probably dead by now. It's been nearly twenty years."

"You can try, can't you?"

We drove up to Albany early in the morning when the Hudson Valley was gilded with haze. I borrowed a newish midnight-blue Electra from an old friend of mine who ran a guidebook publishing company, on pain of returning it in pristine condition with the ashtrays licked clean. Personally I was always pretty careless about what I drove, and it made me nervous to take charge of an automobile that smelled of leather and gleamed so much.

We listened to the radio for a while, but the news from Chicago was overwhelming and unrelentingly painful to hear. The building collapses seemed to have abated, but thousands and thousands of people were killed or missing or injured and the emergency services were stretched to the limit. The greatest feeling this morning was one of hurt and bewilderment—as if somebody had gripped the very heart of America and torn it out.

The President would address the nation this afternoon. But what could he say, except tell us all how shocked and grief-stricken we already knew ourselves to be?

Amelia lit a cigarette, then immediately tossed it out of the car window.

"I'm not *forcing* you to give it up," I told her.

"Don't flatter yourself," she replied. "You never forced me to do anything."

We arrived at Dr Snow's house—the same brick-built house on the outskirts of Albany where we had first met him twenty years ago. Then, the house had been surrounded by tall mournful-looking cypresses, but all except one had been cut down, and the house now looked lighter but shabbier. The yellowed net curtains had been replaced by strong chintzes that looked as if they had been chosen from a mail-order catalogue.

We were greeted at the door by a tall, plain woman with bobbed hair and large feet. She wore a poncho tied at the waist by a fraying silk cord. "I'm Hilda," she said, letting us into the hallway. "Daddy's in the conservatory in back. You won't overtire him, now, will you?"

She led us past the rows of fierce Indian masks that I remembered from my first visit; and the stuffed birds in glass cases; and the dark long-case clock, the clock that had ticked twenty years ago as if it were very weary, and which now sounded wearier still.

"Would you like some herbal tea?" she asked us. I recalled that Dr Snow didn't allow alcohol in the house.

I said, "A cup of black coffee would be good." But she tightly smiled and shook her head.

"Daddy doesn't believe in artificial stimulants."

We walked through the musty living room into a large octagonal conservatory, far too warm and far too dry, in which a profusion of brown-and-yellow palms were gasping their last. The glass roof was emerald with algae, lending the whole conservatory a ghastly morgue-like greenness, and giving Dr Snow the appearance of death.

He sat in a complicated modern wheelchair close to the windows, staring out at his drought-dried garden. He was very shrivelled now, with a fine dandelion mane of intensely white hair, and green-tinted glasses. He wore an off-white bathrobe which—for all its thickness—failed to conceal the skeletal emaciation of his body.

"Dr Snow," I said, to his back.

"Well, well, Mr Erskine," he replied, without turning around. "How is the shaman hunter today?"

"You remember," I said.

He rotated his wheelchair, and confronted me. "Of course I remember. You were the first and only person in the whole of my academic career who ever asked me for practical help."

"Do you remember Ms Crusoe?" I asked him, nudging Amelia forward.

"Mrs Wakeman," Amelia corrected me, and stepped forward and took hold of Dr Snow's hand.

"It's been a very long time," said Dr Snow. He patted

Amelia's hand, and gave her a badly-arranged smile. "A very, very long time." Hmm, I thought. He doesn't believe in artificial stimulants, but he's not averse to some real live ones. But you know me. Eternally jealous, even of the women I don't really want. Or *kid* myself I don't really want.

"Dr Snow," I said, "you've probably heard what's happened in Chicago."

He nodded. "A great natural tragedy. Terrible. I have a good friend there, Dr Noble, at the Cook County Medical Center. Of course I'm very concerned for his welfare."

"I think—" I began, and then I hesitated. The connections that I had worked out between the Greenbergs and Karen and the body-shop homicides in Arizona and the two towns in Colorado and Chicago—well, quite frankly, they suddenly seemed a little tenuous, to say the least. I had forgotten how formidable Dr Snow had first appeared to me, how much of a stickler for logical thought and totally unvarnished argument. He was one of the country's greatest experts on Indian lore and Indian magic, but he wasn't at all romantic or superstitious or even politically correct.

"You're experiencing another problem with Indians," he said. His voice sounded as if he had a mouthful of that white gritty sand they heap in hotel ashtrays.

I shrugged, smiled, and said, "I guess so. Yes. That's about the size of it."

"Of course it is. You wouldn't have come to see me if you weren't, would you? And the truth of the matter is that we shall all experience problems with Indians for ever and ever, amen. Not so much with Indians, perhaps, but the mystical forces in which the Indians believed.

"We tend to dismiss every other religion apart from our own as invented, as make believe. We believe our own religion to the point where the words 'Act of God' even have a legal meaning. But really, you know, in America, the God of the Jews has very little relevance. He's a European fetish, a kindly but not-very-powerful deity from the Middle East.

"We should be worshipping not the gods of Europe: not the gods of Europe's pirates and Europe's adventurers, but the real, ethnic gods of America, just as the Indians did.

These gods are equally powerful; equally vengeful; equally just; equally concerned for our welfare. Even more relevant, they're *real,* and they're *here.*"

"Dr Snow," I told him, "I believe that Red Indian wonder-workers brought down Chicago."

Dr Snow pushed himself closer. His knees were wrapped in a blue and green Buchanan-plaid blanket. He smelled of violet cachous and some indefinable medical rub. "You really believe that?"

"You've seen the way the buildings collapsed. In fact they didn't collapse, they vanished."

"That's right. So what are your suspicions?"

I told him all about the Greenbergs, and Martin Vaizey, and Karen, and then I showed him the newspaper clippings about Arizona and Colorado.

"This is all most interesting," he said. "Would you care for a cup of herbal tea?"

"Thanks, but no thanks. I just want to know if I've lost it or not."

Dr Snow studied the paper; studied my notes; and then took off his green-tinted eyeglasses and closed his eyes. "Greenwich Village . . . Apache Junction . . . Pritchard . . . Maybelline . . . Yes!"

"Did you think of something?" I asked him, but without hesitation he opened his eyes and propelled his wheelchair out of the conservatory and through the living room and out of sight. I looked blankly at Amelia and Amelia looked blankly at me.

"Maybe it was those onion rings we had for lunch," I suggested. I cupped my hand in front of my mouth and smelled my breath.

It wasn't long before Hilda Snow appeared. "Daddy wants you in his study, please," she announced with consummate gloom.

We followed her into the world's most cluttered library. Every shelf was crammed with books and pamphlets and files and letters; and then with pictures and postcards and letters; and then with extraordinary shrivelled-looking Indian artifacts, Apache headpieces and Navaho rattles and medicine-bundles stuffed with eagles' claws and buffaloes' tails.

Dr Snow's desk was heaped with layer upon layer of books and papers, a surprisingly state-of-the-art Japanese typewriter and a carved wooden sundance doll with a tiny, malevolent-looking head. Dr Snow himself was sitting in his wheelchair by the leaded French windows with three large books open on his knees. Through the windows I could see sloping lawns and hedges and pink flowers fluttering. There was a strong smell of new typewriter ribbons and dust and sweet peas.

"Ah," said Dr Snow. "I believe that I've found your connection."

"Really?" said Amelia, circling round the room.

Dr Snow lifted his head and smiled at her. "Women are always so skeptical. I love it."

Dr Snow tapped the books with his finger, as if he were admonishing them. "All of the places you mentioned—although of course they were known to the Indians by very different names—were the locations of noted killings, Indians slaughtered by whites.

"The location on East 17th Street in New York City is the most obscure but one of the most interesting. In the winter of 1691 two British officers raped and killed a Manhattan Indian girl at a place which the Indians called Man of Rock. It was probably no more than a brownstone outcropping, and of course it would have been levelled as Manhattan moved steadily northward.

"The only reason that this incident was recorded was that both officers were court-martialled not for killing the Indian girl but for stealing the brandy on which they got drunk that night."

"Do you know what the officers' names were?" I asked Dr Snow.

"Of course. It's here, in the British colonial records. Captain William Stansmore Hope, of Derbyshire, and Lieutenant Andrew Danetry, of Norfolk."

"Hope and Danetree," I repeated. "Those were the names of the men who were killed at the Belford."

"Well, naturally," said Dr Snow, completely unsurprised.

"What do you mean, 'Naturally'?"

"Let me just explain your connection," Dr Snow asked me, a little testily. "In 1865, seven of Geronimo's braves were captured and tortured by white mercenaries at Apache Junction, Arizona—a place which the Indians called Under The Old One, because it lies just beneath the Superstition Mountains.

"In the early fall of 1864 more than seventy-five Cheyenne Indians were massacred at Pritchard, Colorado, by cavalrymen of the Third Regiment, the so-called 'Bloodless Thirdsters.' This happened a full six weeks *before* the notorious massacre of one hundred and twenty-three of Black Kettle's Cheyenne people at Sand Creek, and if anything the scalpings and sexual mutilations were far worse. It was common practice for the cavalrymen to cut off the men's private parts to use as tobacco-pouches, and to cut out the women's privates, too, as souvenirs.

"The new commander of the Colorado military district, Colonel J.M. Chivington, managed somehow to keep the Pritchard massacre under wraps. It was said that he threatened to shoot any man who talked to the newspapers or the politicians about it. And him a Methodist minister, too.

"In February of 1865, at Maybelline, Colorado, a place which the Cheyenne called Buffalo-Gathering-Place, ninety Indians were slaughtered by white ranchers in retaliation for raids on several of their settlements—which themselves had been carried out in retaliation for Pritchard and Sand Creek.

"In 1870, the Sioux chief Red Cloud was invited to visit Chicago with five of the greatest medicine-men. Red Cloud had already been to Washington DC—where the Commissioner of Indian Affairs had made sure that he visited the Navy yards and the U.S. Arsenal, so that he could see for himself how powerful the white men were. The medicine-men however had refused to accept his account of the white men's weapons, and were still making warlike threats. So the Commissioner of Indian Affairs gave them a guided tour of the arsenal and the railroad yards and the docks, so that they could see for themselves just how futile it would be for them to carry on fighting.

"Red Cloud was all for negotiating peace, but the medicine-men still believed that the white men were full of trickery and lies, which of course they were. One night when Red Cloud was giving a speech to the Philanthropic Institute of Chicago, there was a fire at the Palmer House, where the medicine-men were staying, and all five of them burned to death. It caused a terrific sensation because the Palmer House had just opened, and it was one of the most luxurious hotels in America. The Chicago fire department said that the men had tried to light a campfire in their room; and the Chicago papers said that this was proof that Indians were not much more than savages, and that they weren't fit to live alongside white people, and never would be.

"However that fire was kindled, it wiped out five of the most powerful and influential wonder-workers that the Indians had ever known. In a few minutes it weakened the Indian nations more dramatically than all the years of cholera and cavalry action put together."

I leaned over his shoulder and looked at the books that he was holding on his lap. "So the connection between all of these incidents is that Indians were killed there?"

Dr Snow nodded. "Quite so. And the more Indians who were killed, the more devastating their revenge. A life for a life, so to speak. Except in Chicago, where they appear to be exacting a punishment for the loss of entire tribes."

"But how are they doing it?" asked Amelia. "They're dragging entire buildings right into the ground—people, too."

"Of course they are. They're pulling them down to the underworld, to the Great Outside. What our Western storytellers mistakenly call the Happy Hunting Ground."

"I don't understand," I told him.

Dr Snow snapped his books shut and heaped them back on his desk. "It's very simple. Imagine if you can that the continental United States is a lake, and that we are capable of standing on its surface. Above the surface of the lake is what we like to think of as the real world. But—if we look down—if we look below the soles of our shoes—we can see ourselves standing upside down in another world. A negative, mirror-image world.

"This negative, reflected world is the world beyond death, the Great Outside. It is the world where spirits live. It is the world where the Indians go when they die.

"It is no more real than a reflection is real. But it is undeniably *there,* just as a reflection is *there.* It is the world of Indian understanding, Indian belief, Indian superstition, Indian fear, Indian happiness. It is what the Indians understand their natural world to be.

"In 1869, in Nevada, a Paviotso Indian called Tavibo began to preach the doctrine that all white people would fall into holes in the ground and be swallowed up, while the dead Indians would return to earth. He said he could talk to the dead in trances, and he encouraged the Indians of the Great Basin to dance their traditional circle dance and sing songs which had been revealed to him by the dead.

"The doctrine was called the Ghost Dance because it preached the return of the dead. It spread through California, Oregon, and other parts of Nevada. It only died out when Tavibo's prophesies failed to come to pass.

"The Ghost Dance was preached again by another Paviotso messiah, Wovoka, who died as recently as 1932. Wovoka was stricken by a severe fever when he was thirty-three years old, and almost immediately there was an eclipse of the sun. During the eclipse he was taken by ghosts to the Great Outside and shown the world of the future.

"The Plains Indians had recently suffered terrible defeats in battle, the destruction of the buffalo herds, the introduction of new and often fatal diseases, and confinement on reservations. Wovoka promised that if they danced and chanted, the white men would vanish into the ground, the dead would come back to life, and the buffalo would return to their grasslands. You can see the attraction of such a doctrine to a people who were totally demoralized.

"The Ghost Dance cult was eagerly adopted by the Sioux, the Comanche, the Cheyenne, the Arapaho, the Assinaboin and the Shoshoni. Only the Navajo refused to join in, because the Navajo were afraid of ghosts.

"There have been plenty of learned books about the

Ghost Dance. Anthony Wallace interpreted it as a 'revitalization movement,' that aimed to restore the vitality of a culture under attack. Weston LeBarre preferred to call it a 'crisis cult,' and saw ghost dancing as an adaptive response to misery and despair."

"What about you, Dr Snow?" I asked him. "What do you think?"

Dr Snow jabbed his finger towards the floor. "Beneath our feet, Mr Erskine, there lies a continent of shadows—the Great Outside—in which the Indian notion of America still survives. A continent without highways, a continent without buildings or railroads or ships or automobiles. A continent teeming with game and bison and running with unpolluted rivers. America as she once was, before a single white man set foot on her. The Great Outside."

"You believe it actually *exists*?" I asked him.

"Haven't you seen enough evidence of it yourself? Where do you think your unfortunate friend Miss Tandy is now? Where do you think the Sears Tower has disappeared to? The day prophesied by Tavibo and Wovoka has finally arrived. The Indians are killing, they're looting, and they're taking prisoners—and they're taking everything back to the Great Outside.

"From what you say, I expect they're planning to leave it there. In fact—from what you say—I expect they're attempting to turn back the clock."

"What do you mean?" asked Amelia. She was twitchy, and I expected she was beginning to feel like a cigarette. "How can anybody turn back the clock?"

"My dear, you're a very clever spiritualist, aren't you? You know that it's perfectly possible to send simple material things from the real world to the spirit world and vice versa. You can send a real hat, for instance, to the other side. You can accidentally send a glove, or a pen, or a cufflink. That's how certain small items become irrevocably lost. Very frustrating indeed, sometimes, but that's where they've gone! They've dropped through the surface of our imaginary lake into the world of shadows beneath our feet.

"In the same way, a skilful medium can draw shadows from the Great Outside into the real world. Some people call them 'ectoplasm' but I personally prefer 'shadows' or 'reflections' because that's what they really are."

"I still don't see what you're driving at," I asked him.

"Oh, it's not *that* difficult to grasp! Your Indians appear to have developed enough supernatural power to be able to drag down very much larger objects—and very selectively, too.

"Your Indians appear to be intent on purging America of everything that the white man ever brought here or built here. They are punishing the direct descendants of everybody who killed or hurt them. They are taking just revenge for acts of massacre and treachery. Lives for lives, lodges for lodges. And eventually, I suspect, they will leave nothing at all but prairies and mountains and deserts and swamps."

"Is that *possible*?" I asked him, in disbelief.

Dr Snow took off his spectacles. "Looking back at the environmental and mystical history of our planet, Mr Erskine, I would say that it isn't just possible but highly probable. The Indians want their lands back, just the way they were."

ELEVEN

He wheeled himself across the library and pointed to the top shelf. "Fetch me down that old black book, will you, the one that looks like a Bible?"

I reached up and tugged the book off the shelf. It smelled sour and musty and very old. Inside the black leather cover thick deckle-cut pages had been handsewn inside to make a new book altogether.

Dr Snow leafed through it slowly, and sneezed. "It must be thirty years since I looked at this. It was written in 1863, by Bishop Henry Whipple, the Episcopal Bishop of Minnesota. See—*An Account of the Recruitment by U.S. Military Forces Of Spiritualists & Mediums In Their Conflicts Against the Santee Indians 1862*"

"It's quite fascinating," he said. "The Commissioner of Indian Affairs was aware that the Indians had strong magic powers and took them extremely seriously. In fact, I'd say that the only reason the Indians were eventually defeated was not so much because the white men overwhelmed them but because they lost faith in their own supernatural skills.

"In Minnesota, when he was leading troops and local militia against the Santee, Colonel Henry Sibley employed the services of a celebrated medium called William Hood.

"There are several accounts of William Hood's career in the Old West, but regrettably no pictures of him. Some stories say that he was originally a Serbian vampire-hunter named Milan Protic, and that he had been shipped over to America by the Commissioner of Indian Affairs in secret.

"In O.L. Ward's *Gunslingers,* I discovered a verified report that William Hood lived for some time in Santa Fe, New Mexico, and that he was involved in several gunfights. They nicknamed him the Shadow Boy, because none of his opponents ever succeeded in hitting him.

"He was called in to help Colonel Sibley after the Minnesota Massacre in August 1862, when Santee Indians killed four hundred and fifty white settlers. William Hood went to the scene of the very first killing—the cottage of a settler called Robinson Jones—and carried out days of 'spiritual investigations.'

"Here, Bishop Whipple writes, 'Mr Hood turned out to be a very taciturn young man, with the wildest hair, and dressed in curious leathers and rags. He carried about his belt numerous bells and bones and several pear-shaped bottles, which he called 'shadow-bottles.' His only explanation for the use of these bottles was that warring Indians would often be possessed by a shadow or darkness from the Great Outside, which I took to mean the Indian equivalent of Purgatory. If he could capture any traces of this shadow—even the slightest fragment of it—the shadow would lose its spiritual integrity. It would be wounded . . . it would hemorrhage darkness. If it didn't return at once to the Great Outside it would literally bleed to death.

" 'The Indian would be exorcised, and would no longer have the power or the magical abilities which the spirit had lent him.

" 'I was skeptical of Mr Hood's abilities, I must confess,

but equally I had never seriously believed that the Indian medicine-men were capable of any genuine acts of supernatural power. Mr Hood on the other hand was utterly convinced that they could work real and dangerous magic. He said that he had once been captured by the Cheyenne, and that his soul had been tortured by a Cheyenne shaman. This experience had taught him about shadows from the Great Outside and also how to become so skillful with weapons that nobody would ever be able to best him.

" 'He said that he had learned from the Cheyenne how to momentarily become a *mislai,* a shadow-man, so that bullets would fly right through his body without injuring him. But he never volunteered to demonstrate this skill, saying that magic was for serious purposes, not for exhibition.

" 'Later, Colonel Sibley also recruited a negro man from somewhere in Louisiana. This person was always dressed as if for the opera, and carried a cane with a silver skull for a knob. Sometimes he called himself Sawtooth and sometimes he called himself Jonas DuPaul; but most of the time he referred to himself as Dr Hambone.

" 'I found Dr Hambone to be extremely intimidating and avoided him whenever possible. Colonel Sibley said that he could make the dead speak and took him to question all of the corpses of murdered settlers in order that they could identify their assailants. I never ventured with him, being opposed to this activity, and thus I never heard any of the dead answer him, as he claimed they always did.

" 'One day Dr Hambone ventured out on his own and was apparently captured by Killing Ghost and Runs Against Something When Crawling, two of the most warlike of the Santee braves.

" 'William Hood was dispatched by Colonel Sibley to find Dr Hambone by natural or supernatural means, which he did, although he never told anybody how. He brought him back to the militia's encampment in a condition of trance. Dr Hambone eventually said that he had met a Santee shaman and that he had been shown a future world in which all of the white man's works would be enveloped in darkness, and that white men would be massacred by shadows, and that none would escape.

" 'He then departed for good, saying that the red men and the black men would walk these plains and fish these rivers long after every white man had been buried. Colonel Sibley threatened to arrest him, but William Hood said that in his opinion it was not advisable. Dr Hambone had influences of which William Hood had no experience, and he would not be able to protect Colonel Sibley or any of his men if Dr Hambone should cut up ugly.' "

"There!" said Dr Snow, carelessly throwing the book onto the desk, and causing a miniature avalanche of *National Geographics.* "What do you make of that?"

"It's fascinating," said Amelia. She picked up the book and slowly leafed through it. "I've heard of shadow-bottles, but I've never seen any historical reference to one before."

"Oh—here," said Dr Snow, in a very matter-of-fact way. He went across to one of his cupboards and rummaged around for a while. Eventually he produced a small bottle of thick plain glass, about the size and shape of a lightbulb, with a tarnished silver stopper.

"You've actually *got* one!" said Amelia, in astonishment.

Dr Snow shrugged. "Found it in Baton Rouge. It doesn't look very special, does it? Ghost-hunters in Serbia were supposed to use them when they went looking for vampires. So that gives some credence to the story that William Hood was Milan Protic."

I turned the bottle over and over, and then I returned it to Dr Snow. "What's going to happen now?" I asked him. "I mean—what the hell's going to happen *now*? Are we just going to sit around and watch the rest of the country go under? Jesus!"

Dr Snow shrugged. "Who knows? If your Indian friends are determined to wipe every trace of the white man from the face of America, then presumably they'll carry on trying to do it. Wherever Indian blood has been spilled, they can use that place as an opening down to the Great Outside. And, believe me—apart from those few that they have used already, there are thousands more, all the way from Connecticut to Canyon de Chelly. Thousands!

"In Connecticut, you know, in 1638, Captains Underhill and Mason supervised the torching of a Pequot encampment; and with it the burning alive of five hundred Pequot Indians, men, women and children. Think what an opening to the underworld *that's* going to make! A tribe for a tribe! They'll probably decimate the entire state!"

He seemed almost elated. "They were such magicians! Such great magicians!"

"I expect they're glad that *somebody* appreciates them," I retorted. "But what the hell are we going to do to stop them?"

"Stop them?" he frowned, as if the very idea of it hadn't occurred to him. "Stop them? I don't think we can. I don't think that *anybody* can."

"You're talking about a national disaster that's already killed thousands of innocent people and is going to have a more devastating effect than about a hundred nuclear bombs! You're talking about the end of an entire civilization, on which most of the world depends! You're talking about throwing the whole of America back into total savagery!"

Dr Snow smiled slyly. "That's not a very p.c. thing to say."

"Maybe it isn't; I'm all for noble savages and Indian rights, but I'm damned if I'm going to live in a world where I have to go looking for lunch with a spear."

"You won't have to," said Dr Snow. "They'll probably kill us all. Either that or they'll make our lives not worth living, just as we made *their* lives not worth living."

"Come on, Doctor, there has to be *some* way of getting back at them. And some way of getting Karen back, too."

"You think that Misquamacus is behind all this?" asked Dr Snow.

I nodded. "Singing Rock tried to warn me about it, but he was being got at, and I never really understood the whole message."

"Misquamacus is by far the most likely suspect," Dr Snow agreed. "He always possessed such remarkable powers. He could change the wind, make rivers flow backwards, travel through time, and appear in two or three different places simultaneously. The only *trouble* of course is how he managed to summon the power to draw down half of an entire city."

"Wouldn't the spirits have helped him? The Great Old Ones?"

"It's possible that he could have summoned Tirawa, the great Pawnee god; or Heammawihio, the Cheyenne god of the skies. But all that darkness, you know, all that *dragging-down*!"

He pulled down his fist two or three times as if he were trying to imagine how Misquamacus might have done it.

"You know, there's only one way I can think of," he said, at last. "He would have had to make some kind of bargain with Aktunowihio, the god of the underworld. But according to legend, Aktunowihio never makes bargains. Aktunowihio is something a little too frightful to contemplate, even for a wonder-worker like Misquamacus."

"Do you mean he's some kind of devil, some kind of Satan?"

"Oh, no, the Indians never thought that their gods represented good or evil. They simply had gods that were up above and gods that were down below. Heammawihio, in fact, is the Indian name for that primeval being that used to dominate earth in the very early days of pre-Columbian civilization. The Indians used to say that he came to earth down the Hanging Road, which was what they called the Milky Way. Several fanciful writers have called him Cthulhu. In fact he wasn't a he, but very much an 'it,' and was probably formed out of the collective consciousness of many different species from many different galaxies. If you can imagine a being that thinks like a man, a snake, an octopus, a wolf, and a centipede, all at the same time, then you're probably quite close to understanding what Heammawihio was really like.

"But it was Aktunowihio, you know, who frightened the Indians the most. If you died a noble and natural death, you went to the Happy Hunting Grounds without fear. But if you broke a taboo, then Aktunowihio would claim you when you died.

"Chief Roman Nose once broke a taboo by eating before battle with a metal fork. He was shot almost immediately and went to Aktunowihio. His followers had propped his body in the high branches of a tree in the hope that he would fly upward instead of downward; but on the second night the entire tree was dragged into the ground and Roman Nose's body was never seen again.

"Aktunowihio, quite frankly, is everything you never want to happen to you, all in one. He's supposed to take many shapes—dogs, strange women, men without heads. Even Columbus went back to Spain with stories about men without heads.

"But the most fearsome shape of all is that of the Shadow Buffalo. If an Indian thought he glimpsed the Shadow Buffalo when he was out hunting he would drop everything and gallop back to his lodge in a total frenzy of fear, and none of his fellow braves would think any the less of him for being frightened.

"Aktunowihio is supposed to be able to appear in the real world by possessing the bodies of living men and women. Most of the time he can walk amongst us and we don't even realize that he's passed us by. But if you see anybody staring at you without reason, or if you feel someone touch or tug at you, then it could be Aktunowihio, or part of Aktunowihio—the Great Dead One walking the world of the living."

"I don't know," I said. I sat back in my chair and gave a tight, repressed stretch. "If I hadn't seen stuff like this for myself—if I'd never come across Misquamacus—well, I wouldn't believe a single God-damned word of it. Would you?"

"Oh, once you really *know* the Indians, you'll believe anything," said Dr Snow. "The trouble is, not many people know much about Indians, nor do they *want* to know much about Indians. I've been making Indian business forecasts and giving out Indian-style weather-warnings for years now. I've only been wrong with one weather prediction, *ever*. But will the media believe me? Of course not. Even though my forecasts are so accurate the poor fools prefer to rely on a multimillion dollar satellite which consistently gives them the wrong idea."

"What do you suggest we do?" I asked Dr Snow, dully.

Amelia reached across and held my hand.

Dr Snow made a face, pushing himself backwards and forwards, backwards and forwards. "You need friends, no doubt of it. You need somebody who understands Indian lore instinctively rather than academically. In other words, with Singing Rock gone, you need to find yourself another wonder-worker."

"Easier said than done," I told him. "You don't happen to know any, do you?"

He shook his head. "I used to correspond with Crazy Dog until the beginning of this year, but I haven't heard from him for months. He's either dead or drunk or being chased by the South Dakota cops on bigamy charges. Somehow, you'll have to find your own."

"Thanks a whole bunch," I told him.

"That's not all," he warned me. "You'll also have to have people to back you up, people who understand what you're doing and aren't afraid."

I nodded. "I think I can manage that. What else?"

"Most important of all, you'll have to find out what bargain Misquamacus struck with Aktunowihio, because if my guess is correct, and Aktunowihio is giving Misquamacus the power to drag down all these buildings, then Misquamacus must have offered him something which Aktunowihio badly wanted. All Indian magic is based on bargains. You lend me your magic bonnet, I'll give you my horse. You give me your horse, I'll strike down your enemy dead. You strike my enemy dead, I'll make your pumpkins grow. And so on."

"Do you have any idea what Aktunowihio might have wanted?" I asked him.

Dr Snow shook his head. The afternoon sunlight caught his glasses, like a heliograph signal from a distant butte. "I really couldn't say. But once you've found out—*if* you find out—you'll have to find some way to break the arrangement—some way to cancel the whole deal. Otherwise—*pfff!*—forget it."

We drove back to the city feeling tired and defeated. It was dark by the time we crossed the George Washington

Bridge and Manhattan glittered and sparkled like a city seen in a dream. As I drove southward I wondered how much longer the dream could possibly last. We may have conquered the land surface but we hadn't conquered the darkness that lay beneath it, the darkness of centuries, the world that really *was* America, when you came to think of it.

Amelia said, "Will you take me back to my place? I have to think."

"Think? Think about what?"

"Harry—I want to sit for a while on my own and work out whether I really want to be doing this with you."

I made a face. "I suppose you have that privilege."

"Of course I have that privilege! It's not even a privilege! You're expecting me to involve myself in something totally catastrophic and you haven't even stopped to ask me if I *want* to!"

"I'm sorry," I said. I smacked my forehead with the heel of my hand, a gesture of self-punishment. "You know me. I'm always taking everybody for granted." I continued to drive, glancing at her from time to time.

After a while, she said, "What?"

"Do you want to?" I asked her.

"Do I want to what?"

"Do you want to get involved, of course."

"Harry! For God's sake! I said I needed to *think* about it! I'm scared, if you want to know the truth. I'm absolutely scared to death. I saw Misquamacus's head coming out of that table and I know what Dr Snow is talking about is true. Things *can* be dragged from one world into the other, and vice versa, and, boy, we're talking about something really, really scary here because those worlds are so dangerous and so *strange*! Do you really want to see something like—I don't know, your dead grandfather standing in your bedroom at night? Do you really want to lose people for ever?"

"I have to find Karen somehow," I said. Even saying Karen's name was like cutting my tongue with a tomato-knife. "If he hasn't hurt her—if he hasn't killed her, I mean—then I really have to find her."

"Maybe you're learning some responsibility," said Amelia.

"Oh, for sure. Or maybe there's nothing else in my life that's really worth doing."

New York

Just after four o'clock that same afternoon Martin Vaizey was visited at the 13th Precinct by his lawyer Abner Kaskin. Outside the mesh-protected windows, a sudden summer shower was falling. It sounded as if somebody were desperately throwing raisins against the glass to attract attention.

Martin was sitting at the table in the interview room when Abner Kaskin came in. He was very straight-backed, freshly shaven, his hair brushed and gleaming. He looked pale and a little tired, but his bunk at the 13th Precinct was a great deal less restful than his bed at home in the Montmorency Building.

His sleep had been disturbed by something else, too, apart from shouts and echoes and slamming doors and the constant whooping of sirens.

Abner Kaskin shook his hand and then set his briefcase down on the table. He was round-shouldered, with combed-back wavy hair, protruding teeth, and lips that looked as if they had been painted on with lipstick. He wore an expensive crumpled linen suit, its padded shoulders speckled with rain, and the necktie of the New York Bar Association.

"We're making some progress," he said. "Donna Medina called me from the DA's office just after lunch and said that she might consider a manslaughter plea for Mr Greenberg, providing we make things easy for her."

"Why should we make things easy for her?" Martin demanded. "I didn't do it."

"Martin, you reached down into that woman's throat and you turned her inside out. Then you karate-chopped her husband and broke his neck. The medical examiner's evidence is incontrovertible; the circumstantial evidence is overwhelming; and there are two eyewitnesses who might support your demonic-possession story but who both admit that they saw you commit both killings. That's why we should make things easy for her. Listen, Martin, we're not talking about acquittal here. I'll consider myself a platinum-plated genius if I can get you out of this with two consecutive life sentences."

There was a lengthy silence. Martin sat with his head bowed. "Abner," he repeated, "I simply didn't do it. I was helpless. I was taken over. I no more killed Naomi Greenberg than if somebody had put a gun in my hand when I was fast asleep and squeezed my finger on the trigger."

"Martin," Abner replied, "I've defended twenty-six eminent and respectable people like yourself on charges ranging from first-degree murder to vehicular homicide. I know when people are innocent and I know when people are guilty. It's my job to know. Now, I believe that you're innocent. Don't ask me why. All the evidence is stacked up against it. But whereas all my other clients could be defended with pleas of provocation, or temporary insanity, or stress, or drunkenness—you have no mitigating plea at all. Demonic possession is not yet recognized in US courts as an acceptable defense. Maybe in Haiti, who knows?

"Unless I can raise the devil right in the middle of the courtroom, and *prove* that possession is possible, then we don't have a prayer."

Martin lifted his head and looked Abner steadily in the eye. "You've seen what's been happening in Chicago."

"Sure. It's terrible. I have a cousin at Spertus College, I'm still waiting for news. But what does that have to do with it?"

"That's your proof. That's your devil right in the middle of the courtroom."

Abner eyed him warily. "Am I hearing you correctly? Come on, Martin, you haven't lost it, have you?"

"I had a phone call from Harry Erskine, from Albany. He's been investigating my case for me. He went to see an expert upstate. No—not a spiritualist, nothing like that. A doctor of anthropology. A very respected doctor of anthropology, Ernest Snow."

"Never heard of him, sorry."

"Maybe you haven't, but anyone who's anyone in anthropology has heard of him. And according to Harry, he's totally convinced that the force which possessed me—the darkness which possessed me—is one and the same force that brought down Chicago."

Abner's mouth was already open, about to say something, but then he closed it again. He ran his hand through his wavy hair.

"Martin," he said, at last. "Do you want me to enter a plea of insanity?"

"Don't be ridiculous! I know the concept is difficult to grasp, but believe me, I'm not insane."

"Then maybe this Harry Erskine ought to enter a plea of insanity. And Dr Snow, too. For God's sake, Chicago was hit by an earthquake, not a demon. What do you think this is going to sound like in court? Come on, Martin, this isn't the Middle Ages."

Martin said, "I'll prove you wrong, Abner. I'll prove it."

"Well, so long as *you're* confident."

"Abner—just give me some time. If I can't establish my innocence beyond a shadow of a doubt, then you can make it as easy on Ms Medina as you like. Did you bring me those books I asked for?"

Abner popped open the clasps of his briefcase. He handed Martin three thickish books, and then a faded black-velvet pouch containing something that jingled. He glanced quickly toward the corridor to make sure that nobody was watching, and then handed the pouch over. "This, too, against my better judgement."

Martin loosened the drawstring around the neck of the pouch and shook out two silver three-tined forks. They were tarnished and obviously very old. On the end of each of them was the bulging-eyed face of a dragon.

He held them up. "You see these? Eight hundred years old, at least. I bought them in London."

Abner peered at them unhappily. "Eight hundred years old, hunh? Very nice."

"Do you know where they came from?"

Abner shook his head.

"They came from Massachusetts. They were discovered by Puritans when they were digging graves at Plympton. They're Norse—from northern Denmark originally."

"Is it impertinent to ask what you want them for?" said Abner.

Martin dropped them back in the pouch. "Not for eating. When those were made people didn't eat with forks, only knives. They were carried to America by Viking sailors to protect themselves against malevolent spirits. The idea was that they would hold the forks in front of themselves, handle-first, and the spirit would jump into the handles, like lightning into a lightning-conductor.

"But then the Viking shaman would turn the forks round, and the only way in which the spirit could then escape was through the six prongs, and that would mean splitting itself into six. That was the theory, anyway."

Abner's expression grew more and more miserable with every word. Eventually, he closed his briefcase, stood up, and held out his hand.

"Listen," he said. "I want you to think very seriously about pleading insanity. It doesn't mean you have to be starey-eyed and frothing at the mouth. It simply means that your mental condition at the time you perpetrated the killings was sufficiently unstable as to render you not responsible for your actions. There's no shame in it, Martin. Plenty of people lose it from time to time. I know some judges who should be weaving baskets."

Martin looked up. "I'll make a deal with you, Abner. If I can't bring the proof in twenty-four hours that I was being manipulated by a spirit or a demon, then you can plead more than insanity, you can plead totally ga-ga."

"It has to be proof that I can produce at your arraignment hearing," said Abner. "You have to convince the judge, not me."

"Let's hope we luck out and have one of those judges who should be weaving baskets," Martin replied, although he wasn't smiling.

He was returned to his cell. Through the bars he was faced with nothing but a flaking green-painted wall. A tiny mesh-covered window allowed a faint trapezoid of sunlight to wax and wane on the surface of his fixed wooden table. The table was scratched and gouged with thousands of messages and initials and wildly obscene drawings. He set his three books down on it, and laid his velvet pouch next to the books.

The precinct echoed like the lunatic asylum in *Dracula*. Howls of misery from arrested winos; screams and laughter from crack addicts; doors slamming; keys jangling; a woman arguing high and shrill; and the rattle of nightsticks against bars and brickwork.

Martin pressed his hands over his face. "Samuel, help me," he whispered.

He was summoning his dead brother, his brother who would always be ten years old and never any older. He was asking Samuel to take his hand, and to guide him into the darkest and most frightening landscapes of the spirit-world.

He knew that it was highly dangerous. He knew that he could be putting Samuel at risk, too. But he could see no alternative. He had tried to fight the darkness on his own and it had totally overwhelmed him and made a murderer out of him. He could only guess at how powerful it was. If Harry Erskine was right and it was the Great One from below, Aktunowihio, then it was certainly powerful enough to drag whole cities into the darkness.

He opened one of the books that Abner had brought him from his apartment. *Forces of Darkness,* Professor Calvin Mackie's examination of Celtic and Indian concepts of life after death.

Ever since they had started to write decipherable hieroglyphs, it was clear that the Alqonquin and Micmac tribes had been aware of "the shadow world beneath, and the huge dark horn-headed god, whose face could only be seen through a man's fingers." On a stone at Spiro Mound, Oklahoma, Professor Mackie had discovered the letters M-M, which stood for Mabo-Mabona, the ancient Celtic name for Aktunowihio. Next to the letters was a crude but clear engraving of a beast with round eyes and antlers and a face so wild and horrifying that Martin turned the page to cover it up and pressed his hand over it.

He felt a small kind of madness coming on. The world of spirits was always unpredictable and frightening even when he was doing nothing more than looking for sons and daughters and deceased parents. Moving through the world beyond was like struggling through a dark garden hung with line after line of black, drenched blankets. He was always aware that others were pushing their way through the blankets, too, close but mostly hidden. It was only when a pale cold hand reached out between the blankets that he received any guidance. He would take hold of that hand, however dead it might be, and hurry after it, trusting it.

Sometimes—mostly—his spirit guides were gentle and helpful and would take him where he was anxious to go. At other times their hands would suddenly slip away and leave him disoriented and lost, in the tilted corner of somebody's nightmare, or in the flickering strobe-light crisis of a sudden death—a car crash, a heart-attack, somebody shattering through a plate-glass window. Occasionally they would lead him into actual danger. Darkness, and more darkness, and a thick threatening smell like the breath of wolves.

Then he would have to drain himself out of his spiritual trance. Dwindle, and vanish, and return to the waking world. It wasn't always easy. Only four months ago, he had opened his eyes after a spirit-guidance session to find the back of his hand bitten—*bitten* by something, and blood on his trousers. He had gone to the doctor for a tetanus shot and the doctor had looked at him very strangely.

"You're not going to tell me how this happened, are you?" the doctor had asked him; and Martin had said, "No, I'm not, because you wouldn't believe me if I did." He took out the Celtic forks and laid them on the table, with the tines pointing towards him. Maybe they'd protect him, maybe they wouldn't; but the Celts must have thought that they worked, and if you were planning on taking a walk in an electric storm, it made sense to take your lightning-rods.

"Samuel," he whispered. "I need you, Samuel. I need you more than I've ever needed you before."

The cell remained stuffy and silent. The light from the window brightened and then dimmed again, as clouds passed by. He could see the shadows of the clouds on the backs of his hands, almost like moving pictures.

"Samuel, help me," he urged. "You've always managed to help me before. Please help me now."

He closed his eyes tight. All he could see was blackness. He hoped it was the blackness of spiritual trance; of that dark, wet, blanket-hung garden. But he knew that it wasn't, not yet. It was simply the darkness of a desperate man with his eyes shut.

"Samuel," he repeated. "Wherever you are, Samuel, I really need you now."

And even deeper in his mind, he said, *Samuel, I beg you.*

He thought he heard something.

Somebody breathing, close beside him.

He slowly turned his head forty-five degrees to the left, and then he opened his eyes.

Karen was standing outside his cell. Karen van Hooven, née Tandy, in a yellow linen blouse and a short twill skirt. She looked pale, and her eyes looked strangely colorless and metallic, almost as if they were steel ball-bearings rather than eyes. Her hair was awry, and looked as if it were floating in an unfelt draft.

"Karen?" said Martin, uncertainly. "What are you doing here?" She came up to the bars of his cell, and grasped them in both hands. At first she said nothing, but stared in Martin's direction with her eyes oddly long-sighted, as if she were actually focusing on the wall behind him.

For some reason that he couldn't quite work out, Martin felt afraid of her. There was an unusually *unsettled* feeling about her psychic aura. He had only sensed a similar aura twice before. Once in a woman who was dying from seventy-five percent burns, after trying to rescue her husband from a house fire. Once in a nine-year-old boy whose father was abusing him and who would soon be drowned in a wash-basin.

It was an aura of darkness. The same darkness that surrounds the sun.

It was an almost-visible aura of death.

"Karen?" Martin repeated, although he made no move to get up. "I didn't know you were coming."

Karen said, "I have to warn you."

"Warn me?" asked Martin. "Warn me about what?"

"I have to warn you to take your punishment. We won't be pleased if you don't. You did what you did. Now you have to take your punishment."

"I don't understand what you're talking about."

"I mean you mustn't interfere. Things will be much worse for you if you interfere."

"Karen," said Martin. "does Harry know that you're here?"

"What?" Her voice was silvery and flat.

"Does Harry know that you've come to visit me? And in any case, who let you in here? Don't they usually insist on your having an escort? And a security badge, at least?"

Karen repeated, *"You mustn't interfere."*

With no warning whatsoever, she stepped *through* the bars of the cell and stood beside Martin as calm and as expressionless as if she had walked through an open door. Martin jumped up from his chair and knocked it over.

"Hey, now," he said, lifting one hand to protect himself. "You're not Karen. You're not Karen at all."

"Who else could I be?" she asked him. "Karen van Hooven, flesh and blood. Here, touch me."

Martin backed away. "Thanks . . . but I think I'd better not."

"You want to find what it was that possessed you, don't you?" asked Karen.

Her smile was faint and eerie. Her eyes still didn't seem to be focused correctly.

Martin blurted, "Yes, of course I want to find out what it was. But there's really no rush. I'll try it some other time."

Karen reached out and laid her hand on his shoulder. It was a real hand, gentle but real. At least it *felt* real.

If Karen was a ghost of some kind, or maybe an ectoplasmic projection, she was the best damned ghost that he had ever seen. Apparently solid, breathing properly—*perfumed* even. Ghosts very rarely smelled of anything, although their imminent appearance could be signalled by a strong distinctive aroma associated with somewhere they had lived, or something they had liked.

Martin walked cautiously around her. She stayed where she was, very calm.

"You don't believe I'm *real*?" she asked him.

"Real people can't walk through steel bars. I rest my case."

She turned her head to face him. "Some people can walk through steel bars. It's called willpower."

He hesitated, tried not to smile back at her. "I think it's a little more than willpower, Karen. I think it's material projection. You're here, but you're not really here at all."

Karen looked at him mischievously. "All right, if I'm not really here at all, where am I?"

"I don't know. But that's what I intend to find out."

"You really shouldn't. It's too risky."

"What could be riskier than facing an arraignment for first-degree murder?"

"Martin—you don't know what you're up against."

"That's precisely the problem. And that's precisely why I intend to find out what it is."

Karen lifted one hand, and said, "Martin . . . please don't."

"I can't do anything else. What choices do I have?"

"None, I guess." She looked away, nervously drumming her fingers against her shoulder, nervously biting her lips. "Are you *sure* I can't persuade you?"

"I'm afraid not."

"You're not thinking of going into such a deep trance without an anchor, are you? Somebody to bring you out, in case things go wrong?"

"I don't have any choice."

Karen said, "Let me be your anchor."

"How can you do it? You're not even real."

She stroked his cheek with her fingertips. He reached up and took hold of her wrist.

"Real enough." She smiled.

Martin released her. He picked up his fallen chair and sat down again. "Maybe you're real enough," he said. "But how do I know that I can trust you?"

Karen thought about that. Then she said, "You can trust me because Harry trusts me, and because Amelia trusts me, too."

She said it without blinking. Martin thought to himself: maybe she's lying to me, maybe not. She had walked through steel bars as if they didn't exist, and maybe *she* didn't exist, either. But he couldn't keep her out, could he— even if he wanted to? And he had nobody else who could act as an anchor, while he searched for the spirit that had taken hold of his soul.

Most of the time, Martin wasn't afraid of spirit manifestations. After all, his brother Samuel had been visiting him regularly since he was ten years old. Most of the time, spirit manifestations where caused by a freak intermingling of unfulfilled desires, unfinished feelings, and a twirl of spiritual ectoplasm, caught on an unexpected current. Two things kept spirits coming back to the world that they should have left behind them: jealousy, and revenge. People who had died contented, amongst friends they loved, were always happy to turn their back on the world and look to the future.

Martin rearranged his Celtic forks and clasped his hands together, an almost priestly little ritual. He glanced up at Karen's reflection in the mirror on the wall. For the briefest of seconds, he thought he saw her face darken and distort, but it was probably nothing more than the clouds passing outside.

"You'll have to stay quiet," He told her. "And if it looks like anything's going wrong—ghost or not—you're going to have to get out of here, and as quickly as you can. The creature I'm trying to track down is capable of tearing up a city. I don't think it would have very much compunction about tearing up *us*."

Karen said nothing, but stood beside him with her arms folded and waited for him to begin.

He cleared his throat. Then—placing himself completely at Karen's mercy—he closed his eyes.

"Samuel," he said. "I need you to guide me, Samuel."

He heard Karen move slightly, move around behind him. He was desperately tempted to open his eyes to see what she was doing, but he knew that would only delay things.

"Samuel," he said. Then, "Samuel?"

There was a very long silence, six or seven minutes or more. Martin could feel Karen growing impatient. But this time he could feel that the spirits were moving well. This time he could feel the darkness pouring thick and steady into his mind, filling up his brain, the real seamless darkness of death.

He saw his brother Samuel standing in the corner of the room, white and silent, in his red wool bathrobe.

"Samuel?" he said.

He had never seen his brother look so sad. He had never seen him look so indistinct. It was like seeing a boy through a grey net curtain, a curtain which stirred in the breeze, so that you could never be sure if he were smiling or if he had just been crying.

"Samuel?" he repeated. He didn't rise; but he held out his hand, even though he knew that Samuel would never take it.

"Martin," said Samuel, without moving his lips. "Martin, you should stay away. . . . It's all over, the whole world's turning upside down."

"Samuel, I have to find the spirit that possessed me. I have to. I have to find it, and I have to bring it back here—or part of it, at least. I have to prove that *I* didn't kill those people."

Samuel was silent for a long time. Then he slowly shook his head. "You should stay away, Martin. It's the dark one; the one from underneath. He's going to take all of you."

"Samuel, for Christ's sake! I need your help!"

Samuel brushed back his cow's-lick hair, the way he always used to when he was alive. "I can't help you, Martin. Not now."

"At least give me a guide."

Another long silence. Samuel's image brightened and faded, brightened and faded, in the same way that the sunlight brightened and faded through Martin's cell window.

"All right," said Samuel, at last, and turned his narrow back in a way that he had never done before.

Martin waited and waited, resisting the temptation to open his eyes. He could feel Karen standing close to him, but he knew that if he opened his eyes there could be a considerable risk of disrupting the connection he had formed with the spirit-world, with strange and dangerous consequences. Things could be left in the real world which didn't belong there; and vice versa. He had once come across a simple sewing needle which had penetrated the real world from the spirit-world, and which had pricked everybody who had tried to pick it up.

He waited. He tried to meditate. He tried to think how he

was going to deal with the shadow that had possessed him once he found it.

He hummed "Jeannie with the Light Brown Hair." He drummed his fingers on the table.

At last, he felt a spiritual draft. With his eyes still closed he saw a thin man in a bedraggled blue uniform approaching him, walking (as it were) through walls and doors and windows. As the man came closer, he saw that it was the cavalry officer who had first made contact with him when he had tried to search for the shadow-spirit in Naomi Greenberg's dining room.

The man dragged one of his feet in a weary limp, and his uniform was powdered with white dust. He had been horribly scalped, ears and all, because the Oglala Sioux always preferred their scalps with ears on. His head was matted with blood, thick black clots of it, except where the bone of his skull showed through. His drooping mustache was bloody, too. He came up close to Martin, standing in front of Martin's desk, and eyeing him up and down. Martin could see that the crotch of his cavalry pants was dark with blood.

"I thought once would have been enough," the officer remarked. He was very laconic in spite of the fact that he was dead, and that he still bore the terrible scars of his torture.

Martin was shivering. "I need to find him. I need to prove that he's real."

The cavalry officer said, "He's real all right. Real as rain. Don't know how you go about proving it, though."

"I must."

The cavalry officer looked bloody and reflective. "It'd be a darned dangerous business."

"But you came to help me all the same."

"Yes, sir, I suppose I did."

"Can I ask who you are?"

"I'm Daniel McIntosh, sir, First Lieutenant, Company G, Seventh Cavalry."

"What happened to you, Lieutenant McIntosh?"

"I died at Greasy Grass River, sir, the battle they called the Little Big Horn."

"And what do you know about the shadow?"

"I saw it, sir. I saw it right behind Crazy Horse the first time the Indians came riding up that northerly hill."

"You *saw* it?" said Martin.

"Yes, sir, we all did. It was like a shadow, sir, black as a shadow, with things moving in it, things like snakes or maybe coils of smoke. We couldn't rightly decide. The day was pretty dark in any case, on account of the firing and the gunsmoke."

"What did it do?"

"It moved so quick it was hard to say, a whole great rush of shadow—scared the living shit out of all of us. First it dragged some of the horses down the hill and they was screaming like human women, those horses. It was the worstest thing I ever did hear, apart from the screaming when the men was dragged down the hill after them."

"The shadow-thing was dragging them down?"

"That's correct, sir, exactly that. I felt it myself. It was like the whole hill was moving under my bootheels. I never felt anything like it before.

"I swear to you, it wasn't Crazy Horse or any of his men who killed us that day, it was the shadow that dragged us down, and it was only then that Crazy Horse started counting coup and torturing and all."

"Did you see where the shadow went?"

"No, sir. I was hurt by then. I was pulled to the ground and my back was broke. I couldn't get up to my feet at all. Then there was four or five Sioux standing over me and they shot arrows between my legs into my privates. Then they cut off my scalp and my ears and left me to die. I lay on the ground and I dreamed of my dear mother and it was almost like being a boy again. Then my mother came through the smoke and knelt down beside me and touched my forehead as cool as buttermilk. She said, 'Come on, son, everything's fine,' and then I knew that I was passed over, and all my suffering was at an end."

Martin covered his closed eyes with his hand, but he could still see Lieutenant McIntosh just as clearly.

"Think, lieutenant . . . did anything happen that could have *proved* it was the shadow that killed you, rather than the Indians?"

"Well, I'll tell you, sir, several of the men were turned completely outside in, like gloves, and I don't know how an Indian could have done that, even the strongest."

"But you were all killed, weren't you? Nobody survived to bear witness to that."

"Well, sir, photographs were took."

"Photographs? Somebody took photographs?"

"Mr Kellogg of the *Bismarck Tribune,* sir, although what became of Mr Kellogg or what became of his photographs I never shall know."

Martin was about to ask Lieutenant McIntosh where Mr Kellogg had been standing when he took his photographs when the cavalry officer seemed to shiver and fade.

"Lieutenant, what's happening?"

Lieutenant McIntosh opened and closed his mouth, but if he did speak Martin couldn't hear him. His image grew dimmer and darker, as if a shadow were falling across it, and Martin began to be aware that a shadow was building up in front of him. The temperature in the cell began rapidly to drop, and Martin was aware of a strong and familiar smell. The smell of prairie burning. The smell of Indian fires. The smell of buffalo meat and magic herbs and a wind that stayed silent, because it had too many tragic stories to tell.

He felt Karen moving around behind him. He didn't know what she was doing, but he didn't dare to open his eyes and find out. This was Samuel's trance, using Samuel's spiritual energy, and if Martin were to break it off now, without warning, he might cause Samuel severe harm. He might even silence his spirit forever.

The darkness in front of him was dense and smoky. He thought he could detect things moving about in it, black glistening things that coiled and uncoiled.

"What are you?" he demanded. "What do you want?"

There was a long silence, and then Martin heard a breathy, reverberating voice, more like the wind blowing down a hollow reed than a voice.

"You thought to find me?"

Martin licked his lips. "Yes, I thought to find you."

"You thought to defeat me?"

"You killed Michael and Naomi Greenberg, not me.

That was why I wanted to find you. I wanted to prove that it was you."

"You are a fool."

"Maybe I am. But I'm going to prove that you exist, even if it kills me."

"Are you not afraid to die? I thought that all white men were afraid to die. At the Greasy Grass River they threw down their rifles and they cried out, 'Spare us!' And we spared not a single one."

Martin was shuddering with cold and fear. He had come across dozens of unpleasant spirits before now; mean-minded spirits, angry spirits, bitter spirits. He had talked to murderers, bigamists, you name it. But the spirit that was hiding itself in this shadow was something else.

The spirit that was hiding itself in this shadow was something infinitely old, darkly terrifying, and possessed of powers that Martin could only guess at.

He suddenly understood that he was very, very frightened. More frightened than he had ever felt before.

"You want to see me?" the breathy voice asked him.

Martin swallowed and nodded.

"If you wish to see me, you must open your eyes."

"You're a spirit," said Martin. "How can I see you if I open my eyes?"

"Open your eyes," the voice insisted.

Martin hesitantly opened his eyes.

And *saw.*

And literally jolted with terror. And closed them again, tight, in the hope that it couldn't be real, that it couldn't be true.

But then he felt a sharp, chopping pain in the sides of both his eyesockets. He yelled out and twisted in his chair, but he felt as if his skull were caught in an iron clamp. The pain in his eyes was so intense that he stayed where he was, sitting upright, shivering.

Inside his eyesockets there was a deep, agonizing crunching of skin and flesh and nerve fiber. His eyes were bloodily, forcibly opened, and then pulled right out of their sockets.

"Oh Christ!" he screamed. *"Oh, Christ, don't blind me!"*

It was Karen. She had taken each of his Celtic forks and

dug their blunt, curved tines into his eye-sockets, underneath each eyeball, and literally forked them out. The tines
were an eighth of an inch apart, just wide enough for the
optic nerve of each eye to be caught between them and
stretched out. Martin could still see, even though his eyes
felt as if they were on fire. Blood coursed hotly down his
cheeks and pattered onto the table.

"Karen," he babbled, "oh Christ, Karen, don't blind me.
Karen, what are you doing Karen what the hell are you
doing don't blind me don't blind me don't blind me-e-e-ee!"

"You wanted to see me," the voice breathed. *"So shall you
see me; and so shall you never look away."*

Through a scarlet fog of pain and bursting capillaries, his
bare eyeballs wincing, Martin stared at the apparition that
stood in front of him, half-buried in the wall and the table, a
being that could live both inside and outside a spiritual
trance simultaneously, a wonder-worker of such enormous
powers that the darkness shifted and trembled all around
him as if an earthquake were imminent.

Martin knew who he was, and the fear that he felt was
as great as the terrible thing that Karen had done to his
eyes. He was Misquamacus, the greatest of all the Indian
medicine-men. Misquamacus, who had walked through
time and space. Misquamacus, who had travelled through
fire and death and every level of cosmic consciousness.

It was said that the face of Misquamacus had appeared in
trees and rivers, and that his voice had chanted in the wind.
In the 1870s he had been photographed in a Sioux encampment near Fort Snelling, Minnesota, on the same day that
he had been photographed with Etchemis Indians in north-
eastern New England, more than 1,500 miles away.

But now he was here, in Martin's cell in the 13th Precinct,
and even the air was softly thundering with his presence.

He was tall—almost monstrously tall. His face was slab-
like, impassive, high-cheekboned, and decorated with
flashes of red and white clay. His eyes were totally dark, like
perforations in a curtain.

But it was his headdress that horrified Martin more than
anything else. His scalp and his neck and his shoulders were
completely covered in a swarming mass of struggling, shiny

beetles—cockroaches and black-beetles and weevils and whirligigs and deathwatch beetles. His head was alive with beetles, and as he stood and stared at Martin with dispassion they clicked and struggled and occasionally dropped to the floor.

Misquamacus himself was afflicted by hideous growths on his torso and his upper arms, patches of black insect hair and lumps of maroon, insect-like body sections. On either side of his body, all the way down his ribs, pale tendrils like millipede legs waved and rippled.

What did you expect? he whispered, inside Martin's mind.

The pain in Martin's eyes was now far too intense for him to be able to answer. He thought he was probably having a nightmare, and that he would very soon wake up. But then Misquamacus lifted a huge buffalo mask onto his head—a mask already swarming with beetles—and Martin knew without a doubt what the wonder-worker was going to do to him, and why; and that his chances of survival, blind or not, were almost nothing at all.

"Kill me," he said. "I can't stand to be hurt. Please kill me."

Misquamacus reached out his hand and gently touched Martin's gouged-out eyeballs, running his greasy, ash-blackened fingertips around their cringing, wrinkled surfaces.

"Can you see that?" he asked. He flicked the corneas with his fingernails, and then laughed when Martin screamed.

"Perhaps you don't deserve it," said Misquamacus, his eyes bright, his voice thickly accented. Martin had never heard a Narragansett accent before, but he knew that if he survived he would never forget it. It was amused, declamatory, but there was also a slight hint of self-mockery in it.

"Don't blind me," he said. He couldn't find any other words. He knew that it was probably too late for any surgeon to save his eyes; but so long as there was the smallest chance. So long as he could still *see.*

Misquamacus took hold of Martin's right eye like a man plucking a plum. Martin knew than that the Indian was going to hurt him, and worse than hurt him. He thought he started to scream but he couldn't be sure. His lungs were clenched with dread and he may not have uttered any sound at all.

Misquamacus squeezed his eyeball until it burst. Optic fluid suddenly flooded between the wonder-worker's blackened fingers.

Roaring with rage as well as agony, Martin tried to heave himself backward. All he succeeded in doing was ripping his optic nerve through the tines of his Celtic fork. His face exploded with pain. It was like being hit in the face with a hammer. He thrashed all around him, still roaring. Everything was black. Everything was fire. Everything was blindness and defeat.

Three officers heard him screaming and roaring and came running down to the cells. They found him lying on his back on the floor, his eyesockets as blind as overturned pots of red ink, and the cell walls splattered with blood. Some of the blood formed exclamation points, some of the blood made question marks. But all Martin could do was kick and scream, his body convulsed in pain, and all that the cops could do was call for the paramedics.

"Self-mutilation," said Sergeant Friendly. "It happens a lot with homicide suspects. They're worried we're not going to punish them enough for what they did."

A single cockroach zig-zagged furiously across the floor.

TWELVE

The next morning the humidity was even higher and my
Avis air-conditioner started to cough like Monday morning
on the cancer ward. I eased myself stiffly off the couch and
shuffled through to my dinky little kitchenette. There was a
magnifying shaving-mirror hanging from a cup-hook on the
shelf, and a monstrous bloodshot eye swam around in it.

Last night I had finished off the better part of a bottle of
Absolut, trying not to imagine what might have happened
to Karen, and trying to think what the hell I should do now.
Maybe I should do nothing at all. Maybe I should accept
the idea that just because I had confronted Misquamacus
twice before there was no reason why it was my responsibility to confront him again. Let him do whatever he wanted.

I scooped espresso coffee into my coffee machine, filled it
with Evian water, and switched it on. There was a sharp
crackling noise and a wisp of blue smoke came out of the
plug. Shorted out again. That meant I would have to put on
my trousers and go down to the drugstore.

I was raking my fingers through my hair when my intercom buzzed. I picked it up and said, "Erskine the Incredible—palmistry, card-divining, tea-leaf interpretation—"
But I was interrupted by a voice saying, "Harry, it's me,
Deirdre."

"Oh, Deirdre." I frowned, and checked my Russian wristwatch. It said twenty after five, which was impossible,
whether it was morning or afternoon. "We didn't schedule a
reading for today, did we?"

"I know we don't, but you were quite right about Mason
having me followed. He's found out about Vance. And I'm
worried that John has found out about Mason."

"I see, well, I did warn you."

"Harry, I know I'm being a nuisance, but could you possibly give me another reading right now? Things are happening so fast, I need an update."

How could I refuse? Mrs John F. Lavender was my bread
and butter. In fact she was more than my bread and butter,

she was my Kraft cheese slices too. I pressed the buzzer and as I struggled into my crumpled fawn Chinos I heard her climbing the stairs, two at a time, like an Alpine gazelle. I opened the door for her with one hand and zipped my fly with the other.

She was wearing skin-tight emerald-green satin pants, a floppy blouse of stridently purple silk and a huge yellow straw hat with an extravagant scarlet flower on the head-band.

"Harry," she said, "you look like *hell*."

I coughed. "Had a rough night, I'm sorry."

She picked up the empty vodka bottle and turned it upside down. "Well, drowning your sorrows, were you? I wouldn't have thought that clairvoyants *had* any sorrows. I mean, can't you always see what's coming?"

I shrugged. "Oh, for sure. But just because I can see what's coming, that doesn't always mean that I can get out of the way. Or even that I necessarily *want* to get out of the way."

"Oh," said Deirdre, with a knowing, multi-eyelashed wink. "Affair of the heart, was it?"

I lifted a heap of newspapers and magazines from the chaise-longue. "Just take a seat, Deirdre. I have to shave."

"I kind of like you with stubble," Deirdre flirted. "You remind me of Humphrey Bogart."

I went back to the kitchenette, tugged out the plug of the coffee machine, and plugged in my electric razor. While I shaved, Deirdre said, "I first realized that Mason was having me followed when I was shopping in Bergdorf Goodman. I spent *hours* looking for cyan gloves to go with my cyan evening suit, you know the Ralph Lauren evening suit I was telling you about, when I noticed a man in an awful cheap blazer hanging around pretending to look through the scarves. After that I went to lingerie and he followed me into lingerie. There was no doubt about it; he was a private detective."

"What makes you think that Mason hired him?" I asked.

"Because you said he would, of course."

"Oh, yes, sure," I called back. "Has Mason told you directly to your face that he knows about Vince?"

"Vance," Deirdre corrected me.

"Vince, Vance, whatever. Are you sure that Mason knows for sure?"

"Well, he didn't say so in so many actual words. But he *did* say that if he found out that I was two-timing him, he'd do something desperate."

"Has he done anything desperate yet?"

"It depends on your definition of desperate, I guess. Yesterday afternoon he bought a yellow Hermes cravat in the men's department at Macy's."

"Hmm . . . I guess you'd have to be pretty desperate to do that."

I finished shaving. Then, without any technical ceremony, I cut the plug off my coffee machine with a paring knife, stripped the wires bare, and poked them directly into the socket. There was a moment's pause, and then the machine gave out a satisfying *bloop* and I knew that a much-needed caffeine overdose was on the way. I came back into the consulting room, where Deirdre was lighting up a cigarette. I breathed in match-sulphur, saltpeter and half-burned tobacco, and my stomach gave a *bloop* in sympathy with the coffee-machine.

"I guess you saw that new client of yours on television," said Deirdre. "I told John, that's another client of Harry Erskine's. I've seen her in the flesh, for real. Mind you, I think she looks so much prettier in the flesh, if you know what I mean."

I sat down. I had missed a small patch of stubble on my left cheek, and it felt prickly and uncomfortable. "I'm sorry," I said, "I don't understand."

"Well, I scarcely *ever* watch television, but there was something on the news about a racehorse that belongs to a friend of mine, Douglas Evershed III, you must have heard of Douglas, he's quite an eccentric."

"Yes, I have, but what was this about—?"

"It was that girl, that same girl who was waiting for you downstairs in the hall the last time I visited! They had a news item about some terrible mass murder in Arizona, and there she was, clear as daylight. They were interviewing the sheriff or somebody and she was standing right in the background. There was no mistaking her."

I covered my mouth with my hand for a moment and thought hard. *Karen? In Arizona?* How could that be?

"Can you remember what station that was?" I asked Deirdre.

"Of course, NBC."

"And you're absolutely positive it was her?"

"No question at all. She was standing right behind the sheriff, clear as daylight."

I felt the strangest shiver go down my spine: partly of hope, partly of dread. I guess I shouldn't have been surprised at Karen appearing all the way across the country—even though she had dropped out of sight only the day before yesterday down a bottomless grave in New York City. I knew from experience that Misquamacus was capable of travelling through time and space in the most extraordinary way, and maybe he had taken Karen with him.

I rummaged through my bureau and pulled out a Manhattan telephone directory with a torn cover. I licked my finger and leafed through to NBC. Deirdre watched me, smoking and agitated.

"Have I *said* something?" she wanted to know.

"I'm not sure," I said. "But I want to see that news item for myself."

"Well, for goodness's sake, *I* can help with that," said Deirdre. "I videotaped the whole news, so that Douglas could see it when he came back from France."

For once in my life I actually believed that God and happenstance were both on my side. "Deirdre," I said, "you're an angel from heaven."

She dragged at her cigarette, and then explosively coughed. "Don't kill me off yet." She opened her pocketbook. "Here—call this number. It's my car phone. Tell my driver Felipe to go get the tape for you and bring it back here."

She stretched herself back on the chaise-longue, her skinny thighs wobbling slightly under the clinging emerald-green satin. "And while Felipe is doing that, *you* can give me a fresh reading."

"Oh—yes," I agreed. "What's it to be today? Cards? Tea-leaves?"

"Oh, cards. Those French cards. I really like what they have to say. They give me such *frisson,* if you know what I mean."

I sat down at the table and set out the cards. Behind the beaded curtain, in the kitchenette, the coffee machine continued to bloop. None of my divinations were particularly mystic, but this morning's reading was going to be even less mystic than ever. I couldn't think about anything else but Karen. Was she conscious of what she was doing, I wondered, or had Misquamacus somehow hypnotized her? What was she doing in Arizona? Had she flown there, or had Misquamacus transported her—in the same way that he must have transported himself in the 1870s? Was she really there at all—or was the face that Deirdre had seen on the evening news nothing more than an illusion, a trick, a magical joke?

Deirdre peered through the cigarette smoke at the cards which I was turning up. "Wasn't that terrible, that earthquake in Chicago?" she said, apropos of nothing at all. "Sometimes I think that God's punishing us, you know, for being too arrogant."

I said nothing, but held up the first card. It showed a hillside, with autumnal trees on it, and clouds. Some of the clouds were shining white, others were grey and depressing. You can see why I liked the Lenormand cards so much. They gave me *carte-blanche* to say whatever I thought was most suitable. Or at least *carte*–completely ambiguous.

"What does it mean?" Deirdre asked, excitedly.

"It says *'Clouds brightly shine strung in precision . . . life will be fine with firm decision.'* In other words you have to make your mind up. Make some choices, and stick to them."

Deirdre obviously didn't like the sound of that. "What's going to happen if I don't? Can't I hedge my bets just a little? I *hate* to make choices. I mean I like what I choose, but I can't bear to lose whatever it is I *haven't* chosen. I want it *all.*" She laughed, coughed.

From the kitchenette, I heard a sharp spitting noise, and

then I smelled burning. The coffee machine had overflowed and shorted out the bare wires that were stuck in the plug.

Deirdre waited for me impatiently while I mopped up. "I told you—you should read your own fortune once in a while."

Amelia came over just before one o'clock and we sat and shared a Neapolitan pizza and watched the videotape that Deirdre had lent me.

The anchorman started by saying that "—the tiny desert community of Apache Junction, less than thirty miles east of the state capital Phoenix, has become the focus of the most intensive police operation in Arizona's history . . ."

"Apache Junction," I interrupted, shaking my head. "I should have known. Under The Old One. The place where they tortured Geronimo's men."

The bulletin switched to NBC's on-the-spot reporter, a handsome high-cheekboned Indian girl with glossy black shoulder-length hair. She said, "Here at the used automobile dealership of local character Papago Joe, police are still investigating the horrific deaths of seven men and women, whose mutilated bodies were discovered two days ago in an automobile inspection pit.

"All of the victims were out-of-towners, and five of them came from out of state, including Washington, Minnesota and Maine. Police as yet have no idea what they were all doing here, or who might have been minded to murder them all. Sheriff Ethan Wallace is currently working on the theory that they were all members of an illicit drugs or gambling syndicate who tried to double-cross influential figures in the Phoenix Mafia."

The interviewer then turned towards a hot freckly man in green-lensed Ray•Bans, who stood with his hands parked on his bulging sides, systematically chewing a large cud of gum.

She asked him why he believed this was a mob killing, but I didn't bother to listen to what he was saying. Because Deirdre had been right. Close behind Sheriff Wallace's shoulder, *in the same yellow blouse that she had been wearing on that day she disappeared,* stood Karen: my Karen. The girl who had now become "my Karen," and who had now been taken away from me.

She was listening to the sheriff and nodding as if she agreed with him. Then she turned to one side and talked to the man standing next to her. The man nodded and pointed. After a while, Karen moved out of camera-shot and disappeared.

"Karen," I said to Amelia, standing up.

"No question," Amelia agreed. She took out a cigarette, although she didn't immediately light it. "But what is she doing *there,* in Arizona?"

"Who knows? I guess she's there because Misquamacus wants her there, that's all."

"But how did she *get* there?"

"Misquamacus has a way of appearing wherever he wants, whenever he wants. Don't ask me how it works. He's a spirit, after all, a manitou. I guess that time and distance don't mean all that much to him."

Amelia said nothing, but as I rewound the videotape she looked distressed.

"Misquamacus has no real physical substance," I reminded her. "He's using Karen like a sort of human puppet—the same way he did when he used her body to have himself reborn. He spoke with her voice; he saw with her eyes; he touched with her hands. I guess you could say that she's possessed."

On the videotape, Karen reappeared, running backwards.

"Look at her!" I said. "Look at the way she's staring. She's not even blinking. She probably can't even remember who she is, or why she's there."

Amelia said, "What are you going to do?"

"I don't know. Maybe Martin may have some ideas."

"You think so? I don't know. He's probably far too wrapped up in his own problems. Besides, how are you going to get to talk to him?"

"I'll ask his lawyer. And I don't think he's going to be too wrapped up in his own problems to understand that if I can rescue Karen, then there's a good chance that I can come up with something that will help to prove his innocence, too."

"Like what?"

"How should I know? Maybe a feather out of Misquamacus' headband. Maybe a piece of that shadow-thing, in one of those shadow-bottles that Dr Snow was talking about."

"I hope you're joking."

"Only partly."

I searched through the pockets of yesterday's shirt and found the crumpled piece of paper on which I had written the number of Martin's lawyer. I punched out the number and waited while the phone warbled. Amelia said, "This is all so *frustrating*. It's like trying to catch ghosts."

"Are you kidding me? It *is* trying to catch ghosts."

"Kaskin Moskowitz Kaskin."

"Could I speak to Mr Abner Kaskin, please?"

"Hold on, sir."

I waited and listened to *Tulips from Amsterdam* as played by Robby the Robot. Eventually a brisk secretarial voice said, "Good morning, sir. I regret that Mr Kaskin is out of the office."

"This is Mr Erskine. I wanted to talk to him urgently."

"May I ask in what connection?"

"It's about Mr Martin Vaizey. It could be critical."

"Mr Kaskin's gone to see Mr Vaizey this morning, in the hospital."

"In the hospital? What do you mean—in the hospital? What's happened?"

"Mr Vaizey's had a serious accident, sir."

"Accident? What kind of accident?"

"I'm sorry, sir, I can't say."

"Where is he? Which hospital?"

"If you can hold a moment, sir, I'll—"

"Which hospital?" I snapped at her. "This could be critical! This could make all the difference!"

"Sir, there's no need to—"

"I'm sorry. I didn't mean to bite your head off. Please tell me which hospital. If Mr Kaskin gives you any kind of flak you can lay all the blame on me, I promise you. I'll even tell your fortune for free, how about that?"

"My *fortune*?"

At that moment, however, Amelia tapped my shoulder.

She had ejected the videotape that I had borrowed from Mrs John F. Lavender and there on the TV screen was the mid-morning news. They had flashed up a photograph of Martin Vaizey, with the caption "Homicide Suspect"—then they cut to an ENG camera right outside a Manhattan hospital.

"Did you say my *fortune*?" Abner Kaskin's secretary repeated, in an incredulous whine. But I cradled the receiver without answering. I couldn't hear what the TV reporter was saying, but I recognized the glass front doors of the hospital behind her. Jesus, I should have. It was the Sisters of Jerusalem, on Park Avenue, where Karen had been taken when Misquamacus had first invaded her body.

I guess there was nothing remarkable about Martin Vaizey being taken to the Sisters of Jerusalem. After all, it had a state-of-the-art trauma unit, and one of the finest teams of neurosurgeons on the Eastern seaboard. But I was gripped by the lead-lined feeling that we were all being mocked and manipulated; that we were all dancing to Misquamacus' cruel and vengeful tune—that he was dragging us back to the scene of his first defeat, in order to show us how hollow our victory had really been.

"The Sisters of Jerusalem," I told Amelia. "Wouldn't you just know it?"

"That was where—" Amelia began, but stopped when she saw the expression on my face.

"Did they say what was wrong with him?" I asked.

"Severe eye injury. They didn't say how it happened."

"We'd better get across there," I said.

"Harry—" said Amelia. Then she paused. I stopped by the door, and turned around. "Harry," she repeated. "Not me."

I stared at her. She looked very serious, especially in those owlish eyeglasses. I suddenly saw what I should have seen in myself, if not a long time ago, then well before I started trying to play the part of Karen's knight in buffed-up armor. I saw, simply, middle age. I saw that I wasn't Kevin Costner and that Amelia wasn't Julia Roberts. I saw that in the years that had passed since Amelia and MacArthur had first raised the head of Misquamacus out of a cherrywood table;

since Karen had first struggled for her life against an old and malicious spirit; since Singing Rock had danced and cast his magical spells; that we had grown older, very much older.

"Harry," Amelia said again, and this time her voice was soft, and very regretful.

I shrugged. "It's okay. I understand."

"Do you really?"

"Listen, there comes a time in the life of all clairvoyants when they have to hang up their pointy hats and put away their Tarot cards and call it a day."

"I feel terrible, leaving you to face this all alone."

"I'm not alone. You know that." I waved all round the room. "There are more spirits per cubic inch than you can count."

"That's all right if you know how to summon them up."

"Martin Vaizey said we were *all* capable of talking to the dead, if only we'd listen."

There was a moment between us then of sweet and eloquent silence. Maybe it was the final goodbye that we had never been able to say to each other before. Maybe it was nothing more than the recognition that we had always been destined to go our separate ways, and that a parting was long overdue.

I can see her now as I saw her then, Mrs Amelia Wakeman, in a loose Indian-cotton blouse and a necklace of freshwater pearls, her hair pinned up in a sun-shining bun, pretty and tired and smiling. Then I closed the door and lolloped down the musty stairs and out into the street, where I whistled for a passing taxi, which promptly accelerated and picked up a girl in a short red skirt on the opposite side of the street.

I found Jack Hughes on the 32nd floor, in a large penthouse office overlooking Park Avenue. I walked across about a quarter of an acre of soft, dark brown carpet, and Jack Hughes rose from behind his desk and held out his hand.

I had been prepared for grey hair. I had even been prepared for *white* hair, considering what had happened to Dr Hughes the last time I had visited the Sisters of Jerusalem. But I sure as hell wasn't prepared for totally bald. Jack

Hughes no longer looked like a dashing young medical expert. He looked instead like an old, cross baby. He had lost even his eyebrows.

"Well, well," he said. In spite of the fact Misquamacus had taken three of his fingers, his hooklike grip was still muscular and sure. "I never thought that I'd ever run into *you* again."

I looked around. "Nice office. Nice view. Nice works of art."

"Oh, yes. Nothing but the best for the Senior Administrator. But give me back my operating theater any day of the week."

I prowled about. On one wall there was a dry-brush view of a farmhouse in Cushing, Maine, by Andrew Wyeth.

"Original?" I asked Jack, and he nodded.

"Unfortunately I don't get to keep it when I retire." He came and stood beside me, admiring the painting almost as if he had never seen it before. "You know why Andrew Wyeth liked to paint Maine? He said he liked the nothingness."

"I can understand that."

There was a lengthy silence, and then Jack said, "You didn't come here to talk about art, though, did you?"

"No. I came because of one of your patients."

"Not another three-hundred-year-old pregnancy, I hope?"

I shook my head. "Not exactly. But I think it has something to do with—well, what happened here before."

Jack looked at me level and unblinking and his eyes were washed of all color, like the weatherboarded farmhouse in the Wyeth painting, light but no color.

"I'm not sure I want to know."

"A patient was admitted here this afternoon. His name is Martin Vaizey; he's currently under arrest for first-degree homicide. *Two* first-degree homicides."

"I'm aware of that. We're keeping him on eighteen, under police guard. I doubt if there's much chance of him escaping, though."

"I just heard that he was involved in a serious accident."

Jack looked down at his mutilated hand. "Yes . . . you could say that. He blinded himself."

"I heard that, too. It was on TV."

"Did they say *how* he blinded himself?"

"Unh-hunh."

"Well," said Jack, "it was very unpleasant. In fact I don't even know how he managed to do it. He gouged out his own eyes. It looked like he did it deliberately and that he meant to cause himself maximum pain. There's some evidence that he sat in his cell for three or four minutes with his eyes pulled out on the ends of their optic nerves."

My breathing became suddenly shallow. "Jesus," I said.

"Yes, Jesus. It wasn't your common type blinding. I mean, people *do* blind themselves. Sexual deviants and religious zealots, usually—punishing themselves for what they've seen. We had a case only two or three months ago of a young man of twenty-three who had cauterized each of his eyeballs with a red-hot screwdriver simply because he had walked in on his mother when she was taking a bath."

I sat down on the brown hide couch that was deliberately too low and deliberately positioned at an awkward angle, so that anybody who wanted to talk to Dr Hughes while he was sitting behind his desk would have to sit right on the edge of the couch with their back straight and their neck screwed around sideways. Office psychology, sixties-style.

I said, "I know it's a lot to ask, and that you do have pretty strict hospital policy, but I really have to talk to this guy."

"He's not conscious, as far as I'm aware. He's had an emergency operation on his eyes and he's heavily sedated."

"When do you expect him to be *compos mentis*?"

"Not till tomorrow morning at the earliest. And then it really depends on whether he wants to talk to *you*."

"Can I see him?"

"You mean now? No, that's out of the question."

"Jack . . ." I said, "we went through a whole lot together, didn't we?"

"Yes, we did." His voice was as dull as two stones knocking together on a dry creekbed. He knew that I was going to ask him a favor.

"Jack," I said, "I'm almost certain that Misquamacus is back. He's back in a very different way, but it's the same Misquamacus. More powerful, *much* more powerful. I've been talking to Dr Snow up at Albany, and Dr Snow thinks that he's enlisted the help of some kind of underworld spirit, some kind of shadow thing."

Jack listened in silence, but then he held up his mutilated hand.

"Harry, let me tell you this. I believe in Misquamacus. I believe in Red Indian spirits and I believe that there are forces in this country that most white people can't even begin to imagine. I lost three fingers to a lizard that was half-real and half-imaginary. I saw rats running down the walls and right through the floors. I saw monstrosities that people were never meant to see. So, don't get me wrong—I believe.

"But there's something else I believe. I believe we managed to destroy Misquamacus for good. I believe that we won.

"Sure—we still have nightmares about it, maybe we're still a little paranoid. But we *won,* didn't we? If I can't believe in that, then losing these fingers counts for squat. I've been prepared to sit in this office for fifteen years pushing pieces of paper around because I've always believed that it was worth it. The lives that we saved were more important than my career in surgery.

"So don't tell me that Misquamacus is back. We won, we destroyed him. I know we did. Whatever it is you're up against now, it's all inside *here.*" He tapped his forehead. "It's nothing but ghosts, Harry. Nothing but delusions. I get them too. Dr McEvoy took early retirement. Dr Winsome spent the next five years of his life on tranquilizers. What makes you think that you're any different?"

"Jack," I insisted, "he's back. It was Misquamacus who brought down Chicago. He destroyed two communities in Colorado, too. God knows what he's going to do next."

But Jack continued to shake his head from side to side, over and over, almost as if he were trying to deafen himself. "I'm not listening, Harry. It's over and we won."

"Supposing I tell you that I had to fight him again—him

and a dozen more medicine-men just as God-damned vindictive, in California?"

"I'm not listening to you, Harry. I don't want to know."

"Supposing I tell you that Singing Rock was killed? He was killed, Jack; Misquamacus took his head off. What kind of a sacrifice is three lost fingers, compared with that?"

"You're lying to me, Harry."

"Am I? What would be the point? Anyway, the police and the military were involved in what happened in California—I can *prove* it to you."

"So you're trying to tell me that Martin came again and that you and Singing Rock destroyed him again; and now you're trying to tell me that he's back yet *again*?"

He came around his desk and leaned forward and stared directly into my eyes. I could smell mint on his breath. "Harry, it's over. If you need help in coming to terms with that fact, then I can easily arrange for you to get it. It was a terrible thing that happened and it left terrible mental scars on everybody who was involved in it.

"In your case—without being slighting or personal about it—you never had much status in life. You were always a socially disaffected kind of guy, never able to settle down, never able to make your mark.

"When we fought Misquamacus, when we destroyed Misquamacus, that gave you some temporary social standing. That made you feel important. I can't blame for you trying to regain some of that standing. Everybody wants to relive their finest hour.

"But it's finished, Harry, I promise you. It's all over."

Even while Jack was speaking, my attention was drawn to a faint shivering in the air on the far side of his office, close to the window. It looked like the ripples of visible heat you can see on a sun-baked highway, or flowing from a barbecue on a hot summer day. It distorted the shape of the window-sill, and gave the heavy brown drapes the appearance of being stirred by a warm and languid breeze.

"—everybody likes to feel that they're making a valuable contribution to the community—" Jack was droning on. But my attention was completely held by this shuddering transparent apparition on the other side of the room, this heat-devil or whatever it was.

Very slowly, very faintly, the figure of a small boy began to materialize. He had short hair cut in the pudding-basin style of thirty years ago, and a very white face, with fatigue-smudged eyes. He was wearing a red woollen dressing gown, tied around the waist with a frayed silk cord. He was staring at me unblinkingly, and I couldn't help shuddering, as if somebody had stepped cold-footed on my grave.

"—have to let go at some point, otherwise it becomes a clinical obsession, and that takes years of—"

The boy beckoned. He raised his right hand and he beckoned.

I hesitated, and pointed to my chest and said, "Me? You mean me?"

Jack stopped in mid-sentence and stared at me. "Of course I mean you, Harry. Who the hell else do you think I'm talking about?"

Again, the boy beckoned, and this time I stood up and crossed the room.

"Harry—" Jack protested. "You could at least give me the courtesy of—"

But I wasn't listening. He was wrong, anyway. I knew that Misquamacus had returned, and I knew the kind of revenge that he wanted to exact. It was no good Jack Hughes trying to make out that I was only interested in fame and recognition and social status. I had never enjoyed being the center of attention. I much preferred people to say, "Who *was* that masked man?"

The boy in the dressing-gown beckoned me closer. I was frightened because I knew that he was a spiritual manifestation of some kind; but at the same time he didn't exude that terrible deathly chill that spirits sometimes give off, like an open icebox door. Nor did he have that offkey resonance of dissatisfaction and grief. He seemed anxious, but calm.

Jack Hughes said, "Harry, are you all right? What the hell are you doing?" But I raised my hand to shush him.

"Jack, there's somebody here."

"What?"

"There's somebody here, Jack, a spirit messenger. Somebody who wants to talk to me."

"Harry, have you completely—"

"Ssh!"

The boy said, "My brother's hurt."

"Your brother?"

"Martin Vaizey, he's hurt, they blinded him."

"I know that," I replied. "He's here at the hospital."

So this was Samuel, I thought—the brother whom Martin Vaizey had lost when he was little. He was still only ten years old, but he was still just as determined to look after his younger brother. In spite of the eeriness of the situation, it gave me quite a lump in my throat. I used to have a brother once. I lost my brother, too.

"Martin says I have to tell you three things," said Samuel.

"Oh, yes? What are they?"

Jack Hughes returned to his desk and made a performance of sitting down. "I'll tell you, Harry, I think you've flipped. I really think you've lost it."

"Please, Jack," I begged him. "Just give me a couple of moments more, would you? This is for real."

"For real? What do you mean, for real? You're having a conversation with a window!"

"Jack!" I snapped at him. "There's somebody here, a boy, Martin Vaizey's brother. You may not be able to see him but he has a message from Martin Vaizey and I want to hear what it is. For Christ's sake, Jack, this is the first time that I've ever raised up a real genuine psychic manifestation in my life. So, *please,* will you do me a favor and let me listen to it?"

Jack was stunned. "All right," he conceded, at last. "Go ahead and listen. Jesus H. Gonzales." He punched the button on his intercom to call his secretary.

I turned back to Samuel. His image was wavering and watery, like the body of a young boy floating just below the surface of a swimming pool.

"He said that Mr Kellogg took pictures," said Samuel. His voice was very odd, fading and then growing louder again, but always indistinct.

"Who's Mr Kellogg?" I asked him. "And what did he take pictures of?"

"Mr Kellogg took pictures of the . . . *Bismarck*."

"I'm sorry, I don't understand. Why did Martin want me to know this?"

"He said you must find his forks."

"Mr Kellogg took pictures of the *Bismarck* and he wants me to find his forks?"

Samuel's image was growing darker now. I could feel that the shadows were gathering; the same shadows that had surrounded Singing Rock when he had appeared to me in Martin Vaizey's book of Velazquez.

I was frightened, seriously frightened. Not just for myself, not just for Karen; but for Martin and Samuel, too.

"Samuel," I said, "I don't understand what you're trying to say to me."

"You'll need his forks, that's what he said."

"Forks? What? I don't understand. I don't know what the hell you're talking about."

Samuel's image had darkened so much that I could scarcely make him out at all.

"Samuel!" I shouted.

His red dressing-gown rose and fell like a red patch of seaweed glimpsed on an outgoing tide.

"It's Misquamacus," he said, in that short-wave-radio voice, rising and falling. "He's seen him. It's really him. It's Misquamacus."

The darkness thickened and stirred, and his image was blotted out by a shadow that almost seemed to have a life of its own. But—as he vanished—I heard two tiny words carried across the static of Samuel's psychic aura. "Little . . ." Then, "Big . . ." Then nothing at all.

I turned back to Jack. He was sitting behind his desk watching me, his fingers steepled. "You're sweating," he said.

"Are you surprised? I was scared shitless."

He stood up, came around the desk, and felt my pulse. "One hundred and five," he said, after a while. "A little high for a man of your age, but nothing too much to worry about."

"Jack . . . I saw Martin Vaizey's brother . . . he was standing right there."

"Sure you did. I believe you."

"Jack, for Christ's sake don't humor me. He said something about somebody called Mr Kellogg. Then he said that I needed Martin's forks. Then he said, 'It's Misquamacus . . . it's really Misquamacus.' Then he vanished."

Jack let go of my wrist and stared at me cautiously. "He said you needed Martin's forks?"

"That's what it sounded like. It didn't make any sense."

"Did any of the nurses mention forks?"

"Hey, come on, Jack, what are you driving at here?"

Jack said, with simmering, suppressed annoyance, "When Martin Vaizey pulled his eyes out of their sockets, he did it with two antique forks."

He lifted his hands to his temples and gave me a graphic mime of what Martin had done to himself.

"Jesus," I said.

"Yes, Jesus," snapped Jack. "But *I* didn't tell you that, did I? And if any of my staff told you that, I want to know who it was. The police asked me specifically to keep that under wraps. They wanted to ask questions around the antique stores; and around the museums; and they wanted to do it before the newspapers and the TV people got ahold of it. If one of my staff mentioned forks—"

"Of course none of your staff mentioned forks," I protested. "I found out just the way I told you—about two minutes ago, right here in this room, from a ten-year-old dead boy in a red dressing-gown and grey pajamas."

"You're not discussing this very maturely, are you?" Jack demanded. "I should have remembered what you were like from before. You're about as rational as a Mexican jumping-bean. Listen, forget about Martin's forks. Forget about Martin. It seems to me like you're suffering from terrific stress—maybe you should forget the whole thing and take a few days away."

"Like where? Chicago? Or Maybelline, Colorado? Or Apache Junction, Arizona?"

Jack Hughes said, in a very level voice, "You can talk to Martin when he's feeling well enough. I'm not going to stop you. You can do whatever you damned well like. But I went after Misquamacus once before, Harry—and for me, that once was more than enough, so don't you dare to ask me to do it again. End of discussion."

I laid my hand on his shoulder. I looked around, at the place where Samuel had been. Then I said, "Thanks, Jack. I'm sorry if I upset you. I'm not asking you to go after Misquamacus again. I guess it disturbed some of us more than others."

I knew why I had annoyed him so much. By mentioning Martin's forks, I had proved to him that there *had* been a spirit in his office. And that meant that I was right about Misquamacus—and that he had lost his fingers and his career as a surgeon in vain.

Jack picked up a framed photograph from his desk, and held it too close for me to be able to focus on it. It looked like a plain woman with dark hair and spectacles.

"I'd help if I could, Harry. But I'm married now. We're expecting our second child."

"Sure," I said, and gave his shoulder one more squeeze, and left his office.

Shit, I thought, as I went down to the hospital lobby in the elevator, crammed between a wheelchair and a hugely fat woman in a lime-green pantsuit, *where have all the heroes gone, the guys you could count on?*

What had happened to "give me some men who are stout-hearted men"?

Grown older, I answered myself. *Once they were twenty and didn't care. Now they're forty and all they see is lost opportunity, unfulfilled ambition.*

The years have taken away too much already. They don't want to risk losing anything more.

I must have been feeling exceptionally low, because I poured myself the *burra-peg* to end all *burra-pegs* and telephoned Dr Snow.

To begin with, he was even more cagy on the phone than he had been face-to-face.

"I really can't advise you," he kept telling me. "There's nothing I can do. I'm an anthropologist, Mr Erskine, not an Indian fighter."

"But you said I had to *outbid* Misquamacus. I didn't really understand what you meant."

He paused. He was beginning to feel flattered. "Outbid him? Is that what I said?"

"Yes, and I don't know what you were trying to explain."

"Oh. Well, neither did I. Not beyond the simple fact that Indians never do anything for nothing. And the reason they never do anything for nothing is because the spirits in which they believe never do anything for nothing.

"Remember—you thwarted Misquamacus twice: once at the Sisters of Jerusalem and once at Lake Berryessa. Now he is obviously determined that you won't be allowed to thwart him a third time. That is why he has called on Aktunowihio to give him all the power he needs. But—like all Indian deities—like *most* deities in *most* religions—Aktunowihio must have demanded a price.

"All *you* have to do is find out what that price was; and best it. Then Aktunowihio will return to the Great Outside and leave you alone. Well . . . hopefully, anyway." He gave a peculiarly girlish giggle. "Aktunowihio the Shadow Buffalo has rather an appetite for human souls."

"You're a great help," I told him, with naked sarcasm.

"Always glad to be of practical assistance," replied Dr Snow, not in the least offended. "In fact, I find this conflict of cultures endlessly fascinating. Despite Wounded Knee, despite Sand Creek, despite the Little Big Horn, it's still going on—this shadow-wrestling for moral and political and territorial rights."

"Little Big Horn," I repeated.

"Yes," said Dr Snow, baffled.

Little . . . Samuel had said. Then, *Big* . . . Then, nothing.

But what other phrase in the English language combined the adjectives Little and Big in quite the same way? Apart from that movie *Little Big Man* with Dustin Hoffman, of course, and there was no earthly reason why Samuel should have mentioned *that*.

Little, Big, Horn.

Maybe that was what Martin had been trying to tell me. Somehow the key to Misquamacus' reappearance—maybe the secret to Aktunowihio, the Shadow Buffalo—was somehow involved with the Little Big Horn, Custer's Last Stand.

I thanked Dr Snow for his help. He seemed quite disappointed that I didn't want to ask him any more. I hung up, and then I dragged across a take-away menu from the Mok'po Korean restaurant, and uncapped a ballpen with my teeth. I scribbled down everything that Samuel had told me.

Mr Kellogg had taken pictures of the Bismarck. That was what Samuel had told me. But I could remember that Samuel had left a distinct gap between "the . . ." and ". . . Bismarck," and then another, shorter gap.

Maybe I had failed to hear the whole message. Maybe the message had originally been "Mr Kellogg had taken pictures of the . . . something-or-other . . . and then taken them to Bismarck . . ." or, maybe, "gone to Bismarck."

After all, as every well-informed school kid knows, Bismarck happens to be the capital of North Dakota, right in the middle of old-time Indian territory, where the Northern Pacific Railroad crossed the Missouri River, and it was far more probable that Martin had been trying to tell me something about Bismarck, North Dakota, than, say, Bismarck the German Chancellor or the World War Two battleship *Bismarck,* or the Bismarck islands in the Pacific.

Maybe the message should have been *Mr Kellogg had taken pictures of the Little Big Horn and sent them to Bismarck?*

But it still made no sense. And what the hell did it have to do with Misquamacus? I sat and listened to the air-conditioner rattling and screaming and I decided that I might be Erskine the Incredible, but I wasn't Sherlock Holmes, not by any stretch of anybody's imagination. I stood up and gave the air-conditioner a terrific kick, and it made a terrible clacking noise like a man I had once seen choking on a fishbone.

I set out the cards, to see if I should go to Stars for a large pastrami sandwich, or Maude's for too much to drink.

The very first card I turned over showed a dark marble mausoleum with an eternal flame burning on the top of it. *"Illness is known, sickness is near, Fate has its own ending to fear. You lose your memory, all's hopeless to you. And what's not funny, your courage fails too."*

Terrific, I thought. I'm hungry, sober, perplexed, afraid,

and now I'm going to lose my credit-rating, too.

I tossed the card across the room. The pack would be better without it. None of my ladies would want to hear that little ditty, especially Mrs John F. Lavender. Illness, fate, fear, losing your money? She had enough problems with men.

The phone rang. I picked it up and began the usual litany, "Erskine the Incredible—palmistry, card-diving, tea-leaf interpretation—"

"Harry," said Amelia, "I just had a call from Abner Kaskin."

There was a long silence, as long-drawn-out as saltwater taffy.

"It's Martin," I said.

"What's happened?"

She started crying. I knew that he was dead even before she managed to get the words out. "He was such a sweet guy," she sobbed. "He wouldn't have hurt anybody . . ."

"I know," I told her. I felt like crying too. In fact, what was all this wet stuff running down my cheeks?

She continued to cry while I told her about seeing Martin's brother Samuel, and what he had told me, and I said, "Maybe he can still pay Misquamacus back."

Amelia said, "How, for God's sake? He's dead."

"Sure. But dead is one thing . . . paying somebody back, that's another thing altogether, and you can do that, dead or not. Listen, I'm going to fly to Arizona tomorrow morning."

"To look for Karen?"

"What else can I do?"

"You could stay in New York and carry on being Erskine the Incredible and pretend that none of this ever had anything to do with you."

"Yes," I agreed. "I could do that, for sure. And what about Karen?"

"Harry, you're no match for Misquamacus. Not this time. I don't want to lose you, too."

"I don't want to lose me, either," I told her. "I'll call you from Phoenix." I hung up. Then I picked up the phone again, and punched out the number of United Airlines.

THIRTEEN

Until you fly to the sunbelt, you don't have any idea how many old people there are in America today. There was so much white hair on that 737 that by the time we reached St Louis I was beginning to suffer from snowblindness. Of course I was seriously spoiled and flirted-with. You know what effect I have on elderly ladies. A widow in a powder-blue leisure suit bought me two bottles of champagne and gave me her telephone number in Paradise Valley, and a retired beauty counsellor called Lolly invited me to test her collagen-pumped lips for their kissability.

In a way I enjoyed their company, because it kept my mind off Karen, and the fear I felt about facing Misquamacus. That was if I could *find* Misquamacus. I had tried at La Guardia to find books about Custer and the Little Big Horn, but the only reference books I had been able to find were *How To Make A Million Out Of The Recession, Lose Forty Lbs. The Celery-Stick Way* and *Peak Performance Sex.*

I decided to wait until I reached Phoenix, and try the public library.

I kept doodling around and around the words that young Samuel Vaizey had told me. "Mr Kellogg . . . Bismarck . . . it *is* Misquamacus." But I didn't have enough information to make any kind of sense out of them. I wondered whether I ought to try a séance, to raise Samuel from the other side, so that he could explain himself in a little more detail. But somehow I didn't think I was sensitive enough to be able to do it. Samuel had appeared to me, I hadn't called him. And he had probably appeared because Martin had sensed that I was in the hospital and had sent him to give me a message.

I had called the 13th Precinct early that morning and asked Sergeant Friendly if it would be possible for me to collect Martin's antique forks, or at least take a look at them. But Sergeant Friendly had been very unfriendly indeed, and had told me that the forks were police exhibits and that even after their investigation into Martin Vaizey's blinding, I would have to produce a notarized letter of authority proving that Martin had wanted me to have them.

There wasn't much point in trying to explain to Sergeant Friendly that Martin's ten-year-old dead brother had appeared to me in the office of the Senior Administrator of the Sisters of Jerusalem Hospital and specifically requested that I have them. Most of the time the hardest part about struggling with the supernatural is that nobody, but nobody, will ever believe you. The TV newsreaders were still talking about the Chicago "earthquake," in spite of the fact that there had been no seismological disturbance whatsoever, not even the slightest flicker. Even when a building the size of the Sears Tower disappears into the world of the dead it doesn't show up on the Richter scale.

Lunch was served as we flew over the southeastern corner of Colorado. I toyed with my breadcrumbed Southern-style chicken and my lima bean salad, but my stomach was knotted up like one of those balls you make out of rubber bands. Lolly leaned over, fork poised, and asked, "Are you really not going to eat that chocolate brownie?"

"Oh. No. Go ahead, have it."

"Chocolate is my only weakness, you know. Apart from you-know-what." She kissed the air with her surgically bee-stung and plumped-up lips. She must have been well on the family vault side of seventy-five. Still, who was I to complain? I was thirty years younger but I wasn't having half the fun that she was, and that was for sure.

The cabin staff were taking away the trays when the pilot suddenly came onto the intercom. "Ladies and gentlemen . . . we've just received a report from Phoenix Sky Harbor that there is severe cyclonic weather in the Las Vegas area. Early reports don't indicate how serious the storms might be, but I have to tell you that all connecting flights from Phoenix have been delayed until further notice.

"I'll keep you posted with further information as soon as it becomes available."

There were cries of bewilderment all round the cabin. One woman said, "My husband's in Las Vegas! My husband's in Las Vegas!"

Lolly, with her mouth full of yet another chocolate brownie, said, "This is weird. They don't have cyclones in Las Vegas, do they? I never heard of a cyclone in Las Vegas."

I shrugged. "Something to do with global warming, I guess." But I had a tight, dull, deep-down feeling that it was nothing to do with cyclones. According to Dr Snow's maps, it had been close to the O.D. Gass Ranch in Las Vegas that eighty-six Washo Indians had been killed in 1862 by Colonel Patrick Connor and two hundred and fifty cavalrymen. This was the same Colonel Connor who, the following year, surrounded four hundred Shoshoni Indians on the Bear River in Utah, under cover of a blizzard, and massacred them all. Two-thirds of them had been women and children.

The Mormon civilians who had counted the dead had said that the snow for hundreds of yards around looked like "strawberry ice" because of all the blood that had soaked into it.

I guess I couldn't blame the Indians for wanting their revenge, for wanting their lands back, for wanting America the way it once was. But maybe too many years had passed. Maybe the Indians had to accept that—rightly or wrongly—the old days were over. Who wanted to live in a tepee any longer? Who wanted a world without air-conditioning and Jack Daniels and Cadillacs and implant dentistry?

The 737 captain came back on the intercom. "Unhh . . . ladies and gentlemen . . . the cyclonic weather situation over Las Vegas appears to be continuing . . . so we're going to make arrangements for any passengers who have ongoing reservations to stay overnight in the Phoenix area. If you have any queries, please don't hesitate to talk to your flight attendants."

Lolly said, "Do you know something? This is very weird. Just one weird thing after another. My astrologist said this was going to be a weird year."

I tried to smile. "Yes. Mine too."

The sun hit me like a hammer when I walked out of the terminal at Sky Harbor, over 110 degrees. I had forgotten to bring my sunglasses, so I spent the first fifteen minutes walking around with my eyes squinched shut like Robert Mitchum. I rented a white Lincoln Town Car from the Budget desk. At sixty-one dollars a day, with twelve dollars insurance, it was far more than I could afford, but after the captain's announcement about Las Vegas, I thought, wothehell wothehell. If the civilized world was going to end tomorrow, I might as well be driving a decent car. The young man behind the desk was called Scott. He had a perfect tan and a perfect white shirt and perfect teeth and handed me a complimentary map.

"Just keep an eye out for seniors," he warned me. "They tend to do things unexpected. Like unsignalled U-turns, because they suddenly remembered they left their Zimmer frame at home."

I drove out eastwards on Apache Boulevard through Tempe and Mesa. I can't say that the suburbs of Phoenix have much to recommend them. They're just like anywhere, except that they're hot. Gas stations, souvenir shops, markets, shacks. People standing around looking desiccated and bored. Everywhere heat and shadows and that strange dry smell of desert and cactus and automobile fumes.

No wonder old people retire to Arizona. Apart from the fact that it's permanently hot and permanently dry, it's unreal. It's like living in an episode of *The Cisco Kid,* the sun so glaring and the shadows so black. You might just as well be on TV. And if you're on TV, like Duncan Renaldo and Jay Silverheels and Dan Blocker and James Arness, you never die. Your body might have been consigned to the mausoleum, but there you are, every weekday morning, still riding and shooting and jumping and smiling. How could anybody say that Lucille Ball is dead?

I reached Papago Joe's Oldsmobile dealership sooner than I expected. There was an ochre-painted building on one side of the highway, with a faded sign saying Sun Devil Bar. On the other side of the highway, a chaos of battered cars, dusty and sun-baked, and a spectacularly dented Airstream trailer, and a rickety sign with a buffalo skull nailed to the top of it, announcing PAPAGO JOE BARGAIN USED AUTOS. Nothing Over $3300, CLOSED FOR REFURBISHMENT.

I parked the Lincoln next to the Sun Devil Bar & Grill

and walked across the highway. In the clear, glassy distance, I could see the crumpled heights of the Superstition Mountains, where the famous Lost Dutchman Mine was supposed to lie. The mountain wavered in the heat, in the same way that Samuel had wavered when he had given me Martin's message, and it looked just as unreal.

I had read an article about the Lost Dutchman Mine in my (otherwise mind-numbing) airline magazine. Apparently it had first been discovered in 1840 by a young Mexican boy hiding from his irate father: then by three Mexicans, who had been dumb enough to show it to a homicidal Dutchman called Jacob Waltz. The Dutchman had killed all three Mexicans, and dug the mine for himself, occasionally appearing in Mesa and Phoenix with pocketfuls of gold nuggets. I liked that. I mean, wouldn't you like to roll into your local bar, dusty and sweaty, your pockets bulging with gold nuggets?

On his deathbed, Waltz confessed to a friend that he had killed not only the Mexicans but eight more men who had tried to follow him back to the mine, and gave his friend a map showing where the gold was buried. However he must have been a seriously incompetent cartographer, because his friend couldn't find the mine, and neither have any of the hundreds of prospectors who have combed through the Superstitions since.

There was something about that story that appealed to my sense of the ridiculous. I'll bet that Jacob Waltz wasn't a killer at all, but the biggest hoaxer this side of the Gila River.

I crossed Papago Joe's used-auto lot, and gave a postman's knock on the side of the trailer. Not far away, a shaggy German shepherd barked and yanked at his chain. "Down, Fang," I told him. He carried on barking, but not very enthusiastically. It was almost impossible to be enthusiastic about anything in this heat, even about biting my leg off.

I knocked again. Eventually the trailer door was opened up. I found myself confronted by a thin, pale boy of about nineteen, wearing a Sex Pistols T-shirt and heavy boots and black transparent panties with lace round the edges.

"Yeah?" he said. "Whaddya want?"

"My name's Harry Erskine. I'm looking for Papago Joe."

"We're closed, man. We got nothing to sell. All of our cars got damaged."

"I'm not interested in buying a car."

"Then what?"

"I told you. I want to see Papago Joe."

The boy scratched the back of his neck and winced. "I don't know, man. He's not too excited about talking to anybody right now. All his cars got smashed. He lost his daughter in a custody case. Apart from that, he's been drinking."

It was so damned hot on that lot that I was practically braised. A few tomatoes and onions, and a sprinkle of sage, and I would have made a perfect *costoletta di maiale alla modenese.*

I said, "I don't really give a damn whether he's been drinking or not. I just came all the way from New York, and I need to talk to him."

"You came from New York?"

"I just arrived, about an hour ago."

"You came all the way from New York just to talk to Papago Joe?"

I nodded.

"Hey," said the boy. "That's *extra.* That's really *extra.*"

"Glad you think so," I told him. For some reason— despite the fact that he was such an obvious goofball, and despite his terrible T-shirt and his cock curled up in his see-through panties—I decided that I liked him. There aren't very many originals left, but this guy was obviously one of them.

The trailer door swung shut, juddering on its hinges, and the boy disappeared inside for what seemed like three hours, especially in this heat. I could cope with New York when it was hot. New York was all sweat and grime. But out here, Under The Old One, it was clean and dry like a fan-assisted oven. One breath, and all the hairs in your nostrils shrivelled up. Two breaths, and your lungs were pemmican.

The door opened again. The boy had a serious look on his face. "Papago Joe says okay. But he needs some firewater."

"Firewater?"

"Didn't you ever read cowboy comics? He wants a bottle of Chivas Regal."

"Some firewater," I complained.

"It's all right. You can buy it across the highway at the Sun Devil. Ask for Linda. Tell her that E.C. Dude sent you."

I dabbed my forehead with my crumpled handkerchief. "E.C. Dude? What kind of a name is that?"

"Just tell her, E.C. Dude."

"Does that stand for anything? E.C.?"

He covered his eyes with his hand, as if he were so tired of people asking him what E.C. stood for that he was almost ready to commit suicide.

"I'll bet it stands for Elvis Charisma," I teased him.

His eye appeared through his partly-opened fingers. *So that onlie ye Eyes look'd out.* "You've got to be kidding me. My mother hated Elvis. My mother was into Little Richard and Chuck Berry. Besides, my real first name is Trenton and my real second name is Partridge. E.C. Dude is just a name I made up for myself. Would *you* want to be called Trenton Partridge? I mean, get real."

"So E.C. doesn't stand for anything at all?" I asked him.

He shrugged, looked away. "It does, as a matter of fact. But whether I tell you is down to me."

"You're right," I said, with a serious nod. "I'll go buy the firewater."

I walked away, across the dusty sunbaked lot. I knew that E.C. Dude was still standing in the open doorway of the trailer watching me. That's the wonderful thing about teen-age kids. They try so hard to be different and sophisticated that they all end up acting exactly the same. Mind you, I guess that's true of almost everybody. But I bet myself a hundred dollars that by the time I reached the perimeter fence of the used-car lot, E.C. Dude would tell me his name.

I walked slower and slower. My shadow cowered beneath my feet as if it were afraid to come out. I passed a wrecked Electra and a crushed-up Le Sabre. I had almost reached the perimeter fence. Then I heard E.C. Dude call out, "Extra Cool!"

I turned around, took off my sunglasses.

"Extra Cool!" he repeated. "That's what E.C. stands for! Extra Cool Dude!"

"That's great," I told him. "I like it. Nothing like wearing your heart on your sleeve."

I crossed the shimmering-hot tarmac and climbed the gritty wooden steps to the front door of the Sun Devil Bar & Grill. Outside, you could easily have mistaken the Sun Devil for a concrete blockhouse because that's about all it was. The only giveaway that this was a palace of refreshment was a red-and-blue neon sign announcing Coors beer on draft.

I opened the screen door and went inside. It was so dark after the blinding white desert that I had to stop and blink for a while before I could see where I was or where I was going. The air-conditioning was set to North Pole.

There was a long dimly-lit bar with a vinyl-padded front and a row of chrome and vinyl-padded stools. Behind the bar hung a parody of one of those old-time reclining nudes, only this one looked more like a centerfold from *Playboy,* a glossily airbrushed girl sunbathing on a desert rock. Out of her tumbling brunette hair poked a pair of nubby horns, and in her hand she held a three-pronged toasting-fork.

A juke-box was playing some sentimental Tammy Wynette–type song. As far as I could make out in the gloom, the only other customers in the Sun Devil were a porky little man in a light green suit and white shoes who was perched up on a bar stool with his white Stetson hat and a Bloody Mary in front of him; and a mountainous black-bearded trucker who was sitting at one of the tables, shovelling up corned-beef hash and eggs as if his stomach were a landfill project.

As I approached the bar, however, a young blonde woman came out from the back. She had blue eyes as big as Bambi, and she was wearing a tight white sleeveless blouse. Quite pretty, if you like Western waitresses.

"He'p you?" she wanted to know.

"I want a bottle of Chivas Regal, if you have one to spare."

She nodded her head in the general direction of Papago Joe's. "Joe's got you buying, does he?"

"He's done this before, then?"

"Just about ever' time anybody comes to talk about the murders," she said. She reached down under the bar and produced a bottle of Chivas Regal. "He used to drink Johnnie Walker but not these days."

I gave her two twenties and she gave me the change. "What happened over there?" I asked her.

She shrugged. "Nobody really knows. My son Stanley saw it happen but of course he's only just turned nine. And E.C. Dude saw it, did you meet E.C. Dude?"

"Yes, I sure did. Quite a character."

"All they say was the cars all kind of slid across the lot and crashed into each other. When the deputy came to see what all the noise was about, Stanley kept on screaming that there was somebody inside the workshop. So they opened up the workshop and there they were, all dead, all chopped up."

I frowned. "Had Stanley been in the workshop before?"

"Unh-hunh, it had been locked for years."

"So how come he knew there was somebody in there?"

The young woman shrugged. "I don't know. Childish intuition I guess. Kids can pick up vibes that grown-ups can't pick up, do you know what I mean? They're like dogs and gophers."

"Is Stanley around?"

"Oh . . . sure."

"Do you mind if I talk to him?"

The young woman's eyes narrowed. "Are you a reporter?"

I shook my head. "My name's Harry—Harry Erskine. I'm kind of an investigator."

"Oh, yeah?"

"Did you ever see that movie *Poltergeist*? I'm kind of a psychic investigator."

"You mean you go looking for ghosts and stuff?"

"That's it. I go looking for ghosts and stuff."

"Gee, I never realized people actually did that."

"Oh, they actually do that, all right."

The young woman held out her chilly little hand and I shook it. "My name's Linda Welles," she said. "You stay right here and I'll go find Stanley."

While she was gone, I looked up at the television over the bar. Although the sound was turned down, I could see flickering images of downtown Las Vegas, taken in what looked like the middle of a blood-red night. I saw the ornamental fountains in front of Caesar's Palace churning with debris and fallen statues and crimson foam. I saw a row of casino billboards on Las Vegas Boulevard toppling like bowling pins: the Silver City, the Morocco Motel, the Riviera, the Silverbird, the Sahara. I saw cars tumbling over and over—a stretch limo sliding sideways along Desert Inn Road, trailing a shower of sparks.

People were running, buildings were falling. I saw the pink-and-white striped tent of Circus-Circus collapsing. I saw the Aladdin vanish. Then, in terrible silence, the Landmark hotel-casino tower dropped into the ground—literally dropped right into the ground.

Linda came back, leading a small grumpy boy. I pointed up at the television. "Have you seen that?"

"Sure," she said. "It was on earlier. Isn't it awful? I sure hope we don't get a cyclone like that round here."

"Do you mind turning up the volume?"

She turned it up. A voice that sounded like a strained Dan Rather was saying, *"—fifty or sixty square miles . . . all flights to Las Vegas have been diverted away from the area and highways have been cleared for emergency services . . . so far impossible to estimate how many people have died . . . although the toll of dead and injured could run into thousands . . ."*

We listened soberly. There were interviews with seismologists, meteorologists and engineers. The engineers were anxious that the "tremorless earthquake" could affect the integrity of the Hoover Dam, thirty miles southeast of the city, and that Lake Mead might suddenly burst down the valley of the Colorado River, causing widespread destruction. So far it had been impossible for rescue helicopters to fly through the storms.

"It was red . . . the sky was red . . ." said one exhausted-looking pilot. *"But right in the middle there, where all the hotels were falling . . . we saw something black, like black*

smoke—black kind of tendrils of smoke . . . like a boiling octopus."

The man in the green suit said, "Hey, Linda, switch over to the game, would you mind?"

Linda obediently switched channels to Phoenix playing the L.A. Clippers. The game was almost over. "Have to oblige the regulars," she explained, rolling her eyes up.

Stanley whined, "Mom, I want to go back outside."

"No, Stanley. I want you to talk to Harry first. Harry, this is Stanley. Stanley, this is Harry. Listen, Stanley, Harry wants to ask you some questions about what happened when all the autos crashed at Papago Joe's."

"I don't want to talk about it," Stanley protested, trying to twist his hand free.

"Well, you have to talk about it."

"Don't *want* to talk about it."

"Hey, Stanley," I said. "Come around here. Come on. I want to show you something."

Linda nudged him and Stanley reluctantly came around the bar.

"You have a quarter in your car," I told him.

He stared at me as if I were a prime candidate for the funny farm. But I reached into his ear and produced a quarter, which I turned this way and that, and then dropped into his shirt pocket.

"How did you do that?" he said.

"I didn't do anything. You had a quarter in your car, that was all."

"Are you a fairy?" he asked me.

"Hey . . . do I *look* like a fairy?"

"You're wearing a pink shirt. Only fairies wear pink shirts."

"Get out of here. The President wears pink shirts."

"Exactly."

I said, "How about a root beer? You like root beer?"

"Okay, so long as you show me how you do that thing with the quarter."

"I told you, I didn't do anything. Is it my fault if you walk around with quarters in your ears?"

We sat at a table in the corner. Stanley had a root beer

and a pack of dry-roasted peanuts which he ate greedily and very noisily, with his mouth open.

"I'm going to go talk to E.C. Dude and Papago Joe," I explained, "but first of all I wanted to hear all about it from you."

Stanley chewed for a while, and then he said, "We heard all this crunching and crashing and everything, and all the cars went sliding across the lot."

"Did you see anything else?"

He hesitated, then quickly shook his head.

"Did you see something that looked like a shadow?"

He kept on chewing. He managed to challenge my stare for about twenty seconds, then he had to look down at the table.

"How did you know there was something inside of the workshop?" I asked him.

He looked up again. His eyes were dark. "I don't know. I just did."

"You saw a shadow, didn't you? Something that looked like a shadow?"

He nodded.

"You want to describe it for me?"

He swallowed, and hesitated. Then, very slowly, he raised his hand over his face and parted his fingers so that only his eyes looked out. "It was dark and it was running and it had a great big head and it was all bent over like a buffalo and it ran like this."

Here, he hunched himself forward and gave an imitation of a heavy, uneven loping movement.

"Did you mention the shadow to anybody else?"

He nodded. "Deputy Fordyce, and my mom, too."

"And what did they think about it?"

"They didn't think anything. They thought it was maybe somebody's shadow, somebody running away, and it just looked funny because of the way they were running."

"Did E.C. Dude see the shadow?"

"Yes," said Stanley.

I took a long cold swallow of beer, and then I leaned back in my chair and looked at Stanley intently. "What do *you* think it was?" I asked him.

"I don't know. I think it was a sort of ghost."

"Do you believe in ghosts?"

He shook his head. "Not ghosts like in *Ghostbusters*. Not Slimer or anything."

"But you do believe in the shadow?"

"Yes," he said.

I sat thinking for a while, and Stanley sat watching me. Eventually I leaned forward and found a dollar seventy-six in small change in his left nostril.

"You know what?" I told him. "You're better than a one-armed bandit."

E.C. Dude said, "I'd almost given you up, man."

I climbed the steps into the trailer. Inside, it was frigidly air-conditioned, like everywhere else in Arizona, but *la grande luxe* on wheels it wasn't. The sides and part of the roof were spectacularly stove in, and all the left-hand windows, instead of being glazed, were covered in sun-yellowed plastic sheeting. A television set with no screen sat perched on a broken table, and the only other furniture appeared to be mattresses and broken wooden chairs and Indian blankets. A zigzag-patterned blanket had been hung across the width of the trailer in order to separate it into two "rooms." In spite of the air-conditioning, the trailer was aromatic with unwashed feet, marijuana, pine-scented toilet block and cigarette smoke.

"I brought the whiskey," I announced, holding up the bottle.

"Hey, extra," said E.C. Dude. He lit a Camel and then held out the pack. "Smoke?"

"Don't, thanks."

"That's cool. Wish I could quit. My old man died of lung cancer. I should of tape-recorded some of his coughing, just to remind me, you know. He practically coughed up the soles of his God-damned shoes."

I looked around. "Is Papago Joe here?"

"He'll be out in a minute. He's flossing his teeth."

Somehow it never occurred to me that Indians might floss their teeth, but I guess they're only human, like the rest of us. Even Geronimo must have had to go to the little boys' room now and again.

I said, "The reason I took so long was because I talked to Stanley."

"Oh, yes," nodded E.C. Dude. "Linda's kid. I like him. He's something extra, that kid."

"He told me about the automobiles crashing. He told me about the shadow, too."

E.C. Dude lit his cigarette and looked a little shifty. "Well, he's a bright kid. He's got a whole lot of imagination."

"But the shadow wasn't imagination, was it? The shadow was real."

"A trick of the light, man, that's all."

"Oh, no. That shadow was really real; and I know it was really real because I've seen it for myself, in New York."

He stared at me, hollow-cheeked and stubbly-chinned and white as sour milk. "You've seen it, too?"

"Yes. And I know what it is. Leastways, I *think* I know what it is. You've seen what's been happening in Chicago, and Colorado, and Las Vegas . . . it's all part of that."

"I don't understand you, man. Are you trying to tell me that shadow has something to do with all of those storms and all of those earthquakes?"

"They're not earthquakes. They're part of something else . . . something that's far more destructive than earthquakes. An earthquake, that's a natural phenomenon, right? The ground shakes, buildings fall down, then it's all over. Maybe some aftershocks, but that's generally the end of it.

"But what's happening now isn't a natural phenomenon. What's happening now is, revenge."

"Revenge?" His eyes slitted. "Are you kidding me, or what?"

"Come on, E.C. You saw those cars crashing, all by themselves. You saw those dead people. There are forces underneath our feet that want to drag us down and bury us for good, and they're not going to stop until we're gone. Not just us personally, either, but every last scrap of evidence that we were ever here."

"Who's this 'we'?" E.C. Dude wanted to know.

"We, the white men, the palefaces, the intruders. Every single person who has invaded this land, from the Vikings

and the Celts through to the Pilgrim Fathers and the Poles
and the Germans and the Irish. No distinctions, this is it,
they want their land back the way it was."

E.C. Dude blew smoke out of his nostrils, and coughed.
"That's crazy, man. You're beginning to sound like Papago
Joe. He's always ranting on about white men and Indians
and all that Native American bullshit."

"You think it's bullshit? You saw the beginnings of it
here."

"Oh, come on, man, that's *crazy.*"

I was about to explain about the Great Outside when the
rug that hung across the trailer was dramatically tugged
back. There, wearing a plaid shirt and faded jeans, stood
Papago Joe. He wasn't particularly tall, maybe 5'7", but he
was stockily-built, big-shouldered, which gave him great
physical presence. He had a large sculptured head, with a
hooked, fleshy nose. His eyes were so deepset that they
looked like fragments of broken glass shining at the bottom
of two mineshafts. His hair was long and greasy and pewter-
grey, and tied back in a ponytail. His fingers were yellow
with nicotine.

"Of course you're right," he said, holding out his hand.
"Many of us know that this is the hour that was always foretold."

"You must be Papago Joe," I replied. "Here—I brought
you some whiskey."

He accepted the bottle of Chivas Regal without a word.
"You're not a police detective or a reporter?" he said.

"No," I told him. "I'm what you might call an interested
party, that's all." I was surprised by the cultured, collected
tone of his voice.

He raised an eyebrow. "An interested party? I'd say you
were a *very* interested party. You seem to be very familiar
with Indian affairs."

"I'm very familiar with Indian vengefulness, if that's what
you mean."

"Oh." He paused, and he thought about that. "*Vengefulness.* Interesting word." Then, "You're surprised that we
still feel vengeful?"

His tone was sardonic, but I could sense that he was right on the edge of being deadly serious.

I made a face. "Let's put it this way," I said, "I've always believed that there has to come a time when everybody has to forgive and forget."

Papago Joe unscrewed the cap of the whiskey bottle, found three ill-matched glasses, and filled them. He handed the whiskey round, and said, "Do you think it would be the right thing to do, to forgive and forget—let's say—the Nazis?"

"The Nazis?" I said. "I'm not so sure. The Nazis are a special case. The Nazis wiped out six million people, probably more, and they did it in the most inhumane way that you can imagine."

"I agree," said Papago Joe. "We should always remember the Nazis."

I smelled a trap. "You're trying to tell me that the white settlers were as bad as the Nazis?"

Papago Joe took a mouthful of Chivas Regal, swilled it around his teeth, and then swallowed it. "It depends, doesn't it?" he challenged me. "It depends whether you believe that to decimate a whole civilization is forgivable and forgettable or not."

I said, "Come on, now, the world changes. You can't stop people exploring. You can't stop people looking for something better. And you sure can't blame every single white settler for what the Army and the government did. Plenty of whites were massacred, remember, as well as Indians."

"Of course. But it wasn't your guns that killed us. It was simply you."

"I don't follow you."

Papago Joe swallowed more whiskey, and refilled his glass. "It was simply *you*, my friend. Did you know, for example, that when the Pilgrims landed in New England they found so many dead Indians that, in some places, acres of ground were literally carpeted with bones? It was a landscape like some kind of nightmare. Like hell, like the end of the world. Too many to bury, and not enough left alive to bury them. And do you know *why* so many Indians died? Because four years before, by accident, they had caught measles from European fishermen. Measles! Three quarters of the entire native population from Maine to Connecticut were wiped out.

"Then there was smallpox. You didn't need guns, all you needed was smallpox! In the early days, whole tribes contracted smallpox from just one explorer, or from just one wandering trader. Some of them were entirely wiped out before white colonists ever discovered them. Gone, vanished, without any trace at all, and nobody will ever know their customs, or their culture, or their language, or what they looked like, or even their names.

"You've heard of the Mandans? In just one winter, the Mandans were reduced from sixteen hundred to just thirty-one; and in the same winter, the dreaded ferocious Blackfoot were almost completely wiped out. Not by guns, not by battle, but by *you*. Your being here, alone, was enough to destroy us."

Papago Joe sat down on a backless kitchen chair, and looked up at me with those deep black glittery eyes. "We thought it was magic. Pathetic, isn't it? Our leaders and our loved ones died in our arms. We were stricken with grief, confused, angry, and terrified. We really believed it was magic."

I cleared my throat. I felt pretty damned embarrassed, I can tell you. Partly because of Papago Joe's bitter condemnation of us white folks. I mean, did I feel diseased, or what? And partly because I hadn't expected an Indian who ran a used-car dealership in a one-horse Arizona junction to be so eloquent and so knowledgeable and so *committed*.

I said, cautiously, "Okay, I take your point. You don't want to forgive and you don't want to forget. I guess all that I can say in our favor is that we didn't give you all those diseases on purpose."

Papago Joe gave me a wry smile. "You don't think so? Maybe you didn't, but you tried, my friend, you certainly tried. The British handed out smallpox-infected blankets to the Great Lakes Indians, in the hope that it would start an epidemic; and there were many more deliberate attempts to spread disease amongst what your forefathers were pleased to call 'the dissatisfied tribes.' "

"Well," I said, finishing my whiskey. "What can I tell you? I wasn't personally there at the time, but I'm sorry. I'm embarrassed, I'm ashamed, and if there's anything I can do to make it up to you, I will."

I opened the Airstream's door. The sunlight ran in two parallel lines down Papago Joe's cheeks, like fluorescent warpaint.

"You're not going?" he asked me, still smiling.

I hesitated. "I was under the impression that I wasn't particularly welcome."

Papago Joe laughed. "You shouldn't let me upset you. I do get preachy, at times."

"Maybe, but from what you've said, you're entitled to get preachy."

"Come on back, Mr Erskine," said Papago Joe. "This is good whiskey. If you don't help me drink it, then E.C. will help me drink it, and I can't stand E.C. when he's drunk. He starts reciting all of the names of all of the tracks on all of the Grateful Dead albums."

I thought for a moment, then I closed the door. If Papago Joe knew so much about Indian history, then maybe he could help me track down Karen—and, even better, get her free from Misquamacus.

"I'm going to tell you something," said Papago Joe. "If we taught the real history of America in our schools, then every classroom every day would be awash with tears. What happened to the Indians makes the Holocaust pale by comparison. You preach human rights to the Russians, and talk about Tiananmen Square? You ought to think about what you did to the Indians. It's the biggest whitewash job in all the annals of modern history, but it never went away, it was always there, and now it's eaten this nation's heart out."

I accepted his offer of another three fingers of Chivas Regal. I watched his face in fascination. His skin had the quality of smooth leather, folded into wrinkles under his eyes. I would have given him forty-eight, forty-nine—maybe fifty.

"You're pretty militant," I remarked. "If you'll forgive my saying so, that's pretty unusual in an In—in a Native American your age."

He shook his head. "Why don't you call me an Indian? You think I'm an Indian, for Christ's sake call me an Indian. I can't stand hypocrisy."

"I'm worried about what you might call me in return," I told him.

He thought about that, and then grinned. "Listen, paleface, my father always wanted me to make it big in business. He had worked his ass off for twenty years, and do you know where it got him? Deputy vegetable manager at the local market. Heady stuff, hunh? But he always dreamed that his son could do better.

"He gave up smoking and he gave up drinking and he gave up candy bars and for all I know he gave up breathing. He saved his money and in the end he managed to send me to Arizona State. I was supposed to be taking a business course, but I could tell from the start that I was never going to make a success of it. How could I, when all the white students kept saying 'How!' and calling me 'Tonto' and treating me like something unpleasant that had gotten stuck on the sole of their shoe?

"I began to realize that even my *own* perception of what an Indian was had been totally distorted by cowboy movies and all that noble-savage–*Last of the Mohicans* crap. I didn't know *who* I was, or *what* I was, and most of all I couldn't understand why my fellow students thought that I was so inferior.

"I cut all of my business classes and I went to the university library and I spent a whole year finding out the truth. It's all there. You only have to look for it. And when I *had* found out, I decided that I didn't particularly want to be a businessman any more—the deputy deputy vegetable buyer for some godforsaken supermarket, or the token redskin for some two-bit suburban mortgage-and-loan corporation. I decided I wanted to run my own business, no matter how little money I made; and I decided that I wanted to live the life of a Native American, somebody who was here first."

I swallowed whiskey, watching him.

E.C. Dude said, "You should have realized by now that Papago Joe is one totally three hundred per cent committed

Indian. Aren't you, Joe? I mean, this dude can scalp you just by talking to you."

Papago Joe said, "E.C., go across to the Sun Devil and bring back some ice and some almonds and some potato chips. We're not being very hospitable here."

E.C. Dude said, "What do you think this is? The Biltmore?" But all the same he tugged on his jeans and left the trailer, slamming the door noisily behind him.

Papago Joe said, "I think it's better if you and I talk in private, to begin with."

I said, "You haven't yet asked me who I am or why I've bought you a bottle of whiskey."

"I assumed that you would tell me, given time."

"My name's Erskine, Harry Erskine. I'm a kind of a psychic investigator. You know, like James Randi? I'm looking for a girl who was here the other day, when you were being interviewed on television."

Papago Joe said, "Actually, Mr Erskine, I know who you are, and I know why you've come."

"You *know*?"

"Somebody you know well has already been in touch with me."

"Who? Not Amelia?"

Papago Joe shook his head; smiled. "Somebody closer than that. Somebody who always has your interests at heart."

I was beginning to feel that something was going badly wrong. That first briny taste of uncertainty, and fear.

"Stop worrying," said Papago Joe. "Give me your hand."

Reluctantly, I held out my hand. Papago Joe took hold of it, and pressed it against the crumpled aluminum side of the trailer. The alloy was chilled by the air-conditioning, and it made me shiver. "What's this in aid of?" I asked him.

"You'll see. Do you feel okay?"

"I might feel okay if I knew what the hell was happening."

"Relax," said Papago Joe. He kept my hand pressed against the aluminum.

"What?" I wanted to know.

Papago Joe didn't say any more, simply kept on smiling. But there, in the palm of my hand, the metal began to crinkle and rise. I could definitely feel it changing shape. I frowned at Papago Joe in uncertainty, but his expression was giving nothing away. At first I didn't understand what he was trying to do, but then I felt somebody *breathing* into my hand, and I felt eyelashes flicking against my skin, and I realized that Papago Joe was doing what Martin Vaizey had done for me, back in his apartment, with his book of Velazquez.

Singing Rock.

I tried to tug my hand away from the trailer wall, but Papago Joe gripped it tight and held it there, and gave me a quick negative shake of his head. "Don't break contact. I'm not very highly sensitive. I can only keep it here for a minute or two, at most."

"Singing Rock?" I said, hoarsely.

There was a lengthy pause, but then I felt cold breath, and metallic lips moving in the palm of my hand.

". . . what you have to do now . . ." said the blurry voice of Singing Rock, across fifteen years and the dark frontiers of death itself. *". . . find them, rouse them up, nobody else can help you . . ."*

"Who are you talking about?" I asked him. "Find who? Rouse who up?"

Singing Rock said, in the strangest of voices, *". . . rouse them up, Harry, it's their land, too, they'll help you . . ."*

Papago Joe was sweating and breathing hard. Obviously he found it much more difficult to sustain Singing Rock's image than Martin Vaizey had.

I heard Singing Rock say *". . . your people, your people . . ."* But then, almost immediately, I felt the metal crumple and collapse beneath my hand, and Singing Rock was gone. I stepped back and stared at Papago Joe straight and level. "You're a sensitive?" I asked him.

"I was taught by Blood Hook. I was initiated, and when I was younger I used to see spirits all the time. But in the end I turned my back on it. I found it too depressing, being visited by spirits from the time when men could roam freely. There didn't seem to be any point. After all, there was nothing we could do to change the future; or so I thought. I didn't believe in the Ghost Dance, the dragging-down. I didn't believe it was possible.

"But, three nights ago, your friend Singing Rock visited me when I was dreaming. He spoke to me in riddles, in a spirit language that I didn't understand. But I knew that it wasn't any ordinary dream.

"The next day I took the vision powders, and I found Singing Rock and raised his face out of a buffalo-skin satchel. He told me all about Misquamacus; and what happened at the Sisters of Jerusalem; and how he had been beheaded at Lake Berryessa. He also told me that Misquamacus would be coming here, bringing your friend Karen with him. And then he said that *you* would come, too, looking for Karen, hunting for Misquamacus. He was worried that Misquamacus might set an ambush for you."

"How did Singing Rock know that Misquamacus would bring Karen here?" I asked Papago Joe. Now I was growing excited.

Papago Joe said, "Misquamacus was counting coup."

"Counting coup? What does that mean?"

"Counting coup is when Indian warriors touch their enemies to show their bravado. That's why they used to carry those feathered coup-sticks. Obviously it's braver to touch your enemy while he's still alive, but they used to count coup on dead bodies, too. It's rather like Air Force pilots painting little aircraft on the noses of their fighters, to show how many enemy planes they've shot down.

"But, in this case, Misquamacus has a problem. Because he's only a spirit he can't physically touch his victims. Not unless he possesses somebody's body and uses their hands to touch his victims by proxy. In this case, your friend Karen."

"Jesus," I said. "Does that mean Karen— But why should he *want* to count coup?"

"Every coup makes him stronger. Every spirit he takes makes him greater. When the Indians eventually rise up, Misquamacus will have the scalps of thousands of white men blowing from his lodgepoles. He will have more coups than any Indian who ever lived. You can imagine what will happen then: they will practically make him a god."

"So Karen may still be here."

Papago Joe said, "Yes. If Misquamacus is counting coup, Karen will still be here. She will be looking for all those people who died here, so that she can touch them, and claim their deaths for the greater glory of the great Misquamacus."

FOURTEEN

E.C. Dude came back swinging with a polythene bag full of ice and his pockets stuffed with foil packs of dry-roasted peanuts, but before he could take off his jeans again, Papago Joe said, "Listen, Dan Thundercloud called. He wants that blue Electra over at Scottsdale."

"Oh, man, that's a genuine pain," E.C. Dude protested.

"Of course it is," said Papago Joe, impassively. "That's why I employ *you* to do it."

"I didn't hear anybody call," I told Papago Joe, as E.C. Dude roared off in a huge plume of ochre-colored dust.

Papago Joe said, "No, of course not. But you and me have to do some serious talking."

"About what?"

"About what's happening, about how we're going to stop it."

"From what you were saying about white people, I wouldn't have thought you *wanted* to stop it. Wouldn't it suit you better, a land without palefaces, where the buffalo roam free?"

Papago Joe stared at me as if I had spoken complete gibberish.

"Are you out of your mind?" he wanted to know. "Do you think I want to live like a nomad, scratching my living wherever I can find it? Do you think I want to live in a tepee, or a pueblo, cooking some greasy concoction over a stinking fire? Do you think I want to ride around like an idiot, chasing some tough, unsavory animal, when I can drive into

Mesa in an air-conditioned Buick and buy the best prime-beef cuts, already prepared in a little paper tray, and a bottle of whiskey to wash it down with?"

He closed the trailer door.

"I think I must've misunderstood you," I said.

"No," he replied, shaking his head. "You didn't misunderstand me. What happened to the Indians was appalling. But we can't turn the clock back, and I think that Misquamacus is infinitely evil to want to try. Whether we forgive, whether we forget, those days are long gone, and I don't want to see them come back.

"They were bloody days, superstitious days—days of hunger and misery and terrible hardship. Believe me, Mr Erskine, there was never anything romantic about being a Native American.

"That didn't give you the right to destroy us, no way. But it's over now, it's past, and anybody who wants to go back to those days is even more mindless and destructive than the palefaces were."

I swallowed more whiskey, and ate some dry-roasted peanuts. In spite of the chilly fierceness of Papago Joe's air-conditioning system, I was beginning to feel slightly queasy. "So what are you suggesting?" I said. "Most importantly, I came here to find Karen. As far as I'm concerned, Karen is my number one priority. I don't have even the first idea how to deal with Misquamacus."

Papago Joe said, "There's something in Indian life which we call 'dreaming after death.' That's when somebody who dies with part of their life's destiny still unfulfilled can appear in the dreams of somebody who is still living and ask them to fulfill that destiny for them."

"Go on," I said.

He smoothed his hand over his pewter-grey hair, and tugged at his ponytail. "Your old friend Singing Rock committed himself to destroying Misquamacus. He defeated him once; but when he tried again, Misquamacus beheaded him. Now, however, he has one more opportunity to fulfill his commitment—through me."

"Did he actually *ask* you?"

Papago Joe nodded. "He appeared in my dream in a

cloak of silver eagle feathers and when he spoke, smoke
came out of his mouth. His eyes were like lamps and his
hands were like eagle's claws. He was dead, he was wrapped
in all the trappings of death. But he spoke to me and asked
me to finish what he had begun."

"What did you say?"

"I said that I would do it gladly. Singing Rock was one of
the last traditional medicine-men, one of the great Sioux
shamans. How could I possibly refuse?"

"I see," I said. If he hadn't already known so much about
me, I don't know whether I would have believed him.

Papago Joe leaned forward and laid his hand on top of
mine. "There is a great war occurring in this country, Mr
Erskine, between its present and its past. We have to take
sides, all of us, or else we will be plunged back into igno-
rance and darkness and sudden death."

I looked at him for a long time—into those dark and glittering eyes.

"You're a complicated man, Papago Joe."

"Yes," he said.

"What do we do first?" I asked him.

"We finish this bottle of Chivas Regal."

"Then what?"

"Tomorrow we will enter the Great Outside and search
for Misquamacus."

"The Great Outside? How can we enter the Great Outside?"

He pointed towards the workshop building. "We go
through the place where those seven people were killed . . .
in just the same way that Karen went through the place
where Hope and Danetree were killed in New York. Every
place where an Indian's blood was innocently spilled is a
way through to the Great Outside."

"I see," I told him. I remembered what Dr Snow had told
us about Apache Junction and Wounded Knee and all of
those hundreds of other places all across America where Indians had died. "Have you, unh—have you ever visited the
Great Outside before?"

Papago Joe shook his head. "I didn't expect to go there
until I died. But your friend Singing Rock will guide us."

I was beginning to think that Singing Rock was proving to be more of a liability than a friend. I had flown here to Phoenix to look for Karen—not to take side trips into the Great Outside or the Happy Hunting Ground or whatever you care to call it. Like Papago Joe, I hadn't expected to visit the land of the dead until I was dead, and even then I hadn't expected to go to the Indian quarter.

If I hadn't seen Chicago falling and Las Vegas being swallowed up then I might have dismissed the whole idea as a joke. But for the past few days the whole of the United States had been fraught with tension and suppressed panic and a feeling of terrible weirdness, and in that atmosphere I was ready to believe almost anything. Besides, Papago Joe knew too much. He knew all about me and all about Karen and all about Singing Rock; and all about Misquamacus, too. He spoke in the same dry, informed way that Singing Rock had spoken when he was alive. He gave me the leaden feeling that I was doomed to visit the Great Outside whether I wanted to or not: that my destiny lay beneath the soles of my feet, in what Dr Snow had described as "a dark reflection in a shadowy lake."

Papago Joe said, "I need some things. Deer tails, eagles' claws, dried fingers, rattles, and medicine herbs."

I didn't mock. All those years ago, Singing Rock had worked his medicine against Misquamacus at the Sisters of Jerusalem with colored sand and dry knocking bones, and I knew that Indian magic had convincing protective powers. Not as strong as the powers that Misquamacus could summon up, maybe. Not as strong as Aktunowihio, the living darkness. But I reasoned with myself that we were modern-minded and technological, Papago Joe and me, and what we lacked in shamanism we could make up for in experience, and general coolness, and *nous*.

Papago Joe peered at his ritzy gold Rolex. "Why don't you meet me here at six o'clock tomorrow morning. I should have everything I need by then."

"Should I bring an overnight bag?" I ventured.

Papago Joe levelled those coal-glitter eyes at me, and this time he looked seriously serious.

"Mr Erskine, you and I are going to journey to the land

of the dead. Just bring hope, and imagination, and a great deal of madness."

We finished the bottle of Chivas Regal and then I left the Airstream without any ceremony at all and banged the door shut behind me. I had a sinus headache from the air-conditioned cold in Papago Joe's trailer; and a brain-membrane headache from the whiskey; and a stress head-ache from worrying about the Great Outside.

Then the sun hit me, naked and hot and totally uncom-promising, and gave me an instant migraine.

I crossed the blinding-white lot to my rented Lincoln. While I was fumbling for the keys, Stanley appeared, drag-ging a dusty dead gopher behind him on a knotted string.

"Hi, Stanley," I said. "How's it going?"

"Oh, fine," he said. Then, "You don't look so hot."

"Oh, yeah? Well, neither does your gopher."

Stanley said, very gravely, "My gopher's sick."

I peered at it. "You're right. It looks pretty sick. What's the matter with it?"

"I don't know. One minute it was okay and running around and then it kind of opted out."

Do you know something, I really liked that. "Opted out." That was exactly what I was going to be doing tomorrow with Papago Joe, "opting out." Out of the world of the liv-ing, into the dead. Hallelujah!

I opened the car door and climbed inside. The leather seats were roasting and I had to lift my backside about an inch above them, and start the motor in that famous "cheeks-off-the-upholstery" posture known all across the Sunbelt.

"Your friend was looking for you," said Stanley.

"Is that right?"

"She said she'd try to catch you later."

I let the engine rev for a moment, and then I switched it off. I looked at Stanley closely. Stanley looked back at me. You had to give that kid something, he never blinked.

"My friend was a *woman*?" I asked him.

He snudged up his nose, nodded. "Sure. She said she'd try to catch you later."

"What did she look like, this woman?"

"I don't know. She was just a woman."

"How about her clothes? How was she dressed?"

"Yellow, I guess. She liked my gopher."

Karen, I thought. I felt a sudden thrill of excitement and at the same time, an extremely unpleasant thrill of fear. The last time I had seen Karen, she had been dragged into a hole that wasn't even a hole, on the second floor of the Belford Hotel, in New York. Of course I had glimpsed her on television, but somehow it was possible to believe that whatever you saw on television was an optical illusion, a trick of the cameras, a mirage. Now Stanley was standing in front of me in the blinding white sunlight of Apache Junction and telling me that Karen was really here, and that she was looking for me, and that she would "catch me later."

I took out my billfold and gave Stanley two matching portraits of Abraham Lincoln. "Here, Stanley, go buy yourself something living. You know, like a kitten, or a puppy."

"E.C. Dude has a Gila monster."

"Well, buy yourself a Gila monster."

He waited, frowned, blinked.

"What's the matter?" I asked him.

"Gila monsters cost twelve seventy-five."

I spent the rest of the afternoon at the Phoenix Public Library on McDowell, trying to eat a very messy hamburger without the lady librarians catching me at it (a quick duck of the head, a huge bite, mouth-wipe, chew) and at the same time reading up everything I could find on Custer's Last Stand and the Battle of the Little Big Horn.

Like just about everything else that goes wrong in life, Custer's defeat at the Little Big Horn had been brought about by his own disobedience, his own hotheadedness and his own chronic underestimation of what he was up against. On a June afternoon in 1876, he had attacked a Sioux encampment on the western banks of what the Indians called the Greasy Grass River. Custer had commanded 480 cavalry troopers, split into three contingents. But he had failed to realize that the Indian encampment was protected by well over two thousand warriors., including Gall and Crazy Horse.

While two of his contingents attacked the Indians head-

on at the south of the encampment, Custer and 215 of his
men had raced recklessly up the eastern banks of the river,
trying to outflank the Indians from the north. But Gall and
Crazy Horse had repulsed the attack from the south, and
then crossed the river and caught the bluecoats when they
were all strung out on a ridge, and halfway down a ravine.

The cavalry had scattered, and the rout that followed had
been short, bloody and complete. As they retreated, the
troopers were brought down by spears, warclubs, rifle fire,
and showers of arrows. Some of them, realizing they
couldn't escape, had shot themselves in the head.

Most of the history books that I found in the Phoenix library told much the same story—even the accounts given by
the Indians themselves. But as the sky outside the library
began to thicken into that thick gaudy mixture of mauve
and orange that characterizes a Phoenix sunset, I discovered
the first clue that something different may have happened at
the Little Big Horn. I came across a book of pictographs,
showing the course of the massacre from beginning to end.
They had been drawn by Chief Red Horse of the Sioux—
who had played a prominent part in the battle—with the
encouragement of a US Army surgeon called Charles
McChesney.

McChesney had also taken down Red Horse's narrative
account of the Little Big Horn, and the words were printed
beneath the pictographs.

*The soldiers came on the trail made by the Sioux and at-
tacked the lodges of the Unkpapas.* And there they were, in
childishly-drawn and coloured pictures, Major Marcus
Reno and his contingent, on their way to fight with the
Sioux head-on.

*All the Sioux now charged the soldiers and drove them in
confusion across the river and up into the hills.* Red Horse
had drawn them riding back over their own hoofprints, to
indicate that they were in full retreat.

With Major Reno and his men driven back, this was the
moment when the Sioux had turned their attention to *the
other soldiers*—Custer and his men, riding up the eastern
ridges of the river valley.

But as I turned the page of Chief Red Horse's book, I

came across an extraordinary pictograph which made me literally shiver—and it wasn't the air-conditioning in the library, either, even though the lady librarians had set it to Visible Breath.

The shadow rose out of the ravine and moved across the ridge to the Deep Coulee. The soldiers were crying out and confused. The shadow swallowed them up. Then Crazy Horse blew his eagle-wing-bone whistle, and the Sioux charged into the shadow and killed those soldiers who were not yet dead.

Chief Red Horse had drawn a turmoil of horses of different colors (black, red, brown, blue and even lilac), and up above their heads a huge black cloud. McChesney's comment was:

"The limitations of sign-language made it difficult for me to discover exactly what Chief Red Horse had been attempting to draw. I asked him if it were the smoke from the soldiers' guns and the dry adobe earth kicked up by the horses. In particular the dust must have been choking, because although there was some vegetation on the ridge—sagebrush and Spanish dagger plants and prairie pea vines—it was too sparse to cover the soil, and most of the draws in this part of the river were nothing but barren washes.

"However, Chief Red Horse said again and again that this was neither smoke nor dust, but *shadow*. He further elaborated by covering his face with his hands, and parting his fingers so that I could see only his eyes. I had no idea what he meant by this, and I could find nobody who could explain it to me further.

"I assumed that he must be mistaken when he said that Crazy Horse had blown his whistle *after* the shadow had swallowed the soldiers. The dust and smoke would not have risen as thick as Chief Red Horse had drawn it until the battle was well under way. There was no doubt that the river valley was very dark that afternoon. One account says that it 'seemed like twilight; under the pall, gunflashes winked like fireflies. At times, the blasts of rifles and carbines sounded like the ripping of a giant canvas down the wrinkles of the hills.' But the darkness surely developed *because* of the fighting and did not precede it.

"I was also puzzled by Chief Red Horse's suggestion that

the shadow *itself* had done for a great many of Custer's men. He insisted that Crazy Horse had done nothing more than follow the shadow and dispatch the wounded, although how a shadow could have killed anybody, he refused (or was unable) to explain.

"Whenever I pressed him on the matter, he simply repeated the action of covering his face. He said that he was unable to describe the shadow further, in case he incurred the anger of the wonder-workers."

I examined Red Horse's shadow-drawing for almost twenty minutes. It couldn't have been a cloud, because Red Horse hadn't drawn clouds or sky in any of his other pictographs. Nor had he drawn any dust—even in his illustrations of the most furious fighting. This was the only pictograph in which a shadow appeared and unlike his other drawings, which were light and sketchy, the shadow was drawn thick and black and complicated, as if he had drawn something very detailed but then changed his mind, and tried to obscure it with layer upon layer of heavy pencil-shading.

There was no way of telling what was under all that shading unless I went to the Smithsonian and examined the original pictograph. But all the same, I thought I could make out a mass of coiled or wavy lines, almost like the tentacles of an octopus. At the top of the picture one of these tentacles appeared to have emerged from the shadow and thrust itself into a trooper's stretched-open mouth.

That chilled me more than ever. It reminded me too closely of Martin Vaizey, when he had been possessed by that buffalo-headed shadow at the Greenbergs' apartment and thrust his arm down Naomi Greenberg's throat.

Maybe that same shadow-buffalo had been there, at the Little Big Horn. Maybe the massacre had happened exactly as Chief Red Horse had described it.

I turned over the page, and it was then that I was sure that I was thinking in the right direction. Here was a pictograph of the Indian dead, scattered on the ground in warbonnets, their rifles and their bows lying beside them. *The soldiers killed 136 Sioux, but the wonder-worker performed the necessary rituals to make sure that they would live contentedly in*

*the Great Outside until the day came when all white men
would be buried, when they would again walk free.*

McChesney remarked, "I took this as a reference to the
cult of the Ghost Dance, which claims that one day, white
people and all of their works will one day fall into the
ground and be swallowed up, leaving America free for Indians once more. Because he had drawn him so tall, and in
such great detail, I asked Chief Red Horse to give me the
wonder-worker's name. Chief Red Horse said there was no
sign for the wonder-worker's name, because any warrior
who tried to describe him in sign-language would find that
his fingers caught fire. Instead Chief Red Horse scratched in
the dust some hieroglyphs which looked like two cups and a
curled ear, a lozenge with four horizontal lines on it, and a
bowl with two necklaces on either side of it. I had never seen
a Sioux write hieroglyphs like these before, and I had no understanding of what they might mean. I made a note of
them, however, and some months later in Connecticut I met
the French missionary Father Eugene Vetromile, who was
something of an expert on Indian writing. He studied the
hieroglyphs with great interest and proclaimed them to be
Narragansett, in spite of the fact that they had been written
by a Sioux. Their meaning was: Darkness, Terror, Eternal,
Man—or, He Who Brings The Terror Of Eternal Darkness.
The phonetic pronunciation was m—q—m—c, or mis-
kamakus."

I opened a can of Miller Draft that I had brought into the
library along with my hamburger and other essential items
of sustenance, like a large bag of Ruffles and a several sticks
of beef jerky. I was just about to take my first swallow when
I became aware of one of the library ladies standing over
me.

"Pardon me, sir, but eating and drinking are not permitted."

I turned around. She was small and sweet and quite pe-
tite, a serious brunette in her mid-twenties, wearing a crisp
blouse and a camel-colored skirt.

"I'm sorry," I said. "I haven't eaten today."

"Well, I'm sorry, too," she said. "But we can't have people bringing their meals in here."

"I see," I told her. "A restaurant for the brain, but not for the belly."

She blinked furiously. I don't think she understood me one bit. It was the eastern accent, no doubt, and the eastern sense of humor. They don't have a sense of humor in Arizona, and who would, living in 90-degree heat amid geriatrics and mafiosi, and even some geriatric mafiosi.

"Actually," I told her, leaning back in my chair and crossing my ankles and putting on my full Harold Erskine M.D. act, "actually I'm researching the Battle of the Little Big Horn, and Custer's Last Stand, and I've been finding some very interesting research material here . . . better than anyplace else."

"All the same, sir, you can't eat and drink while you're doing it."

"Can I finish my beer? Would that be allowed?"

"I'm sorry."

"Well," I said, "I'm sorry, too. Very sorry. Just when I thought I was making progress."

She flushed, and eyed the can of beer with uncertainty. "You can stay provided you don't actually drink. The Little Big Horn, that's a real interesting subject. Did you see our book of contemporary newspaper stories?"

I set my beer can down on my desk. "No, I didn't, but I'd like to."

"You'll have to promise me not to drink."

"Hey, come on, Boy Scouts' honor."

She disappeared on squeaky rubber-soled shoes. I sat and drank the rest of my Miller in a leisurely fashion. Outside the windows the night was now glossy and black, like the lake of shadows which lay beneath our feet. Eventually the librarian returned, and laid an oversize book in front of me.

"There," she said. "We're really proud of this book. Facsimiles of newspaper pages, all the way back to 1840."

She had opened the book to the front page of the *Bismarck Tribune,* published in Bismarck, Dakota Territory, on July 6, 1876. The headlines cried, MASSACRED—Gen. Custer And 261 Men The Victims—No Officer Or Man Of 5 Companies Left To Tell The Tale—Squaws Mutilate And

Rob Dead—What Will Congress Do About It?—Is This The Beginning Of The End?

The first paragraph was electrifying. "It will be remembered that the *Bismarck Tribune* sent a special correspondent, Mark Kellogg, with Gen. Custer's expedition. Kellogg's last words to the writer were, 'By the time this reaches you we will have met and fought the Red devils, with what result remains to be seen. I go with Custer and will be at the death.' How true!"

The type was tiny, and my eyes were bleary, but in the third column of the report, I read, "The body of Kellogg alone remained unmutilated and unstripped of clothing. Perhaps they had learned to respect this humble shover of the lead pencil and to that fact may be attributed this result. Perhaps they feared that his photographic equipment had captured their souls, and that he would wreak an awful revenge on them if they desecrated his remains. As it was, his camera remained untouched also, and his photographic plates have been safely returned to Bismarck for development."

I sat back. Jesus. So that was it. That was what Samuel had been trying to tell me. Mark Kellogg had been a reporter and photographer for the *Bismarck Tribune,* and he had actually taken photographs of the massacre at the Little Big Horn.

I couldn't believe that nobody had ever said anything about these photographs before. In spite of the eyewitness accounts from Indian warriors, in spite of all the drawings, the truth of what had happened by the Greasy Grass River had never been fully explained. But if there were *photographs* . . .

The lady librarian came up to me and said, "We're closing now, sir. If you need to do any more research, I'm afraid you'll have to come back tomorrow."

"No, no thank you," I told her. "You've been terrific."

She picked up my can of Miller Draft, presumably with the intention of saying that I could take it outside now, and finish it off. But she realized at once that it was completely empty.

"You *drank* it," she said. "You *drank* it. In contravention of library regulations, and city ordinance, and state law."

Obediently I held out my wrists in the handcuff position. "So arrest me," I said.

I took her for dinner at Mother O'Reilly's up on the hills north of Phoenix, and afterward we sat on the terrace and finished a bottle of Chandon's Napa Valley Brut between us, while the night massaged us, soft and warm and Arizona-velvety, with all the glittery lights of Sun Valley spread out below us.

She told me her name was Nesta and she was twenty-six years old and lived with her parents. She reminded me of those secretaries in true-love comics like *Apartment 3-G* or *The Heart of Juliet Jones*. She was shy and self-deprecating, almost as if she couldn't believe that she was at all attractive. She loved baking and horses and ballet and poetry— particularly Longfellow.

"Once upon a time, I could recite almost the whole of *The Song of Hiawatha*," she smiled.

"As far as I'm concerned, Indians aren't the flavor of the month," I told her.

"Oh, dear! Well, how about *There is a Reaper whose name is Death, And with his sickle keen, He reaps the bearded grain at a breath, And the flowers that grow between.*"

"Cheerful," I nodded.

She said, "Will you read my palm?"

"For sure," I told her. "But let me tell you this: a palm-reading is very superficial. A palm-reading is like the *Reader's Digest*. You know what I mean? Your whole life, condensed into six or seven crinkles. I mean, it'll give you a rough idea of how long you're going to live, and a rough idea of how happy you're going to be. But if you want to be specific and detailed—if you want to know what kind of men you're going to meet, and when, and what color underwear they like the best, and the minute-hour-day when your cat's going to be run over by which particular make of automobile—then you need a full-scale card-reading."

She smiled enthusiastically. "Great! Okay then, a card-reading."

I patted my shirt pockets, I patted my pants. "Oh . . . just a minute. Oh . . . that's a pity. I left my cards back at my hotel."

"Oh," she echoed, and she was much more disappointed than I was. She was wearing a tight black sleeveless sequin top, and she had lovely rounded black-glittery breasts. She needed some frontal orthodonty, but then wandering Lotharios can't be choosers, can they?

"Hey, no worries," I told her. "You can come back and have a couple of drinks and then I can give you the whole shooting-match."

"I . . . unh, I don't think so," she said.

"Hey, what have you got to lose?" I said, and then I wished I hadn't. I sounded like the Fonz.

She glumly shrugged. "I guess I can turn it down because I'm a twenty-six-year-old librarian and you're a forty-five-year-old fortune-teller, and if you think that's any kind of recipe for happiness? Even, what—even *fleeting* happiness?"

I could have said something but I decided not to. She was right and she was wrong. The main thing was that if she didn't feel like it, if she didn't feel like taking the chance, then it was best for her if she didn't. There was no point in her going to the library tomorrow and despising herself. There was no point in me over-exerting myself on a sweltering Arizona evening, just for the sake of company, or lust, or frustration, or God knows what.

We sat in silence for a long time. We saw a faint distant display of shooting stars. She reached across the table and touched my hand.

"I hope you're not angry," she said.

"Angry? Why should I be angry?"

"You expected to take me to bed."

"No, I didn't."

"Then why did you take me out to dinner?"

"Why did you accept?"

She didn't answer for a long time. When she did, she spoke very carefully and very seriously, making sure that her answer was clear, and that she wasn't befuddled by too much sparkling wine.

"I didn't realize what kind of man you are. I'm sorry. I didn't realize that you had some kind of shadow following you. And you *do,* Harry, you can't deny it. There's some kind of darkness about you, I can't describe it. But it's there, I can feel it, and it frightens me."

I could have laughed. I could have cried. "It frightens *you*?" I asked her.

I was booked into the Thunderbird Motel on Indian School Road, an unprepossessing collection of concrete apartments that looked like an abandoned filling-station. It had frosted-glass balconies, every one of which was cracked, and plant-tubs littered with cigarette-ends and an ice-machine that made a grinding, rattling noise all night. Something dusty and scaly was lying in the middle of the walkway that led to my room. It could have been a dead armadillo but I didn't attempt to find out.

The Thunderbird wasn't the Biltmore, but the price of my plane ticket to Phoenix had already stretched my Master-card to the point where I had started stammering when the girl at the United Airlines desk had swiped it through the computer.

I arrived back at the Thunderbird at about ten past eleven, after I had driven Nesta home. She lived in a neat suburban house near Chris-Town. The net curtains had twitched as she pecked me on the lips and climbed out. After the front door had closed behind her, I had switched the car radio onto "Bat Out of Hell," deafened-for-life volume, and swore myself a terrible and comprehensive oath that I would never date a librarian again. All that stuff about, "Why, Ms Hempstead, without your glasses, you're— you're beautiful!" is bull. Nesta had been just as plain without her glasses as she was with them on; and her brain had been plain, to match. And her observation that I had a shadow following me had put me seriously out of sorts.

We all have a shadow following us, for God's sake. That doesn't mean we want to be reminded of it.

I took a six-pack of Coors back to my room, kicked off my shoes and collapsed onto the bed to watch television. The room was small and square and very chilly but surprisingly airless, and *brown.* The carpet was brown, the drapes were brown, the bedcover was brown-and-orange striped. They seem to have a thing for brown in Arizona. The only decorative touches were a huge Indian-pottery ashtray on top of the television, and an amateurish picture of an Apache chief, with the caption, "It is better to have lightning in the hand than thunder in the mouth." I paraphrased that as "It is better to have dollars in the bank than it is to have limitless credit."

I watched *Terminator 2* for a while, and finished a couple of beers. Then I undressed and showered. The tiles in the bathroom were brown. Even the water was brown.

After my shower, wrapped in my old faded-yellow bathrobe, I went out onto the balcony, still towelling my hair. After the deathly Kelvinator chill in my room, the night air was warm and dry and soothing. I could hear a man and a woman loudly and drunkenly arguing, and the distant yowling of coyotes. I felt as if I had arrived here from another planet.

I was just turning back to my open door to fetch myself another beer when I glimpsed a young woman walking quickly across the motel courtyard below me. She was visible only for a fraction of a second before she vanished underneath the balcony, and I couldn't see much more than her shoulders and the top of her head. But the back of my neck fizzed with shock, because I was sure that I recognized her.

I leaned over the balcony. The man and the woman were still arguing. *"—of all the God-damned insane things to do— of all the dumb-ass stupid ridiculous things to do—"*

I listened, but the night was filled with too much arguing and traffic noise and distorted radio-music for me to be able to hear footsteps. I heard a door slam, but that could have been anybody's.

Wrapping my towel round my neck, I walked along the balcony as far as the steps, taking care not to tread on the dead armadillo. I thought I saw a shadow moving, and the sharp shuffle of a shoe on dusty concrete, and I called out, "Karen?"

I waited, straining my ears.

"Karen?" I repeated.

I wasn't at all sure that it was Karen. The odds against it being Karen were about a zillion-to-one. Even if she was still here in Phoenix—even if Misquamacus hadn't spirited her away to someplace else—how would she know where I was staying?

All the same, in that split-second glimpse, I had seen hair that was just like Karen's, and shoulders that were just like Karen's, and there had just been *something* in the way she carried herself that made me think that it *could* be her.

Wishful thinking? Well, maybe. But I stayed where I was at the top of the steps, still listening.

After three or four minutes, the door to one of the ground-floor rooms opened and a fat man with hairy shoulders came out. He saw me and stared up at me suspiciously.

"You got a problem, friend?" he asked me.

I shook my head.

"I'm waiting for somebody, that's all."

He eyed me up and down, spat out of the side of his mouth, and then went back into his room. I thought: classy joints I have stayed in, number two hundred and thirty-six.

I went back to my room and locked the door behind me. I sat on the bed and had a long think, but I was too tired to think of anything sensible. Apart from being tired, I was filled up with one too many beers, and a gnawing apprehension about tomorrow. I knew that visiting the Great Outside was probably the only way for me to find Karen and Misquamacus, but the Great Outside was death. It was what we clairvoyants like to call the world beyond the veil. I wasn't at all sure that I really wanted to make a visit, even if that visit was intended to be temporary.

I switched on the television, and found myself watching *A Day At The Races.* I changed channels to the news, but there were no new updates on what had happened in Las Vegas. *"A hundred square miles of southwestern Nevada are virtually a no-go area . . . rescue pilots have reported running into dust clouds as high as twenty thousand feet."* I switched the television off again, and the bedside lamp, too.

I lay in darkness for a while, listening to the air-conditioning and the sounds of the night outside. It probably took me no more than ten minutes to fall asleep.

FIFTEEN

I was awakened by the feeling that there was somebody standing in the room with me. The feeling was so strong that for a moment I was too scared to open my eyes, in case it was true.

When I did look around the room, however, there was nobody there. A faint light was straining in between the dark-brown drapes, and the single red eye of the television pilot light was still glowing, so if there *had* been anybody there I would have seen them at once. I had probably felt nothing more than the fading vibrations of a nightmare.

I rolled over and checked my watch on the nightstand. It was two-twenty-five in the morning, in those dark and tiny hours when the Reaper is cutting down the bearded grain, and the flowers that grow between.

I lay back on my pillow for a while, trying to imagine what the day was going to bring. But the Great Outside was unimaginable. All I could think of was darkness and more darkness.

I was right on the edge of nodding off to sleep again when I heard a faint squeaking noise from the bathroom. Not a mouse, or a cricket. More like the sound of human skin rubbing against ceramic tiles.

There *was* somebody there, in the bathroom. I lay totally still and held my breath and kept on listening and listening. My heart ran a slow, deep marathon inside of my ribcage, and I could hear my blood rushing through my ears. For a very long time, though, over a minute, I heard nothing at all. A plane droning high in the sky; a truck rumbling and rattling. More nothing. And then *squikkk.*

Slowly, carefully, I climbed out of bed and reached for my clothes. You have no idea how much noise you make when you step into a pair of cotton-twill trousers. It sounds like thirty undisciplined carnie workers putting up a three-ring tent made of cellophane. I buckled my belt and decided to forget about the polo shirt. I stood in the gloom of my chilly room still listening, still listening. *Deep into the darkness peering, long I stood there, wondering, fearing, Doubting, dreaming dreams no mortal ever dared to dream before.*

"Who's there?" I said, in a voice as weak as watered milk. "Is anybody there?"

I glanced towards the door. The chain was still fastened, the door was still locked. If somebody had managed to break into my room, they must have come in through the bathroom window. I didn't quite understand *how,* because although the bathroom window was quite wide it was only about six inches high, not nearly high enough for anybody to squeeze through it.

I padded on bare feet towards the bathroom and stood outside the door for another half minute, listening. The hair on the back of my neck was prickling and I was shivery and goose-bumpy all over, but that was because of the chilly air-conditioning. Leastways, that was what I tried to tell myself. Frightened? *Moi?* Of squeaking noises in the night? I was almost paralyzed with terror.

I waited and waited and waited and prayed that there was nobody in the bathroom. Please God or Gitche Manitou please may there be nobody in the bathroom. But then I knew that I had to push open the door and switch on the light and take a look. There was no escaping it. After all, I couldn't go back to bed and peacefully sleep for the rest of the night without knowing *for sure* that there was nobody there.

I cleared my throat. "Is anybody there?" I asked, man-fully.

Oh, for sure. About a hundred loopy Disney voices are going to shout out, "Nobody here but us ghosts!"

I pushed open the door. It made a light juddering noise, banged against the tiled wall. The bathroom was slightly lighter than the bedroom, because a streetlight was shining through the window. I could make out the tub, the toilet and the washbasin. The light gleamed on the chrome-plated taps. The mirror gleamed dark. A good suicide mirror, that. The kind of mirror which disillusioned husbands stand in front of, and watch themselves cutting their own throats.

What better place to finish a nondescript life, than the Thunderbird Motel?

I frowned at the frosted-glass shower cubicle. It *looked* empty. I hoped it was empty. But there was some kind of shadow in it, some kind of shape, which didn't seem to correspond with the tiling.

I felt as if the floor had dropped away beneath my feet. *There was somebody standing in the shower.* Oh, God. There was somebody in it. This was *Psycho* all over. *Wheep, wheep, wheep, wheep!*

I swallowed a dry, sour swallow. My heartbeat, slow and deep, accelerated into a furious, erratic drumming. There was no question about it. Somebody was standing in the shower, somebody white-skinned and naked, with no water running. Somebody silent, somebody still. It looked like a woman. I could just about make out her eyes, two dark smudges that looked like the blood clots on the yolk of a fertilized egg; and the darkness of her hair.

I approached the shower very slowly, and raised my hand towards the door-catch.

The white figure didn't move, but she must have been watching me closely.

"Karen?" I whispered.

There was a long-drawn-out moment of utter silence. No cars, no radios, no passing planes. I was about to take the catch in my hand, ready to pull the shower door open, and the white figure was obviously waiting for me.

"Karen?" I repeated. "Is that you?"

Before I could touch it, the shower door unlatched itself, and swung silently open. Karen was standing naked in front of me, so white that she could have been dead and bled. She stood with her arms straight down by her sides, her dark eyes staring directly at me as if she were willing me to move, willing me to speak.

The light from the bathroom window made her shoulders and her breasts gleam white, but left the lower part of her face in shadow. It was impossible to tell if she were smiling or not, or whether she was simply standing there, expressionless, waiting for me to say something.

"Karen?" (My heart going crazy now, one of those drum

solos in which the sweat flies and the audience scream and the drummer eventually collapses.) "Karen, how did you get *in* here?"

She slowly lifted one hand. "Aren't you going to help me out of here?"

"Karen . . . the door's locked . . . the window's too small. How did you get *in* here?"

She stepped out of the shower cubicle and stood in front of me, small and frighteningly pale. She lifted her hand and I clasped it in mine. It felt like no hand that I had ever held before, like cold, half-stewed okra. No wonder that, in India, they called okra "Ladies' Fingers." They must have had first-hand experience of touching the spirits of dead women, or reincarnated women, or women who were still alive and who had been possessed by terrible spirits.

I wasn't sure which of those women Karen now was. Or whether this was Karen at all.

"Harry . . ." she said. "It's so good to see you."

"Whaha—" I began, and then I had to stop, because I couldn't pronounce my words properly. "What happened to you?"

"I had to go, Harry, that's all."

I squeezed her hand more tightly. I think I was almost afraid that I would squeeze some kind of cold, clear juice out of her fingers. But she stepped up closer, until her chilly nipples were brushing against my bare stomach, and she lifted her head as if she wanted me to kiss her.

Her face was so bloodless. Her eyes were so dark. If she hadn't been moving and breathing and talking, I would have sworn that she had just been disinterred from the local cemetery.

The question was, when does somebody you care for stop being somebody you care for? When they die, when they go cold, or when they appear in your shower in the middle of the night, white of skin and blank of eye, and demand that you kiss them?

"Karen," I said, "you're cold."

She smiled. "I don't mind being cold. I don't feel the cold."

"Karen, you have to see this from my point of view. You

disappeared into a hole in a floor in New York; and now you're here in Phoenix, with no clothes on, freezing cold—and there's no possible way you could have gotten in here."

"You're worried about me," she said.

"Too damn right I'm worried about you. I'm worried about *me.*"

She wrapped her cold arms around my shoulders. She was still elfin, still enticing. "Why are you worried?" she wanted to know. "I'm *here,* aren't I? I'm safe."

"Sure, you're safe and you're here, but are you *you*?"

She pressed her fingertips to her mouth and gave a stylized, girlish giggle; and if there was anything that was guaranteed to give me a totally chilly shudder down my spine, that was it. "You're so silly," she said. "Of course I'm me. Who else should I be?"

I didn't really know what to do next. But Karen tugged my hand. "Come on," she said. She kept on tugging, and tugged me through to the bedroom. "Do you want me to *prove* that I'm me?" she asked me.

"Listen, Karen, we have to get a few things straight here. When you disappeared through that floor—"

She pushed me back against the bed. "Don't be silly, that was nothing. You don't always have to leave by the door, any more than you have to come in by the door. The world is full of other ways of coming in and going out; not just *doors.*"

"Well, yes, but—"

She gave me a small, sharp shove so that I fell backward. Before I could get up again, she had climbed on top of me and straddled my chest.

"Karen," I protested. "I can't just—"

She leaned over me so that her face loomed over mine. "You can't *what*? You're so cautious, Harry! You can do anything you want!" And with this, she started to lick my face all over, and her tongue was as chilly and slimy as pig's liver. I tried to pull away from her, but she was gripping me firmly between her thighs, and her strength and weight were those of a man, not a lightly-boned young woman. She stopped licking and looked down at me, her mouth glistening with saliva, her eyes as dusty-dead as wood lice.

"You can do anything you want," she repeated, and her voice was low and very harsh. It was then that I knew for certain that Karen was possessed. This wasn't Karen talking to me. This was the manitou of Misquamacus. He had filled her mind and her body like black ink spreading across blotting paper. He had filled her up with his spiritual essence and his tribal ferocity—and his malevolence, too, and his insatiable hunger for revenge.

"Karen," I said, "you'd better—"

But now she was unbuckling my belt, and tugging down my trousers. I tried to stop her, tried to thrash my legs, but suddenly she came back up the bed and slapped my face, hard enough to hurt. I tried to protest but she slapped me again—a cold, hard, stunning slap, and then another, and another, until my cheeks were stinging and my eyeballs were jolted in their sockets.

"Now you're going to do what *I* want to do," she told me.

I gave one last wrestle, but she slapped me again. My head jerked back against the pillow. I almost began to understand how battered wives must feel, when they're faced with somebody who won't listen and won't compromise, and won't do anything but lash out. But quite apart from that, she was still Karen, her body was still Karen, and I didn't want to hurt her. She was so small that one hard punch could have broken her jaw, or worse.

"Karen—" I began again, but she shook her head and said, "Shussh . . . This time it's my turn."

I lay back shivering, my cheeks still hot from all of her slapping. She shuffled her way up my body until she was straddling my throat, and her pubic hair was tickling my Adam's apple. She looked down at me, and said, "I always wanted this. You know that, don't you? Right from the moment we met."

"Karen," I complained, "this isn't right. It just isn't right."

She looked down at me and smiled eerily. "Who says it isn't right? It feels right to me. It feels wonderful to me."

In spite of my fear, in spite of my fear that it was Misquamacus who was making her behave the way she was, I still couldn't stop myself from feeling aroused. It was like one of those sexual nightmares in which you're turned on but terrified at the same time. I had once dreamed that a woman in black leather was trying to cut me with a straight razor, and I had woken in a sweat of excitement and terror. In a peculiar way, the fear made it all the more stimulating. Was this actually Karen, or was it some kind of ghost?

She lifted herself up a little more, so that her sex was only about two or three inches above my mouth. The insides of her thighs were smooth and cold against my slapped cheeks. Although it was so gloomy, I could make out her dark silky fur and the glistening petal-shaped curves of her vulva.

I tensed, waiting for the moment when I could roll out from under her. But she must have sensed what I was intending to do, because she said, in the softest of voices, "Don't, Harry . . . whatever you think, I need you."

"Karen?" I said.

"It's me, Harry, it's really me. Now, ssh."

She reached down between her legs and opened her vaginal lips wide with her fingers, really stretched them wide. The she lowered herself slowly onto my mouth, so that I was offered a kiss of moist wet flesh. At first I kept my lips tightly closed, and tried to turn my head away. But then Karen slowly began to rotate her hips, so that my mouth was smeared around and around with her juices, and I began to think to myself *I was wrong, dead wrong. This isn't Misquamacus. This can't be Misquamacus. This is Karen letting herself go. This is Karen doing just what she always wanted to do, and didn't have the nerve.*

She laughed, and her laugh sounded high and sweet and just like Karen's. I reached up with both hands and clasped her thighs and pressed her even more forcefully against my mouth. I opened my lips and slid my tongue up inside her, licking every fold of her sex, probing as deep as my tongue would allow. I heard her cry out, a thin penetrating falsetto. Her vagina was flushed with even more copious juices, and they ran out of the sides of my mouth.

After a few moments, she climbed off my face, and kissed me. She kissed my hair, she kissed my eyes, she kissed my cheeks, she kissed my mouth. Then she gradually worked her way around my shoulders, and nibbled at my nipples. I lay back on the pillow and closed my eyes in total pleasure as she kissed and bit her way all the way down my sides.

"Karen . . ." I heard somebody say, and it was probably me. I tangled my fingers in her hair as she took hold of my cock and firmly and slowly began to massage it up and down. She kissed and sucked at the glans, the tip of her tongue circling and circling. My cock felt so hard and swollen that I thought it was going to burst. She licked the crevice, teasingly and persistently. Then she took it into her mouth, and I felt it slowly slide in, between her teeth, and her tongue swirling around it, and for the first time in a long time I didn't care about Misquamacus, and I didn't care about shadows that ran along like buffalos, and I didn't care about anything at all except Karen Tandy. I thought to myself, *This young lady and me, we were always meant to get together. Maybe we met through pain and tragedy and rampant evil, but this was always meant to be.*

The feelings that Karen was arousing in me were totally sensational. She had swallowed the whole length of my cock, all the way down to my pubic hair, and she was rhythmically sucking on it, without once pausing to take a breath. What was more, her tongue was actually licking around and around the shaft of my cock, all the way around, with the most incredible swirling motion, almost as if—

Almost as if her head was going around and around.

I had an instant petrifying vision of old man Rheiner at the Belford Hotel, with his head going round and round. But then I opened my eyes and it was worse. *Karen was floating vertically in the air, her bare toes nearly touching the ceiling, slowly spinning around and around.* Her hair gently flew out as she spun, but her eyes were wide open, and each time she came around to face me, she stared at me upside-down, with an uncanny expression of mock-submission, as if she were only sucking my cock to show me how weak and vulnerable I was, and how much like other men. Ready to throw my common sense and my principles out of the window, as soon as I was offered sex. Even ready to throw out my instinct for self-preservation.

I yelled out. I *think* I yelled out. Karen immediately disgorged my cock, and spun over and over in mid-air, like an astronaut tumbling over and over in a weightless space capsule. She landed spreadeagled against the wall in the far corner of the room, beside the dark-brown drapes, where she stood watching me, her face buried in shadow, breathing deeply and evenly, as if she had been running. I grabbed my pants and struggled into them, sweating and shaking in spite of the air-conditioned chill.

"How did you do that?" I asked her. "How the hell did you *do* that?"

"I can do anything, white devil," said Karen, and this time her voice was even harsher and lower. "I can walk through time. I can walk through space. There is nothing that can hold me back now."

"What do you want?" I asked her. I wished I didn't sound so strangulated and high-pitched.

"I want you to be my messenger."

"What do you mean?"

"I want you to take a message to your people. I want you to tell them that their cities are not being swallowed by earthquakes or storms, but by the power of Misquamacus the greatest of all wonder-workers."

"Taking a message to my people isn't going to be quite as easy as it sounds," I replied. I was trying to be brave and challenging but it wasn't very easy. My voice kept shaking and going off track. "Who am I going to take it to?" I wanted to know. "The President? The Office of Indian Affairs? The *Washington Post*? You don't seriously think that anybody's going to believe me?"

"They must be told *why* they have to die," said Karen. "They must know why every single artifact that they ever brought or fashioned must be taken down to the Great Outside, and banished forever. The years of the White Faces are over, forever. It was foretold and now it has come to be."

"I don't know why you're bothering to tell us *why* we have to be swallowed up," I said. "Why don't you just swallow us up and leave it at that?"

"You have to *know*!" Karen retorted. "It is the turning of the moon, the season of darkness that follows the season of light. Just as you believed that it was your manifest destiny to kill us and steal our hunting-lands, we believe that it is *your* manifest destiny to be plunged into the ground, into the Great Outside, and there to meet the god of all shadows, who will be judge and bloody executioner of all."

"I still don't see that it makes any difference whether or not we *know* why we're going to be massacred," I blustered. "Being massacred is being massacred, no matter what the reason for it happens to be."

"It is justice. It is just revenge. They have to know that. Those who survive, those who carry the story to other countries and other continents, they must *all* know why we have done this thing. Otherwise white men will come again, and again, and again, and we shall never know peace."

"Misquamacus," I said, "what you're proposing to do, it's impossible. It's totally impossible! It's way too late to turn back the clock. Supposing you get rid of New York and Los Angeles and Seattle and Denver and Pittsburgh and every place else, what are you going to be left with? A country that's back in the God-damned Stone Age!

"Maybe it *was* unfair that we took your land and killed all your buffalo and changed your life. Maybe it *was* unforgivable that we killed all your women and children, and destroyed your culture. But the world is kind of like that, and human beings are kind of like that, all over the world, not just here. And times change, and people change, and however much you might resent it, you can't put it all back the way it was."

I paused for breath. "It was something we did and maybe it's something we shouldn't have done, or done it differently. Now it's too late. But maybe we've learned a little more humanity and a little more, I don't know, *tolerance,* I guess."

There was a long silence. Karen stared at me with a mixture of suspicion and contempt. In his code, a man didn't apologize for what his people had done. Outside the window it was gradually beginning to grow lighter, and I heard two or three heavy tractor-trailers rumbling past.

At last, Karen repeated, "You will tell your people why they are going to die."

I shrugged. "All right. I guess I can only try. But, as I say, the days of the smoke-signal are long gone. I don't suppose anybody will listen to me."

"They will listen when I have pulled down New York."

"You're going to pull down New York?"

"I have the strength; I can pull down New York. I can pull down any city, anywhere. New York is the place where I was first betrayed by the white devils. By the time I have finished with it, it will have been levelled back down to the rocks."

I stood up, and looked Karen directly in the eye. "Believe me, o mighty wonder-worker, I'm going to do everything I can to stop you."

She laughed, although she couldn't have found it all that funny, because she stopped laughing abruptly, and said, "All those who came to this land from other lands shall be swallowed up and die; and all their descendants shall be swallowed up and die; and every artifact they ever made shall be swallowed up. And the soil will cover them, and grass will cover the soil, and one day I will stand in this land and I will see tall trees and clear rivers and the lodges of many thousands of Red men, stretching from one sky to the other sky. And beneath our feet, in darkness, you will be running from Aktunowihio, who will want your souls the way that he has always wanted souls."

"Okay, then," I said. "If you want me to take a message to my people, I'll try. But don't get disappointed if they think I'm two cans short of a six-pack."

"There's something else that I need," said Karen.

"You'd better tell me what it is."

"I need your seed. That is why I came here."

"I beg your pardon? You need my seed?"

Karen nodded. In a voice that was half hers and half that of Misquamacus, she said, "I want your child."

"You want my child? You mean you, Karen, want my child; or you, Misquamacus, want my child?"

Karen didn't answer me directly, but she soon told me what I wanted to know. "I had two sons. When I left the time in which I was naturally born, so that I could be reborn in your time, I left my sons behind. They were caught by the Dutchmen who were searching for me. They were tortured and beaten. One died of a sickness and the other was hanged. Through all these centuries I have had no heirs. But now, through you, I can."

"I don't understand you."

"Whosoever I possess, their body is mine as well as their spirit. When this woman gives birth to your child, that child shall be *my* descendant, not hers."

I couldn't believe what I was hearing. "You're trying to tell me that if I make Karen pregnant, she's going to give birth to Misquamacus Junior?"

Karen's eyes suddenly blazed. "Don't mock me! The time of your ripping-apart is almost here!"

There was a low, soft thundering noise. I felt the air shake and I smelled the sharp grassy smell of burning prairie.

I backed away. I could sense that something very frightening was about to happen, and I thought I could guess what it was.

Through the wall behind Karen's back, straight out of the corner next to the door, stepped a huge tall figure in a black glistening headdress. I could see him distinctly, although he seemed to have less substance than Karen. It was like seeing somebody through three layers of black chiffon, or somebody standing on the opposite side of a heavily-smoking bonfire.

"Oh, holy shit," I said. It was all I could think of. It was Misquamacus.

He walked around Karen or he may have partly walked *through* her. He approached me and stood over me and he looked more threatening than I had ever seen him before. In his first manifestation at the Sisters of Jerusalem, he had been damaged by X-rays before his rebirth, and so he had been shrunken and dwarfish. Now he had regained his full height, and he was a dark greasy cliff of muscle and bone, with a face that would have looked at home on Mount Rushmore. His cheeks were smeared with magical designs in red and white, and his headdress was crawling with grave-beetles.

What horrified me more than anything else, however, was the way in which his shoulders appeared to have partially transmuted into insect-flesh, hairy and lumpy and clustered with scabs. And all down his sides, he was growing white tentacles that reminded me of potato-roots, pale and semi-translucent.

He wore no loincloth, but his genitals were tied up tightly, almost cruelly tightly, with an elaborate cat's-cradle arrangement of beads and twine. His shins were wrapped in filthy grease-matted leggings of buffalo fur.

"You and this woman are one," said Misquamacus, although it was still Karen who was talking. "But this woman and I are one, also. All three of us are joined by fate and by bodily closeness. Three has become one."

He paused. He may have been a spirit, he may have been nothing but a dim stirring-together of fear and memory and half-developed ectoplasm, but I could feel his breath on my face and it was colder than the air-conditioning, and I could hear his disgusting creepy bugs literally *dripping* from his headdress onto the carpet.

"Twice you have been my nemesis," he said. "Twice you have hurt me. But this time you shall be my savior; and the bringer of an heir; and this time you shall pay for what you have done to me a thousand times over."

I backed away. The back of my leg bumped against the end of the bed. I was trying to work out whether I could vault over the bed and reach the door before Misquamacus could get to me. I thought that I probably could—and even if I *couldn't,* Misquamacus looked as if he didn't have enough physical substance to be able to stop me. The only unknown factor was Karen. Since Misquamacus had completely possessed her, it was quite possible that she would stop me, and I had already had a taste of how strong she was.

Misquamacus said, "You must lie with this woman and give her your seed."

"Well, I'm sorry," I told him. "I can't make love to order. I need a candlelit supper to get me in the mood, if you know what I mean, although you probably don't."

"I am not a fool, white devil. You will give this woman your seed."

He turned, and raised his arm, his headdress still showering cockroaches and black-beetles. Karen obediently moved away from the corner and climbed onto the bed, with her legs apart and her knees slightly raised. Her eyes were dreamy, as if she were high on crack. She was cupping her breasts in her hands. Small white breasts like cups of milk, with darkened nipples.

"Listen—" I told Misquamacus. "I can't just—"

"You must," said Karen. "You have no magic. You have no power."

"But I can't possibly—"

"You must!" Karen insisted.

And then—*"You must!"* screamed a high-pitched voice, directly behind me. *"Oh, God, Harry, you must!"*

It was a voice that I hadn't heard for thirty-seven years, but I recognized it instantly. I twisted around, every nerve in my body tingling with shock. Only inches away from me stood my younger brother David, grey-faced, *green*-faced. He was wearing his black funeral suit, the suit we had buried him in, but he was still dripping wet from drowning. Nine years old, and I hadn't been able to save him.

My mouth opened and closed. I knew this couldn't be true. I had seen David lifted from the swimming-pool. I had seen a tearful lifeguard closing David's eyelids with his gentle thumb. I had stood in the rain at David's funeral and watched as his droplet-beaded coffin was carried past.

I knew what this was. This was what the Indian medicine-men called the soul-torture. This was when they went deep-sea fishing in your psyche and came up with all the agonies that affected you the most, and made you live them and live them until you couldn't stand to live them any longer. Men went out of their minds after soul-torture. That was how Martin Vaizey had ox-felled Michael Greenberg back in New York, by dragging something out of his subconscious that Michael couldn't bear to think about.

"You must," chorused David and Karen.

"David," I said. My throat was congested with emotion.

"You must," David repeated.

"You're not even real," I told him. "You're dead, David. You've been dead for thirty-seven years."

"You know that the dead can come back. You've seen it for yourself. How would you like it if I came back and kept on

coming back and never left you in peace?"

"You're not real!" I yelled at him. My fear and my grief and my terrible guilt were making me tremble with physical pain, the kind of pain that makes you plead inside of yourself, stop, stop, please for God's sake stop. This was mental dentistry, drilling right on the nerve.

"Do you want to touch me?" grinned David. *"You can touch me, if you like."*

I edged away from him, and skirted around the bed. The shadowy figure of Misquamacus remained where it was, in the corner, watching me. David was standing by the single armchair, on the opposite side. His fingers were lightly resting against the brown vinyl arm of the chair, just lightly. But what frightened and hurt me more than anything was that water was running out of the sleeve of his sodden black funeral suit, and dripping onto the floor. If he wasn't real, if he was nothing but a figment of my guilty imagination, then I must have a pretty God-damned brilliant imagination.

"I want your seed, white devil," Karen insisted.

I looked at David and David, greenish-grey, his hair stuck wetly to his forehead, gave me a nod. Then, without another word, he faded—faded as if he were nothing more than fog—except that drops of water still remained on the arm of the chair.

"David?" I said. I hadn't even had the time to tell him that I was sorry—that I would have saved him if I could.

I turned back to Misquamacus. He was darker and less substantial than a shadow, but he was still there. *"I need your seed,"* he demanded, through Karen's lips. *"Otherwise, your deepest shame and your deepest sorrow will revisit you every day for the rest of your life."*

Karen lay naked on the bed, waiting for me.

I felt as if I had just suffered an electric shock. My brain felt totally out of kilter. I didn't know what was real any more, what was shadow, what was spirit, what was hallucination.

Karen whispered, "Come on, Harry, it's the best way."

"I can't," I said, shaking my head.

She lifted the sheet, inviting me to lie underneath it with her. "You're not worried about Misquamacus? He won't see . . . and what is he, after all? Only a spirit, only a ghost."

"Is that you talking?" I jabbered. "Or is that *him* talking or is that both of you talking?"

"Harry . . ." she said, lifting the sheet a little higher.

"I can't . . ." I told her. I was aching. "It's out of the question."

"Harry," she warned me. "You must! Do you want David to follow you forever?"

Outside, in the motel courtyard, a lid fell off a trashcan, and rolled noisily across the concrete. I could hear something else, too. The sound of the wind rising, the scurry of leaves and newspapers. The drapes began to stir, and the cracks around the door set up a thin whistling sound.

"Harry . . ." said Karen, her voice deeper and harsher. Misquamacus lifted both of his arms, with beetles showering from his headdress.

"Obey me." Karen roared at me. *"Obey me, or I will rip your body into shreds, and then I will tear your soul into shreds, and you will never know anything for all eternity but pain and pain and pain!"*

Then she threw back her head so that her neck bulged and screamed out, *"Ak! Ak! Ak! Ak! Ak! Akkkrraaaaaaaaaa!"*

"Stay away from me!" I screamed back at her. I jostled my way round the bed and flung back the heavy brown drapes. The dawn was blood-red, and the sky was thunderous with clouds. The dried-up palms in the courtyard of the Thunderbird Motel were being lashed by a hectic gale, and dust was flying across Indian School Road. I saw a corrugated-iron fence collapse and then slide across the street.

But far more alarming than the storm outside was David, my dead brother David, who was standing on the balcony outside my room in his dripping wet funeral suit, his wet hair stirred by the wind, staring at me with sad, accusing eyes.

I turned back to Karen. She was sitting up on the bed now, with her arms stretched out toward me. Her lips were stretched back over her teeth in a canine snarl, and her eyeballs had rolled up into her head so that only the whites were exposed. She looked just like Naomi Greenberg had looked, in those last grisly moments of Naomi's life. Every muscle in Karen's naked body seemed to *crawl* with tension, as if it had a worm-like life of its own.

"*Nish-neip, nish-neip,*" she growled at me. "*Nepauz-had . . . nish-neip!*" Then that blood-chilling war-cry again, "*Ak! Ak! Ak! Ak! Akkkrraaaaaaaaa!*"

She climbed with a kind of stiff balletic movement off the end of the bed and made her way toward the shadowy over-bearing outline of Misquamacus. As she neared him, as she passed him by, his shadow seemed to superimpose itself on her. I kept on backing away, keeping my hands raised in front of me to protect myself, my mind jangling with fright and panic. I jumped across the bed and onto the seat of the armchair and stepped down on the other side of the room. But when I looked at Karen again I had to peer at her intently in the gloom to make out what had happened.

Somehow, she and Misquamacus had become one, merged together. I could still distinguish the faint darkish outline of Misquamacus' headdress of living beetles, and the clay-painted lightning-flashes on his cheeks. But now his headdress was Karen's hair, too, and his cheeks were *her* cheeks, and their eyes seemed to double-focus together. The nearest way I can describe how they had intermingled is to say that they looked like two photographic negatives, placed one on top of the other, so that they matched. It was uncanny, and it was frightening, too, because it showed me just how much one person could enter the body and spirit of another. It showed me that I was no longer individual, no longer safe. Not even inside my own soul.

Karen lifted her arms and Misquamacus lifted his arms, too, although his arms were so vague and shadowy that I could scarcely see them. Karen's muscles continued to ripple, and with her arms uplifted her ribcage was as bony and prominent as a crucified martyr. "*Aye! Paukunnawaw! Wajuk! Nish! Aye-aye-aye-aye-wejoo-suk!*"

I kept on backing away. In the distance, I could hear a deep rumbling barrage of thunder. Storm rising, I thought. And what a storm. I reached out behind me and felt the handle of the bathroom door. If Karen had somehow managed to squeeze in through the bathroom window, maybe I could squeeze out of it. Or maybe wrap a towel around my fist and punch out the glass.

I opened the bathroom door behind me, hesitated for just one moment, and then dodged inside, scratching my arm on the sharp tongue of the lock. My hands were juddering so much that I could barely manage to twist the lock. I doubted if a plywood cavity door could keep Misquamacus out for very long, but it might just give me the time I needed to escape. I pressed my forehead against the door and took three deep breaths, and told myself that I had fought against Misquamacus before, and beaten him, and that I was going to beat him again.

The day after David drowned, my father said to me, very gravely, "Harry—you're going to have to find more courage inside of you now than you ever knew you had." I said that to myself then, with my forehead pressed against that flimsy door.

Courage, that's what I said. Then I turned around and David was standing in the bathroom, his face pale and decaying, his funeral suit dripping onto the tiles.

"You must," he whispered.

SIXTEEN

He walked past me, only a couple of inches away, but I couldn't bring myself to touch him. Maybe I should have done, but I couldn't. He unlocked the door with his white, water-swollen fingers, and pushed it open. Water dripped from his ears, and into his collar. "You *must,*" he told me.

Karen was standing by the bed, waiting for me. I stepped mechanically back into the bedroom. The wind was singing under the door, and outside I could hear clattering and banging and somebody shouting. I turned back to David and he was still there, still watching me, and this was soul-torture, believe me.

Karen's eyes were dark again, dark and introspective. Her muscles seemed to have stopped twitching, and apart from a strange shadowy look, she could have almost appeared normal, like the Karen I had known before Misquamacus possessed her. But how could I possibly make love to a woman whose soul was filled up with the soul of a man, a woman whose whole being belonged to some barbaric reeking savage?

"You must, Harry," she echoed.

I gave it one last shot. I strode to the front door, and grasped the handle, and snapped at Karen, "You want seed, you bastard, you go to a God-damned garden center." Then I flung open the door, and there he was, standing in the wind, in his sodden funeral suit.

"You must," he insisted.

I looked back at Karen. *I'm going,* I thought. *David may have upset me, but he's only a kid. I'll shove him out of the way now and worry about the spiritual implications later.*

But without any warning at all, Karen strode forward and seized my arm. Karen? It looked like Karen, it felt like Karen, but it was strong and quick and I didn't stand a chance. She flung me onto the bed, and then she slapped my face and my forehead so hard that she gave me a nosebleed. When I tried to get up, she slapped me again, and then she slapped me again, just because she felt like it.

Without a word, she tugged open my trousers and wrestled them down my legs. I tried to sit up again, but this time she seized hold of my hair and screwed it around, and slapped me once, twice, three times, and then pushed me back onto the bed. I shoved her away with the heels of my hands, but she double-slapped me across the face, so hard that my ears rang.

"Get off me!" I yelled at her. "Get the hell off me!"

But now she seized my left ear in one powerful clawlike hand, so tight that I could hear the cartilage crunching. And with her other hand, she grasped my cock and began feverishly to rub and tug at it, her fingernails digging into the skin. In spite of the pain, in spite of my fear—or maybe *because* of them—my cock began to stiffen. Karen kissed me and bit me with a dreadful urgency, and her breath was cold, so that I didn't know whether I was being raped by a young and lustful white woman, or a three-hundred-year-old medicine-man who wanted my heart and my soul and my only offspring, too.

She lifted herself over me. At the same time her fingernails imprisoned my balls in a dangerous sharpened cage. I felt the skin of my scrotum crinkle. Fear, physical fear, but strangely masochistic excitement, too. I didn't speak, I didn't move. My heart pumped, my blood rushed, I could feel thunder shaking the whole motel. I looked into Karen's eyes and I couldn't have told you whether it was really Karen or not. They were bright eyes; twinkling and sharp. But whose eyes? And were they looking at my face, or staring into my soul?

"Who are you?" I asked. But she didn't answer. Instead, she piloted the head of my cock in between her legs, and massaged it for a while, and then slowly sat on me.

"Who are you?" I repeated, but she shook her head, to show me that she wouldn't answer, and lifted her finger to her lips. She started to ride up and down on me, faster and faster, deeper and deeper, until with each downstroke my balls were crammed into the crevice of her bottom.

I tried to sit up, but Karen slapped me yet again, *slapped* me, with both hands at once, and I could feel my nose spring blood. Then she tilted herself forward, and squashed her breasts against my chest, and reached down with both hands and seized my buttocks, digging her nails in deep. She thrust and plunged and thrust with her hips, and then she raked her nails across my bare, unprotected flesh, and clawed at my scrotum, and I climaxed. A thick, pumping ejaculation.

"Ak! Ak! Ak!" she shrieked, throwing her head back, and even before I had finished, I felt a surge of shame and disgust and fright. I slapped at her, and tried to struggle out from underneath her, but then she hit me with her clenched fist, right on the bridge of my nose, and I dropped back onto the pillow with tears bursting out of my eyes.

She leaned over me and I could see that she was no longer Karen. I saw angular cheeks and a hard-chiselled nose, and eyes as blank as coulee-washed pebbles.

"White devil," he said, so softly that I could scarcely hear him. "At last you have given me what I want. An heir, white devil. A son that I can call my own."

He leaned back, and whooped, a high soul-chilling whoop that reminded me of all the cowboy-and-Indian movies I had ever seen. Then he looked down at me again, and he was Karen.

I stayed where I was, flat on my back on the bed, while she slowly climbed off me. "See," she said, as she stood up. "The greatest act of contrition that you ever could have made." And with that, she parted her vagina with her fingers so that I could see the sperm that had filled it. A drop of it slid shining and hesitant down her thigh, but I knew as well as she did that Karen was pregnant again, with another wonder-worker, the unnaturally-conceived heir of Misquamacus.

"Now what?" I said, and my voice was no more than a croak.

She dragged one of the blankets off the bed and wrapped herself in it. "Now you have paid for your treachery," she said. Her eyes slowly rolled upward, until she was staring at me with solid whites. "Now you must die."

I edged crabwise across the bed, still on my back. Karen was already changing, already altering. She grew taller, and darker. I had to remember that she and Misquamacus were sharing the same body and the same soul, and so sometimes (if he let her) *she* could predominate, just like she had on the bed, but sometimes *he* could predominate, and that meant serious violence, such as being turned inside-out, or being ripped into pieces, or having your soul torn up like confetti.

I had seen what had happened to George Hope and Andrew Danetree, and I never wanted that to happen to me. I would rather have died, instantly. I would rather have shot myself directly in the head, like the desperate troopers at the Little Big Horn.

Karen said, "It's a good day to die." She circled the end of the bed, and she didn't take her eyes off me once.

I retreated toward the opposite side of the room. Karen came after me, but I noticed that the further away from the wall she went, the slower she became, in the same way that Martin had slowed down at the Greenbergs'. The shadow

on the wall was all-important. It obviously gave Misquamacus strength—and the further he retreated from it, the
weaker he became. Comparatively, that is. Misquamacus'
weak was still devastatingly strong. He was probably capable of tearing out my lungs with his bare hands, and he
probably wouldn't hesitate to do it. Not for an instant.

"Karen," I said, "try to be strong. Try to be yourself.
Don't let this sucker take you over completely. Come on,
Karen, fight!"

Karen took one step toward me, then another, her eyes
still blinded white.

"Aye-aye-aye-nayew," she chanted. *"Aye-aye-aye-aye-
wejoo-suk."*

I hit the armchair and reached behind me to steady myself. I felt the drops of water that David had left on the
vinyl. I circled around the back of the chair, never once taking my eyes away from Karen, never once lowering my
guard. But then I felt that wetness, those few drops of water,
and I suddenly remembered what Martin Vaizey had told
me, and how I had chased off the shadow at the Greenbergs'
apartment.

*Water. White man's water, Dead water, as far as the Indi-
ans were concerned, because it was filtered and chlorinated
and cleaned, and given added aluminum for brightness. But it
was our water, the water of white civilization, and it was always on tap if we needed it. Like now.*

Karen took another step closer. "You will grow to like
the darkness," she told me. "You will grow to like the pain,
too, in the end, after many years. You will wonder how you
ever managed without it."

"Back off," I said. "I'm warning you."

Karen laughed, a deep, multilayered laugh. *"You* are
warning *me?"*

I stepped sideways into the bathroom doorway. Karen
came after me, one slow movement at a time. Then—as
quickly as I could—I slammed the bathroom door, and
scrambled into the shower, and spun the faucet to full. I was
drenched at once by an explosion of freezing-cold water,
and I shouted out in shock.

Karen slammed open the bathroom door. She was still

Karen, still naked and skinny, but her muscles had started up that knotty convulsion again, and her head seemed to have grown larger, so that it was more like a mask than a head.

"Leave me alone!" I shouted at her. "You got what you wanted! Now get the hell out of here and leave me alone!"

"You have to die!" she roared at me. *"For everything you've done, you have to die!"*

I thought: *water, for God's sake, turn into a rattlesnake. Turn into anything that Misquamacus is afraid of.*

Karen approached me slowly, her eyeballs white, her head swaying from side to side, her teeth exposed in a maniac grin.

I thought of rattlers and water moccasins and cobras and every God-damned snake in the book, my eyes squeezed shut. I tried to imagine that the bathroom was full of them, hissing and writhing and twisting and tangling.

I felt a chilly sliding movement across my foot, and I opened my eyes, and it had happened. The whole shower basin was filled with snakes—shining and transparent, all swarming over my bare feet—and the more water that gushed out of the shower head, the more snakes there were. They poured out over the bathroom floor, and slid towards Karen with loathsome enthusiasm.

Karen took only one more step forward, but a water moccasin lunged at her toes, and she shuddered, and quickly retreated. She lowered her head, and I sensed in her posture the same sudden defeat that I had sensed in Martin Vaizey when I had created that rattlesnake, back on East 17th Street.

Karen's head was lowered, but the shadowy head of Misquamacus rose above it, his face stony with rage, his headdress teeming with black, excited bugs.

"You will pay with your soul, white devil," he told me, through Karen's lips.

He turned, and Karen turned with him, casting one dark resentful look at me from under her tousled fringe.

"No!" I ordered. "No! You can't take her with you!"

But Misquamacus thundered out of the room, dragging Karen behind him, and I heard the door wrenched open and the door slammed shut. I looked down at the bathroom floor. It was awash with water, and I was drenched, but there were no snakes anywhere. I paddled my way out, crossed the bedroom and opened the front door. I thought I glimpsed a tall dark shadow and a fleeting figure in white, just turning the corner by the Thunderbird's office. But it was impossible to tell for sure. The streetlights were out. The sky was as dark as congealing blood. And the wind was whipping up a blizzard of sand and dust and stray fragments of fencing and trash and broken siding.

I stood on the balcony and looked around me. I knew there was no point in trying to run after Misquamacus. He was gone, and Karen was gone, too. They could have been anywhere at all between here and hell and Pennsylvania. But something was happening here in Phoenix. I could hear windows breaking and sirens whooping in the distance, and as I stood on the balcony I felt a distinct *pulling* sensation, as if some magnetic force were trying to tug me right through the frosted-glass panelling and down to the courtyard and along the street and—*where?*

This was it. This was what had happened in Colorado and Chicago and Las Vegas. This was the Ghost Dance, the dragging-down, the day of all shadows. And now it was happening here.

Outside, I heard a crunching, scraping noise, and when I looked out of the window I saw a Dodge van being pulled on its side all the way down Indian School Road, and a man in a baseball cap desperately and unsuccessfully trying to stop it. In the Thunderbird Motel's parking lot, a Winnebago suddenly crashed onto its side, and a brand-new red Allante rolled onto its roof.

My television swung around on its castors and knocked against the wall. My bed began to slide towards the door. I heard shouting from almost every room in the whole motel, and a woman screaming; and then there were people running down the steps and across the courtyard, and a devastating crack of thunder that seemed to break the sky in half from Paradise Valley to the Manzanita Race Track.

In a jumbled way, I began to understand what Misquamacus was doing.

First, he was calling together the direct descendants of all of those pioneers and troopers who had killed or murdered Indians, back to the very same places where the killings had taken place. How he was managing to call them, and why they felt compelled to come, I simply couldn't say. Maybe he had plucked some chord in some sort of long-buried inherited memory, who knows? Misquamacus had very strong powers of suggestion.

He was calling together people like George Hope and Andrew Danetree—like the seven who had died in Papago Joe's inspection pit. Once they were assembled, Misquamacus had been able to open up the door to the Great Outside and let Aktunowihio have his way with them. Aktunowihio, the Dark One, who had stormed up the hill at the Little Big Horn and massacred Custer and all of his men. Aktunowihio, whose smoke-like tentacles had forced their way into old man Rheiner's body, and pulled him into hell.

Misquamacus was travelling around America, summoning the guilty, and having them killed, and counting coup. And *then,* in all of those places where the white man had spilled Indian blood, he was opening up the very gates of the land of death, and dragging down everything that the white man had created—his buildings, his railroads, his television sets, his highways, his airports, everything.

It was revenge on a scale that was almost unimaginable. You destroyed my culture, white devil, now I'm going to destroy yours.

I felt the floors of the Thunderbird Motel shuddering beneath my feet. I decided it was time to leave. If only I knew where Karen had gone. I dressed, and then I quickly stuffed my shirts and my shorts into my overnight bag, and hurried along the balcony to the steps. The dead armadillo had gone, so I guessed it couldn't have been dead after all. The steps were already cracking, and as I gingerly climbed down them I felt them tilt and the steel handrail dislodge itself from the concrete.

My rental car had slid fifteen or twenty feet sideways across the parking lot, and was resting up against a low concrete retaining wall, with its nearside fender badly dented. It was quite a risk, driving in these conditions, but I needed to get after Karen as quickly as I possibly could and there wasn't time to walk.

Maybe I was wrong, but it was my guess that Misquamacus was taking Karen back with him to the Great Outside. If that was the case, I needed Papago Joe to guide me there, and I needed him now.

I climbed into the car and started the engine. As I started to negotiate my way out of the parking lot, a Cherokee truck came sliding past me sideways, its tires singing a deep rubbery protest song. It struck my car a glancing blow on the front bumper, which turned it round in a quarter-circle, but that allowed me to drive through a gap in the retaining wall without having to do one of my famous 103-point turns.

I drove east on Indian School under low, hurrying clouds. The light—what there was of it—was a thick grainy red. To my left I could just make out the hump of Camelback Mountain. It was nearly six-thirty now, but it looked as if this was going to be the darkest morning that Phoenix had ever known.

Trying to drive in that storm was like trying to drive in a strange dream. Even though my foot was pressed down hard on the gas the Lincoln was struggling to hit thirty miles per hour. The engine was straining and the transmission was whining like a lost dog. The dragging sensation from behind me was so strong that I felt as if I was driving up a very steep grade. I could manage to steer due east without much difficulty, but when I turned right on Alma School Road to head towards Mesa, the car was pulled so powerfully and consistently to the west that I had to keep the wheel twisted off to the left, and by the time I finally managed to reach Apache Boulevard, where I could turn due east again for Apache Junction, my hands were aching with the strain and the wheel was slippery with sweat.

The sky grew darker and darker, particularly behind me, over downtown Phoenix. I saw hardly anybody else on the streets, although I came across rubbish and fencing and billboards and baby buggies and God knows what else, all being dragged westward along the highway. Just as I reached the outskirts of Mesa, I saw a huge red gasoline truck sliding sideways along the highway towards me and I had to steer onto the pavement to avoid it. In my rear-view mirror I saw it roll over onto its side in a cascade of sparks and start to burn.

More vehicles came rolling and tumbling along the highway, and my car was struck twice—once by a driverless van, and once by a station wagon. I wasn't sure if there was anybody alive inside the wagon, the windows were blanked out with blood.

Outside of Mesa, I saw sheds and houses being slowly dragged across the landscape. I saw groups of people, too, trying to escape to the east. They were plodding along the side of the highway, their backs bent, as if they were trying to climb a mountain. I felt like stopping to give three or four of them a ride, but if I had a full load of passengers I doubted if the car was powerful enough to keep going. As it was, it was beginning to smell of hot rubber, and the transmission was whining even more loudly.

The wind blurted and howled against my windshield, and the combined rumbling of houses and cars and tumbling rubbish was deafening. I tried the car radio, but all I got was a blurt of static and—for a moment, very faintly—a bluegrass station from somewhere far away. It sounded like a song from another world.

I met her when the rains began to fall.
I met her and I loved her from the first sweet kiss.

Four miles out of Mesa, a red flashing light on the instrument panel warned me that the car was overheating. It faltered and shuddered, and I began to worry that I wouldn't make it. The engine ground slower and slower and the warning alarm started up, a high-pitched penetrating noise and a red light that demanded STOP ENGINE NOW.

There was a moment when the car was travelling so slowly that I thought that I would probably get to Papago Joe's a whole lot faster if I abandoned it by the roadside and tried to hike it. But then something curious happened. The car began to roll just a little faster, just a little more easily. After two or three miles, it picked up even more speed. The warning alarm died away and the red light blinked off as the engine was relieved of the strain of having to pull against such an overwhelming force.

With fewer than eight miles to go to Apache Junction, the car began to travel at fifty, then sixty, then seventy. It was when I hit seventy-five that I realized what was happening. The car hadn't simply broken away from the force that had been dragging it back towards Phoenix, it was being dragged *forwards* in the direction of Apache Junction. The blizzard of dust and trash that was blowing all around me had changed direction, too, and I began to hear pieces of fencing and empty Coke cans and all kinds of detritus knocking and pattering and clanging on the back of the car.

Frightened by my rapidly-mounting speed, I jammed my foot on the brake, but the highway was slippery-dry with dust, and the car slewed from one side of the blacktop to the other, tires screaming, almost out of control. My offside wheels jounced and slammed against the rough stony edge of the highway, and my front bumper snagged a length of twisted wire fencing. I took my foot off the brake, and steered myself back to the right-hand side of the road. There was nothing I could do but let the force drag me forwards, unimpeded, otherwise—shit—I was going to end up killing myself.

At least I was being dragged where I wanted to go. All I was worried about was what would happen when I got there. How the hell was I going to stop?

As I approached Apache Junction, the speedometer needle was nudging eighty-five. The highway was littered with debris and derelict cars, and I had six or seven noisy but not serious collisions. It was only when I started running over bodies that I began to panic. Right on the outskirts of Apache Junction, twenty or thirty people lay dead or dying in the road—men, women, and children—and I was driving right through them before I even realized what they were. But suddenly an old silver-haired man was flung up onto the hood of the car, and then a girl in a jeans and T-shirt was slammed up against the windshield, and my wheels went *bumpity-bumpity-bumpity* over arms and legs and bodies.

I shouted out something, I can't remember what. I stepped on the brakes. The car skidded around and around and hurtled off the road into the side of a shed. Wooden planking exploded all around me, and then I was crashing through shelves of paint and jars of methylated spirits and boxes of screws and paintbrushes and staples, and then I was out the other side of the shed and the car was still skidding from side to side, plowing up dust and bursting into a henhouse. Brown feathers, chickens, straw, netting, wire, and then back onto the highway again with a slam of suspension that must have finished my shocks for good.

Shaking, sweating, swearing under my breath, I looked into my rear-view mirror and saw that the highway was strewn from side to side with bodies. Not far away, a bus lay on its roof, its sides split open. It must have been travelling as fast as I was, if not faster, and overturned. I just prayed that all of those people were already dead when I ran over them.

Through the blurry dust and the dim red light, I saw Papago Joe's signboard up ahead. I was travelling at eighty-five now, and I had no idea of how I was going to pull up. I guessed that the only way was to drive straight into his lot, and hope for the best. I switched my headlights onto high beam and pressed my hand hard on the horn and said, "Please God, don't let me die just yet."

At the last second, just as I reached the entrance to Papago Joe's lot, I saw a man lying in the road. I swerved, and missed the entrance, and crashed straight through his newly-repaired fencing. But that swerve probably saved my life. I pulled up yards and yards and yards of fencing; one fence post after another was whipped up out of the ground, but it acted like an arrester net on an aircraft carrier. By the time I collided with the heaps of Buicks and Oldsmobiles which Papago Joe was still trying to clear from the last disaster, I was only going at about twenty miles per hour. All the same, a head-on collision at twenty miles per hour is no joke, and I was flung around like a puppet. I hit my head on the top of the steering wheel, and knocked both of my knees against the underside of the instrument panel.

I lifted my head and looked around me. Papago Joe's lot was crowded not just with second-hand automobiles but with sheds and signboards and boxes and trailers and all kinds of rubbish, including a sagging clapboard wall that looked like half of somebody's house. I turned around and saw that the Sun Devil Bar had partially collapsed. Its roof was sagging on one side, and all of its outbuildings and garages had been dragged across the road and were shunted up against Papago Joe's Airstream trailer.

I forced open the door of my car and immediately the interior was filled with a blinding, swirling hurricane of dust. The wind was literally screaming, and the air shook with thunder.

I was just about to climb out of the car when I saw Papago Joe struggling towards me, wrapped in a large grey wind-whipped blanket. He was waving to me and shouting something. I waited until he had reached me, and I was glad that I did.

"Stay where you are until I've protected you!" he shouted. "Otherwise you'll get pulled right down into the ground and that my friend—that'll be the end of you!"

"What's happening?" I shouted back at him.

"It's opened up!" he told me. He jabbed his finger in the direction of his workshop. "The place where those people were killed, it's opened up. It's pulling down everything—cars, people, cattle, you name it."

"The same thing's happening in Phoenix," I said.

He nodded. He was pulling a necklace out of his pocket, and making heavy weather of untwisting it. "Much worse in Phoenix," he said. "We saw it on TV, at least till the TV went dead. The airport, the State Capitol, the Art Museum, the Civic Plaza, everything's gone. Not a building left standing on Van Buren Street. They called in the National Guard but the last we saw they'd lost two helicopters and thirty-eight men."

"Why's it so bad in Phoenix?" I asked him. At last he had succeeded in unravelling the necklace.

He put the necklace over my head, and said, "Many more Indians died in Phoenix. Over a hundred and fifty Indians were massacred in 1887 when they tried to protest about the railroad running through their lands. Thirty-eight men, the rest were women and children. Nobody ever knew who killed them. In fact, nobody knew that they had died until a prospector found their bones scattered in a canyon up in the South Mountains."

"What's this for?" I said, lifting up the necklace so that I could take a closer look at it. It wasn't exactly designer jewellery. It was a combination of coarse, tightly-plaited hair, dull red beads, and discolored teeth.

"It's a medicine-necklace," said Papago Joe. "They used to be worn by Hohokam Indians when they had to walk through sacred burial-grounds, to ward off the power of shadow-spirits. It will protect you from being pulled down into the Great Outside."

"You're not wearing one," I observed.

He smiled. "I don't have to. I'm an Indian. Only white people and white artifacts are being pulled down. Well, Mexican, too."

"I've seen Misquamacus," I told him. "The girl I'm looking for, Karen, she came to my motel during the night . . . Misquamacus was with her. Or kind of *in* her, I'm not too sure which."

Papago Joe took hold of my arm. "I know what you mean," he said. "We Papagos call it 'Two-Becomes-One.' Anyway," he said, "come on over to the trailer, I'll tell you what I plan to do."

I eased myself out of the car. I was pretty bruised and shaken up, but I managed to walk with nothing much worse than a slow, heroic limp. Papago Joe took my arm but he didn't really need to. The day was so dark now that I could hardly see from one side of the lot to the other. Grit lashed at our exposed faces, and tumbleweed tangled around our ankles. From the direction of the workshop, I heard a terrible groaning crash, and Papago Joe said, "More cars going. It's the end of everything, as far as I'm concerned. My whole business—everything."

I still felt a slight tugging sensation as we walked across the lot. It was almost like somebody walking too close to you on the sidewalk, and continually nudging you into the gutter. But the medicine-necklace did its stuff. Its hair prickled with static, and by the time we reached Papago Joe's trailer some of the loose ends were beginning to smoulder and burn, but Papago Joe simply patted it with his hand,

and put the smouldering out. I sniffed in the smell of old, burnt hair, and it reminded me of something very old and very cremated and very dead.

Inside the trailer, six or seven candles were burning. The light swivelled and dipped as we opened and closed the door. Extra Cool Dude was there, along with Linda from the Sun Devil, and her little boy Stanley.

"Some driving," remarked E.C. Dude, appreciatively. "You came through that fence like shit off a shovel."

"I was lucky, that's all."

Papago Joe didn't waste any time. He went to the far end of the trailer and returned carrying a raggedy bundle of old, stained buffalo hide, decorated with beads and feathers. "I went to the reservation last night and their medicine-men lent me this bundle. Well, I've done them quite a few favors in the past. Fixing their automobiles, lending them bail-money when their kids get into trouble."

The trailer creaked on its wheels, and I heard something heavy bang up against the side, close to the door.

"How come this trailer doesn't get dragged away, too?" I asked Papago Joe.

Papago Joe glanced up at me with those black, coal-mine eyes. "After the last time, I made sure that I protected it. I made a circle of blue sand and crows' blood, and I asked Heammawihio to guard it, and to keep it in the land of light. It's the same protection that we would have asked for our lodges, back in the days when we had such things. The fact that it's an Airstream trailer instead of adobe is—in magical terms—neither here nor there."

"You see?" said E.C. Dude. "No flies on Papago Joe."

Stanley turned round and stared solemnly at Papago Joe as if to make sure that he really had no flies on him. His mother bent over and whispered, "It means he's smart. Like, he thinks of everything."

All the same, the wind rocked the trailer, and I heard glass breaking outside, and then a long screech of metal that set my teeth on edge, and I wasn't at all convinced that blue sand and crows' blood were going to keep us upright and out of that hole for very long.

Papago Joe untied the bundle and laid out a collection of

bones and sticks and leather pouches. Everything looked dried-up and stained and decayed, and was tied up with hanks of hair and dried-up shreds of rawhide. There was a strong smell of rotting leather and grease.

"This is what we'll need for visiting the Great Outside," said Papago Joe. "In this pouch here is the powder which will induce a state of hallucinatory death."

"Hallucinatory death?" I asked him. "What the hell's that?"

"That means that—once we've taken this powder—we will be tricking our conscious brains into believing that we're dead. Clinically, we *will* be dead. But we will continue to be conscious on a much lower level. We will still be able to function as human beings, we'll still be able to walk and talk and think, and we'll still be capable of coming back to life."

"What's in it? The powder?"

"I'm not sure of *everything* that's in it. But I know it contains human ashes, and peyote, and macerated huajillo leaves, and bitter cactus, as well as one or two other berries and herbs."

"Yecch," put in E.C. Dude. "Think I'll stick to the speedy Alka-Seltzer."

I felt my heart start to palpitate. "Papago Joe—when you say clinically dead, what exactly do you mean by that?"

Papago Joe tapped his forehead. "No more brain activity. Not that a doctor could detect, anyway. But we shall still be able to see and hear and talk and think, but much, much deeper. Down there, in the Great Outside."

"Is it, uh, safe?" I asked him.

"*Safe?*" he asked me. "It hasn't been tested by the FDA, if that's what you're getting at."

"I didn't mean that. I meant, we won't suffer any kind of brain damage, will we, or physical trauma, or anything like that?"

Papago made a face. "How should I know? I've never done it before."

"Hey, *encouraging,* man, or what?" said E.C. Dude.

"You've never done it before?" I asked him. My heart was palpitating even more furiously, and my tongue felt as if it were lined with saguaro cactus skin, crusty and dry.

"Hardly anybody has, these days. The old ways of the wonder-workers are long since gone." He paused, and then he said, "We don't *have* to do it. Nobody said that we're obliged to save civilization as we know it; or even to save your girlfriend. It's only Superman who has to do things like that."

I didn't say anything. I was the only person in the world who had any kind of a chance of rescuing Karen, and Papago Joe was probably the only person in the world who could help me to do it. Maybe I wasn't Superman, but I knew what I had to do, even though it scared me.

"All right," I said. "Supposing we take this death-powder stuff, then what?"

Papago Joe held up a handful of sticks, each of which was decorated with strands of hair, and tipped with a hooked bird's beak.

"Eagle-sticks," he said. "They will allow us to travel almost instantaneously anywhere we like—and without losing our way. Misquamacus used these. That's how he managed to give the appearance of being in two different places at the same time. In fact he *wasn't*—but he had travelled very swiftly through the Great Outside. It's a little bit like having a shortcut through time and space. There's nothing magical about it, nothing supernatural. Even Einstein knew all about it. The shortest distance between two points in the Universe is a curve; and that curve becomes even shorter when you are actually *inside* the Universe, rather than outside it."

I picked up one of the sticks, and turned it this way and that. "But these . . . these look kind of superstitious."

Papago Joe said, "Yes. In a way, they are. But each of them carries different markings, do you see? And those markings represent the landmarks that birds use to navigate themselves across North America. They may look like nothing but sticks to you . . . but in fact they constitute a complete set of highly-sophisticated natural compasses. You could fly a 747 with these."

"What else do we have?" I asked him. I suppose I ought to have been much more skeptical, but I had seen too much

Indian magic today to challenge Papago Joe's medicine-creed. He was educated, he was confident. In his dark, glittery way he was almost fatherly. And, as I said before, I didn't have much in the way of choices.

He sorted through the medicine-bundle. Outside, I heard a heavy collision, and then an extended rumbling roar, as if about three hundred trees were falling down, except that there *were* no trees, not for miles around.

"Only two more things that are going to be of any use to us on the Great Outside," said Papago Joe. He held up another pouch of powder. "Sunpowder, which can cloak us in light, as a protection. Again, it's scarcely supernatural. It simply uses the same chemistry that illuminates fireflies. And here, this is the powder which can restore us back to a normal level of consciousness, when we want to return. Not to be lost, this powder."

"Well," I said, "I sure hope you know what you're doing."

"Most of it, Harry, will be trial and error. I can't promise you any better than that. I'm not a real wonder-worker. I'm nothing more than an enthusiastic amateur."

I gave him a humorless grin. "Thank you for being honest. I'm just about ready to crap myself as it is."

"But we won't be alone," Papago Joe assured me. "I shall be using your dead friend Singing Rock to guide me. In fact, technically speaking, I shall *be* Singing Rock."

"I don't follow you."

"It's very simple. A person can only enter the Great Outside in one of two ways. Either they're dead, or else they've been possessed by the spirit of somebody dead. That's how your friend Karen was able to enter the Great Outside . . . how she came so quickly to Arizona. She's been possessed by Misquamacus. The advantage to him of course, is that he can use Karen to do all of the living things, physical things that he can no longer do for himself, like counting coup."

"But I *saw* him. Not just Karen. I saw the actual Misquamacus. His face, his necklaces, everything. He had this totally grossed-out headdress made out of bugs."

"Of course you saw him," said Papago Joe. "You're quite psychically sensitive, that's why—quite suggestible. And apart from that, you'd seen him before, and so you believed in him. Most people wouldn't have seen him—*couldn't* have seen him."

I thought for a moment about what Papago Joe was suggesting. "So when you go into the Great Outside, you're going to call on Singing Rock to possess your body?"

"That's right. And that means I can borrow his wisdom and his magical experience, as well as his spirit."

"But if *I'm* going to be coming with you—"

"Exactly. *You'll* have to call on somebody to possess you, too."

"Jesus." The idea sounded pretty damned creepy.

"It feels a little strange," smiled Papago Joe. "But I promise you it doesn't hurt."

"Who can I use?"

He shrugged. "Anybody you know who's dead—preferably somebody you liked. It would help if they had some spiritual skills."

"Can it be anybody at all?" I was thinking of David, my own drowned brother.

Papago Joe looked at me narrowly: in the same way that Singing Rock used to look at me. "Don't choose anybody too close to you. You might have to sacrifice them, for one reason or another, and if they've been close to you—well, they'll be dead already, but you could easily hesitate, at a moment when it might be very dangerous to hesitate."

I suddenly thought of Martin Vaizey. I had liked Martin, in a peculiar way. I had found him fussy and scoutmasterly, and a little old-fashioned. But I had admired his psychic skills and I had admired his manners. What more could I say? He was the kind of guy who kept his shoes polished and never belched in public, if he belched at all.

I was sorry he was dead, so sorry that it hurt, because he wouldn't have died if I hadn't involved him in fighting with Misquamacus. If I could give him half a chance to get his revenge, then that was the very least I could do.

"There's a guy called Martin Vaizey," I told Papago Joe. "He died in New York just a couple of days ago."

Papago Joe looked at me for a long time without blinking. "You want to tell me more?"

"He was a psychic, and a good one. He contacted Singing Rock for me, showed me his face. I couldn't choose anyone better."

"Okay," said Papago Joe. "Martin Vaizey—you want to spell that?"

I spelled out Martin's name for him and then I checked my watch. It was almost five, which of course was impossible. Even a Taiwanese watch would have been better than a Russian watch. "I think we'd better leave pronto," I said. "The longer we leave it, the worse it's going to be. Misquamacus could have taken Karen miles away by now."

Papago Joe said, "Listen, don't worry about it. He can travel so fast that it really makes no difference. He could be in Fairbanks, Alaska, by now."

E.C. Dude said, "Fairbanks, Alaska? What would he want in Fairbanks, Alaska?"

"That's just a for-instance," said Papago Joe. "What I mean is, it's possible for dead people to cross the continent in literally seconds. They're not restricted by the same reality as we are. They don't have to contend with time and distance and kinetic energy and friction and all that nonsense. They set their course, and they cross, and that's it."

"Rapid transit, hunh?" asked E.C. Dude. "Beam me up, Geronimo."

Papago Joe said, "Did you ever shiver, like you thought somebody was stepping on your grave?"

E.C. Dude said, "Sometimes I shiver when I really need a leak bad."

"I'm not talking about needing a leak, for Christ's sake. I'm talking about *shivering.* Do you know why that happens, hunh? Did you ever stop to think about it, just for once? You're standing on the sidewalk in downtown Phoenix waiting for the traffic signals to change, and all of a sudden, you don't care whether they've changed or not, because something *cold* goes through you, something cold and dark that really makes you shake; but when you look around there's nobody anyplace near you. Do you know what causes that? Have you any idea?"

"Bad circulation?" asked E.C. Dude, in all innocence.

But Papago Joe shook his head. "It's dead people," he

said. "It's dead people, passing through you, going so fast you can barely feel it. But that's what it is. Think about it."

E.C. Dude looked amazed and annoyed. "Dead people go through me?"

Papago Joe nodded. "Dead people pass through most of us two or three times a week, sometimes more. If you stay really still, you can *feel* them."

"Hey—" protested E.C. Dude. "Dead people go through me and they don't even say 'pardon me'? That's trespass."

Papago Joe wasn't even amused. "You don't have many privileges when you're dead. But that's one of them."

"Hey," said E.C. Dude. "So what are you going to do—travel around with these dead people? Go through other people?"

Papago Joe said, "Harry here wants to find his Karen. He also wants to find Misquamacus, and I want to find Misquamacus, too. And I'll tell you for why. If we *don't* find Misquamacus, then life is liable to come to a dark and horrible and very shadowy finish, and if you knew what I know about Aktunowihio, the Shadow Buffalo, then you'd be crapping those women's panties you wear."

"Hey, these are Cybille's."

"And where's Cybille?" demanded Papago Joe.

"I don't know. Home with her parents I guess. I hope. Unless she's been seeing that meathead Gary again."

"Have you taken a look outside? She may be home with her parents, but where's her parents' home?"

E.C. Dude climbed off the couch and went to the trailer's window. He opened the Venetian blind, but all we could see was billowing dust and the flickering reflections of candles. E.C. Dude turned back and said, "It's a storm, man. That's all. Hurricane Whoever."

Papago Joe emphatically shook his head. "That isn't a storm, E.C. According to all of the Indian legends and all of the Indian predictions, this is it. This is All Shadows' Day, the day that the Ghost Dance comes true."

The trailer swayed, much more violently this time, and I heard something collide with its outside panelling, something soft and heavy. It could have been a sack of flour; it could have been a young pig; it could have been a dead dog.

It could have been a child.

"You're going then?" said E.C. Dude. "You're just going to split, and leave us?"

"You'll be all right," Papago Joe told him. "Take care of Linda, take care of Stanley. That's all you have to do."

"Man, I want to come with you," said E.C. Dude.

"What?" asked Papago Joe.

"I want to come with you. Come on, man, you're talking about spirits and being possessed and stuff and travelling through time. It sounds totally extra, man. I want to come with you!"

Papago Joe said, "No. I want you to stay here and protect Linda and Stanley."

"And what do I do if the trailer tips over?"

"It won't. The spells will hold it, even if it sways."

"Well, man," said E.C. Dude, crossly. "I wish I had your confidence."

I felt like agreeing with him. Especially since Papago Joe and I were about to set off on a journey under the soles of our own feet—a trip through the underground that made me feel almost nostalgic for the New York subway. At least on the New York subway the dangers were palpable. And even when your fellow-travellers acted violent and threatening, and started screeching and vandalizing and mugging, at least they were *alive*.

I watched Papago Joe measure out the powder which would give us hallucinatory death. I saw the candle-flames dipping and swaying in his eyes. I heard the scratching of the razor blade on the mirror. I knew now why Amelia hadn't wanted to go on chasing Misquamacus any further. I knew why MacArthur had made her give up spiritualism, back in the days when she had first raised up the head of Misquamacus from out of that cherrywood table.

Papago Joe divided the powder as neat and sharp as if he were laying out lines of coke, except that this stuff wasn't white. This stuff was grey—grey with cremated ashes and peyote.

"What do you do?" I asked him. "Do you swallow it or inhale it?"

He rolled up a crisp new fifty dollar bill. "I'm sorry, you have to breathe it in."

"Jesus," said E.C. Dude. "How can you snort a stiff? That's disgusting!"

Papago Joe ignored him, and handed me the rolled-up bill. "You first, Harry."

I accepted the bill with shaking hands. In fact I was shaking so much I was worried I was going to shake all the powder off the table.

As I leaned forward, Papago Joe rested his hand on my shoulder, to comfort me. I looked up into the darkness of his deeply-buried eyes and I saw something in that darkness that made me feel as if I was beginning, just a little, to understand the secrets of the universe. "We all have to die sometime," he said, although I wasn't at all sure that he had said it aloud.

New York

Amelia awoke just before dawn, with the strong sense that something was badly wrong. She had a feeling that—during the night—the world had somehow unbalanced itself, and was wobbling on its axis like a child's spinning-top that's just about to run out of momentum.

She lay in her rumpled bed for five or ten minutes, listening, frowning, trying to decide what was different. Then she sat up, and switched on her light. Her bedroom was yellow, with vases of dried sunflowers, and gold-framed prints by Currier & Ives, yellow-dominated scenes such as Reading The Scriptures and The Dream of Youth.

She could hear a low, vibrant, rumbling noise, but it didn't sound at all like traffic. It sounded more like a thunderstorm, approaching from Jersey, or a subway train approaching round the bend, or the city being shaken by its very roots. She picked up her spectacles from the bedside table, and climbed out of bed in her XXL Indianapolis Colts football shirt. Jerry—her ex—had been a Colts enthusiast. Her mother (one cold and cloudy day, as she had died of cancer), had taken her hand and told her that she should never have married a Hoosier. "Hoosiers are always dire, darling. It's in their genes."

She went to the window and opened the yellow Venetian blinds. It was still dark outside, although she could make out a dim crimson streak in the eastern sky, like blood soaking through a black dress. She listened again, really listened, and the rumbling went on. The window frame began to judder and buzz, and she could feel a deep shaking sensation through the floor.

It wasn't traffic, although she could see headlights in the streets below, and horns parping and protesting. It was much more fundamental than traffic. It was the kind of rumbling that disturbed dogs and canaries and neighborhood cats, and made milk curdle in the carton. And it was growing, too. It was growing stronger and deeper and louder. She could hear the cups and saucers in her kitchen jingling.

She went to the bathroom, and as she sat on the toilet seat she could feel the whole apartment building *thrumming*. She was worried now. Late last night on the television news, she had seen the jumbled-up panicky reports from Phoenix and Las Vegas, where hundreds of people had been killed—even thousands—and the buildings had fallen as completely as if they had been dynamited.

There had been no warnings that the same thing was likely to happen here in New York, but she was very aware that it might. After all, Manhattan had seen as many Indian massacres as anywhere else in America—massacres by fire, massacres by shot and shell, massacres by disease.

The site of every one of those killings could be opened up by Misquamacus as a gateway to the Great Outside; through which buildings and people and everything else that the whites had ever created could be dragged into darkness, and sealed over, and buried, forever.

Amelia went through to the kitchen and punched out the number of the Thunderbird Motel in Phoenix. She was greeted yet again by a busy signal. She had tried to call Harry repeatedly, all through the night, but she guessed that all the phone lines to Arizona were down. She just prayed that Harry's usual instinct for self-preservation hadn't deserted him. She still felt guilty that she had refused to help him search for Misquamacus, but not so guilty that she wished she were there, in the Sunbelt, where cities were collapsing and people were being dragged right into the ground.

She filled the percolator with decaf and then she took a cigarette out of her pocketbook and made a fuss of lighting it. I'm not smoking this because I need to smoke; I'm smoking this because Harry Erskine always makes me smoke. Damn Harry Erskine. He's a walking disaster. Everywhere he goes, he causes more trouble than he ever manages to sort out. He thinks he's some kind of Renaissance man, able to do everything and anything, and do it more brilliantly than anybody else. He had built her some shelves for her apartment, and six days later they had all dropped off the wall, breaking her tropical fish aquarium and four out of five rare Mexican figurines.

He had tried to cook her *steak Diane* once, and set fire to the kitchen. Now he had gone charging off like some latter-day knight errant, like some storybook hero, looking for

Karen Tandy in a world of shadows that probably didn't even exist. Not in the way that *he* thought it existed, anyway. She blew smoke, paced around the pale limed-oak kitchen, and listened to the thunder rumbling.

At six-thirty it was still dark. Amelia stood on her small cramped balcony, amongst her pots of geraniums and alyssum, and stared up at the sky. She had tried to call her friends more than thirty or forty times: first Renee, who lived quite close, on West 99th, then Peter and Davina, who lived on the other side of the Park; then Bill Dollis, who had always wanted to marry her. Everybody's phone had been busy, and when she had heard sirens whooping and firetrucks blaring, she had known that her instincts were right. The world had gone badly wrong in the night; and she began to realize that the sun wasn't going to rise, not today. Maybe not ever again.

She had tried to switch on the TV, but the TV was dead, too, only a high-pitched whining noise. She could still pick up two or three radio-stations, but one was country-and-western and one was local news from Hackensack, New Jersey, and one was an interview with Robbie Robertson, the rock musician.

The clouds were crimson, heavy crimson, and they looked as if they were boiling. There was a strong burning smell in the air, a smell of grass and aromatic roots and mesquite. Looking downtown from her balcony, Amelia could see that in most of the major buildings, the lights were still blazing: the Citicorp Center, the Chrysler Building, the Empire State. There were hundreds of automobiles on the streets, but they seemed to be crushed together in impossible gridlocks, at every intersection, and when she leaned over her balcony and looked westward down the length of West 98th Street, Amelia could see six or seven automobiles wedged together on the sidewalk, their lights glaring, and she could hear men shouting at each other.

Robbie Robertson was saying, "I'm half-Mohawk, yes. And I do have some inside information, a couple of connections with the spirit land."

Amelia tipped out the coffee from her percolator, rinsed it, and refilled it, but then she decided she didn't want any more. What she needed now was communication, somebody to talk to, somebody to share her rising sense of panic. For the first time, she heard people screaming in the streets, and then the heart-wrenching sound of two vehicles colliding, and she thought to herself: this is it, this is where it ends. This is where Misquamacus finally gets his revenge on us. She lit another cigarette and then immediately crushed it out. She wanted to get out of the building. It might not stand on the site of an Indian massacre, but she didn't want to take the risk. Better off escaping. Better off leaving the city altogether. This was disaster time.

She dressed quickly, in jeans and a loose white cotton sweater with a low neck. She ransacked her desk in the living room, and took out all the important papers she could find. Insurance certificates, marriage certificate, divorce decree. She took her precious photograph album, too. Pictures of MacArthur, in those early days, outside her knickknackery store in the Village. Pictures of Harry on the Staten Island ferry, squinting against the sunshine. Pictures of her mother, so frail and ill that she was practically transparent.

The rumbling started up again, and a picture dropped off the wall, its glass shattering across the carpet. No time for nostalgia, thought Amelia, and hurriedly stuffed sweaters, socks, panties and dresses into her black canvas weekend bag.

Robbie Robertson said, "I do have in my background people whose gifts I could recognize from their connection to the earth, to father sky, mother earth. Everything's alive, we're all part of this thing, you take care of father sky, mother earth, and they do likewise for you. Mistreat these things, they mistreat you."

She left the apartment, locked it, and stood for a while in the hallway feeling foolish. Nobody else seemed to be leaving the building, in spite of the deep and persistent vibrations, nobody else seemed to be panicking. But after a while she picked up her bags and walked as rapidly as she could to the stairs. Although she was only eight stories up, she didn't want to take the elevator in case it jammed. Not only that, she had always been haunted by that story about the day in 1945 when a plane had crashed into the Empire State Building, and a young elevator operator had fallen seventy-nine stories inside her damaged elevator. Amelia's mother had been a nurse at Bellevue, and had seen the girl when she was brought in. "She died, but then she found she wasn't dead, and the realization that she wasn't dead, that almost drove her out of her mind. I've seen it hundreds of times. Sometimes dead is better."

Amelia clattered down the staircase, carrying her bags. She had to rest on the third floor, her head back against the wall. She didn't think; she tried not to panic. She breathed the way that her aerobics teacher had taught her to breathe. Then she carried on down.

The building was already trembling. She could feel its strain, feel its anxiety. She heard windows cracking and radiator pipes bursting; she heard a woman whoop in fear. But finally she reached the street, and pushed open the doors, and found herself in noise and chaos and dust and total fear. It was like one of those 1950s science-fiction movies when everybody panics at the appearance of giant lizards.

She walked quickly northwards. She didn't know why she headed northwards: for some reason she felt that it was going to be safer. She heard men shouting, and then she saw a firetruck approaching, on the wrong side of the street, sliding sideways. Its siren was still blaring and warbling; its lights were still flashing; but it was out of control, its tires screaming on the pavement. Its crew was still clinging on to their platforms and ladders, but they were completely helpless. All they could do was wave their arms and scream, "Get out of the way! Get out of the way! Get out of the God-damned way!"

They passed her by, like a strange surrealistic comedy. But then they were followed by the battered wrecks of several other cars, their drivers slumped over their wheels, their windows spattered with blood. Then a bus, screeching along on its side, half torn open, trailing bodies and pieces of bodies all along the street. Amelia saw an arm, and most of a leg, including half of a bloodied pelvis.

Amelia herself felt a strong, deep tugging, and by the time she reached 103rd she was beginning to tire. All around her, people and vehicles and objects were being dragged south-ward. Every scrap of trash and abandoned tires and news-paper stands and bubble-gum machines, chained down or not. Bicycles and railings and baby carriages and billboards and sofas and chairs and *everything*—all of it sliding along the street in a scraping, jostling, whispering, clattering river.

An old Jewish woman with fraying white hair came up to her and clutched her sleeve and shrieked at her, "It's the end, isn't it? It's Armageddon! Judgment Day!"

Amelia managed to prize her loose. "It isn't the end, lady. All you have to do is keep on your feet; and pray."

"Pray, yes!" the woman shrieked back at her. "Pray, that's it! Pray!"

Shaken, Amelia continued to plod northwards, although she found that it was harder and harder to walk with every step. She was knee-deep in newspapers and trash, she could scarcely drag one foot in front of the other. She was like a woman trying to walk through deep snow.

However pretentious and careless Harry might be, she would have done anything right at that moment to have him close. He was the kind of guy who wouldn't have taken Ar-mageddon too seriously.

A tumbling cascade of broken plates and tureens clat-tered past her; then cruets and napkins and broken bottles, and then heaps of silver cutlery, slithering along the gutter like a shoal of sardines. *Some restaurant's been devastated,* she thought and carried on walking.

But the cutlery had reminded her of something, and after less than half a block, she slowed, and stopped. She thought of what Martin's dead brother had said, about Martin Vaizey's Celtic forks. *The forks that were supposed to trap the devil.*

She remembered how angry Harry had been because the police at the 13th Precinct hadn't allowed him to take them.

"I don't know what they are, for God's sake. I don't even know what they're supposed to do. But from the way that Samuel was talking about them, they could be the only way of ridding ourselves of Misquamacus for good."

Amelia hesitated, and turned her head downtown. She heard cars and trucks colliding, and she saw glittering window glass falling on every side. Maybe there was a chance that *she* could get the forks. Sergeant Friendly had been adamant that Harry couldn't take them. But things were a little different now. The city was starting to fall apart. Maybe she could persuade Sergeant Friendly to lend her the forks, for just a few hours. Her uncle Herbert had been a judge in Connecticut, so she wasn't badly connected; and her mother had organized charity dances for the NYPD benevolent fund.

She looked back uptown. Lightning was flickering like cobra's tongues over the George Washington Bridge, and she could feel a warm wind rising, a wind that was aromatic with burning grass. There was no question in her mind. This was the day when New York was going to suffer the same fate as Chicago. All Shadows' Day. Whichever way she went, she was going to have to struggle her way through sliding debris and collapsing buildings. She might just as well go back downtown and try to do something helpful.

She walked quickly. In fact she found that she was hurrying faster than she wanted to, in the same direction as all the rubbish and tumbling chairs and tables and news-stands and bicycles. More and more cars and taxis were being dragged along the roadway, their tires smoking, and by the time she reached Columbus Circle the smashed-up vehicles were three-deep, with more and more of them piling into the wreckage all the time. She heard people screaming in pain, deep within the caverns of cars. She saw twenty or thirty people beating desperately at the windows of a half-buried bus. Cars and vans were piled on top of the roof, and more were piling up by the minute. As Amelia watched in helpless horror, the bus roof collapsed under the weight, and the passengers were crushed into an aluminum coffin that, in places, was no more than nine inches high. One man had managed to force his head out of one of the windows, but as the roof came down he was guillotined, and his head came tumbling down the heaps of cars, while his neck jetted blood in a grisly parody of an ornamental fountain.

Amelia hurried on. The noise in the city was deafening and frightful, completely unlike the sound of the New York she knew. She was so used to the high-pitched roaring of

traffic and the echo of car horns and sirens that usually she
scarcely heard them. But this was a low, thick, sinister rumbling, overlaid with the long-drawn-out scraping of twisted
metal and the endless warning-bell ringing of falling glass.

She was a little more than halfway along Central Park
South when she saw the unthinkable happening, right in
front of her eyes. The sidewalk was crowded with people
who—like her—had decided it was safer to stay away from
tall buildings. She was jostling her way across the tide. Almost everybody else was trying to get into the park. But
then a man's voice hoarsely screamed, "Look! My God!
Will you look at that! The Plaza!"

Amelia couldn't understand what was happening at first.
But then she managed to struggle up against the railings,
and lift herself up a little, so that she could see over people's
heads. With an awesome thundering noise, the huge grey
bulk of the Plaza Hotel was slowly sinking, its green cha-
teau-like rooftops dropping faster and faster toward the
ground.

It wasn't collapsing. It was disappearing. Floor by floor,
gathering speed, gathering momentum, until the upper
floors were rushing into the solid rock with a rumble that
blurred Amelia's vision and blocked up her ears. With a last
shattering explosion and a wind-whipped plume of dust, the
Plaza had vanished, leaving nothing but rubble and broken
brick, and a twisted bronze elevator door that stood like a
surrealistic memorial, a door that led nowhere at all.

There was a moment of shocked silence. Then the crowds
all around Amelia began to scream and shout in panic. They
rushed into the park in hundreds, pushing and trampling
and waving their arms. Amelia saw a young black girl
pinned against the railings by the weight of sixty or seventy
people. Her eyes were bulging and her lips were frothing
with blood and bile. She was being forcefully and effectively
crushed to death, and there was nothing that Amelia could
do but watch her die.

A security guard pushed Amelia against the railings, too,
bruising her shoulder.

"What the hell are you doing?" she screamed at him.
"Have you all gone crazy?"

A fat man in a sweaty undershirt gave Amelia a shove with his shoulder. "Get out of the way, ya bitch!" he yelled at her.

And a red-haired woman echoed, "Bitch! You want us to die? Get out of the way!"

It took her nearly an hour to reach the 13th Precinct. The sky hung over her head like black bedsheets filled with blood, and although it was well past eight o'clock in the morning, it was suffocatingly gloomy. Lights still glimmered in most of the buildings, but all of them seemed to have a glowering, reddish tinge, as if blood were running thinly down the windows.

She made her way down Fifth Avenue because Seventh had been barricaded with derelict automobiles and there were black-and-orange Walpurgisnacht fires burning all the way along the Avenue of the Americas. She heard a woman saying that Radio City had gone; and the Hilton, too; and the Simon & Schuster Building.

Even Fifth Avenue was blocked with a slowly-moving tide of abandoned cars and buses, although most of the pavements were still passable. A huge refrigerated tractor-trailer lay on its side, scraping its way gradually southward. Its rear doors had been torn open and it was dropping beef carcasses all the way along the street.

Glass and masonry showered sporadically from the buildings all around. A huge stone head dropped only a few feet in front of Amelia and shattered like a bomb. All that remained was a sculptured snarl, and part of a nose.

She climbed awkwardly over the dented hood of a maroon Lincoln Town Car, and then over a tangle of motorbikes and bicycles and baby-buggies. The body of a young woman was lying in the street, her face white, her mouth slack, her eyes staring at nothing. She seemed to have no injuries at all. Amelia watched her in terrible fascination as she slid across the sidewalk, softly collided with a fire hydrant, and then continued her slow, dead swim down Fifth Avenue, drawn by magical forces which, in life, she had probably never known about.

By the time she reached the precinct house she was exhausted—not so much from walking or climbing over car wreckage, but from fighting against the dragging sensation which kept pulling her more and more powerfully southward. She was surprised how few people she saw. It seemed as if most New Yorkers had decided to stay in their apartments and close themselves off, and hope that this blood-red day of judgment would simply pass them by and leave them alone. She saw a few looters—a crowd of teenagers of all races, smashing in the windows of camera stores. But they were obviously finding it difficult to fight against the dragging force, too; and she saw one youth being pulled on his knees across the sidewalk, his jeans literally smoking from the friction, yelling in pain, but desperate not to drop the three JVC video-recorders which he was cradling in his arms.

At the brownstone precinct house, three squad cars were lying wrecked against the front wall, and Amelia had to climb over a thicket of wooden POLICE LINE barriers before she was able to reach the front doors. A thickset uniformed sergeant with prickly hair was manning the desk, although he was gripping the edge of it with one hand to prevent himself from being slowly dragged away.

"Don't tell me," he greeted Amelia, even before she had opened her mouth. "It's the end of the world and you need somebody to hold your hand."

Amelia said, "It's the end of the world and I need to see Sergeant Friendly."

The sergeant stared at her with piggy, pale-lashed eyes. "Friendly's busy. We're *all* busy."

"I'm not a crank," said Amelia. "But Sergeant Friendly has something in his possession which may be able to stop this happening."

"Friendly has something in his possession which may be able to stop this happening? Are you kidding? The north Trade Tower just vanished."

"Please," said Amelia. "I've walked all the way from 98th Street."

The phone rang. The sergeant picked it up and put it down again without even bothering to answer it.

"Please," Amelia begged him.

"I'm sorry," said the desk-sergeant. "Friendly isn't here."

"Is he coming back?"

"Who knows? It's a war-zone out there. You've seen it for yourself."

"Well, could I talk to one of his colleagues?"

"Lady, why don't you just come back when this has blown over?"

Amelia pounded her thin-knuckled fist on the desk in front of him. "This isn't going to blow over! This is going to get worse! This is going to be worse than Chicago and worse than Las Vegas and worse than Phoenix! You're right! You don't even know that, do you? You're right! This *is* the end of the world!"

The sergeant kept his grip on the edge of his desk. "Listen, lady, Sergeant Friendly isn't here, and that's the truth. He went back to check on his family, if you want to know the truth. There's nothing else we can do, except to look after our own. I mean, what would *you* do?"

Amelia said, in a low and forceful voice, "Sergeant Friendly is holding onto two antique forks. They don't belong to the NYPD and they don't belong to me, either. But they belong to a man who could stop this happening, given luck. So what I'm asking you is, do you think somebody could check out the evidence relating to the death of Martin Vaizey, the psychic medium, and *find those fucking forks before it's too late!*"

The desk sergeant lowered his head for a moment so that Amelia could see right into his prickly scalp. Then he turned, and snapped his fingers to a pimply young uniformed officer who was standing in the doorway, his back wedged against the architrave in order to stop himself being dragged away.

"Officer Hamilton, escort this lady to Sergeant Friendly's office and give her all the assistance she needs."

Amelia breathed a deep sigh of relief. "Thank you, sergeant. You won't regret this, I promise. They may even give you a medal."

The sergeant fixed her with a pale stare. "*Who's* going to give me a medal? It's the end of the world, remember?"

Amelia blew him a kiss, "With any luck, pal, it won't be." She followed Officer Hamilton up to Sergeant Friendly's office. Officer Hamilton didn't seem to appreciate escort duty and hummed monotonously all the way. When Amelia smiled at him he didn't smile back. The elevator made an alarming screeching noise as it slowly hauled them upwards, but at last they reached the seventh floor and the doors juddered open. Officer Hamilton managed to say, "This way," through one nostril, and led her along the silent, wax-floored corridor. He walked in a kind of arrogant mince, and his shoes squeaked, but just like Amelia he had to keep his hand against the wall to prevent himself from being dragged sideways.

Through the windows, Amelia could see that the sky was even darker and even bloodier. Lightning crackled like burning hair, and for a moment she could see the Empire State, veiled in static. *By the old Moulmein pagoda, looking lazy at the sea.*

They reached a frosted-glass door that said SGT J.P. FRIENDLY in chipped black lettering and Officer Hamilton opened it up, asking, "What is it you're looking for?"

To Amelia's relief, the forks weren't at all difficult to find. In fact they were lying in Sergeant Friendly's out-tray in a sealed plastic envelope, only half-concealed under a sheaf of letters and reports, with a scribbled note saying *M. Vaizey: these are what he used to blind himself.*

Amelia held up the forks and said: "These. These are what I wanted."

"Okay, help yourself," said Officer Hamilton. "Take 'em back to the desk and Sergeant Zuwadski will give you a receipt to sign. That's all."

They walked back along the corridor. Officer Hamilton hummed, and his shoes squeaked. Amelia lifted up the forks in their plastic envelope and gently jingled them. They looked very dull; and extremely old, and she couldn't imagine how they could be used to fight Misquamacus; but she would leave that to Harry. She was pleased enough that she had been able to get hold of them. In fact, almost triumphant.

They reached the elevator and Officer Hamilton pressed the button with the flat of his hand. They waited and waited, but the elevator didn't respond. They heard winding-gear clicking and faltering, and electric motors whining, but still no elevator.

"Better take the stairs," said Officer Hamilton.

He opened the mustard-painted door to the staircase and they began to climb down through the gloom, their feet chip-chipping on the bare concrete treads. The staircase smelled of stale air and urine and industrial bleach. They could still hear the elevator whining and clicking as they passed the fifth floor, and carried on down to the fourth floor. "Whole city's collapsing," said Officer Hamilton; and there was something in the tone of his voice, a rising note of panic, that made Amelia realize that he wasn't being surly, just scared. After all, how old was he? Twenty-three or four, and Manhattan was falling around his ears.

Amelia said, "There's a chance we can save it."

Officer Hamilton glanced back at her. "Oh, yeah? How do you stop an earthquake?"

"This isn't an earthquake. We don't have earthquakes in New York. It's solid bedrock, no volcanic faults."

Officer Hamilton wasn't even listening. "Did you see the Chrysler Building go down? It just vanished, like it never happened. I can't even *imagine* New York without the Chrysler Building."

They had just reached the third-floor landing when they felt the precinct house give a lurch beneath their feet. Then another lurch. Then windows broke, with a sharp ice-puddle crackling noise, and a length of metal banister came clanging and careening all the way from the fifteenth floor. Officer Hamilton pushed Amelia against the wall as the rail bounced past them, and then they both stared down at the darkened bottom of the stairwell, until they heard the rail crashing into the basement.

"It's going," said Officer Hamilton, in complete panic. "The whole damned precinct's collapsing!"

Amelia heard a whistling, whirring sound, long-drawn-out, and then a flurry of snaky whiplashes. That must have been the elevator plunging all the way down to the lobby, followed by its broken cables. A dull smash confirmed that she was right.

"Come on!" she urged Officer Hamilton. "We have to get out of here!"

"Jesus!" said Officer Hamilton, and she could tell by the shake in his voice that he was almost hysterical. "Jesus frigging Christ!"

It was then that the building began to drop beneath their feet, just like a giant elevator. It fell faster and faster, gathering a huge and irresistible momentum. Amelia was clinging onto the nearest door handle, trying to stop herself sliding sideways across the landing. She collided with the stair-railings, she collided with Officer Hamilton's back. Then she lost her grip and rolled over him, and she was hurtled down the stairs, banging and bruising all the way down to the next landing.

She could feel the building shaking and roaring away as it was dragged down into the ground. Below her, she could hear terrified shrieking—so high-pitched that it was impossible to tell whether it was a man or a woman. Officer Hamilton screamed, too.

She suddenly thought to herself: *this is it, this is the end. I'm going to be buried alive.*

The walls of the building were vibrating fiercely, as if it were determined to shake itself apart. Dust boiled up the stairwell, and there was a grating, ripping noise as the concrete staircase was wrenched free from its reinforcing rods.

Amelia smelled death rushing up to meet her. She grabbed at the nearest banister, and managed to stand up. At the end of the landing, only fifteen or twenty feet in front of her, was a frosted-glass window, yellowed with years of dirt and cigarette smoke.

The only way out. And even now, it was probably too late.

But even as her mind spelled out *probably too late,* she was already running towards it, straining every muscle, remembering her high-school sprinting days, *come on Amelia, come on Amelia,* and then she crossed her arms over her face and flew into the window and thought that she would probably die.

She smashed through the window and circled in the air with all the slow-motion grace of an acrobat. Fragments of glass glittered and spun all around her. She was a ballet dancer, an athlete, an angel in shattered fire. Then she hit the gritty street and knocked her head and rolled over bloody and winded and bruised.

But at least she was alive. Because she twisted herself round, and sat up and looked, just in time to see the window from which she had jumped disappearing into the bedrock, and then the rest of the precinct house following, thunder and dust, until its water tanks and its elevator housing and its radio antennae had been swallowed up completely, and there was nothing but rubble and an empty lot.

She was weeping, when she finally managed to climb to her feet. She had sprained her wrist and hurt her back and grazed both of her elbows. But she still had the forks. If only she could get in touch with Harry.

A black woman in a torn blue cardigan confronted her at the next corner, looking forlorn. "Where's the police station?" she wanted to know.

All that Amelia could do was point behind her, at a vacant acre of dust and brick.

The black woman said, "I don't understand."

Amelia's cheeks were streaked with tears. "Neither do I," she told her. "Neither do I."

SEVENTEEN

At first, I felt nothing at all, I mean nothing I imagine feels like *death*. Only a choking, dizzy sensation, like I'd accidentally sniffed up half the contents of a vacuum-cleaner bag. I looked at Papago Joe and Papago Joe looked back at me and asked me, "Well? What do you think?"

I took my own pulse. "I'm not dead yet," I told him. "In fact, I'm not even sick."

He gave me a slow smile. Then he leaned over the table with the rolled-up bill in his right nostril, and inhaled the rest of the powder. I glanced at E.C. Dude and shrugged. I was beginning to feel a little foolish, to tell you the truth. Apart from that, I wanted to sneeze. What would happen if the powder didn't work, and we tried to enter the Great Outside without any occult protection at all? It was bad enough to *hallucinate* that we were dead. I didn't fancy dying for real.

Papago Joe closed his eyes and sat up very straight-backed. He began to chant something under his breath, over and over, something that sounded like *"Nepauz . . . nepauz . . ."* It reminded me of Naomi Greenberg's chanting, hypnotic and strange, words that I could scarcely get my tongue around.

E.C. Dude said, "I should be coming with you, you know that? How are two old geezers like you going to stop the world from falling apart? There's no way. You need youth, man, you need extra cool."

I was inclined to agree with him. After fighting with Misquamacus and struggling with Karen and driving all the way to Apache Junction through storm and wreck and disaster, I was pretty much exhausted. My adrenalin had all ebbed away, and I was feeling my age. I would have done anything for a good breakfast and a pot of hot coffee and a couple of hours' dreamless sleep.

All that kept me going was Papago Joe's obvious determination and the sounds outside the trailer of breaking glass and screeching metal and—worse, the faint sounds of screaming. They were the sounds of a world that was gradually being torn apart, like a sackful of toys and live rabbits.

I was just about to say to E.C. Dude, "How about a Coke? I'm parched," when the inside of the trailer went totally black. My first thought was: *power cut,* but then I remembered that the power was out anyway, and that we had been sitting in candlelight. I said, "Joe? What's happened?" and my voice echoed in my ears, with a high metallic singing noise, and then I thought: *I'm dead. That's it. I've snorted that powder and that powder was poison and I'm dead.*

"Joe!" I shouted out. I began to panic. "Joe, what's happened? Where the hell are you? Joe!"

I flailed my arms round and struck the side of the trailer. Then I felt somebody seize my hand.

"Joe?" I asked, anxiously. "Is that you, Joe?"

"Relax," I heard him saying, close to my right ear. "Everything's fine, everything's going to be fine. It takes a while for your eyes to become accustomed to the darkness."

"I thought I was dead there for a moment," I told him, my voice shaking.

"To all intents and purposes, you were. I mean, you *are.*"

"What?"

"This is it. This is hallucinatory death. Your conscious brain believes that you're dead. You're functioning now on the very lowest levels of your psyche."

I swallowed. I didn't know what to think. I was fascinated, impressed, but mostly frightened. I had been close to death's door a couple of times, in my run-ins with Misquamacus, but I had never actually stuck my head round it.

Very gradually, my eyes became accustomed to the condition of "death." The interior of the trailer was almost swallowed up in shadows. Even the candle flames were flickering so dimly that I could barely make them out. I could distinguish E.C. Dude sitting back on the couch, his ankles crossed, but he appeared more as a fitful image of pale green flame than he did as a real person. Linda looked like a flame, too, but steadier, and burning more warmly. Stanley's flame was the brightest: bright and white.

I turned towards Papago Joe. His outline was blurred and

mauvish, a shadow laid on top of shadows; but then I lifted my hand and saw that mine was, too.

"Technically, you're blind," explained Papago Joe. "What you can see is not our bodies but our spirits. You can only see this trailer because it is invested with memories and associations, and the labour of the men who made it."

"Its manitou," I said.

"That's right. Everything has a manitou; even an automobile, even a chair. Of course the strongest manitous are those of men and the natural world around us. But even so . . . everything should be treated with equal respect. We reap what we sow."

"What do we do now?" I asked him.

"We take our leave of these friends of ours and enter the Great Outside."

He stood up and gestured to me to stand up, too. I saw E.C. Dude moving, and I thought I could vaguely hear his voice, but I wasn't sure.

"Can he see us?" I asked Papago Joe.

"Of course, to him we look normal, our normal selves, except that our eyes are turned up into our heads so that he can see only the whites. You see how little Stanley is backing away from us. We look a little scary, that's why."

"I don't blame him," I said. I remembered. Naomi Greenberg with her eyes rolled up, and Karen too, and that had been enough to give me nightmares forever.

Papago Joe reached forward and opened the trailer door and led the way down the steps. Every move I made seemed muffled and slow, like Neil Armstrong landing on the moon. It was just as black outside as it had been inside—black like a photographic negative. I could see newspapers and trash slowly swirling in the wind, and I feel the steady sting of grit on my face. Automobiles were being dragged across the highway and into Papago Joe's parking lot. But the noise they made was blurry and insulated, as if I had cotton stuffed in my ears.

I turned and saw E.C. Dude's flickering blue spirit waving to us, with Stanley's bright white spirit close behind, hiding behind his legs. I waved back, and then Papago Joe and I made our way across the used-car lot toward the workshop.

"Watch out for debris," warned Papago Joe. A sheet of aluminum siding came hurtling past us, followed by broken window frames and roofing and scattered torrents of bricks. A Volkswagen camper rolled by, over and over, roof and wheels, until it reached the workshop and tumbled into nothing and disappeared.

Papago Joe took hold of my sleeve. "This is it," he said. "This is the gateway. We'll have to be real careful. I mean, *real* careful, body and soul. Are you ready?"

"I'm ready," I told him, with huge bravado. What else could I say? "I'm out of here, end of the world or not?" Or, "Great Outside? Who are you trying to bullshit?"

We rounded the corner of the workshop wall, the same wall on which E.C. Dude and Stanley had glimpsed the hunched and jumping shape of Aktunowihio, the Shadow Buffalo. The rest of the workshop had collapsed. The roof had fallen in, and most of the walls had been reduced to scatterings of broken cinderblocks. I saw all this in dim, glowing outline, with the deep, spiritual perception of the dead.

In the center of the workshop floor, a wide hole had opened up—a hole just like the hole in the Belford Hotel—a hole which led to nothing at all but darkness and emptiness and death. Everything around us was being dragged into it—everything *white*, that is. Trailers and pick-ups and sheds and motorcycles and miles and miles of fencing and telephone wires and water piping.

Everything tipped into the gaping hole in a thunderous Niagara of tearing metal and protesting wood and the horrific screaming of everybody who had been caught up in it. I saw a young farmboy sliding across the parking lot on his back, his denims half-ripped-off, his right shoulder bloody-black and raw, and he was screaming at me, *screaming* at me, *Help me! Help me! Stop me! Help me!*

I saw pale-faced children, some of them still wearing bloodied pajamas. I saw two young women who had been dragged through razor wire; their flesh cut into diamond patterns, like a butcher scores pork rind. I saw a man whose thighs were both ripped open in a chaos of muscle and bone. I saw another man impaled through the chest with a length of scaffolding pole. He kept trying to stand up, trying to stand up, trying to wrestle that pole out of his ribcage, but with the eyes of somebody who was technically dead, I could see that his spirit was dimming, I could see that his life was flickering out.

A huge cement truck was dragged through Papago Joe's lot, and I saw it topple over just as it reached the edge of the hole, and crush a little girl who was trying to crawl away, crush her flat.

"Oh, Jesus, Joe," I told him. "I don't think that I can take this."

He turned and looked at me, dark-eyed and serious. "You don't have a choice, do you? Neither do I. This is our destiny. This is what we were born for. We can't back down now."

"You want to know the truth?" I yelled at him. "You really want to know the truth?"

"I know the truth already," he replied. "The truth is that you're scared to death, and so am I. So let's get on with it, can we, before any more children get killed?"

He paused, and then he said, "We *have* to do this, Harry. There's no question of opting out."

I took a deep breath, and then I said, "Okay, I'm sorry. Let's get going. I guess I'm dead already, so what does it matter?"

As we approached the hole, we had to wade our way knee-deep through rubbish and dust and detritus: magazines, automobile tires, telephones, calendars, tinned food, bottles, cartons, and cardboard boxes. Anything and everything that wasn't native to pre-Columbian America was being dragged away, and falling into the hole in Papago Joe's workshop with a steady, earth-trembling roar.

I had visited Niagara only once, with my grandparents, soon after David had drowned. I guess they had taken me away to help me get over his death. I had stood watching Niagara the way I watched this torrent now, fascinated, terrified. *The waters which fall from this horrible precipice do foam and boil after the most hideous manner imaginable, making an outrageous noise, more terrible than that of thunder.* That was what some French cleric had written, back in the seventeenth century. That was what I felt like now.

"What the hell do we do?" I shouted at Papago Joe, as we stood right on the very brink of the hole, with debris cascading against our legs.

Papago Joe pointed downward. "We take our chances, I guess."

I looked around. I saw a signboard that could be a make-shift sledge, but it was whirled away down the hole before I could reach it. Then I saw a ten-foot length of boardwalk sliding towards me through the rubbish. I waited until it had almost collided with my knees, and then I plunged onto it, chest-first, riding it like a surfboard. I heard Papago Joe shouting, *"Wait for me!"* but I was already being dragged towards the hole.

Up until then the most nerve-racking stunt that I had ever performed was swinging across to the balcony at the back of the Belford Hotel. But this was heart-stopping, although it was sensational, too. I dropped straight into nothingness, into pitch-black nothingness, surrounded by the deafening rumble of cars and concrete—even chunks of tarmac—and the higher-pitched sounds of corrugated-iron roofing and window glass and people screaming in total terror.

I fell over and over and for one unforgettable second I thought that I was going to go on falling forever, into space, into time, into the bottomless black-lined coffin of death. In that unforgettable second I was sure that Papago Joe's "death powder" had been nothing but hearth-sweepings, nothing more than milk powder and crushed-up paraceta-mol, and that I was just about to die for real. But then— instead of falling—I found that I was swinging like a trapeze artist, swinging in a wide parabola, and that gravity was pulling me back *upwards.* There was a long, long moment of no sensation at all, weightlessness, blindness and deafness. Then my feet collided with black grass, and rich black prai-rie soil, and I was thumped on the shoulder and pummelled on the side of the head, and then I was rolling helplessly sideways down a long slope.

I lay back on the grass and I knew that I was here. I was actually here. I was lying in the darkness of the Great Out-side. But what I hadn't anticipated was that the ground would be up and the sky would be down—that I would be clinging onto the ceiling of the world like some kind of fly. This was what Dr Snow must have meant when he described the Great Outside as a lake of shadows, a dark reflection of the real world. Just like a man reflected in a lake, I was hanging by my shoes, and below my head was the total infinity of sky and space and forever. *Below me,* for Christ's sake, and I had the world's worst case of vertigo.

I shut my eyes tight. I gripped my fists tight. I was clinically dead and I was upside down, and my brain was beginning to refuse the evidence of my senses. I felt closer to madness at that moment than I ever had before—even when I had seen Martin Vaizey pull Naomi Greenberg inside out. Even when Misquamacus had appeared in my motel room, with his chiselled face and his warpaint and his headdress of living insects. My sanity was clinging on like the last shred of tarpaper clinging to a hurricane-devastated roof. Flapping, twisting, just about ready to go sailing off into the darkness.

"Papago-Joe-what-the-fuck-is-happening-Papago-Joe-where-the-fucking-hell-are-you?" I screamed out.

It was then that I heard a thumping noise close beside me, and a sharp rustle of grass. Papago Joe collided with me, and lay beside me, and said, "Shit."

"This place is upside down," I told him.

He took two or three breaths, very deep breaths. "I know. I hate heights. I really hate heights. I'm not just frightened, Harry, frightened is the wrong word. I'm shitless."

"Maybe we'll get used to it," I said, trying to comfort him. "Maybe—I don't know—maybe our perceptions will adapt. Do you know what I mean? Do you remember that experiment where they made this guy walk around with a kind of periscope in front of his face, so that he saw everything upside down? After a couple of days his brain worked out what was wrong, and turned everything round the right way for him, so that he saw it normally."

With great caution, Papago Joe sat up. He looked east and then he slowly looked west. "There's no doubt about it, is there?" he said, at last. "There's gravity here. But, holy mackerel, it's pulling us *up.*"

I sat up, too, and looked round. In every direction, there was sweeping prairie—undulating hills, deeply-cleft draws. Black prairie, with black grass, under black star-prickled skies. An upside-down prairie under an upside-down sky. I heard the wind rustling through the grass and I smelled burning. I smelled cooking fires and horses and smells that I had never smelled before. I smelled *history*. I smelled Indian history. The same smells that Sitting Bull and Crazy Horse must have smelled.

"This is it," I said, with a sense of enormous awe—because this was the place that you'd always heard about in cowboy books and Indian movies and here it was—the Great Outside, the Happy Hunting Ground. To put it bluntly, this was Purgatory, and we were in it.

But there was a difference. This wasn't the realm of puffy clouds and cherubs and twanging harps. The Indians didn't believe in heaven—not the way that we believed in it. They believed in dark and they believed in light, they believed in Heammawihio and Aktunowihio, that was all. And they had made a bargain with Aktunowihio to drag the white man and all his inventions into the realm of darkness, so that they could have the realm of light.

The prairie rumbled, the prairie shook. Over to the northeast, in an awesome fountain, hundreds of automobiles and houses and signboards and pieces of shattered wood were being thrown up into the air, and thunderously falling into the grass. They were being dragged into the Great Outside from the world above, and spewed out into the darkness. The wrecked, the broken, the dead, the maimed.

I saw a gasoline truck flung into the air, and explode in a bellowing orange fireball, and then crash burning into the grass. I saw houses burst apart, windows and doors and shingles, and children flying through the air like Raggedy Anns and Raggedy Andys.

I managed to stand up. I knew that the sky was *below* me, rather than *above* me, but I managed to persuade myself that I couldn't fall upward, and I didn't. I held out my hand to Papago Joe and said, "We'd better get hunting . . . looking for Misquamacus."

Papago Joe nodded. "Of course," he said. "But first we have to seek our spirit-guides."

I sat down again, and he opened his borrowed medicine-bundle and produced two dried-up-looking sticks. He tapped them together in a slow, complicated rhythm, occasionally interspersed with a burst of faster tapping.

"Hey . . ." I said. "You're good at that."

He frowned. I could hardly see his eyes in the darkness. "What do you mean? I'm making this up as I go along. You don't think *all* medicine-men didn't make things up as they went along?"

"I guess they must have," I said weakly. And all these years, I'd thought that Indians had these really complex tappings and drum-messages that they totally understood. Singing Rock had told me that most Indians hadn't been able to interpret smoke signals. His favorite joke was that it was puff after poff except after puff-puff.

But Papago Joe kept on tapping, and tap-tap-tapping, and at last he said, "We are dead men, brothers. We are newly dead. We are seeking friends and guides in the Great Outside. We are seeking people to lead us."

He tapped again. *Tap-tap, tap-tap.* "We are seeking friends and guides," he repeated. "We are newly dead, and need assistance."

He paused, and then he said, "We are asking for the Sioux called Singing Rock and the white man called Martin Vaizey."

We waited for almost twenty minutes. The prairie was black and the sky was black; and if Papago Joe was feeling anything at all like me, he was dizzy and detached and completely out of touch with any kind of reality. I think I could have vomited, at that point. Just hanging on to an upside-down world made me feel nauseous. I mean, I seemed to *sway* every time I leaned sideways.

But at last I saw a quick dancing of light across the prairie, a quick flicker of spiritual flame; and then somebody was standing right behind Papago Joe with a faint benevolent smile on his face and it was Singing Rock.

Right then, I think I could have wept. I trusted Papago Joe—well, I *mostly* trusted Papago Joe. But Singing Rock

had tussled with Misquamacus right from the very beginning, and defeated him, and even though he and I had never
been close, not really close, we honored and respected each
other, and we would have died for each other, which he had
eventually done for me.

I could still see his beheaded face, flying away from me.
You don't even want to imagine what his expression was—
his brain still functioning, his eyes still seeing.

"*Hallo, Harry,*" said Singing Rock.

I raised my hand in greeting.

"*Playing dead now?*" Singing Rock remarked. "*My uncle
used to take the death-powder . . . said it made him strong.
Said he saw the buffalo-country, the way it was before the
white men came. Well . . . you know and I know . . . he was
only partly telling the truth.*"

I said, "We have to find Misquamacus. You can see what
he's doing. We have to stop him."

Singing Rock turned around and looked at the fountain
of falling cars. "*I warned you, Harry. I warned you. He wants
everything back. The mountains, the rivers, the prairies. He
wants it all back, the way it was before. He wants you gone.*"

I looked at Papago Joe, but all that Papago Joe could do
was to shrug. "And what do you think?" I asked Singing
Rock. "Do you think he should take it all back?"

Singing Rock said, "*Time goes forwards, Harry, not backwards. Whatever happened before . . . however tragic it was
. . . it's over now, and we have to look ahead.*"

He looked smaller than I remembered him: better-
spoken, more frail. More like an insurance salesman than an
Indian wonder-worker.

"*I know what Misquamacus is doing,*" he said. "*I know
where to find him, too.*" He looked down at Papago Joe and
said, "*It was you, then, who chose me as a spirit-partner?*"

"Yes," said Papago Joe.

At the same time, I felt a hand on my shoulder and I
turned around. It was Martin Vaizey. It was actually *him,*
looking the same as he had when I first met him at his apartment in the Montmorency Building. He gave me the faintest
of smiles and said, "*Hallo, Harry. It looks as if it's your turn
to be possessed.*"

I grasped his hand. "Hallo, Martin. How's tricks?"

He looked around, the black wind ruffling his hair. *"I'd seen this place before, through the eyes of other people . . . I didn't think that I'd be coming here so soon."*

Papago Joe stood up, and I stood up, too. It was then that a really weird and wonderful thing happened. Singing Rock *stepped into* Papago Joe, literally stepped right into him, and the two of them became one.

"How did you do that?" I asked Papago Joe, in amazement.

"Your friend is only a spirit. He can enter anything and anybody he wants to. The beauty of it is that I now possess his wonder-working skills, and all of his knowledge of the Great Outside."

I was about to ask Papago Joe what it *felt* like, having a spirit entering your body, when I found out. A warm sensation came over me, warm and totally enveloping, like immersing myself in a huge old-fashioned tub of hot water, and putting my head under, too. I suddenly realized that I was not only me, but Martin Vaizey, too; that his mind and mine were intermingled inside of my head, all of his memories and all of his education and all of his ideas. I suddenly *knew* what had happened in his cell at the 13th Precinct. I suddenly *knew* what the Celtic forks were for.

I laughed out loud. The sensation of being inside somebody else's mind was exhilarating. I had memories of oceanside vacations at Cape Cod. I had memories of meals and birthday parties and Christmas trees and summer days, and they were all Martin's memories, not mine.

"Martin?" I said. But it felt like talking to myself.

"I'm here," said Martin, his voice reverberating inside of my eardrums.

I had often heard of people being possessed, or "taken over," but I had never experienced it, not first hand. All I can tell you is that it made me feel awed and impressed by the powers of the human mind. But it also made me feel love for another person in a way that I'd never felt it before. I felt all of Martin's strengths, all of Martin's frailties. I was Martin and Martin was me. I knew that he could be sympathetic and devoted and self-sacrificing and funny. I knew that he had a dry sense of humor. I also knew that, during his life, he had lied a lot, and that he always felt that he had under-achieved.

Jesus, I even knew that he liked veal Holstein.

Papago Joe said, "Come on, Harry. We have to find out where Misquamacus is now. Then we have to decide how to deal with him."

"How are we going to locate him?" I wanted to know.

"We use these eagle-sticks. They're spiritually sensitive, as well as geographically directional. Indian wonder-work-ers discovered a long time ago that wherever a spirit travels, he leaves a trail behind him . . . the spiritual equivalent to footprints. And if they leave a trail, that trail can be fol-lowed. Where was the last place you saw Misquamacus?"

"Back at my motel room."

"Very well, then . . . that's where we'll start."

Papago Joe sorted through the eagle-sticks until he found one that would take us westward. "This is where Singing Rock's talents come into play," he told me, holding up one of the feathered sticks. "I never could have found this so quickly, not without him. Come on, take a hold. We're about to go travelling places."

I stood beside him in that darkest of worlds, and together we grasped the eagle-stick. I didn't dare to look upward, be-cause I knew that there was nothing above me but empty sky, and I was terrified that I was going to fall. But Martin did a lot to calm me down and steady my nerve. He had al-ready experienced enough of the Great Outside to know that the only real danger came from the spirits and shadows who roamed it—spirits of shamans and wonder-workers, shadows of demons and men who were not only men, but wolves and buffalo, too.

I felt the eagle-stick's spiritual sensitivity. I felt it so quickly and acutely that I whipped my hand away, as if it had caught fire. Martin of course was highly responsive to spirits—much more responsive than I normally was. But I hadn't been prepared for the flash of razor-sharp darkness that cut westwards straight through the air towards Phoe-nix, and the Thunderbird Motel.

"Hold on!" shouted Papago Joe. "Don't let it go again!"

I gripped the eagle-stick and it was then that we flew. Well, we didn't actually fly, not in the sense that we flapped our arms and went up in the air. But the darkness flashed past us with an earsplitting *kkrakkkkkkkkk!* and we were someplace else altogether.

I almost lost my balance. I staggered, slipped, and then managed to stand up straight.

"Careful," said Papago Joe. "The last thing you want to do now is sprain your ankle, or something stupid like that."

I looked around us. At first I couldn't understand where we were. There were no lights, no signs, no streets, no nothing. But then I saw a dark and shadowy hump in the distance, and there was no mistaking that dark and shadowy hump. That was Camelback Mountain, just outside of Phoenix. In fact—when I looked around—I realized that we were standing on the exact location of the Thunderbird Motel, except that the Thunderbird Motel wasn't here anymore, or maybe it hadn't been built yet. The landscape was dusty and rutted and cracked with drought, and not far away a dry riverbed twisted its way toward downtown Phoenix; or what had once been downtown Phoenix, or would be, or *might* be, I couldn't decide which.

"What is this?" I asked Papago Joe. "The present or the future? Or what?"

But even before he could answer me, I heard Martin Vaizey's answer inside of my own head. *Not the future. Not the past. This is death. The land of the dead. Time never passes. Nothing ever changes. The dead never grow old, Harry. Not like you and Karen and Papago Joe are going to grow old.*

Papago Joe was fumbling with his eagle-sticks again. "Here—"he said. "Here. This is where Misquamacus walked. This is where Misquamacus went to. Harry! Follow me . . . I've got traces of him everywhere!"

We walked westwards, almost as far as 24th Street—or at least as far as the dusty burro-track where 24th Street would eventually be, or *was,* in some alternative reality. The whole thing was beginning to confuse me badly, and I was glad that we didn't run into Misquamacus right then, because I think that he could have taken me out like a cheap candle. I was scared, shocked, and was seriously uncomfortable with the idea of being dead.

Phoenix had been forcibly dragged downwards—down to the Great Outside. The city looked like nothing more than an isolated mountain range, its foothills formed from twisted automobiles and collapsed motels and crumbled adobes—its high-rise office buildings marking out the peaks. In spite of the wreckage, in spite of the windblown trash, Phoenix still retained a dark funereal dignity, because most of the major buildings still stood, here in the darkness of Indian magic, here in the darkness of death. They had been dragged downwards into their own mirror-image, and stood together like so many brooding gravestones: the Valley National Bank and the Arizona Bank and the First Federal Savings Building and the Hyatt Regency, the pride of Sun Valley, all in darkness, all suspended like stalactites over a sky that would never see the sun.

The Great Outside was becoming what Misquamacus and all of the Ghost Dance preachers had predicted it would be: the cemetery of white supremacy.

Papago Joe said, "Here . . . I've found his trail here . . . off to the northeast."

"How far?" I asked him.

"I'm not sure . . . six hundred, maybe seven hundred miles."

"Colorado?" I suggested. "He dragged down two towns in Colorado. Maybe he's counting coup there, too."

Papago Joe looked serious. "You realize something, don't you? If you and I don't stop him, this is going to be worse than any nuclear holocaust. This is going to be worse than anything you ever believed possible. When we bombed Iraq, we talked about bombing them back to the Stone Age. Well, Misquamacus is going to do that to us, *now,* for real. He's going to drag us back to buffaloes and bows-and-arrows and living like savages. It *wasn't* wonderful, it *wasn't* idyllic, it *wasn't* paradise. It was only white men's fiction that made it sound that way, and Dee Brown being dewy-eyed. The truth was that it was hard and it was dirty and it was wasteful and it was primitive. Fuck Hiawatha. Fuck *Dances With Wolves.* We were a throwback, an aboriginal people who outlived our time; and that's all there is to it. And if I'm not being a good proud Native American and politically correct, then so be it. But at least I'm telling it like it is."

I stared at him. "I never heard an Indian speak like that before."

"They daren't, usually," said Papago Joe. "But a lot of us feel the same way. If there's anything worse than being killed by cholera and rifles, it's being killed by understanding."

He lowered his head. I didn't know what else to say to him. But at last he looked up with those dark glittering eyes and said, "Come on. We're after Misquamacus. By the time it gets dark tonight, I want that son-of-a-bitch's scalp on my lodgepole." With the same rush of darkness and the same instantaneous *krrrrakkkkkkk!* we found ourselves in black undulating grasslands, amid the wreckage of a small town.

We walked towards the wreckage slowly. It didn't take us long to find out where we were. Pritchard, Colorado, population 335. The sign lay close beside us in the grass, twisted and spattered with blood.

We circled the debris that was scattered on the prairie, but there was nothing we could do. We saw little children lying dead; we saw women with white faces, their lips already tinged with green. We saw dogs and cats and a turned-over Caterpillar earthmover, and a gas-station canopy, and hundreds of cans of 7UP.

"Let's carry on," I told Papago Joe. "We won't find anything here."

He used another eagle-stick to sense where Misquamacus had gone next. Then *krrrrakkkkkkk!* and we had arrived in another part of Colorado. This was high prairie country, buffalo country, where the wind was blowing black and shrill. Across the banks of a slowly-winding river, a town had been torn to pieces. We stood on the summit of a low slope, and looked around at the bodies and the bits and pieces: the tragic debris of a devastated community.

"My guess this is Maybelline," said Papago Joe. He poked at the rubble with a stick. "You know something, Harry? This isn't revenge any longer. This is even worse than genocide. This is killing the future. This is going back."

"What now?" I asked him, dully.

"We keep on hunting him, that's what now."

"But supposing we never find him? I mean, he's not stupid. He must *know* that we've thought about tracking him down."

"Perhaps. But he could be arrogant enough not to worry about it. You know what they say. Pride comes before a pratfall."

"Oh, yeah? Who says that?"

"How should I know? The United Stiltwalkers of America? Who cares? The main thing is that we keep on chasing after him and never let up. This Misquamacus of yours is Mr Relentless, from what you've told me. The only way to fight Mr Relentless is to be Mr Double-Relentless. Beat him at his own game, hunt him down, harry him, chase him; and when you've found him—"

Papago Joe didn't have to finish his sentence. We both knew that neither of us knew how to deal with Misquamacus, once we'd found him. We would have to play it by ear. Misquamacus was already dead. He was even deader than we were. But he had entered a realm of spiritual reincarnation where he was powerful and vengeful and highly magical, and where he was almost ready to sit at Gitche Manitou's right hand. A favored warrior, a great wonderworker, the greatest of all the wonder-workers, probably.

How do you finish off a man with those kind of credentials?

Papago Joe sorted through the eagle-sticks, until he found one that tingled to his touch.

"He's headed northeast again, quite a long stretch. Close on a thousand miles, by the feel of it."

"Chicago," I said. It made some kind of sense, after all. Misquamacus was travelling from one place to another, touching his victims, counting coup. Every dead enemy he touched would gild his reputation even more brightly, and make his eventual glorification all the more certain. By the time he had finished, he would probably be counted as the most destructive Indian warrior who had ever lived. Or died. Or whatever.

I stood next to Papago Joe and grasped the eagle-stick. As I did so, however, I saw something moving in the grass. Not something, *somebody.* At first I thought it was an injured bird, trying to fly. Then I suddenly realized that it was somebody running. A young girl, running.

Without saying a word to Papago Joe, I ran after her. My legs thrashed through the grass. At last I caught up with her and snatched at her arm. She twisted around, staring at me wildly.

"It's all right!" I gasped. "I'm not going to hurt you!"

"Who are you?" she panted. Her face was deathly pale. She was young—no more than fourteen or fifteen, and yet there was an expression in her eyes, an odd, watchful darkness, that made me think for just an instant that she had to be older. An old personality, wearing a young and flawless mask.

"It's okay," I repeated. She was panting and I was wheezing. "I'm a friend. I'm not even dead. Not properly, anyway."

"Well, no more am I," she declared.

"You're not dead? Then what are you doing here? You know where this is, don't you? The Great Outside: the Happy Hunting Ground. This is where people go to die."

"I'm looking for my brother," she said. "He was lost in the storm, and I'm trying to find him."

"Come on," I said. "Come and meet Joe. He knows more about this than I do."

"I'm not a child, you know," she told me. "I *can* look after myself."

"Hey," I appealed. "Did I say you couldn't?"

I led her back across the grass. As she approached, Papago Joe leaned forward and held out his hand. "What's your name, sweetheart?" he asked her. I thought he could have tried to look less sinister, and talked less gravelly, but the girl seemed to place her trust in him immediately, and implicitly. I guess it was something to do with him being a father, which I had never been, and having a way with teenage daughters.

"My name's Wanda—Wanda McIntosh," she said. 'I''ve been looking for Joey, my brother Joey."

"Did you live here, in Maybelline?" asked Papago Joe.

Wanda shook her head. "I used to live in Pritchard, with my mother and Joey. Well, not any more. My mother's dead; I saw my mother dead. And my friend Maggie, too. Maggie's bathroom window broke and all the glass dropped into the bath and she was cut in two."

Her eyes looked blank. I could only guess what horrors she had experienced. I reached out towards her, but, "So how did you get here?" I asked her. "Pritchard—that's hundreds of miles away."

"I was looking for Joey. I couldn't find him in Pritchard and the black man said that the medicine-man might have taken him along. So the black man brought me here. I don't know how he did it: it was like sort of flying, only it wasn't."

"But your brother wasn't here?"

Wanda shook her head. "There was already a storm here, too. The black man said he couldn't help me any more, and he went off someplace. I went back up to the proper world, but I couldn't find Joey anywhere there because of the storm and all the buildings falling down. A helicopter nearly crashed into me, and so I ran away and hid back here. In any case I guessed there was more chance of finding Joey if I stayed here."

Papago Joe lifted the pendant around Wanda's neck and examined it narrowly. "This black man . . . did he tell you his name?"

Wanda said, "Yes. He said his name was Jonas DuPaul and that if anybody was ever to ask me how I came by this pendant, I was to say that it came from Toussaint L'Ouverture himself, and then to him, and then to me, and that it would protect me even in the valley of the shadow of death."

"I see," said Papago Joe. Then he held up the pendant a little higher, and asked me, "Do you know what this is?"

"It looks like a premium for Kentucky Fried Chicken."

"It's voodoo. A voodoo amulet. Very rare, very magic. If it came from Toussaint L'Ouverture himself, then it's something very special indeed. Look on that sacrificed cockerel and tremble. Toussaint L'Ouverture was the guy who led

the slaves in Haiti, and kicked out the British slave traders.
He was practically a god."

I reached out and touched the pendant. As I did so—
instantly—

*thunderous drumming, drumming that pounded and
pounded and wouldn't stop—*and—*blue-painted faces staring
and grinning—*and—

*black naked bodies twisting and convulsing and shuddering
arms and legs—*then—*a knife slicing a cockerel's throat and
blood spraying everywhere—*a naked girl drinking the blood
and letting it pour down her chin and smear all over her
breasts—*and—

*a chalk-white face with black glittering eyes that looked
like beetles feeding on his eyelids—*and—*gripping the girl's
hair and dragging her head back, exposing her throat—*and—

*cutting a thin smile all the way across her throat, from one
side to the other, and blood and air exploding out of it—*

I dropped the pendant, shaken. I stared at Papago Joe
and then at Wanda. "Jesus," I said.

Papago Joe made a dryly-amused face. "Remember that
you now possess all of Martin Vaizey's sensitivities, apart
from your own."

"You felt it, too?"

"Very faintly. I'm not as sensitive as Martin Vaizey. But
even if I couldn't feel it very clearly, I know exactly what it
is. It's a voodoo charm. It's a way of passing magical powers
from one person to another, so if a witch-doctor was dying
he could give the charm to his son or his friend or whoever
and, as soon as they put it on, that person would immediately inherit all of his greatest strengths. Presumably that's
why this Jonas DuPaul gave it to Wanda—so that she
would inherit his magical strength, and be able to survive in
the Great Outside."

"But why would he do that?" I said.

"Search me," said Papago Joe. "Maybe he simply took a
shine to her. Whatever the reason, this is real genuine voodoo."

"Voodoo, hunh?" I asked him. "I never had anything to
do with voodoo. I saw *The Evil Dead* on late-night TV. I

guess I thought that I'd be safe enough if I stayed away from shopping malls."

"I said *real* voodoo," said Papago Joe. He picked up the pendant again, and turned it over and over. "Jonas DuPaul was one of the most feared of all voodoo witch-doctors ever. I mean he still enjoys a reputation very much like the reputation that Misquamacus enjoys amongst Native Americans. In New Orleans, mothers still scare their kids by warning them that Jonas DuPaul will come get them, if they misbehave. Jonas DuPaul is supposed to have teeth that are filed to a point, and like crunching up newborn babies' heads."

Wanda said, "That's not true. I saw Jonas DuPaul's teeth and he has regular teeth. They're all yellow but they're not pointed."

"Wait a minute . . ." I said. "Jonas DuPaul . . . that name rings a bell for some reason."

I racked my brains, and then I suddenly remembered Dr Snow, quoting from Bishop Whipple's diary. *"Later Colonel Sibley also recruited a negro man from somewhere in Louisiana. This person was always dressed as if for the opera . . . sometimes he called himself Sawtooth and sometimes he called himself Jonas DuPaul; but most of the time he referred to himself as Doctor Hambone . . . Colonel Sibley said that he could make the dead speak, and took him to question all of the corpses of murdered settlers, in order that they could identify their assailants."*

"Doctor Hambone," I said. "That's who it was. He was a voodoo witch-doctor brought in to help the US Cavalry fight against Indian magic. I can't remember when it was, eighteen-hundred-fifty-something."

"That's right," said Papago Joe. "Hey, you know more about this than I gave you credit for. The only puzzle is, where does Doctor Hambone fit into all of this Indian magic? Or is he just stalking around, scavenging, collecting up the dead, the way he was always supposed to—finding new bodies for his army of zombies?"

"When I first saw him, he said he was just passing," put in Wanda.

"Did he say why he was giving *you* the amulet, in particular?"

"No, except that I was praying so hard, and he thought that it was good to have so much faith. The way he talked to me, I think he just felt sorry for me."

"Well," I said. "I guess that even the scariest people can have their soft side." I glanced across at Papago Joe. "If we're going to Chicago, we'd better think about making a move, hunh, *kemo sabe*?"

But Papago Joe was still frowning. "This has thrown me off," he said. "What the hell is a voodoo witch-doctor doing *here*, now, in the middle of all this? I mean, he might have been recruited to fight against Indian magic in the past, but he doesn't seem to be fighting against it now. I mean, what's his angle?"

I tried to remember what else Dr Snow had told us about Doctor Hambone. "There was some story of him being captured by the Santee, and how some Santee shaman showed him this kind of dream of the future, when all the white settlers would be killed by shadows."

"I see. Is that all?"

"I guess so. After he was rescued, Doctor Hambone split for New Orleans, as far as anybody knew, and that was the last that anybody saw of him."

Papago Joe said, "Okay, I guess we'd think of splitting, too. What are we going to do with young Wanda here?"

"Do you have any relatives you could go to?" I asked her.

"I guess my uncle and aunt in Denver."

"Okay, then . . ." said Papago Joe, sorting out his eagle-sticks. "If you don't mind the fastest trip of your life, we can take you there."

I took hold of Wanda's hand and squeezed it tight. "Believe me, this is just as much fun as a rollercoaster."

But the second I squeezed her hand, I recoiled. It didn't feel like a girl's hand at all. *It was a man's hand, calloused and muscular.* I looked down at her in shock and saw that she didn't look like Wanda at all. *Her face was grey and her scalp was bloody, and she wore a bloodied, drooping mustache.*

"Daniel McIntosh, sir, First Lieutenant, Company G, Seventh Cavalry."

"What?" I shuddered. "What do you want?"

Papago Joe looked across at me in bewilderment. Obviously, he couldn't see the face that I could see. "Harry?" he said. Then—more concerned—"Harry!"

"This is my great-great-granddaughter, sir. The negro saved her because of me. I saw the negro at the Greasy Grass River, sir. He was there, with Gall first and then with Crazy Horse, I saw him with my own eyes. When we were running, and the Sioux were catching us and scalping us and cutting off our privates, he said, enough, but Crazy Horse wouldn't listen. The negro hates white men, sir, but he felt sorry for the men who died at the Greasy Grass River; he felt sorry for the way they died. That's why he saved my great-great-granddaughter, sir, and my great-great-grandson, too."

I opened my mouth, hoping to ask Daniel McIntosh a question, but his face had faded before I could speak. In one dissolving moment, I was back to holding Wanda's hand again, and looking at *her* face, instead of that bloody horror who had died at the Little Big Horn.

"Did you *feel* that?" I asked her. "Were you aware of what happened to you then?"

She rubbed her upper lip as if she half-expected to find that she still had a moustache. Then she looked up at me, bright-eyed. "I felt it. I really felt it! And Joey's safe, isn't he? I know it. I don't know how. But he's safe, isn't he? He's truly safe?"

Papago Joe took hold of Wanda's other hand. "Denver?"

"Denver," I nodded. "Then Bismarck."

"Bismarck?"

'We're going to get ourselves out of this death-hallucination and visit the *Bismarck Tribune*. There's some photographs we have to find. And we have to find them *now*.'

EIGHTEEN

I never knew that when you woke up from the dead, you had a hangover. But by the time we reached the offices of the *Bismarck Tribune* on that warm, still afternoon, the membranes of my brain were throbbing and my mouth felt like a gopher had slept in it.

There isn't much you can say about Bismarck except that it's *there*, in the middle of North Dakota, on the Missouri River, on the line between Mountain and Central Time, a collection of warehouses and insurance buildings and featureless streets. Rooftops, hardware stores, telephone lines and hamburger restaurants with rows of dusty pick-ups parked outside. If there hadn't been a river and a railroad, Bismarck wouldn't have been there at all—there would have been nothing but rustling grasslands, and distant horizons, and a haze of summer heat.

Papago Joe and I had risen from the dry soil only a half mile out of town, like two resurrected corpses. A buck rabbit had seen us and bounded away, zigzagging through the grass in terror but, fortunately for us, he was our only witness.

We brushed ourselves off and squinted around. The bright sunlight was explosive after the blackness of the Great Outside and the heat was almost unbearable. We could see downtown Bismarck and the sparkling curve of the Missouri, and the skyline of Mandan beyond. We started to walk.

We had left Wanda in Denver, as near to her uncle and aunt's house as possible. We could only enter or leave the Great Outside through the nexuses created by spilled Indian blood, but there were plenty in Denver and it hadn't been too difficult to locate one close to the Mountain View district where Wanda's uncle and aunt lived.

Wanda stood in the darkened grass for a moment and looked around, and then said, "Thank you. I hope I see you again some day."

"We do, too," I told her.

Without a word, she took off the voodoo amulet and handed it to Papago Joe. "Here," she said. "Maybe this will help to keep you safe."

Papago Joe shook his head. "No, child. You hold on to it. This business isn't done yet. There's no place safe—not here, not anywhere. You're in danger, child, wherever Indian blood was spilled, and that means almost everywhere. You hold on to that amulet."

"But I want you to have it. You saved me. It should be yours."

"I don't have need of it," said Papago Joe.

Wanda took hold of his hand, and reached up and kissed his cheek. "Jonas DuPaul will keep me safe," she told him. "You need something more."

There was a moment's pause between them, but it was like that moment when two strong magnets are about to lose their grip on each other.

"Please," said Wanda, and Papago Joe said, "All right," and took the amulet in his hand, although I noticed that he didn't hang it around his neck. Then he shook Wanda's hand, and I kissed her; and she slipped down through the grass as if she were diving into a rushy, overgrown lake. I saw her hands uplifted for the briefest of moments, and then she was gone.

"Nice girl," I remarked, and Papago Joe nodded.

"Aren't you going to wear that amulet?" I asked him.

He shook his head. "One of Wanda's greatest strengths was her youthfulness. If I put this amulet on now, that's what I'm in danger of inheriting from her."

"What's wrong with being youthful?"

"Harry, I may regret growing old, but I have no burning desire to be fourteen again, thank you."

"Oh," I said, although I wasn't at all sure that I understood what he was trying to tell me.

It was leaving the Great Outside near Bismarck that caused Papago Joe some problems. We had walked backwards and forwards underneath the city, searching for a way out. But at last his eagle-sticks had twitched like dowsers' rods at the place where three Indian women, straggling behind their tribe, had been overtaken, raped, and shot by US Cavalry scouts.

Their blood had been spilled over an area just wide enough for Papago Joe and I to force our way up through the surface and into the sunlight.

Saying goodbye to Singing Rock and Martin Vaizey had been the strangest experience. I felt as if my whole insides had taken a step back from the rest of me; and when I turned around in the darkness, Martin had been standing there, sad, smiling, pale as ash; and Singing Rock had been standing next to Papago Joe.

"We'll catch you guys later," was all that I could think of to say.

Singing Rock had raised his hand in the Sioux sign that means "my heart was empty when you came, but now it is full to overflowing."

My heart felt just the same way.

The *Tribune* office was closed for lunch when we arrived, and the iron-haired woman behind the reception desk wouldn't open the door for us for anything—not even when I pressed my hands together in mock-prayer, and then squashed my face against the glass and blew my mouth out, Bart Simpson-style.

We went across the road to The Crossing Restaurant, and sat at a small corner table with a red-checked cloth and ordered steaks and onion rings and beer.

Our waitress had bouffant black hair and scarlet lipstick and a beauty spot on her upper lip with a black hair growing out of it. She kept winking at me and she gave me extra onion rings, "On the house, honey, because you look like you could use them."

Papago Joe looked at me with those deepset eyes, chewing. "You know something," he said. "There's nothing so useful when you're fighting a bloodthirsty wonder-worker as extra onion-rings, don't you agree?"

"I'll be able to waste him just by breathing on him," I agreed.

When the *Tribune* reopened, we found our way to the photograph archive, a stuffy little room lined wall-to-wall

with grey filing cabinets. A short bald man with jazzy braces
directed us to the files for 1876.

"We're looking in particular for photographs that were
taken at the battle of the Little Big Horn," I told the archivist.

He blinked at me. He reminded me of Mickey Rooney
back in his Andy Hardy days. "I'm sorry, I don't believe
that any photographs were taken at the battle of the Little
Big Horn. If there were, I've never seen any. They would be
famous, wouldn't they? Actual photographs of the Little
Big Horn, my goodness!"

"The *Tribune* sent a reporter to the Little Big Horn along
with General Custer. The reporter's name was Mark Kellogg. I understand that Mark Kellogg was quite a photogra-
phy buff, and took his own cameras with him. He took
pictures at the Little Big Horn and even though Mark Kellogg was killed, the negatives survived."

"I never heard that story," said the archivist, shaking his
head. "You can look if you like, but I've catalogued all of
these photographs—especially the historical collection—
and I've never seen any pictures from the Little Big Horn."

We searched through scores of large brown envelopes.
We found photographs that had been taken by Mark
Kellogg—even a portrait of General Custer by Mark Kellogg, lounging outside a tent with his Indian scout Bloody
Knife and two mangy-looking mongrels. But after two
hours we had to admit that there were no photographs of
the Little Big Horn.

The archivist came back. "There's one thing you might
try," he suggested, "and that's the Kellogg family home.
They still live in Bismarck, on Edwinton Avenue East. According to the special edition we printed back in 1876, Mark
Kellogg was killed by the Sioux but he wasn't mutilated,
and his clothes and possessions were eventually returned to
his mother and father."

"All right, thanks," we told him, wearily, and left the
building.

On our way to Edwinton Avenue East, we walked past a
TV store. I stopped to comb my hair in my own reflection.
But as I did so, I noticed news pictures of crumbling build-

ings and crushed automobiles and bodies being dragged along cluttered sidewalks.

"Look—" I told Papago Joe. "It's happening again."

A passing old-timer paused for a moment to stand beside us and watch the news pictures, too.

"New York," he remarked, and spat.

"That's New York?" I asked him, in horror.

He nodded. "Serve 'em right for building so high and stooping so low."

Mrs Keitelman sat in her tapestry-covered armchair with the yellow blinds drawn, so that the afternoon sun wouldn't fade the furnishings. The sitting room was crowded with hefty, ugly furniture, most of it darkly-varnished oak, in the gargantuan style favored by Sears, Roebuck catalogues of years gone by. Next to me, on a pedestal table, a glass dome covered a bevy of stuffed songbirds, faded and molting and dull-eyed; while just above a huge rolltop bureau the size of a Wurlitzer organ a morose carp swam in a garishly-painted lake.

Mrs Keitelman said, "We were always a family for keeping things, yes. My whole attic is crammed with clothes and books and toys and ornaments and goodness-alone knows what! But Mark—great-uncle Mark—well, his things were always our special pride. We even have his pocket telescope, you know!"

"It's just the photographs we were interested in," I told her. "For the time being, anyway. I mean, we'd love to come back sometime, and look through the rest of the stuff."

She smiled. She was a well-preserved woman of seventy-five going on eighty. Her skin was very pale, almost transparent, and her hair was white and fastened with an Alice-band. She wore a loose-flowing cotton dress in hyacinth blue, which matched her eyes. For some reason I felt she looked exactly like the grandmother I had never known.

"Well, I only saw those photographs once," she said. "They were supposed to have been brought back to Bismarck from the battlefield, along with poor Mark's clothes and his valise, and his pocket watch, and all of those bits and pieces. They didn't bring his body back. The paper said he wasn't mutilated but my grandfather wrote in his diary that he probably was; the same as all the rest. That was why they didn't send the body home."

"The photographs . . . are they prints or are they negatives?" I asked Mrs Keitelman.

"Oh, we have both. The original glass negatives were sent to the *Tribune* and they made three copies of each print—one for the paper, one for the Army and one as a record. But the paper never published any of the pictures—or any engravings based on the pictures, as they would have done in those days—and the Army said they had lost their copies, and in any case they didn't believe that great-uncle Mark had really made a true record, or some such nonsense. There was even some suggestion that he might have faked them. But we still have a set of prints here, as well as all the negatives."

She left us alone for three or four minutes, while the clock on the mantelpiece ticked away the afternoon, and large cups of weak creamy coffee grew colder and colder beside us. I said, "I can't believe that. The Army actually refused to believe that Kellogg's photographs were authentic."

Papago Joe tiredly pinched the bridge of his nose. "You don't expect anybody to believe what *we've* done, do you? Sniffed up death-powder, visited the Happy Hunting Ground? They'd send us straight to the funny farm."

"I don't know," I told him. "I still can't believe how people can be so skeptical about spirits when they're *there* . . . right in front of our noses. *Talking* to us, guiding us. Mingling with us, you know, just like any crowd of people. The only difference is that some of us are dead and some of us are still alive."

Papago Joe grunted in amusement. He sat back and crossed his legs, and exposed an expanse of bare leg and a red-checked sock and a worn-down cowboy boot. "I never thought I'd ever hear a white man say that."

"And I never thought I'd ever see a Native American in argyle socks."

Mrs Keitelman came back with a photograph in a brass frame and a large, well-worn envelope. First of all she showed us the photograph. It showed a podgy, serious-faced young man with his hair parted in the middle and a wing collar.

"That's poor great-uncle Mark, taken at Fort Yates, Dakota Territory, on September 17, 1875, the year before he was killed at the Little Big Horn. Fort Yates is where they buried Sitting Bull, you know. You can still see his grave today."

She brought over a small card table, set it down in front of us, and unfolded its green baize top. Then she carefully opened up the envelope and drew out six large sepia photographs, which she laid out in two rows of three.

"The Army refused to believe they were genuine," she said. "They said that somebody had fixed them, somebody who wanted to make the Department of Indian Affairs believe that the Indians had extraordinary occult powers, which the Army wouldn't be able to beat. They said that these photographs were some kind of crude retaliation for the way in which the Sioux chiefs had been brought to the east and shown around our shipyards and our munitions plants, in order to convince them that it wasn't worth them fighting for their lands."

Papago Joe and I studied the photographs minutely. It was plain that Mark Kellogg had taken them under the most harrowing conditions, and four out of the six were quite blurred. But they clearly showed a deep coulee, its sides dotted with sagebrush, and a barren hill beyond it. In the first photograph, soldiers were riding up from the coulee, towards the hill; and although the sky above the hill looked unusually dark, that could have been faulty exposure.

But the next photograph showed *something* coming up over the brow of the hill. Something dark, with writhing tentacles, like a giant squid made out of smoke. The leading cavalry officer was half-turned around, and his horse was rearing up. Behind him, some of the other troopers had already tightened their reins and prepared themselves for a hasty retreat.

"This is another aspect of these pictures that the Army didn't care for," said Mrs Keitelman. "Quite simply, they show the famous US 7th Cavalry turning tail and running away. But you can hardly blame them when you see what happened next."

What happened next was that a huge black bulky shape rose up over the horizon, and three troopers seemed to have fallen—or been dragged—off their horses. One of them was crushed by his falling mount; the others tried to escape, but were wrapped in black smoky tentacles before they could ride back more than fifteen yards.

The massacre that followed was even more grisly than I had imagined it would be. But in the fourth photograph in the sequence, there was still no sign of the Indians. The cavalry were being torn from their saddles, stripped and slaughtered. Their horses lay dead and injured all around, like gutted sofas, and I saw a young Santee woman walking from one to the other, stripping off saddles and belts and boots and rifles.

There were two more pictures. One of them showed a huge shadow rising up, and some of the troopers must have fired at it, and hit it, because I could see smoke and fragments of what could have been ectoplasm.

The last picture was the most stunning, though, and if I hadn't known that such things could exist, I wouldn't have believed the evidence of my own eyes. It was hard to believe, but there it was, on its original print paper, faded and yellow.

The date, scribbled in pencil on the back of the original, was Sunday, June 25, 1876—the actual date of the Battle of Little Big Horn, the very Sunday on which Custer and all his troopers had died.

The picture showed cavalry troopers desperately riding for their lives down the slopes of the coulee. Even in this fudge-colored old print their eyes showed up white in screaming panic. Close behind them—and already catching up with some of them—was a monstrous thing that you'd have to invent a new dictionary to describe.

It was like a black cloud concealing all of your worst nightmares. Inside the cloud, I could just make out a kind of *face,* a face like a human shriek. Out of the face curled tentacles like snakes. But it wasn't the snakes that upset me so much. It was the creature's underbelly, which seemed to be made up of a tangled mass of human heads, hundreds and hundreds of human heads; and the smoky squid creature was running across the hilltop in a terrible spindly uneven rush, *on human arms, on hundreds of human arms.*

"Christ," I said, and sat back, in awe.

Mrs Keitelman raised an eyebrow, disapproving of my blasphemy, but satisfied because she could see that I believed.

"This is authentic, isn't it?" she said. "*You* believe that it's authentic. There's no photographic trickery here. This is real."

"Ma'am," said Papago Joe, his voice hoarse from tiredness but very controlled, "I've seen drawings and paintings of this thing here ever since I was small. I've heard stories about it that kept me awake, night after night. But I never thought for one moment that I'd ever get to see a *photograph* of it."

"You know what it is?" asked Mrs Keitelman.

"Yes, ma'am, this is Aktunowihio, the Native American god of darkness. And this is the reality of what happened at Little Big Horn. It wasn't Crazy Horse who killed Custer; it was Aktunowihio.

"But look—Aktunowihio normally couldn't leave the Great Outside, the dark place, the place of the dead. He didn't have the strength and he didn't have any way of moving himself about. He was smoke, he was slime, he was everything black. Usually, he swam in darkness, but he couldn't swim around in daylight. So he had to find a way of walking . . ."

"All of those heads," I said. "All of those arms. They're *black.*"

"That's right," nodded Papago Joe, his nostrils flaring in triumph. "*That's* why Doctor Hambone's been involved—*that's* what he did when he was captured by the Santee. He made a bargain. Look! In exchange for his life, in exchange for his freedom, he gave Aktunowihio the use of his zombies, the dismembered bodies of American slaves—alive but dead! Look at it! Shadow and death, joined together! Invincible!"

Mrs Keitelman studied the photograph for a long time. "I

had a feeling that it might be something like that. But, of course, what could I say? Everybody told me the photograph was just a fake. In those days, they used to fake photographs of fairies and dinosaurs and nonsense like that, and people believed them.

"If you happened to have a photograph showing that Custer had been killed by an Indian demon, instead of by Crazy Horse, think of the stir! You'd upset the church, the politicians, the Indians, the whites, the military, the historians, everybody!

"But," she said, and here she produced one more photograph. "He couldn't have been *completely* invincible. Because, look."

She showed us a photograph taken from a different angle, farther down the hill. How Mark Kellogg had managed to struggle down the coulee with all of that luggage and photographic equipment, I shall never know. Judging from the photographs, he had probably been far enough away from the first attack to realize what was happening, and to have run away—escaping both Aktunowihio and Crazy Horse's braves. But he had chosen to stay, and to record what had happened for posterity. It was a particularly bitter touch that, up until now, nearly 120 years later, posterity would choose to believe that Mark Kellogg had given his life for nothing, and that his photographs were no more authentic than pictures of Big Foot, or the Loch Ness Monster, or the Yeti.

But Aktunowihio wasn't any of those. Aktunowihio was the embodiment of darkness and death. Aktunowihio was the shadow that floats in your mind, when you're asleep up and down, up and down, on the black currents of your unconscious—the ultimate predator, swallowing the private darkness on which your sanity subsists—and, in the end, your life, too. And here he was, running across the banks of the Greasy Grass River, in the worst white massacre of the Indian wars.

This last photograph, though, told a different story. On the extreme left, a figure was standing—a thin, raggedy figure in a wide-brimmed leather hat. He was holding out something in his left hand. It was difficult to distinguish what it was, but it appeared to have smoke issuing out of it.

Or maybe not *out* of it, but *into* it.

I pointed him out to Papago Joe. "You see him? I didn't know he was there, at the Little Big Horn. But I'll give you two hot tips at Belmont Park if that isn't William Hood, or Million Protein, or whatever his name was. The Shadow Boy—the vampire-hunter that the US Cavalry employed to fight the Santee Indians. And there—you see, he's holding a shadow-bottle. It looks like he's using it to trap a little bitty piece of Aktunowihio."

Papago Joe nodded soberly. "I've heard of that. All that a shadow-catcher had to do was trap a small piece of shadow, and the main shadow would be hurt so much that it would have to retreat to the Great Outside. Otherwise light would bleed into it and it would die. It couldn't touch the shadow-catcher himself because a shadow can't survive in the real world unless it's complete . . . it would be just like somebody stealing your mouth, say, so that you couldn't eat and you couldn't breathe and you couldn't talk. And if you tried to get it back . . . all the shadow-catcher would have to do is to top up the bottle with sulfuric acid, and dissolve that little piece of shadow for good. Some shadow-catchers used to keep hundreds of shadow-bottles and sell them to people who wanted to raise up shadows against their enemies, or against unfaithful wives, or business partners they wanted to get rid of.

"They said that Billy the Kid was the victim of a shadow that Pat Garrett paid good money for. You know how the story always goes that Billy stepped into a darkened bed-room, and Pat Garrett shot him? Well, think about *why* that bedroom was so dark. And think about *why* Billy's last words were '*Quién es?*'—'Who is it?' "

We thanked Mrs Keitelman and I wished that there was more that we could have given her than thanks. I offered to read her tea-leaves but she didn't believe in fortune-telling. Strange, really, for a widow in Bismarck, North Dakota, who was prepared to believe that a shadow-squid from hell had massacred General George Custer and his men. But then the West is made up of incongruities like that, and full of superstition, and stories of demons and ghosts and soil that whispers.

You stand out there, like Papago Joe and I did, that summer night, after a day spent in magical darkness, and tell me that the West isn't haunted.

That evening we stayed at the Mandan Hotel, southeast of the city, an odd grey clapboard building that stood alone in its own scrubby lot, with the same proportions but less charm than an up-ended steamer trunk. The owner was a grey-haired old lady with a disconcerting habit of suddenly twitching her head to one side when you least expected it. But in a floral-wallpapered dining room, home from home, she served us a good sturdy supper of pork'n'beans, and there was plenty of whiskey to be had, and the convivial company of two travelling salesmen who had flown in that afternoon from Kansas City, Missouri, to interest a client in prefabricated warehousing space.

That night, we had two slim strokes of luck, and for the first time since Karen had arrived at my consulting rooms I began to feel that I knew what I was doing, and why; and that we had a chance of fighting this thing, and maybe— well, maybe not destroying it, who could destroy the god of all darkness?—but maybe driving it back to the Great Outside, and keeping it there.

After Little Big Horn, after all, it looked as if William Hood had managed to beat Aktunowihio back and keep him trapped below ground for more than a century—and anything William Hood could do, I was sure we could do equally well, if not very much better. I mean, we were much more technologically advanced, right? We were much more sophisticated, when it came to science and natural phenomena. And we had just travelled all the way from Phoenix, Arizona, to Bismarck, North Dakota, over a thousand statute miles, with nothing more than human ashes, peyote, a bouquet garni of weird herbs, and a collection of dried-up sticks.

The time had come, however, to use the telephone. More than anything else, I was worried about Amelia. On TV we saw jerky live-action newsreels of the Woolworth Building vanishing into the bedrock, then the GM building and the

Pierre, then the Guggenheim. It was all dust and chaos and flashing helicopter spotlights, and mountains of abandoned cars.

For the first hour of trying I got nothing but a busy tone. I was almost ready to give up, but Papago Joe, swallowing whiskey out of the bottle, said, "Go on, you never know. Give it one more shot." I punched out the number—and almost immediately I heard a crackly voice say, "Yes? Who's that?"

"Amelia? Is that you, Amelia?"

"Harry? You sound like you're calling from the moon!"

"Amelia, what's happening? Are you okay?"

"I'm fine. A little bruised. I wanted to leave the city but there's no way. The roads are all blocked and there's some kind of curfew. Harry—where *are* you? I tried to call Phoenix but all the lines are dead."

"I'm in Bismarck, North Dakota."

"Harry, listen, you know the forks that Samuel Vaizey was trying to tell you about? The Celtic forks? The ones they used to trap evil spirits? Well, I went down to the precinct house and I got them!"

"Oh," I said. "Good."

There was a short pause. Then Amelia almost screamed, " 'Good'? What the hell do you mean '*good*'? I almost got myself killed! The whole precinct building collapsed and I had to jump out of a window!"

"I'm only saying 'good' because I guess that they're important but I don't know what they do."

"You don't know what they *do*? I'm all bruises and cuts and I look like shit and you don't know what they *do*?"

"Listen, Amelia," I told her. "Stay where you are. We're trying to fix up a couple of things and then we're going to come and get you."

"Oh, *fine*. Do you want the forks or should I add them to my dinner service?"

"Amelia . . . please. I'll have to ask Martin."

"Martin is dead, Harry, and you're not sensitive enough to ask him anything."

"Oh, yeah? As a matter of fact, Martin and I have gotten

pretty close, and I don't think I'm going to have any trouble asking him a simple question like that."

There was a very long silence. I heard crackling, and the high-pitched singing of long-distance wires. Then Amelia said, "I'm sorry, Harry. I'm scared, that's all. Buildings are coming down all over. There's no warning at all, they just come down, with everybody inside them, and there's nothing that anybody can do to stop them."

"I think there is," I told her. "And in fact I think we're doing it right now."

Another long silence. Then, "Any sign of Karen?"

"Unh-hunh."

"I still worry about you, Harry."

"Listen—the feeling's mutual. Always will be."

We swapped kisses over the phone. Papago Joe swallowed more whiskey and rolled up his eyes and said, "Gitche Manitou, spare me."

Papago Joe sat crosslegged on the end of the bed. "This is the way I've been thinking," he said. "The last time that Aktunowihio was powerful enough to come out into the real world, that was Little Big Horn, when Doctor Hambone gave him enough black souls to allow him to walk on the real earth.

"Now he's strong enough to be pulling all of these cities down, buildings, people, everything—and he's edging his way out into the real world again, little by little, the way he did with your friend Martin Vaizey. At the same time, we hear that Doctor Hambone's been prowling around. Him or his spirit. So it strikes me that Doctor Hambone has maybe made him a new deal, maybe through Misquamacus, so that black and red can rule this continent together, and finally be rid of the whites."

"But thousands of blacks have died, haven't they, as well as whites? And maybe a few Indians, too?"

"Casualties of war," said Papago Joe, in a matter-of-fact voice. "Think how many whites died, winning the West. That didn't stop you, did it, not for a moment? Besides . . . any black who dies will rise again, as one of Doctor Hambone's zombies."

"I can't believe this," I said. "I really can't."

"Believe it!" Papago Joe snapped at me. "If you don't believe it, then we're finished; and Misquamacus will bring your white civilization down to basement level, where it probably belongs."

"What is this deal, then, that Misquamacus struck with Doctor Hambone?"

"Souls, I guess," said Papago Joe, as if "souls" were no more unusual than "negotiable bonds" or "soybean futures." "That's what Aktunowihio feeds on. Souls are his staple diet. The souls, that is, of anybody and everybody who's died unjustly. The souls who die justly die content; and they go to Heammawihio, the spirit of light, and Heammawihio takes them up to spend the rest of eternity as stars. Peaceful, content, twinkling.

"Probably the first time—back at the Little Big Horn—Doctor Hambone gave Aktunowihio the spirits of dead slaves. But after nearly one hundred and twenty years, I'm sure he has plenty more discontented spirits to offer. Millions more. And that's why Aktunowihio is now so *strong*. I mean he couldn't be nearly as strong as this, not with just Indian souls. But with blacks, think of it! Think of all the blacks who were lynched by the Ku Klux Klan. Think of all the blacks who died through poverty, or hardship, or neglect. The blacks who died on the civil rights marches. All those spirits must be giving Aktunowihio tremendous power—power like you wouldn't believe possible. I'm sure of it: it's the black souls that are helping him to pull down everything you arrogant white bastards built up."

I thought about that, finished my can of beer and crumpled it up in my fist. "Do you think you're *right*?" I asked him. "I mean—you're making my head spin here."

He tapped his forehead with his finger. "I *know* I'm right. Believe me. Papago intuition."

"So what are we going to do?"

"The way I see it: three things. We go for Doctor Hambone, get him out of the way, and set all of his spirits free. That's going to leave Aktunowihio without the physical strength to drag any more buildings down. Then we catch his shadow, which will keep him trapped for as long as we want. Then we finish off Misquamacus, once and for all."

"Oh, yes, and how do we do that?"

He sniffed. "I don't know. I haven't thought about it yet."

"And how do we get Doctor Hambone out of the way?"

"I don't know. I haven't thought about it yet."

"And Aktunowihio? Or haven't you thought about him, either?"

"Oh, sure! I've thought of that. We get Aktunowihio by catching part of his shadow in a shadow-bottle, the same way that William Hood did—you know, the shadow-catcher."

"You said that shadow-catching was a specialized art . . . that hardly anybody knew how to do it."

"That's true. But we can get around that little difficulty. We call on William Hood's spirit."

"Well, that makes some kind of wacky sense, I suppose," I conceded. "How do we go about finding him?"

"The same way we found your old friend Singing Rock and Martin Vaizey, simply by going back to the Great Outside and summoning him. Then we can use the eagle-sticks to travel to New York and face up to Misquamacus and Aktunowihio."

"And Doctor Hambone? What about him?"

Papago Joe gave me a toothy grin. "Time for *my* phone call now. To Sissy LaBelle, in New Orleans, a very old friend of mine. I got to know Sissy through the wise guys. Sissy will know what to do."

Like me, Joe had to punch out the number he wanted twenty or thirty times before he was finally connected. Chicago had collapsed, Las Vegas and Phoenix lay in ruins, and now New York was falling: it was hardly surprising that all of the communications systems all across the United States were jammed solid. If only we could have persuaded the Federal government that Papago Joe and I were probably the only two people who could salvage the rest of the nation—just we two with our death-powders and our eagle-sticks and our mumbo-jumbo chanting—they would have given us hot-line priority. But that's always the way. You don't get any help when you're trying to save the world, and you don't get any thanks if you do it.

Mind you, if *I* had been something big in the government, *I* wouldn't have believed me either. I still find it hard to believe myself now. It was more than a nightmare; more than a dark hallucination; and I guess it always will be.

"Sissy?" said Joe, in the brightest voice that he could manage.

Then, "Oh. I'm trying to get in touch with Sissy."

Then, "Oh. I see. Oh, you're Loni. How're you doing, Loni? It's Papago Joe. Do you remember me? Papago Joe, from Phoenix? That's right, the Indian guy you met with Anthony Funicello. That's right. That's it. How're you doing? Listen . . . if Sissy's not around, I need a favor. Do you happen to know anybody who can do a little jiggery-pokery for me? Know what I mean? I need a mama, that's right."

He hesitated, clamped his hand over the receiver. "Sissy's cousin; quite a girl. She should be able to help us." Then, "Hi, Loni. Yes, good. Well, I'm nearer Chicago than Miami. Okay. That's okay. Well, give me both, in case she's not around any longer. Well, with Chicago you just don't know. For sure. Fine. Good. Thank you."

He wrote down two names and addresses, thanked her again, and then put down the phone.

"Get some sleep," he suggested. "Tomorrow, we're heading for Chicago."

NINETEEN

We arrived at the brown-brick house near Avalon Park at a quarter past two the following afternoon. We had travelled the normal way: by American Airlines, paid for by Papago Joe's gold American Express card. I hadn't been able to face another *krrrakkkk!* through the Great Outside, not so soon after the last experience, and in any case Papago Joe said we were running low on the hallucinatory-death powder. We would need two substantial nose-fulls for our final confron-

tation with Misquamacus and Aktunowihio, and we didn't
want to risk wasting it.

In spite of the devastation in Chicago, there was still a
limited air service flying into Midway, and we managed to
catch a plane that was taking a collection of engineers and
medics into the city. We sat in the back of the plane and
made a point of avoiding any small talk. We didn't like to
tell any of these professional optimists that the damage they
had seen so far was nothing compared with what Misquamacus had in mind.

In a few weeks, even these ruins could have disappeared,
and Chicago would be nothing but sandbars, rocks, and
grassland.

I had noticed something strange as we sat in the back of
the taxi, on our way through Chicago's southern suburbs;
and I pointed it out to Papago Joe. People were walking
around the streets, black people, some families, some cou-
ples, some by themselves. They were finely dressed, most of
them—in fact, *formally* dressed. Men in dark-blue three-
piece suits and shirts and neckties, women in cream and yellow frocks, with plenty of petticoats. Children dressed in
Sunday-meeting suits, with gloves, too. But none of them
wore hats. Not one.

"Looks like everybody's dressed up for church," I remarked.

Papago Joe soberly shook his head.

"Use some of that psychic sensitivity of yours," he suggested. "Those people are *dead.*"

I looked around the streets with rising disquiet. *"Dead?"* I
asked him.

"Sure . . . this is Misquamacus' end of the bargain. Doctor Hambone gave him black souls to help raise up Aktunowihio . . . and in return Misquamacus is raising the
dead . . . just like it was foretold by Tavibo, in his Ghost
Dance doctrine."

On the corner of 82nd Street and Champlain Avenue—
when we had almost reached Avalon Park—I saw a black
family standing staring at nothing at all—grandfather,
grandmother, uncles, aunts, and children, even a little girl of
three or four, with a lemon-yellow party-frock on, and yel-

low gloves to match. Their faces were grey and their eyes were the color of red-hot embers in an ashy fire.

"Zombies," I said, in awe.

Papago Joe nodded. "Technically speaking, yes."

We paid off the taxi driver. Papago Joe said to him, "Careful who you pick up, my friend. Some of your customers may not be all that they seem."

The taxi driver pulled a dismissive face. "I know the difference between dead and alive. And I ain't picking up no dead. Dead ain't got the fare."

I didn't know whether to laugh or not. It sounded like a Steve Martin movie: *Dead Men Don't Take Taxis*.

We climbed the stairs to Mama Jones' apartment. We had to ring the doorbell twice before it was answered by a handsome-looking black woman in a flowery summer dress. She was very well-groomed and smelled of expensive perfume.

"Did you want something?" she asked.

Papago Joe said, "My name's Joe and this is Harry. We're on kind of a mission."

"A mission? What are you? Jehovah's Witnesses? I'm sorry . . . we got plenty of religion of our own right here. Apart from that, I believe in blood transfusions."

"No, no," said Papago Joe. "We're not Jehovah's Witnesses. We're looking for Mama Jones."

The woman looked at us with deep suspicion. "Who sent you?"

"Sissy LaBelle. You know Sissy LaBelle?"

A flicker of the eyelids. "My grandmama knows Sissy La-Belle. I heard her speak of her, once in a while."

"That's Mama Jones, your grandmama?"

"That's right."

"Is she here?"

"I don't know. I'll go see."

Out of his pocket, Papago Joe took the cockerel pendant that Doctor Hambone had given to Wanda. "Show her this," he said.

But there was no need. A thin grey woman in a long grey gown was standing in the living-room doorway, resting on the arm of a pretty young girl with a bow in her hair. The sun caught the lens of the old woman's smeary, magnifying spectacles, and made shining half-moons out of them.

"Sissy LaBelle sent you? You'd better come along in."

As she led us through to the living room, I glimpsed a thin black youth in a leather jacket standing in the kitchen, his hands by his sides. I nodded a greeting to him but he didn't seem to see me. He had sharply razored hair and earrings, and he would have looked pretty smart if his face hadn't been so grey, and his eyes hadn't burned so dull.

The kitchen door was abruptly closed in my face. Mama Jones said, "Hurry along. That's Nat, my great-grand-daughter's intended."

"He looks kind of—" I began, but Papago Joe silenced me with a sharp look.

Mama Jones stared up at me defiantly. "You can say it if you like. He looks kind of dead. The reason for that is, he *was* dead. He was buried in the hi-fi store where he works. He was dead and he was buried but he rose again. Hal-lelujah. Not that I'd have him here, if he wasn't the father of Trixie's baby."

We sat by the fireplace with its creepy assembly of post-cards and paintings and voodoo relics. Mama Jones lit a cig-arette and blew smoke out of her nostrils while Nann and Trixie went into the kitchen to fix us some coffee. It was plain that Nann didn't approve of us coming here one bit, but this was Mama Jones' apartment and Mama Jones wanted to talk about Sissy LaBelle and all the people she had known on St Philip Street back in "the old days"—peo-ple like Chief Bo Rebirth and Evangeline Charmant and Jack Quezergue—which sounded like a useful name to know when you were playing Scrabble.

Eventually, though, Mama Jones sat back and said, "You didn't come here to talk nostalgia, though, did you?"

"No, ma'am," said Papago Joe.

"You're Injun, aren't you?" Mama Jones asked him.

"Yes, ma'am."

"But you ain't?" (Turning to me.)

"No, ma'am, I'm not."

"Thought not. No aura." Mama Jones sucked at her cig-arette, and coughed. Then she said, "I ask myself, what do an Injun and a white man want with a voodoo woman? And I answer myself, it's because of the Ghost Dance, the day of All Shadows, the day of dragging-down, that's why it's because."

"Well, you're right," said Papago Joe.

"We're looking for Doctor Hambone," I put in.

"You mean you're looking for the zombie of Doctor Hambone? Because Doctor Hambone he was a friend of Toussaint L'Ouverture, and he died a long, long time ago."

"Zombie, whatever," shrugged Papago Joe.

Mama Jones eyed us narrowly. She must have realized that we knew quite a lot about the Ghost Dance and Doctor Hambone; and about spirits and spirit manifestations in particular, because you can't usually sit in your living room drinking coffee and start talking about zombies without people raising an eyebrow or two. But neither Joe nor me were raising any eyebrows.

"What do you want Doctor Hambone for?" asked Mama Jones. "He's one magical son-of-a-bitch, I hope you know that."

Papago Joe explained. It wasn't easy—and after all, most of it was guesswork—but Mama Jones was a patient listener, and when Joe had finished she sat and smoked and nodded, and lit another cigarette from the butt of the one before.

"You got it all worked out, pretty well," she said. "Doctor Hambone and Maccus met each other way back centuries ago, and worked out a common destiny for red men and black men. That was on the day we call Soul Day, even now. But then Doctor Hambone got himself involved with the Catholics and the miracles of Christ, and decided he had more of a taste for God's power than he did for the power of Gitche Manitou. He went back on his word. He started to work for the white men, tracking down Indian wonderworkers and scotching their magic.

"That went on till the Injuns caught him and persuaded him to change his mind. Maybe persuaded is too kind a word. Those Santee wonder-workers took him to the edge of space and back, to the very limits of the cosmos, believe me, where things are frothing that you can't even *think* about without going crazy.

"Now, you're right, he's given all the souls that he owns to the Shadow Buffalo, or whatever you want to call it, the Injun god of darkness; and together they're pulling down the white man's world, brick by brick."

"And you're *pleased*?" I asked her.

She turned and looked at me with rheumy, crowlike eyes. "You don't have any idea what black people have suffered over the years. You don't know what Chicago was like, back in the slum days, and it's still no better, if you're poor and you're black. There are black babies being born on Grand Avenue with a crack habit, sir, even now, even today, and if that's the white man's world then we don't want to live in it."

"So what are you going to do?" I asked her. "Are you going to live like the Indians used to live, in tepees? Do you know how *cold* it can get, in a tepee, on the shores of Lake Michigan, in the dead of winter? And how are you going to get around? Are you going to learn to ride palominos? Are you going to catch buffalo for lunch? Can you imagine what it's going to be *like*, for Christ's sake? No hospitals, no sanitation, no schools, no highways, no railroads, no supermarkets? Are you seriously trying to tell me that you want your granddaughter and your great-granddaughter and your great-great-granddaughter to live in the Stone Age?"

"It's revenge," said Mama Jones, fiercely. "They took us from Africa like animals. They crushed our culture; they crushed our pride. But now look! Where are those highways now? Where are those proudful towers? We brung you low."

"Listen, Mama Jones," I said, leaning forward. "History rolls on. You can't go back, ever. Your best hope is to change the way things are, not to destroy them. Do you want Trixie's baby to grow up without medication or dentistry or any hope of travelling the world? I don't know about Nat, but I'm damn sure that Trixie doesn't."

Mama Jones said, "They crushed us. You God-damned white folks. You crushed us." There were tears trickling down her wrinkled cheeks.

Papago Joe said, very gently, "Could we *talk,* do you think, to Doctor Hambone? Can you do that for us? Just *talk.*"

She sniffed, wiped her eyes, and shrugged.

Papago Joe glanced at me. I took hold of Mama Jones' clawlike hand and stroked it. "If we could see him . . . talk to him. It sounds like he was compassionate, you know, as well as fierce. He protected a little white girl we met. Maybe we can work something out. You know—revenge, but not total revenge."

At last Mama Jones nodded. "All right. But just talk, mind. Doctor Hambone has very superior magic, you understand, and if anything go wrong . . . well, I don't know if you know anything about eternal damnation, but Doctor Hambone has it in his power to give it you, c.o.d."

We watched the television news in the kitchen while Mama Jones prepared the living room for our séance with Doctor Hambone. To my relief, Nat had retired to the bedroom. In New York, it looked as if the Upper East Side and the financial district had been totally flattened, and unconfirmed reports said that the Midtown Tunnel had flooded and the Brooklyn Bridge was partially collapsed. I watched it with a growing numbness, like your feet growing cold on a snowy day—a feeling that I didn't realize until very much later was bereavement.

I could understand how the Indians had felt bereaved when they had lost their homelands, their magic, and thousands of their loved ones; and they hadn't even had anybody to tell them why.

Mama Jones beckoned us back to the living room. The drapes were drawn tight, so that the room was in smoky darkness, except for a single candle in a red glass globe.

Mama Jones had spread out a faded red candlewick tablecloth; and on this cloth she had arranged the skeleton of a cockerel, a tiny shrunken skull, and a row of cheaply-painted statues of the saints.

"Remember," she said. "Just talking, nothing else."

She closed the door, and then we all took a seat around the table. We sat still for such a long time that my left foot began to go numb. Mama Jones said nothing, but stayed quite still, except for the faintest trembling of her left hand.

After ten long minutes, she said, "Jonas DuPaul, I humbly beg to speak with you. Can you hear me, Jonas DuPaul?"

Nothing happened. My foot felt as if it had grown to five times its normal size, and now my back was beginning to ache, too. I had never taken part in any kind of voodoo ceremony before, and I didn't know what to expect. If voodoo was going to be as tedious as this, I told myself, I was going to stick to tea-leaves.

But then I saw Papago Joe frowning and jerking his eyes sideways.

"What's the matter?" I mouthed.

He jerked his eyes sideways again, and mouthed something in return. I got the feeling that he wanted me to turn around and look behind me.

I turned around, and I almost had a heart seizure on the spot. Standing right behind me, literally six inches behind me, no more, was a tall spindly black man in a dusty-shouldered tailcoat, with a face like a mask. His eyes gleamed and his teeth were yellow as rats' teeth.

"Jonas DuPaul," said Mama Jones, in a thin, phlegmy voice. "Welcome, Jonas DuPaul."

The black man seemed to glide around the table without even moving his legs. He stood above the red-glass lamp and it made him look even more ghastly, as if he had been drenched in blood.

When he spoke, his voice came not from his mouth, but from a small wooden cupboard in the corner of the room. I was almost tempted to go across and fling it open, to see if there was a hidden loudspeaker in it. But I was afraid there might be something else—something seriously voodoo, like a skull that could talk, or some kind of shrunken monkey.

"I'm a busy man these days, mama," said Doctor Hambone. "Why are you calling on me? Don't you know that it's All Shadows' Day? Can't you see that we're bringing down the towers of greed, the towers of slavery, the towers of oppression, hallelujah."

"Hallelujah," echoed Mama Jones.

Doctor Hambone's head turned as if it were set on thickly-greased ball-bearings. His grin was horrendous, like that of a cannibal. I had faced many weird spirits and manifestations and supernatural creatures; but Doctor Hambone frightened me more than any manifestation had ever frightened me before. This was a dead man who could walk; a dead man who owned the souls of other dead men. This was a spiritual slaver.

"What do you want of me?" asked Doctor Hambone. "You better speak quick. You better speak good. And you better speak truthful."

I said, "We want you to call back the souls you gave to Misquamacus. We want you to reconsider your position."

Doctor Hambone stared at me, and I couldn't help shuddering. He rested his fists on the tablecloth, and as he did so, his knucklebones tore through his skin.

"You want me to reconsider my position? Is this a white joke? Today we are bringing down your great cities, and you want me to reconsider my position? Ha, ha, ha! Ha, ha, ha! Mama Jones, you conjured me here for this white man to ask me this?"

But Papago Joe said, "Mr DuPaul . . . when my friend says he wants you to reconsider your position, he doesn't mean that he wants you to laugh. He means that he *wants* you to reconsider your position, and to call back all of those souls."

"Sir . . ." said Doctor Hambone. "I think you've made a serious mistake here. I think you don't understand who I am."

"Oh, sure I do," said Papago Joe. He reached in his pocket and he took out the cockerel pendant, and let it spin and shine in the lurid red candlelight. "You're Sawtooth, Jonas DuPaul, the great and magical Doctor Hambone."

I was literally grinding my teeth with tension and fright, but Papago Joe seemed to be quite unperturbed. He let the pendant spin around and around, and then he said, "Toussaint L'Ouverture gave you this amulet, didn't he?"

Doctor Hambone couldn't take his eyes off it. He half-lifted one of his half-mummified hands towards it, but Papago Joe drew it away.

"The question is, who gave the amulet to Toussaint L'Ouverture, and why? You know, don't you, Doctor Hambone? It was given to him by a voodoo witch-doctor, so that he would always be protected against zombies and demons and loogaroos. The amulet always passes the qualities of one wearer—whatever they were—on to the next. The witch-doctor was immune from zombies, and so were you. But Toussaint L'Ouverture gave it some of his own qualities, didn't he? And when you started wearing this amulet, that was when you turned your back on your Soul Day bargain with Misquamacus, wasn't it? Because Toussaint L'Ouverture was prepared to fight on the side of progress, and light, and even to accommodate the white men, when it suited him.

"So you gave the amulet to a little white girl, and for the short time that *she* wore it, that little white girl became fearless and magical and wise beyond her years, just like you. But what would happen if I gave it *back* to you?"

Doctor Hambone stared at Papago Joe with his eyes almost bursting out of their sockets. Then he turned to Mama Jones and roared so furiously that the cupboard doors burst open, and swung on their broken hinges. *"You traitor-woman! What did you call me for? You traitor-woman! I am going to fix you for ever in pain! You see!"*

But Papago Joe had already thrown up the amulet. It flew across the room in what seemed like slow-motion, its chain looping like a lasso. Doctor Hambone lifted his head as it circled towards him, and tried to lift his hand to catch it, but it encircled his head and dropped down around his neck.

Doctor Hambone let out a bellow that made the glass chandelier shake. He dragged aside the tablecloth and cockerel bones, and statues and glass beads showered everywhere. The lamp rolled over and dropped onto the floor and set light to the fringes along the bottom of the curtains.

"Harry!" shouted Papago Joe. "The curtains!"

I stamped on them furiously, and then dragged them apart, so that I could open the window. The living-room was flooded with sunlight.

Doctor Hambone stood rigid, his eyes still bulging, his

hands grasping the chain of the amulet, his lips stretched back in a hideous grimace.

In front of my eyes, he began to shrink and collapse. His tailcoat caved in, and then his legs crumpled beneath him. I saw his eyeballs dry up like two prune pits, and drop out of their fleshless sockets. I saw his wristbones tear through his papery skin. His head fell back, and then he dropped onto the floor, with the softest of noises.

From the open cupboard, I thought I heard an echoing, diminishing cry; but then I could have been imagining it.

But there was no question about the cry that we heard next. A thick, roaring scream from the kitchen. A cry of agony and hopelessness and terrible despair. The living-room door was flung open and Nann stood in front of us with her eyes wide.

"It's Nat! Grandmama! It's Nat!"

I followed Papago Joe into the kitchen. Nat lay on the floor, crushed and crumpled, blood foaming from his lips. One leg stuck out from underneath him at an impossible angle, and his whole body trembled and shuddered.

Trixie was kneeling beside him with tears streaking her face.

"What's happening?" she begged, in a shrill, unbalanced voice. "What's happening?"

There was nothing we could do. Nat had been dead already and now that his spirit-master had gone, he was dying for a second time. Crushed by tons of concrete, broken by falling girders.

Nann crossed herself and then pressed her hands together in prayer.

"Isn't there anything we can do for him?" cried Trixie. "He's hurting so much!"

Papago Joe laid a gentle hand on her shoulder. "I'm sorry. He wasn't meant to die. But then he wasn't meant to come alive again, either. These things have a way of coming full circle."

Outside in the streets, we could hear shouting and sobbing and people running. Papago Joe glanced at me and we both knew what had happened. The hatless people had collapsed, too. I crossed to the kitchen window and looked out, and saw an elderly couple lying face down on the sidewalk, while a middle-aged woman knelt beside them in grief. She had buried them once before: now she would have to bury them again.

Hoarsely, Mama Jones cried, "What have you done? What have you *done*?"

Papago Joe said, "Come take a look." He led us back to the living-room and stood over Doctor Hambone's fallen body. "Come on, Harry, take a look."

I went over reluctantly and took a look. To my amazement, Doctor Hambone's dusty tailcoat contained the corpse of a young boy, no more than thirteen or fourteen years old. He was desiccated, his skin was stretched like beige leather over his bones, but I could see that he had once been handsome. I looked up at Papago Joe and said, "What? I don't understand."

"Very simple," said Papago Joe. "Wanda wore that amulet and gave it her youth. Doctor Hambone became a child again. A child who didn't know voodoo; a child who didn't have the strength to keep a dead spirit alive in a dead man's body."

He turned to Mama Jones, who was standing ashen-faced and shaking in the doorway.

"Mama Jones," he said. "There's one more thing you have to do."

"I can't," whispered Mama Jones. *"I can't."*

Papago Joe took hold of her hand. "Yes, you can. You can bless this body here, in accordance with the voodoo ritual. You can do it now. This body owned hundreds and thousands of discontented souls, and you've got to give those souls peace and contentment. Help them to cross back over Jordan, where they should rightly be."

Mama Jones crossed herself. "All right," she agreed. "It's gone so far, it had better be finished. I'll do that thing."

Papago Joe triumphantly squeezed my shoulder. "That's it—that's taken away all of those black spirits that Misquamacus has been counting on. You mark my words, Harry, once Mama Jones has done her stuff, and those spirits have been laid to rest, Aktunowihio won't have the strength to pull down an outhouse, let alone a skyscraper."

"You're a bright guy, Joe," I told him. "I never would have thought of that amulet stunt, not in a hundred years."

He looked away, and gave my shoulder one last squeeze. "You want to know the truth? I didn't think for one split second that it would actually work."

"You're kidding me. I thought you had it all planned out. What were you going to do if it *didn't* work?"

He shrugged. "I don't know. Kick him in the nuts?"

TWENTY

E.C. Dude arrived at Midway Airport at seven o'clock that evening, wearing jeans with elaborately-ripped knees and cowboy-boots and a Grateful Dead T-shirt and carrying a large canvas shoulderbag studded with Mr Smiley faces and Nixon for President buttons. He looked tired and unshaven and his face was waxy. More like Jim Morrison than ever.

We greeted him and relieved him of his bag and took him out to our waiting taxi.

"How're things in Phoenix?" I asked him.

"Oh, quietened down now. The wind's died down, anyway, and the houses have stopped sliding. But the place is a mess. You wouldn't even recognize it. Shit."

"Chicago's not much better. Most of the downtown area has been wasted."

E.C. Dude leaned forward in his seat and said to Papago Joe, "You practically scared the shit out of me, you know that?"

"What do you mean?" asked Papago Joe.

"Well, sending those guys to collect me. I couldn't believe it when this big black limo turned up outside the trailer. These two Apache guys got out, with headbands and sunglasses and Armani suits, right, they're built like adobe shit-houses, right? They told me they were taking me off for a ride. I thought I was dead, man, I mean it. I thought they were going to take me out to the desert and put a bullet through my ear."

"Sorry," said Papago Joe. "But the phones were out, and the best I could do was to call Jim Grey Wolf in his car. How was your flight?"

"Little bumpy. But those LearJets, they're something, aren't they? I wish I had one."

"Jim Grey Wolf has two," Papago Joe explained to me.

"Useful friend at a time like this," I remarked.

Papago Joe systematically cracked his knuckles. "He owes me sort of a favor."

I looked at E.C. Dude but E.C. Dude pulled a face that meant, "Don't ask me, man." I was beginning to think that there was more to Papago Joe than met the eye. But then, isn't there always more to everybody than meets the eye?

We had booked a room at the Four Lakes Lodge a mile west of Downer's Grove. "What a downer, man," E.C. Dude remarked. But it was quiet and it was anonymous, just one of those tedious Chicago suburbs, with nothing to distinguish it but a shopping mall and acres of concrete parking lots and orange sodium lights that stained the sky the color of Fanta. At least the Indians, out on the Plains, had seen the stars.

We ate dinner in our room, steaks and fries. E.C. Dude ordered a salad because he had decided (yesterday) to become spiritual, and at one with nature, which meant that his digestive system had to commune with lettuce leaves and Belgian endive and nothing else. I told him that the President was a Belgian endive enthusiast but that still didn't deter him. "Vegetables aren't political, right? Did you ever see a fascist carrot?"

Papago Joe explained to E.C. Dude what we intended to do. E.C. Dude munched lettuce and green peppers and alfalfa and nodded. "Okay, that's extra. That's cool. I'll do anything, man, believe me."

All the time we kept the television switched on, in case there was any more news of what was happening in New York. From the time that we had visited Mama Jones' apartment, no more major buildings had gone down, although the city was still jammed with smashed-up automobiles and mountains of loose debris, and the toll of dead and missing was running into tens of thousands.

I tried calling Amelia but for most of the evening the lines were busy, and when I did get what sounded like a ringing tone, nobody answered.

Papago Joe said, "We may have taken out the black souls that gave Aktunowihio his extra strength, but don't let's forget that he's still a formidable spirit to deal with. I mean seriously powerful, the god of darkness. And don't let's forget that Misquamacus means business, too. He's cruel and he's wily and he'll do anything to stop us. Absolutely anything."

"Sounds cool to me," said E.C. Dude. "When do we leave?"

We slept for two-and-a-half hours; and then, at seven minutes past three Central Time, we dressed and sat around the table, while Papago Joe carefully divided out our remaining death-powder.

"I just hope the heat don't decide to rush in," said E.C. Dude. "I'd hate to be busted for sniffing up somebody's sacred remains."

Papago Joe sniffed first, then E.C. Dude, then me. Then we all sat back and looked at each other.

"Hey man, this is a downer," said E.C. Dude. "No wonder they call it Downer's Grove. I'm not even *high*."

But in the next instant, he turned and stared at me wide-eyed and yelped, "It's all gone dark, man! Who switched off the fucking light?"

Papago Joe reached out and took hold of his wrist. "It's all right, E.C. No need to panic. We're all experiencing the same experience. We're dead."

"I don't want to be dead!" E.C. Dude shouted, jumping to his feet. "Fuck this, man! I don't want to be dead! I changed my mind!"

I grabbed hold of his sleeve and pulled him down again. "For Christ's sake, you're not really dead! Your brain is hallucinating that you're dead, that's all. If it didn't do that, you wouldn't be able to get through to the Great Outside, would you? Living people don't get to Heaven, no matter how much they may want to go there."

E.C. Dude petulantly tugged his sleeve away. "All right, I'm not dead. All right. That's extra. Let's forget it."

Led by Papago Joe, we walked Indian-file out of the Four Lakes Lodge, and across the parking-lot to a scrubby building-site. The concrete foundations had been poured, but it looked like the developer had run out of money. The rest was wild grass and rusting concrete mixers and reinforcing rods and broken fencing. The night wind whistled mournfully through the chicken-wire.

Papago Joe said, "The reason I chose the Four Lakes Lodge was because of this site."

"Well, it's cool," said E.C. Dude. "But, you know, I wouldn't spend the summer here or nothing."

There was a dark drainage trench dug into the soil; and we climbed down into it, glowing as dark as the dead men we were; and broke through the crust of the soil with a rusty-bladed shovel. Below the soil was darkness, and emptiness—an emptiness that fell as far as infinity.

E.C. Dude peered down into it, and then looked at Papago Joe, and then at me. "No fucking way, man. That's *eternity.*"

Calmly, Papago Joe said, "Harry and I have been there. Harry and I have both come back. You can do the same."

I slapped his arm. "Come on, E.C. You can do it."

"I can't do it, man!" screamed E.C.

For the first time since he had opened that trailer door and blinked at me sleepy-eyed, E.C. Dude annoyed me. I took hold of his shoulders and pressed my nose flat against his nose so that our eyes were so close that we couldn't even focus on each other.

"You're going to do it, okay?" I breathed into his face. "You don't have any fucking choice."

E.C. Dude took a deep, quivering breath, and then he said, "Okay . . . okay. I just freaked out is all. I'm okay now. No problem. Everything's extra, okay?"

Papago Joe went first, climbing/slipping/falling into the blackness. E.C. Dude went next, clutching onto my hand as he did so, and I heard him scream out, "Oh, *shhiiiitttttt!*"

Then I followed, dropping into darkness, dropping into death. There was something familiar about it now; something soft and warm and welcoming, like dropping into bed. Maybe death welcomed you, when you were older. Maybe death knew that you would soon be joining it, ashes to ashes, darkness to darkness.

We found ourselves on a dark windblown prairie, under the stars. Lake Michigan was too far away for us to see, but we could feel the breeze blowing off it. Papago Joe said, "Come on, now, let's gather together. Let's call up those spirit guides. Let's get this Ghost Dance finished, once and for all."

He took out his sticks and tapped in rhythm. E.C. Dude watched him in fascination. "That's a cool rhythm, man. That really is. We could make a demo of that, you know, with some kind of rap. You know, the Death Rap or something."

I gave a cold-rivet stare, so he shrugged, and sniffed, and said, "I'm sorry, okay? I wasn't trying to be tasteless or nothing."

Papago Joe said, "I'm calling on spirit guides . . . spirits to help us . . . I'm calling on Singing Rock and Martin Vaizey and one more spirit. I'm calling on William Hood, the shadow-catcher."

We sat in that windy prairie, listening to the grass rustling, and then we saw two flickers of light. They were small and flickering and dim, way off across the prairie. But they were Singing Rock, no doubt about it; and Martin. Soon they were flickering lights no longer, but shining spirits, beautiful shining spirits, and they walked towards us through the grass, and we embraced.

And—as we embraced—they vanished inside us.

Possessed us.

E.C. Dude stared at Papago Joe and then he stared at me. "Pardon me for being nosy," he said. "But those guys . . ." He paused, and looked around, baffled. "Where did those guys go?"

"They're still here," said Papago Joe. "They're right inside of us."

E.C. Dude peered into my eyes. "I don't see nothing."

"I know," I told him. "But I feel something."

He shook his head. "That's extra, you know? That's something extra."

I felt Martin inside of me, sharing my brain cells, sharing

my consciousness. I closed my eyes and said, "Welcome."
The warmth of his personality flooded my arteries and ran
through my veins, and together we were one.

"Listen," I asked him. "What about the forks? What do
the forks do?"

"What does it matter? The forks are lost."

"But they're not lost. I talked to Amelia. She went to the
precinct house and rescued them. She has them now."

*"She has them now? She really has them now? Then you can
catch Misquamacus for good."*

"How, for Christ's sake? I couldn't kill Misquamacus
with a sawed-off shotgun. How am I going to get rid of him
with two forks?"

*"They're very simple . . . very logical. Celts made them,
back in Wales, centuries and centuries ago."*

"Yes, great, but how do I use them?"

*"Like dowsing rods, like lightning conductors. The Celts
learned how to make them from the Egyptians. You see—
when the Egyptian seafarers first discovered the New World
there were demons and spirits walking the land everywhere. If
they wanted to land, if they wanted to explore, they had to
protect themselves."*

"There were demons and spirits just strolling about? Is
that what you're saying?"

*"Of course. They were able to walk about openly above
ground because the land was innocent and the Native Americans believed in them, and gave them food and milk and buffalo blood. Columbus saw some of them . . . men without
heads, and wild dogs who walked on their hind legs. In those
days, even Aktunowihio walked above ground, in the shadow
of buffalo and discontented men."*

"But how can we use these forks?" I pressed him.

*"I told you. It's simple. Every spirit has an electrical
charge—that's all a spirit is, really. If you hold the fork handles toward it, it will jump into them. Then all you have to do
is to cover the handles with rubber or any insulating material,
and the spirit will be faced with only one way out—through
the tines of the forks, all six of them. It will have to split itself
up into a magical number—six—and it will need to find two*

more spirits similarly split before it can make itself whole again."

"Three spirits, split into six?" I asked him. "That's six, six, six."

"*Exactly. The number of the beast. Always has been, always will be. It goes back much, much farther than the Bible.*"

Papago Joe had been sorting through his eagle-sticks. "We're ready to move," he said, impatiently.

"So where's this Hood character?" asked E.C. Dude.

"I don't know," said Papago Joe. "If he doesn't come now, we'll have to leave without him."

"Hey . . . too dangerous, man," said E.C. Dude.

"I wouldn't worry about it," Papago Joe retorted. "You wouldn't have to come with us. You couldn't, without a spirit-guide."

"Pardon me for being relieved," said E.C. Dude.

We waited and waited, under that ink-black sky, on that ink-black prairie, in the land of the dead. The wind smelled of mesquite and other smells that modern America would never know. At least, I *hoped* they would never know them. I suggested to Papago Joe that he should call William Hood yet again, but Papago Joe said no; and inside of my mind Martin Vaizey agreed with him. A spirit can only be called for once; and if he or she doesn't choose to answer—well, that's another of those prerogatives of being dead.

I had almost given up hope when we saw a dim greenish flame on the horizon. A thin greenish flame that danced gradually nearer, and waxed slowly brighter, until it resolved itself into a figure—a thin youth in a wide-brimmed hat who was striding toward us in a big hurry. A youth in ragged leather, with bottles and flasks hung around his waist. He came right up to us and stopped, and looked boldly from one to the other. He was needle-nosed and sharp-eyed and his chin was prickly with blond stubble. A ratcatcher's face.

"Are you William Hood?" I asked him.

"*What if I am?*"

"You're a shadow-catcher, right? We need to catch a shadow."

"*What shadow?*"

"The biggest shadow that ever was. Aktunowihio."

"I could catch Aktunowihio. I caught him before."

"I know. You caught him at Little Big Horn."

William Hood stared at me chillingly. *"How did you know that?"*

"I saw the photographs that Mark Kellogg made."

The chilling stare slowly melted. The thinnest of smiles. *"Well, then, you're a believer. That's good to know."*

"Do you know what's happening now?" I asked him. "Aktunowihio has pulled down half of New York; half of Chicago; as well as Phoenix, and Las Vegas, and scores of small communities."

"The dead can hardly fail to notice more dead, my friend. Apart from all those buildings, and all of that junk. I never saw such junk."

"Will you help us?" I asked him. "You can take over E.C. Dude here, he's about the same age as you. He can show you what it's like to be living again. That's if you can show him how to catch a shadow."

William Hood thought, and then he nodded. *"All right . . . I don't mind. Eternity's a long time, don't you know? Anything helps to break the monotony."*

Papago Joe lifted his eagle-stick. "Here," he said. "Grasp it. Let's go."

Both E.C. Dude and William Hood stepped forward to grasp it, and as they did so, their outlines merged. Light rippling through light, shadow rippling through shadow. E.C. Dude looked left, and then right, and then turned around and looked behind him. But then he clapped his hand against his chest and said, "Shit, Harry! He's *inside* me! He's me!"

"Yes," I said. "He's you."

Clinging to the eagle-stick, along with Papago Joe and E.C. Dude and all of those spirits who possessed us, I heard a small compressed *kkkkrakkkkkkkk!* and then we were there, back in New York, standing on a rocky brownstone outcropping. All around us, in the darkness of the Great Outside, there were nothing but rocks and trees and scrubby bushes. But the dimmest of lights was shining up through the grass. This was the gateway through which Misqua-

macus had first snatched Karen. This was Room 212 at the
Belford Hotel, right beneath our feet. It was the only gateway back to the real world that I knew of, that I could find
for certain. We stood around it for a while, looking down.
We could see the springs beneath a divan bed, and part of
the ceiling. Then one by one we climbed down into it, and
gravity reversed itself, and we found ourselves standing in
the room where George Hope and Andrew Danetree had
died for the sin of being ancestors.

This time, we didn't leave our spirit-guides behind. They
came with us, deep inside our souls, Singing Rock and Martin Vaizey and William Hood the shadow-catcher.

We carefully opened the door, and looked around.

"Everything's cool," said E.C. Dude. "Not a deek in
sight."

"Hey, wait a minute," I asked him. "If you're going to go
shadow-catching, what about a shadow-bottle?"

"God-dammit," said Papago Joe. "I hadn't thought of
that. Didn't you tell me that Dr Snow had one?"

E.C. Dude frowned for a moment, as if he were concentrating on something inside of himself. Then he said, "It's
okay . . . William says it's okay. We don't need a special
bottle, any bottle will do. That bottle he brought from
Serbia. It's a vinegar bottle he stole from a restaurant."

I looked at Papago Joe in exasperation. "Jesus . . . the
great magic shadow-bottle, and what does it turn out to
be?"

But Papago Joe was busy with his eagle-sticks. "I can
sense movement . . . enormous movement . . . Something's
happening here in New York . . . something bad."

"But you finished off Doctor Hambone . . . you pulled the
plug on Aktunowihio . . . what's happening?"

Papago Joe lifted his head, and listened. I could hear sirens, and helicopters flackering overhead, and the slow,
chunky sound of falling masonry. But I heard something
else, too. A deep-chested rumble; a low seismic reverbera-
tion through the brown Manhattan bedrock. And then
lightning cracking; and glass breaking; and people screaming.

"The last stand," said Papago Joe.

"The last stand? What do you mean?"

"The last stand—just like Custer's Last Stand. And he's going to bring down everything he can!"

"Listen," I said. "Let me call Amelia . . . we need those forks right now."

I don't know what made me think of that. Well, yes I do. It was Martin, inside of my mind, telling me what to do.

We hurried down the stairs, and I vaulted the hotel desk and found the phone. While Papago Joe and E.C. Dude waited impatiently, I punched out Amelia's number. After ten attempts, I finally got through.

"Just give me one second!" I told Papago Joe.

We pushed open the doors and clattered down into the street. The destruction was much, much worse than I could have imagined. It had recently been raining, and the streets were heaped with wet rubble and wrecked automobiles and hotdog stands and stalls and rubbish and overturned trucks. We had to climb over a mountain of bricks to reach Madison Square, and the square itself looked like Berlin, after World War Two. Strewn with masonry, strewn with twisted ironwork, strewn with hideously broken and torn-apart bodies.

There were no vehicles anywhere around, apart from a firetruck which screamed uptown on Madison, its red lights flashing. But the ground continued to rumble and shake, and chunks of stonework dropped from buildings all around us, and shattered in the roadway, and so many windows fell that their jingling sounded like Christmas.

By the time we reached 29th Street and Fifth Avenue, we were gasping and sweaty and exhausted. But the quaking in the ground was so severe now that we knew we must be reaching the epicenter. The asphalt cracked open and thunderous showers of abandoned automobiles dropped into the subways, and the sewers, followed by dusty avalanches of bricks.

Fifth Avenue was deep in darkness, apart from the nervous twitching of lightning, over to the west. The three of us walked along the sidewalk side by side, like three gunslingers in *High Noon*.

"He's here," said Papago Joe, packing away his eagle-sticks at last. "I thought he'd be here."

As we approached the grey, megalithic spire of the Empire State Building, we saw him standing on the sidewalk. Standing two or three inches *above* the sidewalk, hovering in supernatural rage. It was Misquamacus, the greatest of all the Indian wonder-workers, his arms folded, his eyes glistening with fury, his headdress swarming with grave-beetles. The sidewalk literally shook beneath his feet, and we could hear windows cracking all the way up the building.

We approached him, and stood in front of him, and the three of us were not afraid, I can say that for certain, because we had died and come to life again; and our friends had died, and we had met them again. In fact, we had brought them with us, inside us, as witnesses to this final confrontation.

We knew now what Misquamacus had always known—that death is never the end, but just a different way of living. He had always drawn his power from our fear of him, and from our fear of being killed. But tonight was different.

He stared at us, and said, "You deceived the black man, didn't you?"

"That's right," said Papago Joe. "We deceived the black man."

Misquamacus shook his head, and bugs rained from his headdress onto the concrete. "You . . . Joseph . . . and you who hides inside Joseph . . . Singing Rock . . . I know you for what you are . . . rats and cowards and running-dogs, white men's pets."

"No," said Papago Joe. "We're nobody's rats, and nobody's cowards, and nobody's pets. Tomorrow belongs to us, you'll see . . . the way it once belonged to you. But tearing down all of these cities and slaughtering all of these people . . . that isn't the way to do it. The old days are gone, Misquamacus. Nobody wants to live that way anymore. You should let it stay what it always was . . . just one moment, do you understand me? Just one quick moment in the hand of time."

"I saw the buffalo running," said Misquamacus, with a sweep of his hand. His arm remained outstretched; his eyes focused on something long ago and far away, and that was the only time that I ever felt sorry for him.

Papago Joe approached him, one cautious step at a time. "It's all over, Misquamacus. It's finished. The Great Outside is waiting for you. Dark, and peaceful, and running with buffalo."

He stepped nearer and nearer, one hand lifted.

"It's finished, Misquamacus. Can't you see? The days of magic are gone for good."

It was a plea for forgetfulness, even if it wasn't a plea for forgiveness. The buffalo were dead; the tepees had all been struck; the lodge-fires had long since burned down to ashes.

For one tense, stretched-out moment, I nearly believed that Misquamacus was going to surrender. But then he stretched his mouth wide, and let out a deafening roar, and as he did so the sidewalk suddenly split open, right beneath our feet. Huge lumps of concrete were thrown up into the air, and thundered all around us. Utility pipes and electricity cables were ripped out of the soil and flung haywire, as if Manhattan had been gutted.

Papago Joe fell back, and was buried up to his waist in sand and shattered concrete. As more sand sifted down, he lifted up his hand to shield his face.

"Joe!" I shouted, and ran toward him. But he turned and screamed at me, *"No, Harry! Save yourself! Look!"*

With a deafening rumble, a dark shape rose out of the hole that had been blown in the sidewalk. First, a waving tentacle of black smoke, then another. Then something heaved itself out of the sidewalk, something huge and black *ye Bigness of many Ground-Hogs.*

"Oh, shit," said E.C. Dude, and dropped to his raggedy knees.

The black shape grew larger and larger, until it seemed to blot out even the night. It was difficult to see what it was really like, but I could make out glistening tentacles that coiled around and around like snakes, and paler parts that could have been faces. It smelled of cremation fires, and blood, and the nauseating sweetness of death.

Finally, out of the hole, I saw hands grasping at the sidewalk, disembodied hands. The whole hideous creature,

smoke and tentacles and all, was supported by a maimed
and creeping mat of human beings. They jerked and
moaned and shuddered as they tried to heave the creature
into the living world, so that its grisly serpentine bulk
swayed unevenly from side to side, like an emperor being
carried in a palanquin by lepers.

Many of the humans were already dead: summoned back
to heaven or hell by the demise of Doctor Hambone. Their
arms dragged brokenly on the street, and their intestines
hung in putrefying loops, so that Aktunowihio left behind
him a grisly glistening trail of rotting flesh and reeking
fluids.

God knows how powerful he would have been, if all of
Doctor Hambone's souls had still been able to support him.
There must have been thousands of arms and legs under-
neath him; thousands of vengeful souls.

"E.C.!" I yelled. "For God's sake! The shadow-bottle!"

E.C. frantically looked around. "There's no bottles,
Harry! There's no bottles!"

Papago Joe shouted in terror. Then he started screaming.

I saw plenty of smashed bottles, littered across Fifth Avenue. But then the lightning flickered again, and I glimpsed a
ketchup bottle, standing on the table of a hamburger bar
opposite us.

"There!" I shouted.

E.C. Dude loped across the street. The hamburger bar
was locked. I heard him rattling the door handles.

"Oh, fuck this," I heard him say; and he picked up a massive chunk of concrete, and hurled it through the plate-glass
window. He came loping back, furiously shaking ketchup
out of the bottle as he ran.

But for Papago Joe it was too late. Misquamacus wanted
Papago Joe, the same way that he had wanted Singing
Rock. They were traitors, as far as Misquamacus was concerned, betraying the Red man, betraying his gods, betraying his heritage. Misquamacus shrieked out *"Nepauz-had!
Nepauz-had!"* and a spindly black twitching claw came out
of the smoke and dug its nails into Papago Joe's face.

"No!" I shouted. I turned in desperation to E.C. Dude,
but E.C. Dude was still wildly shaking out ketchup.

With sickening elegance, the claw probed into Papago Joe's nostrils. I saw the black chitinous skin disappearing into his nose. I saw his eyes go bright with pain and panic.

There was a frantically optimistic moment when I thought I might have saved him. But then the claw dragged itself upward, and the whole of his face was ripped off, with a sound like tearing linen, and Papago Joe was screaming out of a bloody eyeless skull.

The claw dropped Papago Joe's face like a bloody latex mask, and then relentlessly came back again, and probed down into his screaming mouth. I saw yard after jointed yard of insect-like claw disappearing down Papago Joe's throat, and it was then that I turned around and sicked up bile and drink and badly-chewed breakfast.

But now E.C. Dude dodged around me, and he was holding up the empty ketchup bottle. He was shouting out something, but I couldn't understand what it was. He shouted again and again. *"U'lwau! U'lwau! Almaui! Almena!"*

The black cloud shuddered a little, and boiled, and beneath it, I saw the twisted mass of human limbs rippling like centipedes' legs.

In a last vicious gesture, it dragged its claw out of Papago Joe's throat, bringing out bulging lungs and bloodied heart and softly-collapsing stomach and everything else, heaps of intestines, liver and pancreas and kidneys, all slithering onto the sand and grit, and pulsing with Papago Joe's last few seconds of life.

But E.C. Dude continued to stalk it without any apparent fear, waving that ketchup bottle at it and shouting, *"Almaui! Almaui!"*

"E.C.!" I shouted. "For God's sake be careful!"

He ducked and weaved nearer; but as he did so, three or four of those shadowy tentacles snaked swiftly towards him, and poured around his ankles. He tried to kick himself free, but one of them twined itself around his left leg, and slid up into his open shirt.

"Almaui!" he cried out. *"Almaui!"*

"E.C.!" I screamed at him. I remembered what happened to old man Rheiner, back at the Belford Hotel, and I was cold with panic. "Get yourself out of there! E.C.!"

E.C. was still trying to catch some of Aktunowihio's smoky substance in his bottle, but now another tentacle had wound around him and was dragging the shirt from his back. He struggled and thrashed, but I saw blood spraying from his fingertips, and I could see that the tentacles were tearing at his skin.

I looked around, frantically trying to find some kind of weapon. I saw a scaffolding pole, but it was partly wedged under a wrecked automobile, and I couldn't lift it.

It was then, however, that I saw a pale flickering above Papago Joe's grisly ripped-apart body. I stared at it more intently, and I realized that it was the faint faltering outline of Singing Rock.

A voice inside of my head—Martin Vaizey's voice—said, *"Sun-powder . . . he's telling you to use the sun-powder. Aktunowihio is a thing of shadow . . . he hates the light."*

Lying scattered on the sidewalk next to Papago Joe's bloody hand were all of his eagle-sticks and death-powders and flasks and bones. I turned back to E.C. Dude and he was struggling and yelling, almost completely entangled in shadow-tentacles.

"Get the fuck off me, you God-damned octopus! *Almaui! Almaui!*"

I scrabbled around until I found the small rawhide pouch filled with "sun-powder." I wrenched open the hempen string that was tied around its neck. Inside was a handful of blueish-looking salt, and that was all.

I turned back to the flickering outline of Singing Rock. "What do I do with it?" I asked, in panic.

"Throw . . ." I thought I heard him whisper, but I couldn't have been sure. All the same, I rushed up to E.C. Dude and threw the powder at the darkest part of Aktunowihio's boiling body.

Instantly, there was a spitting, crackling sound, and I was totally dazzled by a brilliant white light.

It formed an incandescent, totem-like shape, but it was so bright that it was impossible to look at it directly. It kept on popping and spitting, like a Fourth of July firework crammed with magnesium, and with every second it burned it seemed to flare brighter.

Aktunowihio made a noise that was unlike anything I had ever heard before—or ever want to hear again. It was an insectlike screeching, as if it had been torn out of a throat that was lined with bristly black hairs. The shadowy tentacles recoiled from the light, and slithered away, running back down E.C. Dude's legs and retreating from his feet.

As they did so, I saw murky flashes of light within Aktunowihio's bulk. I saw things that looked like red, glowering eyes; and I saw something that looked like a humped, grotesque buffalo. For a moment, as the sun-powder flared its last flare, I saw the Shadow Buffalo more clearly; and I don't want to say what it looked like, because I don't want to remember what it looked like. It was everything that hides in every shadow. It was everything that makes the night terrifying.

Misquamacus had frightened me many times; but he had never shaken me right down to the roots of my sanity, the way that the Shadow Buffalo did.

It was black and it writhed and the only way that you could look at it was through the chinks of your fingers, so that only your eyes looked out.

E.C. Dude circled and backed away. But then he saw one shrinking tentacle, close to his feet, and he stamped on it with his boot-heel, and caught it. He ducked right down with his ketchup bottle, and prodded the tip of the tentacle until it coiled itself around the neck of the bottle, and then probed inside.

"E.C.!" I shouted. "For Christ's sake! That thing's lethal!"

"Piece of cake, man," E.C. called back. He held the tip of his tongue clenched between his teeth, until the shadow had almost filled up the bottle. Then, without hesitation, he capped it, and screwed it tight.

"Extra-a-a-a cool!" he whooped, in triumph. "Extra-a-a-a-a cool!" And he threw up the bottle and caught it again, and did a wild fandango on the sidewalk.

Misquamacus rose out of the gloom, his face distorted with anger. "What have you done? What have you done? What have you done? Your blood will be spread across the sky, from Pole to Pole."

But Aktunowihio, the shadow god, the terrible one, was thrashing and writhing in confusion. Unless he was whole, he was unable to survive in the world of light, the world of the living; and now he was squirming in agony, like a slug dropped onto a hotplate.

He coiled his tentacles and thundered and screamed; but he was like a deepsea diver whose pressure suit has been pierced. His darkness was shrinking; his blackness imploded. In a sudden welter of shadow and tentacles and clawing human limbs, he poured into the sidewalk and disappeared, leaving behind him a shower of dust and a rockslide of concrete rubble.

E.C. Dude stepped back to join me, still holding up the shadow-bottle. "Did you see it?" he crowed. "Did you see it?"

"How did you *do* that?" I asked him.

"It's like tickling a trout, man. That's all. You lift up the bottle and you say the words and the words mean, "There's all eternity, in here," and the stupid God-damned shadow-thing can't resist checking it out, just to make sure that all eternity *isn't* in there. Gets 'em every time, that's what William Hood tells me. Nice guy, but foreign."

He looked at me, grinning. But then, just beyond me, he saw the bloody remains of Papago Joe, and his grin gradually dissolved.

"I'm going to grieve later—in private—okay?" E.C. Dude challenged me.

I raised my eyes toward Misquamacus. The wonder-worker remained hovering over the sidewalk, his expression so dark that I thought that he was in danger of exploding.

"You think that you have defeated me again," he told me, his voice tearingly harsh. "You think that you have seen the end of me. But I will take your heart with me, in my hand, my friend. I will take your heart and I will bury it deep, in the darkest corner of the Great Outside."

He slowly sank down towards me, his robes softly rumbling in the wind. His face was like a primitive mask. The god of human sacrifice. The god of pain. I stepped back two or three paces, but he continued to float after me, his feet almost scraping the roadway but not quite.

E.C. Dude tried to make a snatch for his sleeve, Misquamacus swung his arm out without even looking and knocked him flat onto a heap of rubble. E.C. Dude came back again, winded, but Misquamacus swung at him again, and he was hurtled into the side of a wrecked Pontiac, hitting his head. He tried to claw himself up, but sagged, and coughed, and dropped to his knees.

Now Misquamacus reached out and pulled at my shirt, catching me. He circled his hands around my throat like a necklace made of hardened horsehair, and pressed my Adam's apple until I gagged. His breath thundered into my face. His breath that reeked of death and decay; of bodies buried on stilts; and of days that would never come back.

"You," he said. "You are all that is worst in the white man."

I couldn't speak. My throat was too tightly constricted.

"You are death," he said.

There are one or two moments in everybody's life when they're convinced that they're just about to die. For me, this was it. My whole life didn't flash before me. All I could think of was: I can't breathe, for Christ's sake.

Misquamacus pressed my throat harder and harder. He could easily have broken it, one twist, just like that. But he wanted to enjoy me dying; and after all the problems I'd given him, I don't suppose I could blame him.

But just as I was beginning to see scarlet flashes in front of my eyes, I felt a gentle hand take hold of my right hand, and another gentle hand take hold of my left hand, and I felt two cold metal objects pressed firmly into my palms.

Amelia. She'd come, and she'd found me.

Amelia. She'd brought me the forks.

Indistinctly, I heard Misquamacus saying, "Before you die, I'm going to pull your heart out, little brother, so that you can see it for yourself."

I couldn't think of anything smart to say. I couldn't speak.

But I stretched both arms out wide, and bunched up my muscles, and then I rammed both fork handles deep into Misquamacus' sides.

For nearly ten seconds, I thought it hadn't worked. He

stared at me and I stared at him. But then suddenly he began to convulse, and sparks began to crackle around his face, and static-fried insects started to drop from his headdress. Blue electricity jumped and twitched out of his body, and into the forks, until the forks were smoking with built-up charge.

He opened his mouth and let out a scream that they must have heard in hell.

Gradually, Misquamacus disassembled himself in front of my eyes. Face, hands, body, arms, like a speeded-up movie of a jigsaw puzzle, in reverse. In front of me, instead, stood Karen. She was white, and wide-eyed, and almost mad with shock; but then who wouldn't be, if an ancient Indian wonder-worker had possessed them?

I took two paces back, holding up the forks. My wrist-tendons were twitching with shock, and I didn't know how much longer I could hold them.

"It's all right," said Martin Vaizey, inside of my head. *"All you have to do is put them down. He can't escape now. You've trapped him forever."*

Gingerly, I laid both forks on the sidewalk, and stood watching them as they crackled and smoked. Karen came up to me and clung on tight, and then Amelia came up, too, with E.C. Dude limping beside her.

"Amelia," I said, swaying with exhaustion, my throat still sore.

"Harry," she replied.

"I owe you, Amelia. I owe you forever."

Amelia shook her head. "I don't want anything from you, Harry. I never really did."

"What are you going to do now?" I asked her.

She smiled wanly. "I'm going to take this friend of yours home, and bathe his wounds. What are you going to do?"

"I don't know. Stand and think."

At that moment, however, E.C. Dude said, *"Look!"*

I didn't know what he meant at first. But then he said again, *"Look,"* and I turned around.

Over Papago Joe's torn-apart body stood Singing Rock. His image was pale and unsteady, but I could see that he had one hand lifted in triumph; or maybe it was simply fare-well.

Behind him, though, arranged in grey and orderly ranks, stood scores of young men. They wore faded uniforms and gloves and boots. Their faces were as white as history.

While we stood and watched, they recited their names. A roll-call of honor; a roll-call of names that had at last been avenged, and laid to rest. Their voices were scarcely audible above the fluffing of the wind and the crackling of burning buildings, but I knew who they were. The five companies of the 7th Cavalry who had been killed at the Little Big Horn by Aktunowihio, and by Misquamacus who had raised him.

We stood and watched and I'm not ashamed to say that I had tears in my eyes.

"Corporal Henry Dallans . . . Corporal A.G.K. King . . . Lieutenant-Colonel W.W. Cook . . . Blacksmith P. Manning . . . Acting Assistant Surgeon J.M. DeWolf . . . Private F. Gardiner . . . Private F. Hammon . . . Private F. Kline . . . Arthur Reed, civilian . . . Chas. Reynolds, civilian . . . Mark Kellogg, civilian . . ."

Two-hundred-and-sixty-one names, recited in the night. And one by one, as they spoke their names, the men faded into the darkness. Soon there was only one man left visible, and he spoke the last name of all, *"Major-General George A. Custer."*

I wiped my eyes, and when I looked again, Singing Rock had vanished, too; and there was nothing to be seen but the faintest flicker of light. I heard distant sirens in the night sky. I felt strangely detached from myself, as if I were some-place else. Dead, perhaps. I don't know.

"Come on," I said to Karen. "Why don't we go back to my place and see if it's still standing?"

I looked around and found a red insulated rubber glove, property of ConEd, lying in the gutter. I picked it up and came back to the sidewalk with it, with the intention of dropping the forks into it, and taking them home. Some-place where I could keep a close and constant eye on them.

As I leaned forward to pick them up, however, there was a blitzing crackle of discharge, and six dazzling fingers of electricity jumped from the tines of the forks, and touched the steel window frames on the side of the Empire State Building.

I said, *"Shit!"* and jumped forwards, but I was seconds too late. The electrical sparks ran up the sides of the building, six of them running in parallel up the decorative strips of chrome-nickel steel. They vanished for a moment when they reached the fifth-story setback, but then they reappeared again, and I saw them sparkling up the tower to the eighty-sixth floor observatory, until they were nothing but the faintest of twinkles.

There was a moment's hesitation, and then an ear-splitting crack of lightning from the mast on top of the Empire State Building. This time, however, the lightning jagged *away* from the building, and into the sky; and all we were left with was the half-ruined city, and the faint smell of burning, and the first pricklings of drizzle.

Oh, and each other, of course.

TWENTY-ONE

Well—as you know, the experts are still blaming geological plate-shifting and cyclonic weather-conditions for what happened; and it's probably better that they do. If everybody believed in Indian spirits and shadow-demons and the black infinite lake that lies beneath our feet, I guess the whole country would be chaos. Even more chaotic than it is already.

Better to be pragmatic. Better to bury the dead and clear up the rubble and build new buildings, in the good old pioneer tradition.

America, after all, belongs to us now, and not to the shadow-demons.

It's seven months now since all of this happened, and I think I've gotten most of it straight in my mind . . . although I still ask myself questions like, what happened to little Samuel? And what happened to David, my younger brother? I'd like to believe that, somewhere in Heaven, or whatever you want to call it, they got together, and made friends.

I wonder what happened to Trixie, in Chicago. I wonder if Mama Jones is still alive. I tried to call but she never answered.

I had a postcard six or seven weeks ago from Wanda, in Denver. There was a picture of Minnie Mouse on it. Wanda lives with her uncle and aunt now, and so does Joey. A demolition crew found Joey asleep in a wrecked car, two miles outside of Pritchard, hungry and dehydrated, but safe.

Amelia still teaches. I call her now and again, and we talk for a while, but as time goes by we have less and less to say to each other. I like Amelia. I probably love Amelia. But I'm no good for her. We both know that.

E.C. Dude went back to Apache Junction. Cybille came and took all her panties back and went to live with Gary instead. Now he and Linda and Stanley live together in that dented Airstream trailer and sell second-hand Jeeps.

I still tell fortunes. Come on up one day and I'll peer at your tea-leaves. I've been known to be pretty accurate, now and again. I told Mrs John F. Lavender to *"Beware of the ground sinking from within,"* and what happened? On All Shadows' Day, the ground had opened up, right underneath her chauffeur-driven Mercedes, and that was the last that anybody saw of her.

Fifty-one thousand died in Manhattan. Seventy-three thousand died in Chicago. Nine thousand died in Las Vegas; six-and-a-half thousand in Phoenix. Altogether, countrywide, more than two million. Talk about an eye for an eye.

On my bookshelf in my consulting-room I still keep the Heinz ketchup bottle which E.C. Dude used to catch Aktunowihio's smoky tentacle. Occasionally, I peer inside it, but it's as dark as bonfire smoke inside; as dark as the Great Outside. The only thing I *don't* keep on that shelf anymore is books. I found that—after they'd been standing next to the shadow-bottle for a week or so, the print would fade, and after a month the pages would be totally blank. Karen thinks it's sinister. I think it shows that I've still got Aktunowihio where I want him.

As for Karen—Karen's very pretty, and Karen's fine.

We've been living together since it happened, and we manage to rub along pretty well, most of the time anyway. We've actually been talking about the m-word, you know, marriage.

Karen's a little iffy about it, but I think we ought to—and as soon as possible, too, before the baby's born.

"When I was a kid, I'd go and visit the reservation in the summertime, and I had these cousins whose senses were finely-tuned, senses that we don't use: they could smell in the air that it was going to rain later on that day, they could feel the ground and tell things.

"And whereas in the outside world people would talk about God and the devil, these Indians said, we have no concept of the devil—what is it, a man in a red suit running around? We have no devil—the devil came over in a boat with Columbus!"

—Robbie Robertson